BAD
MANNERS

BAD
MANNERS

Amy Beashel

Harper
North

HarperNorth
Windmill Green
24 Mount Street
Manchester M2 3NX

A division of
HarperCollins*Publishers*
1 London Bridge Street
London SE1 9GF

www.harpercollins.co.uk

HarperCollinsPublishers
Macken House
39/40 Mayor Street Upper
Dublin 1
D01 C9W8

First published by HarperNorth in 2024

1 3 5 7 9 10 8 6 4 2

HB ISBN: 978-0-00-852647-4
Printed and bound in the UK using 100% renewable
electricity at CPI Group (UK) Ltd, Croydon

'This world, which is the same for all, no gods or human beings have made; but it ever was, is now, and ever shall be an ever-living Fire, with measures of it kindling, and measures going out.

All things are an exchange for fire and fire for all things, even as wares for gold and gold for wares.'

Heraclitus

She is surprised by the details that stick. The grit on the carpet that grinds tiny searing holes into her elbows when she attempts to force herself upwards. How silently fire sends its warning through the small gap between the floor and the door. The clarity with which she knows the hotel isn't the only thing burning. That her rage is also incendiary. That her intention is fatal when she bites down and twists enough to grab her shoe. That a heel is sharp. That an eyeball is soft. That, tonight, she will make him pay.

BEFORE

CASS

Gramps likes that rhyme about sugar and spice and all things nice. He one hundred per cent believes that's what little girls are made of. Or his little girl at least. I'm not so sure. Right now, I'm made of nerves and paranoia. And the others in this girls-only room are made of smooth bare legs and pouting glossed lips, as we listen to my aunt Sophie deliver a pep talk in the spirit of a dare.

She strikes a spoon twice on her glass. 'It's OK, recommended even, to accept a drink if it's offered.' Leading by example, she sips her Champagne. 'It makes the men feel good to think it's not only them who are enjoying the evening. And when *they* feel good...' She raises a hand in the air, rubbing her thumb against the tips of her fingers. 'Well, we *are* here for the money,' she reminds us, laughing, then, as if maybe we've misunderstood. 'For charity,' she says, and I clock how *she* is made of contoured certainty and that bright-white electric smile.

'Can I just ask...' The other girls turn to look at me. A slack-jawed model-type with dewy skin and an apparent intolerance for newbies, furrows her brow and clicks her cherry-red nails.

'Go on.' My aunt's onceover is sharpened by our earlier conversation in which she had suggested, if there was time, I should think about fake tan.

'Why is the dinner men-only?' Heat rises in my cheeks when the lithe well-seasoned pro rolls her black-lined eyes.

Sophie puts her glass on the dressing table, tucks her short blonde hair behind her ears and shrugs, like, *isn't it obvious*. 'They behave differently when their wives aren't watching.' Her tone is collected. Every word long. 'That's great for the charities. And great for you too if you play the game well.' She tilts her head in a gesture implying empathy. 'Your choice.'

She'd said the same towards the end of our call this afternoon. 'It's In the Event Of's showcase event, Cass; it'd be good to have family eyes on the scene.' I'd asked if my cousin, Will, could do it. 'As brilliant as my son is, he doesn't quite fit the bill. I need *you*,' Sophie had said. 'Your choice, though,' which it was, of course. There wasn't a gun to my head. But it's not like my job at Subway is enough to fund my hoped-for Australian gap year. And 'Easy money,' was how Soph had put it. 'It's waitressing, darling. High-end though. You remember, Liv helped out last year?' I did remember. My best mate's tips had left her flush enough for a cut *and* balayage without having to bat her eyelashes and hold out a palm to her mostly absent daddy. So, I'd said yes and come, fairly last-minute, with only part of the uniform stuffed into a Tesco's bag-for-life. When I'd arrived, Sophie told me not to worry. 'I've got just the thing. Get the girls to pour you some vino. I'll be back with them in a min.'

A small blonde had passed me a thin throwaway cup of warm, yellow wine. 'Not exactly the standard we'll be serving later.' She winced with the acidity of her sip. 'S'alright though.' She'd knocked back the rest of her Lambrusco Bianco like a shot before slipping into the obligatory heels, skirt and shirt that would have been so nothing-to-see-here if it wasn't for their height, its length, and that sheer white cotton that did nothing to conceal the obligatory black bra beneath.

'T minus ten,' Sophie says now, and I imagine Mum's face if she could hear the NASA-style countdown to what's effectively a fancy dinner for a bunch of men with nothing better to do on a September night in the Midlands. Only these aren't just any men, as Sophie reminds us for the third, fourth time. These are *generous* men. She reads one of the information cards that will sit on each of the eight-person tables, detailing the local charities that stand to benefit from tonight's fundraising. 'With *your* undivided attention and *their* unguarded benevolence, our guests will be doing untold good for animals, children and women.'

She pauses, giving us time to comprehend the importance of our work. And, it seems from the way she points a bony finger at her fixed grin, the importance of a smile. 'If you're happy, they're happy. And if they're happy, the charities will be too.'

Speech done, she comes over, hands me a pair of glossy, black shoes.

'Jesus, are these —?

'Yep,' Sophie nods. 'Never underestimate the power of Louboutin. Our diners aren't barbarians, Cass. They're the sort to recognise, and appreciate, class. Go on,' she says when I'm strapped in and wobbling on the too-high heel. 'They might feel a bit much at first, but once you get used to them, you'll be fine.'

Guardian alert: Police
have said they are
"increasingly concerned"
over the disappearance of
Lucy Corrigan, 19, who
has not been heard from
since Tuesday night when
she was walking home from
her boyfriend's flat in
the Harborne area of
Birmingham.

EVE

'Oi, oi!'

I hear them before I see them.

Before that though, I *feel* them, just as I watch a similar *feeling* make itself visible in her.

She's, what, thirty feet ahead of me, a gap I engineered then maintained after we almost collided in the park. Our two separate paths were merging and so, because it would be awkward to run alongside a stranger, I knelt to re-tie an already perfectly tied shoelace before silently vowing to keep at the same yet distant pace.

Not that she's competition. More motivation maybe. There's nothing like a sculpted twenty-something to make you chase your own vanishing youth. Sure, I'm old enough to be the girl's mother, but I still have it. I *do* still have it... right?

And while it's not like I actually believe matching a stranger step for step will prove anything, there's no denying the buzz that comes with mirroring her stride, which was wide and strong until the *oi oi*, when it turned hesitant without wanting to slow.

Approaching the pub with its outdoor tables and chairs, something about this other runner is less. Not her stride, which, despite the cobbled path, remains steady (and faster than I would usually manage), but her demeanour. Only that's not quite right because *demeanour* suggests conduct or behaviour, and that's not what's changed. Rather, she shrinks with the understanding maybe of what the pub and its punters might mean.

'Oi, oi!' Again.

Calls of what – admiration? – rattle across the empties in a ricochet of whistles and grunts, landing on her shoulders like hailstones. She curls. The movement is so slight the drinkers wouldn't clock it from the beneath the shade of their parasol, which makes it impossible, perhaps, for them to see whoever's directly in front of them as whole. It occurs to me, then, how hailstones, despite also consisting of water, never have the same cleansing affect as rain.

'Fit,' one shouts. A single word that could be a compliment. But there's that *feeling* again.

When we were kids, or not only then, really – she still says it now – Mum likened our shoulder blades to wings. 'Up,' she told me at age twelve when I was slouched over an old copy of *Smash Hits*, reading and rereading the lyrics of Mel and Kim's *Respectable* until I knew them by heart. 'Seriously, Eve, on your feet.' She wanted me to know what standing tall felt like. 'Like Sophie,' Mum said, pointing out how well my older sister pulled her shoulders back and down. 'Because if your blades *are* wings, your entire body must point upwards if you want it to fly.'

The way Sophie looked down at me it was as if she were already soaring.

Honestly, though, I didn't care about flying. All I cared about was nailing the words *and* Mel's dance moves in the music video because my friend Kelly was coming round in an hour and had told me repeatedly in our previous night's telephone conversation that spanned the length of both *Home & Away* and *Neighbours* that she had definitely nailed Kim's.

No matter how hard I rehearsed, my muscle memory failed to recall the combination of hip dips, Tootsie Rolls and T-arms-into-splayed arms Kelly insisted we'd need mastered to have a hope in hell of winning the school Summer Talent Show. The choreography might not have stuck but, like the chorus of any decent Stock, Aitken and Waterman pop song, Mum's advice held firm in the decades since.

'Shoulders back,' I say too often these days to Cass, who rolls her eyes like hers is the first generation to contend with the infuriating predictability of parents.

I adjust mine now, inwardly urging the girl in front of me to do the same. But she's making herself smaller, tucking beneath the canopy of scaff boards framing the building opposite, as if the shadows will provide the cover that stops her from being fair game.

'Come out, come out, wherever you are.' It's playful. A hint of those soggy-bread-and-jam scented lunchtimes of hide and seek, when my friends and I would crawl under bushes and slide behind doors, relishing the fleeting invisibility.

The runner – the *other* runner, for I too am running – emerges into the glare of the afternoon light, a faceless silhouette of a woman's body hurrying away from the vibrations of the lads' calls. Her hands are clenched into fists.

It's a rigidity, I suppose. A preparedness. Quietly, mind. Because most of the time it's nothing.

It's true, most of the time, there is absolutely nothing to fear.

She is headed for the horizon now, which makes it my turn.

I wish – once she's at a safe distance – she would stop and watch how I've learnt to handle these moments, these men. I have twenty years on her. At least. Time enough to have understood I don't need to take this shit. This narration of my body when I work. When I walk. When I eat. When I eat swim, drive, dance, think, shop, run.

'Wings, Eve,' I mutter, no qualms about sounding like my mother. I hope by the time Cass is my age she is proud to sound like her too.

I wipe the sweat from my brow, keep my pace steady and look straight ahead, awaiting the *oi oi*'s take two.

The pub pummels its R&B tunes into the September air. Feet tap. Pints clink. There is noise, but from the men's mouths: silence.

I run by without them saying a word.

What. The. Fuck.

I was prepared to stop. I was prepared to stand with my hands on my hips and tell them I didn't quite catch what they'd said. To suggest they repeat themselves. And when they did, I was prepared to ask them would they speak that way to their daughter, their sister, their mum?

But in their obliviousness, all I can do is keep on moving.

Unscathed. And, unlike that other runner, unseen.

I know disappointment when I feel it. But *this*? This is boggier than that, a bloated collision of – what? Envy? Shame?

'Hypocrisy?' My friend Charlotte suggests when I call her on the ten-minute walk I justify as a cooldown because I've lost any will to continue my run home. 'Aren't you always telling our daughters to find their value in their brain and,' – her voice assumes a weighty, self-righteous tone – 'if not in that, then in their ability to treat others with faith and kindness?'

Shit. Am I really that worthy?

'You know how tempted I was to double back on myself and run past the pub a second time?'

Charlotte scoffs. 'Why would you do that?'

I know this is one of those deeply pathetic thoughts I should stifle but, 'In the hope there was some sort of misunderstanding, and I do indeed warrant at least one whistle. One oi-oi. Honestly—'

'Eve!' Charlotte cuts in. 'I'm not sure I need any more honesty.'

'*Honestly*, I'd even take one *look-at-the-tits-on-her.*'

'Jesus Christ.' My friend's voice is spliced with derision and a hint of genuine concern. 'Why do you not sound like you're joking?'

'You're right.' On our doorstep now, I rummage in the pocket of my running belt for the key but can't find it. 'Maybe it's the speed I was running. Or the lack of oxygen.' I find the key, not in the belt but in the pocket of my leggings. 'Or maybe it was my body heat, which, when you come to think of it, more likely means it's the peri-fucking-menopause. Because isn't that, according to you and Sophie – and *Woman's Hour* – responsible for every single mental and physical peak and trough of my life right now?'

'You *are* forty-five.' Charlotte says, like my withering womb is a foregone conclusion.

'*You're* not far off, and you're – what did that judge call you? *Well-racked?*

'Eve.' Charlotte's tone is her barrister special. The deep authority she says is required for court. 'Please tell me you are not about to suggest a comment that forms part of a possible sexual harassment claim is the kind of ludicrous affirmation you're still seeking?'

'Not now, I'm not.' I close the door behind me and almost bump into Harry. 'Clearly, there's no way I'd want some old Rumpole praising my fabulous tits.'

The pile of fresh and neatly folded laundry my husband's carried up from the basement is as teetering his brow.

'I should think not.' Charlotte's voice is dense with reproof.

'And don't worry, I wouldn't actually want such dodgy comments from men who've downed too many beers this early on a Saturday evening either. That said...' I narrow my eyes at Harry in the hope he might, for the first time in a long time, use my obvious outrage as a prompt to show me a smidge of aesthetic appreciation. '...If a good and decent man happened to mention my breasts look wonderful, that might not be so offensive.'

Harry's making his way upstairs. 'Wow,' he stage-whispers. 'So this is what women are really like?'

I cover my phone with my hand. 'Hashtag not all women.' I catch myself in the hallway mirror, don't even attempt to disguise the sigh. 'We still walking to your exhibition together?'

'Yup. I'm on my way home from Sainsbury's now. Need to change. Check in with Shayan and the kids, so I'll be at yours for, what, eight-fifteen?'

'Perfect.'

'I won't bother knocking.' My friend's smile is audible. 'I'll just shout *look at the tits on her* through your letter box, and you'll no doubt come scuttling, delighted, to the door.'

Look Good, Feel Good

Questionnaire issued to Year 11 girls as part of the Smart Thinking in Business Day for all Year 11 students at Oakfield College

	/10
Is my blouse buttoned up and my cleavage hidden?	
Have I polished my shoes?	
Are my nails clean, cut and nicely shaped?	
Have I taken a shower today? (10 yes, 0 no, 5 if yesterday)	
Do I smell good?	
Is my hair brushed and nicely styled?	
Am I fresh faced?	
Do I have on clean (and un-holey) underwear?	
Am I smiling nicely (always 10, often 8, sometimes 5, never 0)	
Is my skirt long enough?	
Total (room for improvement if less than 100/100)	

CASS

When I was seven and first started playing Scrabble with Gramps, he'd rope in Mum, so he and I were never really opponents. Instead, we'd huddle side by side, glass of orange juice and a bowl of Maoams on the table, colluding.

'It's like I say at the station,' he said. 'Strength in numbers. We're much more likely to come out on top if we band together. Whether it's the police or family, Cass, we do better when we work as a team.' It's been palpable, that strength, among the *girls* this evening, waving each other's hair and slipping on shoes with weapon-sharp heels, which push us several inches taller. Strutting around the dressing room, though, I'm not sure it's our height that makes us invincible. One of the bolder girls suggests it's the lipstick.

'*Lady Danger*,' she reads from the bottom of the tube after meticulous application, passing it to the blonde next to her. Unlike our nails, which are either a mouth-matching scarlet or a less-attention-grabbing black, on our lips, we are all to wear the exact same red. She pouts, undoing an extra button of her shirt and declaring it a "power move". 'Putty in my hands,' she says, wiggling her fingers to cast a magic spell. If we hadn't been told to leave our phones in our bags from the second we arrived, I'd have filmed her "button trick" and sent the video to Maya and Liv. I imagine the accompanying text, 'Mark this waitress out of ten for the following question: Is her blouse buttoned up and her cleavage hidden?' An adapted quote from a questionnaire Mr Herring distributed at school during a careers-day lecture about preparing for interview. He'd issued it only to the girls.

One hundred per cent, this uniform would not pass Herring's muster.

Tonight reminds me of dress-up with Liv, when we'd progressed from the princess-stage to a more attainable kind of woman: our mothers. Scouring their wardrobes and make-up bags, painting our faces and striking poses from magazines, the sort of sultry glare and jutted hip that sells anything from cars to watches to jeans.

Not for the first time, I wish Liv were here. God knows how, but she talks this language, gets the difference between Tempranillo, Muscat, Sauv Blanc. Like always, I'd be more comfortable, more confident with my best mate by my side.

But she's busy. She's always busy these days. Don't get me wrong, I'm not lonely or anything. There's Maya and George. But, point is, I'd not been surprised when Liv said 'Can't, Cass,' after I ended this afternoon's call with Aunt Sophie, who'd been keen for my friend to work tonight's gala again. But when I passed on the message, Liv was a hard no. 'I'm already a working girl, remember.'

'You do a couple of shifts at Zara, babe.' I held up two fingers ostensibly to reiterate the number but handily also forming our favourite physical swear. 'I'm not convinced Sheryl Sandberg's heralding you as a beacon of *leaning in*.'

'Mean.' Liv sat up on the bed, play punched me on the shoulder. 'I do have other things in my life besides the fast-fashion that pays me shit money for all those precious hours I sacrifice every weekend.'

Her scowl suggested it wasn't a good time to remind Liv that the *shit money* she's earning is, as far as I have seen, serving her very well. Styled brows. Manicured nails. Threads that look like they've come from stores a level or two up from the one where she gets the benefit of staff discount. I'm starting to wonder if she's reneged on her vow not to accept more handouts from her father.

'Stand tall.' Sophie says now. And maybe it's best Liv's not here because my aunt's instruction is exactly the kind of physical pedantry that riles my mate, who, when we were told by Herring on careers day to remember our body language, was adamant she knew

18

exactly the story her body is destined to tell. What I mean is, everything Liv does, she does with intention. Like a dancer, there's a choreography to each of her moves that adheres to a larger longer plan.

Sophie's not so different in that sense. Standing at the front of the dressing room, she takes her own advice and gains an inch or so in height. Her chest too is made more prominent. A shift, despite its subtlety, that could be described as a manoeuvre. 'Listen,' her smile is equally subtle, 'the diners' eyes may wander. And I appreciate in other circumstances that may well make you uncomfortable, but this evening, *we* are the ones in control. You're like a flock of birds…' She pauses in front of me, adjusting my collar and removing a loose strand of someone else's dark hair from my sleeve. 'Starlings, isn't it?'

'A murmuration.' The word in my mouth is as soft and beautiful as every one of the girls in this room.

'Exactly.' She nods. 'They're the perfect team. Work together, and you'll be hypnotic.' Happy we are all presentable, she claps her hands twice and tells us, then, 'It's time.'

In our neat line, we walk in position behind the heavily ornate doors.

'Stunning.' It's not clear if Sophie's compliment is directed at us or at the room, where the tables have been decorated with floral centrepieces which, in fact, contain no flowers but are instead vases filled with tall grass and sharp curled acid-green leaves.

Somehow, without her saying so, we know we are not to talk.

Rather we stand.

We wait.

And we smile.

Like animals trooping onto Noah's Ark, the men come mostly in pairs. Similarly bow-tied and suited, they are predominantly but not exclusively white. And prompt, arriving only a few minutes either side of seven-thirty for canapes and, 'Something sparkling?' The way I teeter on these too-high heels could be off-putting. When I pour the first top-up, foam spills over the glass. The bottle shakes in my hands.

And even though right now I am made of inexperience and naivety, the men are kind. Understanding. 'No matter,' they say, words slipping so sincerely between their whitish teeth and sloping smiles they could almost be paternal.

'OK?' Sophie swaps my already-empty for a still-smoking bottle of Champagne.

'Think so.' I wouldn't say it out loud, because, truth is, I'm probably over-thinking, which everyone says I tend to do, but I wonder if our murmuration isn't punctured already? The jostling over which of the guests each of us girls should serve. The sense of sisterhood that was seeded in the dressing room has felt slightly less rooted since we've been in the company of the men.

And perhaps my pathetic need for someone to lean on is obvious, because 'It's a shame,' Sophie says, leaning ever so slightly towards me. 'That Liv couldn't make it. She was a real hit last year!'

I can believe it. Mum calls Liv a disco ball because she reflects whatever light shines on her in all directions, amplifying the mood of the room. I imagine her here now, long red hair cascading down her back, smiling at each of the men in turn as if he is the first to suggest her beauty is pre-Raphaelite. Then the rolling eyes when she turns to me, like, *fuck's sake, these dudes are so cliché.*

While the last of the sun begins to glide down the floor-to-ceiling windows, the temperature and light inside remains comfortable. Everyone is, mostly, at ease.

One man though is louder than the rest, his face increasingly puce. He fingers the gap between his neck and his collar, argues the pleasures and frustrations of golf. There is a dress code, of course, and most of them stick to it, but only seventeen minutes into the evening, this gentleman removes his black tie.

I pour him a third glass of Champagne and look to Sophie, whose eyes flit from me to the rebel. She nods approvingly, her tiny gesture confirmation: his needs are more important than the rules.

EVE

Look at the tits on her.

The first time, I was barely thirteen. Crop top, high-waisted jeans, and hair fortified with Elnett snuck from Mum's bathroom once I got a whiff of brewing coffee and toast. She'd inhaled when I came down to the kitchen, pulled a lighter from her handbag and said something about the flammability of hairspray before kissing my forehead and rubbing her thumbnail over the ridges of the sparkwheel so it tick tick ticked. She was teasing, of course. She would never have ignited the flame.

The men who catcalled me were no different in that sense. Their words too were sparks not actual fire. And so I'd smiled, then, when they rubbernecked through their van window, the bald one running his tongue over his teeth before looking me up and down and declaring in a volume so loud it can't only have been for his mate's attention, 'Imagine what they'll be like when they're fully grown.' They rounded the corner, I went to breathe again, and they sounded a last impression with their horn.

'Old? Like *how* old?' Fifteen minutes later, Kelly was sliding down the inside of her bedroom door, jamming in my secret. For even though they'd not made them in whispers, I already knew the men's observations were most definitely something to keep quiet. Why else would my cheeks have blazed with an itchy flush of disgrace?

'Twenty-nine? Thirty?' With hindsight, they may have been forty. At that age, anyone over twenty-five was ancient. And while there was some gratification in the attention of boys like Spencer Jenkins and Chris Bourne at school, there was greater kudos in being noticed by grown-ups.

'What did you say?' Kelly's legs were crossed, the skin of her left knee taut. She was picking a scab, a warrior wound from her first attempt at shaving.

I shrugged, unsure what to do with the crick of discomfort that rubbed against the hum of pride. 'Not a lot.'

She licked her finger and stemmed the blood running in a thin stream from her knee before it reached her shin. A beat passed between us, and her gaze settled on her toes. 'Your boobs aren't even that big though.'

She was right. They were, *are*, small. The under-wired bra I put on after my post-run shower this evening gives them a little something, but they've never been remarkable. Not quite true. There were those ten, eleven months when I was breastfeeding and got the boobs I'd always thought I wanted. C-cup. Large enough to command attention. That adage *be careful what you wish for* proved true. I wasn't exactly bereft when they shrank again, though their smallness was different for having been briefly large.

I turn side on – take the inevitable breath in – and check the mirror for the *explosion of flesh* Nineties makeover-TV had repeatedly warned could spill from a too-tight bra. The mirror is tall and thin, like that other younger runner. Though she had none of the mirror's sharp corners and hard surfaces but was, instead, made of perfectly round edges and perfectly soft skin. Not too round and not too soft though. She was the Goldilocks of women.

My fingers settle on my waist.

My Nanna's voice, gentle but certain, bounces off the glass. 'Pinch an inch,' she says, and it's not my own face I see in the reflection but my mother's, when she was about my age and my nan – her mum – suggested – no, stated – that Mum had let her forties get the better of her. 'Clare,' Nanna's whisper betrayed the shame embedded in Mum's sin, 'you've let yourself go.' Thankfully, there were things she could do – milkshakes instead of meals, or meetings in a local village hall – that would return her to that ideal size 10. 'It so easily creeps up on you,' Nanna said. Mum nodded and later, at dinner, gave Sophie and me her share of the salted fries.

I suck myself in.

You've let yourself go.

It's not my Nanna's voice now but that other one.

The one that comes from the guts of me.

Hushed.

Perceptive.

Mean.

Fat, she says. *Disgusting*, she says. *Old*.

Her words – though never original – are always snarled and dogged and true.

As with all playground bullies, I should ignore her. At the very least, I should attempt to walk away. I turn, though, obliging, so she can assess me from behind.

When she tells me to squeeze the flesh, I do it. I let her, enable her, encourage her, to see me at my worst.

I don't remember when I first heard her. When the prods and pokes and pinches began.

Did I really believe this lingerie would do the trick? I've not worn it, or anything similar, in years. Unable to purge the irritation of inattention, I wanted – *needed* – to coerce and clip myself into something young and unmotherly. And so, as my husband whistled unidentifiable tunes while he washed and shaved in preparation for an impromptu night out with "the boys", I crept down to the basement, dragged the box where I kept out-of-season clothes from the shelving he built last summer and was surprised not only by the fabrics of my underwear stored there but the colours too.

Turquoise. Orange. Red.

I pull again at the white flesh around my middle. Tuck my pelvis. Exhale.

I am a cliché.

A middle-aged woman clawing at her body.

'Fancy,' Harry says when he walks into the bedroom and catches me peacocking. It's not that I freeze, but I do wait, curious if I should feel silly. But he doesn't laugh. Doesn't even smile. Barely even looks.

A touch would be something. Not sexual (necessarily). My neck or shoulder would do.

His hands, though, are in his drawer.

Something like sadness pools in my stomach. Sadness is too passive maybe because this feeling is as needy as hunger, as longing as regret. I should say something.

'I'm proud of you,' is what I said to Cass a few months ago, when she asked if I'd take her to the doctor, telling me she wanted – *needed* – to go on the pill.

'Proud of me? For having sex?' My daughter's voice was curdled in the sarcasm she'd developed overnight at thirteen. Five years on though, it's mellowed, not sharp but warm and infused with laughter that suggests she may well believe her mother is lame, but there is also a part of her that believes she is cool.

'For talking things through.' My finger hovered over the light switch on her bedroom wall, tempted to turn it back on but knowing that despite her maturity, her honesty, Cass prefers, like me, to have these more awkward conversations in the dark. 'With George,' I said. 'About when, how, where.'

'My body, my choice.' She'd chimed it, almost weary, a frayed and over-used mantra. But despite that persistent flicker of sarcasm, when I closed her door behind me, I congratulated myself on a job well done.

Because wasn't she doing what I'd always wanted. Exploring safely with curiosity and control.

'Got it.' Harry pulls a bowtie from beneath the cluster of his grey and black boxers, the same style he wore when I met him when I was twenty-one.

Does he even remember?

Another mirror, wider, taller than the one I'm standing in front of now. To the side of a super-king in Edinburgh, where I was stripped of everything but this underwear, its pink almost gaudy against the winter pale of my skin. But colours were different in his shadow. He twisted my neck so I could observe him via the glass, watch ourselves and each other as we… what? What was it then? When the curves and smells and gasps of our bodies were so deliciously – so obsessively – new?

He arched my back, and my throat opened in a thirsty groan that came, I realised even then, from two versions of me. The one who felt and the one who performed. I closed my eyes, opened my mouth and dropped to my knees on the floor.

I remember dressing for dinner afterwards, catching this just-fucked glimpse of myself and wondering if I'd ever be this attractive again.

Our desire lingered. The air was so thick with it we cancelled our reservation and ordered instead to the room.

What if this evening we didn't have our separate plans? Would Harry stop dressing, stop whistling. And if he did, would I tell him, as I did that night, to push the knickers aside if he liked, but no matter what happened, I wanted them on because I loved how I both felt and looked in them. Lucien – my first boyfriend – had set that trend, laying my first matching set on his bed ready for my arrival. He liked the idea of me wearing them with my uniform, only the two of us knowing my power in what lay beneath.

When that relationship ended, I continued buying the expensive bras and thongs. The fact I barely had any money didn't stop me. Isn't that the point of a credit card? To allow you to become the person you couldn't otherwise afford to be. But while it's crass, perhaps, to say so, the money I didn't have but spent anyway in Agent Provocateur and Coco de Mer meant something. About me and the value I saw in myself. Or at least I thought it did at the time.

Our bed now is soft when I fall onto it, the ceiling unreflective, plain. I shut my eyes and will myself into the twenty-something body that felt so furiously. The body that affected men like Lucien and Harry and – as much as I don't want to give more light to the tiny and pathetic part of me that aches for it – men like those drinkers this evening. Whether my skin goose-bumped or flinched would depend on who was doing the looking. Whatever, wherever, whoever, though, I came to expect it, *need* it, that hungry heat from men's fervent eyes.

'New undies?' Harry's lips press into my forehead for just long enough to erase my frown. I run my hand across my belly, grateful for the pseudo flatness that comes with lying prone.

Undies doesn't speak to lace and passion, does it. It speaks to the overworn M&S bikini-brief five-pack in my drawer.

When I open my eyes, Harry's back is to me, at the bedroom door already, his arms pushing through the sleeves of his jacket, hands brushing dust from his cuffs. He turns before he leaves.

'We could?' His words alone aren't a question, but there's no denying the whispering nerves that have crept into our marriage and settled between our sheets. 'Later, I mean.'

'That would be nice,' I say, immediately wishing I'd paused, allowed time for a better adjective, something more seductive than a word I'd use to describe my mother's home-made jam.

I roll over, reaching for the inevitable, remembering the flood of pleasure I used to get so regularly with Harry but making do now with its more easily obtainable relation: the alert of an Instagram *like* interrupting the mindless scroll of my phone.

MAIL ONLINE

The Minister for Housing and Urban Development, Lionel Morgan, well known for his exuberant sense of humour, has come under fire after allegedly suggesting a female Ofsted inspector was 'in need of a good shag'. The Shrewsbury and Atcham MP's comment was said to have been made on a night out with fellow parents from his children's school. Heard joking that one of the women from the group of inspectors assessing the local primary appeared to 'suffer from resting bitch face', Morgan also allegedly suggested the school stood a better chance of maintaining its Outstanding status if 'one of the dads stepped up to take one for the team'.

Morgan has denied the allegations.

CASS

In the quickly darkening ballroom, this close to the scourge of black suits, I am made of untanned skin that glows a moonish pale.

Sophie has warned, no hissed, we are running ten minutes behind schedule. In a more familiar mood, she'd told me she'd been in my shoes. But if that were true, surely she'd know exactly how tough it is to gather dirty plates and pour Champagne or wine or whisky when there are jokes demanding laughter, gestures for missing cutlery and requests for friendly light-hearted chat. There are other, grander gestures now too: bids on a racing-car experience, a weekend in Marbella, a signed poster of a 1970s footballer and, 'one for the absent wives,' the auctioneer says, a pamper day at a nearby spa.

In this first half of the auction, run during crème brûlée and stilton, the money is coming hard and fast, the lots are a distraction for the men and a break for us, the guests' mouths and fingers busy with spending. They may have been too preoccupied to read about the work carried out by these benefacted organisations but, if their donations are anything to go by, the men care, genuinely, about helping those less fortunate than themselves.

'Benevolent,' is how Sophie had described the bidders. And it's true. What one of them paid for an A3 photo of a man heading a ball is triple what I could earn in an entire month of full-time waitressing. The more intuitive diners are aware of this; the way they're sliding notes into girls' palms, their cash a kind of apology, fused with a tremble of appreciation. Or glee.

'Here,' one of them says now, beckoning me with a slight lift of his chin. Reaching into his pocket, he removes a fifty from a money clip his wife probably gave him for his sixtieth birthday. His cheeks plump when he grins.

When he'd asked me earlier about hobbies, I'd said, 'With studying and work, hobbies aren't something I really have time for,' which, like the accent I adopted, wasn't exactly true, but something stopped me from revealing anything too personal.

'What *would* you do?' He presses now. 'If time, *money* allowed?'

Travel, I think. *Far far away.* I glance at the huge portrait on the wall. 'Paint?'

He doesn't notice how it comes out like a question. 'A little extra then.' He leans in closer so he can say it quietly, as if not wanting to make a fuss of his gift. 'For you to have fun with.' He bites his bottom lip. 'Think of me, won't you, when you buy yourself canvas and oils.'

33

My smile is enough, I hope, to show my gratitude. Not so big though that he'll know I've never touched a fifty. Seen one, sure. You don't go to private school for five years and not witness flashes of that kind of money. The ease with which he hands it over though suggests a new level of wealth. Or a new level of expectation. There's a sharp twinge in my gut. Anxiety? Excitement? Ms Standing told us in a year-ten public-speaking workshop that, physiologically, they're practically the same thing. 'It's what you do with the feeling that counts,' she said. 'Think about whether the situation you're in is genuinely dangerous or if, instead, it's a chance for good things to come your way.' Hadn't Sophie called tonight an opportunity? 'If you focus on the positive,' Standing's face had softened into a smile, 'you'll present not only as more capable, but as friendlier too. Friendly is good, girls,' she'd said. 'Friendly will serve you well.'

'Thank you,' I mouth.

Money-Clip's pinkie brushes my hand.

A man, much like all the other men, red-faced, booming and bow-tied, approaches. 'Evening, Rodg, will I see you at the after party this year?'

'No can do.' Money-Clip stretches his arms wide, oblivious to the fact he almost knocked several drinks from another's waitress' tray. 'I'm heading off after this. Let's just say I have something especially sweet waiting at my hotel.'

'We're approaching our final lot before we break for some entertainment.' The auctioneer's call sends a rumble of anticipation through the crowd.

Money-Clip clicks his fingers, demands eight tequilas. 'Dutch courage. After his miserly avoidance tactics last year, Scrooge here promised me he'd bid tonight.' He waggles a thumb in the direction of one of the more sedate guests who, when an earlier request for bread turned into a joke about large baps, had leant back in his seat, twisting his head away from his fellow diners to ask me quietly if I was OK.

'Generosity comes more easily to some than others, eh.' Money-Clip winks, nodding at my fist, where the fifty, despite how easily he'd folded it, is unwieldy, heavy almost, in my palm.

On my way to get their drinks, I do what I've seen the other girls do and tuck the money inside the band of my skirt.

'I've never liked tequila,' the sympathetic Scrooge says when I place a shot in front of him a few minutes later. 'Or auctions,' he mumbles. 'Or my boss for that matter.' He throws his head back to swallow the shot. A violent shake after, and he lifts his index finger the way the other men have when they've wanted to place a bid.

Money-Clip takes his own glass from my tray and raises it. His face is made of ruddied cheeks and satisfied smile. 'Attaboy!' he says, and Sympathetic Scrooge shrugs, like, *what's a man to do.*

I stand aside.

The auctioneer switches to the next slide on his PowerPoint, a photo of a beautiful white woman with short black pen lines forming an almost semi-circle beneath her eye. There is a hand holding a scalpel and another gently cupping her chin. 'How apt that we've already had interest from one of this evening's sponsors.' He points aggressively at my table. 'Weston & Mayfair, gentlemen. Shropshire's leading estate agents and so very used to dealing with what's known in their trade as a "fixer upper". This lot is perfect for you then, Sir.' He eyeballs Sympathetic Scrooge. 'Rumour has it that "fixer-upper" is exactly how your fellow agents describe your wife!'

Money-Clip roars.

Sympathetic Scrooge snatches the shot glass I'd placed in front of his neighbour and necks it. His eyes glass over, and I can't tell if he's buoyed or shamed by the foot stomps and applause. He no longer looks at me or asks if I'm OK.

Money-Clip waves his hand at the table, indicating I'm to clear away his plate. There is half a cracker and a soft crust of expensive stinky cheese.

The bidding starts, and there's much excitement when the auctioneer asks if there's anyone in need of filler.

'Your wife?' Money-Clip shunts his chair backwards a foot or so and calls to Sympathetic Scrooge. 'I'd filler,' he says, spreading his legs significantly farther apart, blocking the narrow path I've been weaving through.

That stab in my gut again.

'You okay, Cass?' Sophie's hand is gentle on my back. 'The after-dinner speaker is on in ten, and it seems your guests are in need of a top-up.'

'A top-up?' My voice is as off as that congealed stilton.

'We're not here to judge.' My aunt's tone and that small shake of her head suggest otherwise. Thing is, I don't think it's the drunks Sophie is judging, it's me. 'The guys getting a little lively? Don't worry, they'll have something far more interesting to gawp at in a minute.' Everything about Sophie is suddenly softer. 'Their attention won't be on you when Luke Rock's up there on the stage!'

'Luke Rock? But he's —'

'Huge!' Her eyes are wide.

"Huge" is true. Luke Rock *is* one of the UK's biggest stars, though I could think of other adjectives to describe him.

'A sexist, racist, classist pig,' is how Maya put it when Liv and I met her outside the headmaster's office, where she was suspended by Herring, having already been cautioned by the police for burning library books by what the *Shropshire Star* had called a "much-loved comedian". 'You know what makes it even worse?' Maya asked fifteen minutes later when we were sat in a greasy spoon. Her fingertip toyed with the salt and pepper grinds sprinkled across the red-and-white checked cloth. 'When Luke Rock first made that gross foreign-ade joke, I talked with the school librarian about banning his books from the library, and it was escalated to Herring, who said that was censorship, and he wasn't in favour of *supressing ideas or information*, especially, he said, when those ideas or information belong to a man who's doing so much to help others battle addiction. That man has people blinkered.'

Maya's right. When Dad brought up that same news story about the secret recording of Rock saying a high-end brasserie might do better if its staff weren't "off the boats", Mum wasn't as outraged as I expected by the punchline that all migrant waiters doss about at the bar drinking their bloody foreign-ade. 'At least he's apologised,' she said.

I wonder what Maya would say if she could hear Sophie's announcement now: 'Luke Rock, everybody!'

The funny-man-come-reality-TV-judge-come-sobriety-guru makes his way to the stage.

The room is a pre-emptive standing ovation of long and burly applause. His first move, once the crowd is seated, is to nod at Money-Clip, who has summoned me with a mere tap of his glass to pour him yet more Pinot Noir.

'I'll have whatever you're having,' Rock says. When he points, it's not at the wine. He's, what, twenty feet away, but the end of the comedian's finger is a cigarette end burning into my chest.

I get it now, why Liv didn't want to return.

EVE

A message from Charlotte tells me she'll be fifteen minutes. The slightly too-tight band of my nostalgic bra digs in deeper when I sit on the sofa. I am not – and will never be again – the same woman who wore this ridiculous underwear with sensuality and poise. I press the power button on the remote, and the TV screen fills the sitting room with its cool invasive light. A man in a green-striped shirt and matching tie is keen to reassure the newsreader and viewers that the police are doing their utmost to find nineteen-year-old Lucy Corrigan. This is, he says, an isolated incident, no need for more widespread concern. The camera cuts to a pink missing-person's poster stuck to a lamppost with a photograph of a beautiful blonde woman, who looks not that dissimilar to my only child.

My call to Cass goes to voicemail. I leave her a message, WhatsApp her too.

> Me: Hope this evening's going OK. Please get a taxi when you're done. Any problem, call me. Your

```
dad's  out  with  mates
tonight,   last   minute
thing, and I forgot to
tell him you'd taken this
job  with  Sophie.  Don't
stay too late  XXX
```

On the news, the presenter is direct to camera, his steady, baritone voice, no matter the world's hysteria, instils a sense of calm. Not quite mollified, though, I call my sister.

'I can only be quick,' Sophie whispers. 'But Cass is fine. Doing a grand job. From your earlier message, sounds like you need to focus your attention elsewhere.'

I'd told her about Harry's proposal.

'I get six months is a pretty long time, Evie…' I don't tell her it's more like sixteen. '…but your hymen won't have grown back, you know. You're married. You've had sex with Harry, like, a million times already. How hard can it be? No pun intended.'

I pour myself a second glass of rosé though can't really remember drinking the first.

Sophie's exhale when I don't say anything isn't exasperated but contrite. 'I've got to go. The entertainment's in full swing and,' she pauses and, in a conversation I assume is with one her staff, says something about playful banter and understanding the mood of the room. 'Listen,' she says, switching to a softer wiser tone that always confirms my position as the younger of the two of us. 'You know *my* feelings about men. I only have a hundred of them here tonight because it's so good for the charities. But Harry's one of the good ones. What was it you said when you met him? That he was your *Head over Feet* guy?'

'Oh god, I did, didn't I.' It was a reference to Alanis Morissette. One of the few tracks on the *Jagged Little Pill* album our dad could abide because 'for once the woman doesn't sound like an angry wailing banshee'.

'Like in the song,' Sophie says. 'Harry was different from the others. Sweet.'

'Right.' It's true. Harry *was* patient and healthy and brave. 'But.'

'But what? Have you thought perhaps…' Our call is audio only, but that doesn't mean I can't picture my sister's face. The gentle chewing of her inside lip that means what she's about to say is potentially awkward. 'Is it always on him? My point is, do *you* ever make the first move?'

'I.' I start, but how to continue. 'I *did*. Before, I mean. When things… when *I*—'

'Typical.' She might be whispering, but my sister's contempt when she cuts in is loud and clear. 'I realise it's not exactly your forte, but if you want something, Eve, it's up to you to make sure you get it.'

Despite its price tag, the wine is acid on my tongue. 'Like my Alanis album you stole? I seem to recall making it very clear I wanted *that*.'

'You're seriously citing an example from twenty-eight years ago?' Sophie's laughter verges on unkind. 'Talk about clutching. And the way I remember it, you listened obsessively for weeks then *gave* it to me. Said something about Laurence or Lucien or whatever you insisted on calling your boyfriend despising Alanis and suggesting you focus instead on *a more sophisticated* Blur. Amazing what influence comes with a bit of charisma!' Sophie sighs. 'Speaking of, my VIP's on stage. You'll understand later why I can't possibly not give him my undivided attention.'

'Sure,' I say. 'I'll see you tomorr—'

But before I can even finish my sentence, my sister is gone.

I put my phone on the kitchen counter, resist the urge to Google *Lucien*. My infamous ex. Another alert about Lucy Corrigan. Her parents have issued an appeal for information.

The two ticks next to my earlier WhatsApp to Cass aren't yet blue. If she's not read the first, a second message won't make a difference, but I can't stop myself.

> Me: I don't want to nag
> but... TAXI! Please. I can't
> stop thinking about the
> news x

CASS

The air is clotted with a slightly greasy expectation that forms a film, so the other girls aren't quite visible, quite themselves. It's on my own skin, this slipperiness, too.

A tap on my shoulder.

Shit. Sophie. I stand taller. Smile.

'I need you.' She nods towards the far side of the room by the huge glass doors. I've not ventured beyond my own corner all evening. We were instructed to stay in our zone. 'Can you please help the girls over on six.'

Feet raging against the three-inch heels, I scan the table numbers displayed in tall silver horse-shoe-shaped holders. There is no six. Huh, hilarious what the guests have done. Taken the two back-to-back pieces of cardboard on which the numbers are printed, flipped one on its end before reinserting them side by side together so that it now reads... 69.

When he catches me staring at it, the loudest of the bunch, flanked by two empty seats, broadens, his weight balanced precariously on the two back legs of his chair. I come closer, and he jerks forward.

'So glad you could join us.' He brushes my hip.

This isn't right. Three words. OTT. Silly, even. But they come to mind anyway.

'Oh yeah? Extra pudding, Bry?' The question, hurled from a nearby table, is steeped in glug after glug of wine.

This isn't right. And you'd think they'd be a starting gun, that I'd be running, or walking, at least, in these shoes that don't belong to me. But these three words, This isn't right, aren't the road out I imagined they'd be. Rather they stack like giant bricks to form a wall.

Using the fabric of my skirt, Bry coaxes me to his side, one hand pincering the hem as the other points towards the stage. He tilts backwards, an invitation for me to lower my ear to his mouth. 'It's Luke Rock.' His lips don't quite touch my lobe. 'Watch with me. He's a funny guy.'

The comedian, deep into his spiel now, is talking about his ex, holding up a hand, fending off demands to know her name. 'A gentleman never tells, chaps, and you know I would never disrespect a lady. But as we're a small and private gathering, and since "lady" is such a difficult word to define, I will say she's a model.' He rolls his eyes. 'I know, what a cliché,' he says, as if the joke is on him. 'She penned me a Dear John.' A photo of the letter appears on the large screen, and Rock pulls what I initially think is a ruler from the inside of his trousers. Like a child with a wand, he flicks it, and it unfolds. 'Not the only thing that gets significantly bigger when unleashed from there!' He winks then uses it as an old-fashioned pointing stick to indicate the different sentences he's referring to in his breakdown of why his ex's summation of their relationship is so utterly wrong.

His patter is slick, every word, gesture, expression dipped in oil.

There's a pause, and I make to move.

Bry's knuckles, taut from the hold he still has on my skirt, graze the back of my thigh.

'Wait,' he mouths.

I don't know why, but I do.

'She says I'm cold.' Luke Rock's mouth droops, eliciting the sympathy of the crowd who boo and hoot.

'Frigid bitch,' someone yells.

'And on this front, Daisy De Souza — Oops!' He makes a show of putting his hand over his mouth. 'Forget I said that. Let's start again. On the me being chilly front, the model was right because, gents, I have Raynaud's disease. Anyone here familiar?' On the big screen now is a video of the comedian wiggling his fingers which, when the camera zooms in, are a whitish yellow. 'Poor circulation. Fingers tend to go a bit numb, which, as you can imagine, can be a late-night silver lining now I'm single man.' He quirks his brow and, from the table next to the mic-stand, picks up what I assume is Daisy De Souza's letter, which, once again, appears on the screen.

'You'll see here how the model says she's learnt something from our relationship. All I can say is, it's about bloody time because, not to be an arse about it, but I'm not sure she learnt much at school. Other than how to look pretty.' He pretends to flick his hair. 'Look, she hopes I can learn something too.' He pauses, as if there's a joke that needs time to land. 'What she hopes is that this, her well-penned letter, can be of benefit to me and help me to move on.'

It's him on the big screen now, a live camera trailing him as he tosses his pointing stick across the stage and picks up what looks like a serviette before quickly dropping it, blaming the Raynaud's which he says makes it hard for him to control his fingers. He tries and fails several times to retrieve it from the floor.

In close-up, Rock crouches next to a shin-high silver cylinder his minion brought on stage prior to the show. With his free hand, he pulls a large-pen shaped instrument from his jacket pocket and, looking straight to camera, flicks a switch on its side. A flame shoots from its end.

'You know what, I really could benefit from this letter.'

He teases the lighter to the paper, which instantly catches. Luke Rock drops it into the cylinder, and fire shoots upwards before settling into a less rampant but still significant burn.

Rock holds his hands above the flames. 'Ahh,' he says. 'That's nice. What better way to get a cold man warm.' Back on the stage and on the big screen Rock is genuinely delighted. 'Circulation restored, I'm not nearly so butter fingered.' He retrieves the serviette from the floor. 'Seems the model is right, too, about the letter helping me move on.' When he unfolds the napkin, there's a Sharpie'd phone number and name: Holly. 'Nice bush apparently.' He winks. 'My agent told me tonight would be fun. Back in five,' Rock says. 'Just need to make a call.' He makes a pumping gesture with his groin and leaves the stage.

The roar that follows is guttural.

Bry's fingers are twitchy with applause.

EVE

'Wasn't it, I dunno, awkward?' I tilt my head to get a better view of the naked woman in front of me and lean closer to the framed nude. 'Is that crayon?'

'Philistine.' Charlotte jabs my side with her elbow, casts a quick eye around the gallery to check no one's overheard my basic-bitch question. 'Pastels, Eve. I'm not five.' She makes as if to take my glass of cheap – well, free – white away from me, 'Seriously, how much rosé did you have earlier?'

I narrow my eyes, tracking the sparse lines of her portrait which, given it's from my friend's first ever term of evening class, really isn't too bad. 'Why are some of the limbs yellow when most of them are red?'

'I'd like to say it was an artistic decision.' She tugs me away from her masterpiece. 'The yellow pastel snapped. I had to switch. Nicky though – my tutor – thinks the *tonal contrast complements my delicate flow.*'

'Last you told me, your flow was so *in*delicate nothing could hold it.'

'Sshhh,' she says, a reaction that's likely less about me publicly referencing her "near-Niagra-level peri-meno periods" than a concern one of the youths here

50

will somehow report back to Charlotte's daughter, Diya, that her promise to switch to reusable period pants hasn't been entirely fulfilled. 'We've raised them too well, Eve,' she said a few weeks back when Cass called me out – fairly – for using the wrong pronouns for one of her favourite bookstagrammers. 'Our girls have no tolerance for lip service. They really are the generation that'll get things done.'

'Sorry,' I swipe a finger, zip-like, across my mouth now. 'Can we talk about the fact she's nude then?'

A sigh. 'What is there to talk about?' Charlotte moves on to the next piece.

'Look at the tits on her,' I say, perhaps too loudly because there's my friend's elbow again. 'I'm not being entirely facetious. I swear, it's actually very good. *They* are very good.' I nod at the very good breasts. 'Did the model really just stand there like that, boobs out, arms behind her back, no qualms about you lot gawping.'

I was embarrassed for my own husband to see me in front of the mirror this evening. Honestly? I was embarrassed even when I was on my own.

'We were *not* gawping.'

'Looking then.' In the drawing, there's a scar on the model's shoulder. A mole on her neck. The visible section of her forearm is mossed with fine hair. The thought of such detailed inspection. 'Imagine having

that confidence. To not mind being so, I dunno…'
I think of the near invisibility that riled me earlier.
How this, its opposite, is equally – if not more –
frightening. '…so *seen*.'

Charlotte moves into the corner, another fellow
student's painting, oils, maybe, sits proud on the wall.
'Now this,' she says, 'is beautiful.'

I squint but don't see it. What *was* beautiful about
the model in the other pieces has been distorted here.
'Find a husband who looks at you the way my friend
looks at an abstract life painting,' I say, mimicking
the #couplegoals so rife on Insta. My voice really is
low-level now. 'Harry barely noticed me earlier. It was
humiliating.'

Charlotte, who already listened patiently to this
story on our walk into town, glances away from the
picture for the mere purpose of briefly looking at me
with what can only be described as a frustrated and
furrowed brow. 'Have you thought perhaps Sophie
has a point?'

'Sophie?'

'Yes, Sophie. Didn't she say you should be more
vocal about what you want.'

'And what Sophie says goes, does it?' I follow
Charlotte's gaze back to the artwork. 'Because what
Sophie also says is that I should get a vibrator.'

Charlotte almost spits out her wine, but any sense of my suspicions around my sister's theories being vindicated is fleeting because, 'It's not that Sophie would suggest a vibrator that's shocking, babe, more that you don't already have one. Seriously, it might not do you any harm to spend a bit of time working out what *you* like.'

'And when in the day or night do I have *a bit of time* for that? Oh, sorry, guys, I'm going to have to reschedule tonight's dinner *and* my run *and* my PTA meeting because I need *a bit of time* with my Grey Greedy Girl rabbit.'

'The triple G.' Charlotte winks. 'You've already done some homework.'

A small shake of my head indicates just how ridiculous she's being. 'Sophie sent me a link actually.'

'Of course she did. Maybe she and I will club together and buy you one for your next birthday.'

'Sophie doesn't care about my birthday, remember.' She had bailed, short notice, on my 45th-celebratory dinner.

Charlotte's chest rises with her exasperated inhale. 'Will you two ever not be trapped in your unresolved adolescent tension?'

'All I wanted was a bit of attention from my sister on my birthday.'

Charlotte throws her hand in the air. '*And* from those pissed-up Neanderthals today?'

'I was kidding about them,' I say, though we both know I sort-of wasn't.

'What would you say if Cass came home bolstered by *attention* from the men at this evening's dinner.'

I take a swig of my wine. 'Not going to happen.'

Charlotte's brow curves – again – into a steep arch. 'How can you be so sure?'

'Because – as you like point out – we've raised our girls to be better than us at this shit.'

'Sure, the *girls* might be better at this shit, but the diners at tonight's gala, aren't they all men?'

'Ye—'

'Of a certain age?' A leading question, the type Charlotte's mastered in court.

'Yes, maybe, I don't know. Didn't Sophie make a point of telling us about her *diversity quota*?'

'She did.' Charlotte scoffs. 'The same night she asked if I thought Shayan would be buying a ticket. When I said he had plans with his brother, she suggested they both go. *If only for the canapes*, she said. She could make sure the photographer got a few snaps of them then. I mean, god forbid Sophie miss out on an opportunity to get a brown face in her promo.'

'Harsh.'

But Charlotte has already moved on, is chatting to a woman I think is her tutor.

I return to the abstract picture.

A flash of myself in the mirror earlier. Disappointed hands squeezing fleshy bits. Maybe it's not the artist who distorted the model. Maybe it's me.

I take a photo of the painting with my phone.

Across the room, a young woman is looking at Charlotte's drawing.

Behind her, a middle-aged man is looking at her. His eyes rest on her arse.

My daughter will be fine, I'm sure of it, but I tap out a message anyway.

```
Hey, bub. Me again (I know,
sorry!). Just checking
everything's okay. Let me
know when you're on your
way home. X
```

CASS

One finger, Bry's pinkie, I think, unfurls.

How that one finger moves me, I don't know. But it does.

I am standing in front of him again, my back to the other men on the table, though their collective gaze is a wet heat on my neck, my spine, my —

'Fuckssake.' Immediately behind me, this soaked voice is a new one. I think of the two empty seats when I first came over. Is this one of the missing diners coming back? I attempt to look at this new man, but Bry's one finger holds my chin in position so it's only him I see.

'IsBryatitagain?' That new voice says behind me. New yet familiar. So familiar I should be able to pin it to a person, but it's not only his speech that's slurred. Everything else around me is made blurry and distant by Bry's hand sliding down then around and up to the inside of my lower thigh, which could, at a push, be described as my knee.

A knee isn't sexual. Four new words. A mantra, because if I say it and believe it then this... now... *I...* will be okay. *A knee isn't sexual.* Especially not when the touch is casual. Almost like I just happen to be standing where his hand just happens to be. There's no physical pressure is what I mean. To stand here. To stay here. To listen to whatever it is he's trying to say.

'What's your name, dear?' Bry's question, like my knee, like the touch, *isn't* sexual.

'Hesalreadylostusonewaitress.' Again, the new-yet-familiar voice drawls. It's close but, like everything else, made separate by Bry's hand, which puts the rest of the world behind increasingly impenetrable glass.

Bry's thumb is still thick on my skin, which is too thin to stop his touch boring through its layers into my flesh and bones and whatever it is that lies at the deepest part of me.

Head down, I stare at his lap. *This is not sexu—*

The folds of his trousers are strained.

I should be made of fight or flight but instead I'm frozen in You Should Have Seen This Coming. In You Must Have Known How This Would Be.

'Stop,' I try. But from behind that smeared glass, there's the returned and swaggering comedian, the drunk and howling crowd, and the giggles of another nearby girl who must think this room, these men and their hands and fingers are fine.

They're all laughing. All smiling.

'Stop,' I repeat. My one-syllable word hasn't a hope in hell. I think of the fifty tucked inside the waistband of my skirt. How does money like that smell when it burns?

'Jesus!' The temper of the voice from behind me hollows my lungs of breath because maybe he'll do what I can't and put an end to this. 'Seriously he carries on like this there will be no one to bring us more of that excellent port.' So, it's the port, not Bry's hands, that concerns him. 'Letherdoherjob.'

Bry sits upright, drags that hand back up my leg, my arse, my waist, my shoulder, until his arm is fully stretched at my neck, where he tugs at the open collar of my shirt. 'There,' he says, a smile like he's done me a favour. 'That's straight now.' One finger slips from cotton to clavicle and stays there. 'What's your name?' I hear it, Bry's not yet gratified leer, and see it when I force my gaze from his disgusting lap to his disgusting mouth, which is suddenly illuminated by the slow swoop of headlights turning on the hotel's wide stone driveway and penetrating the room's darkness through the window's full-height glass.

'Wewanttheport,' The new-yet-familiar voice comes this time with a new-yet-familiar hand. Two taps in quick succession on my arse. 'DoIhavetokeepasking?'

Bry stands, swiping at this intrusion, sending me spinning on the too-high heels.

I squint, caught blind in the headlights' glare.

'Whatthe?' The new-yet-familiar man grabs me by the shoulders, his hands rougher than before. Not impatient but angry and no longer slurred but firm. 'HOW COULD YOU LET HIM TOUCH YOU LIKE THAT?'

The dazzling light fades, and I see for the first time who he really is.

This second man to put his hands on my body is not only familiar.

He is known.

Loved.

Trusted.

He is made of fury, and I am made of noise-bleached screams surging red-hot lava in my throat.

Only one word pounds my brain now.

Run.

YOU

You want to tell her it was an accident. That you would never have smacked her bum, but, 'HOW COULD YOU LET HIM TOUCH YOU LIKE THAT?' is the only thing you manage to say before she runs, almost tripping, pulling off those shoes, which are too high and too sexy, and what you want then is to run after her. To hold her. To persuade her to stay.

Shit. You weren't even supposed to be here.

'Johnno can't make it,' Paul said on the footy pitch this morning while vigorously and victoriously shaking your hand. 'Some fancy dinner the wife's company sorted. No need to pay for the seat or nothing. Let's call it compensation for your loss.' He winked. 'Few drinks'll help you forget about that three-nil score line too.'

It wasn't the result that bothered you so much as the way a few of the lads had kicked off at the ref. How dismissive a couple of them were when you spoke to them about respect and good manners after.

You wanted to go home, chill.

No, you weren't being a sore loser, you told Paul. You were tired, you said. You weren't sure where you'd

60

stored your tux, and even if you could find it, chances are it would be too small.

But Paul was as persistent with the invite as his Under 16s were with the ball. 'You get your glad rags, and I'll get the details from Phoebs and send 'em over later.'

So, you had a nap, found your tux, tried it on and stood in front of the bedroom mirror, whistling with pleasant surprise not only that the suit fit but that, at fifty-two you were still game for an impromptu night out; Paul still hadn't sent those promised details, merely told you to meet him at seven-fifteen.

Walking to his place, unaware you were already too late to share his taxi, you thought how good your wife had looked laid almost naked bar some scanty underwear on your marital bed. Trying to count how many weeks, months maybe, it's been since you've had sex, you planned to message later, telling her you'd be sure not to stay out too late.

But then, realising the night was your sister in law's gig, you drank white with your starter, ordered a full-bodied red to accompany your main. You saw Sophie, briefly, from a distance. She'd nodded in surprised greeting, sent a girl over with a bottle of your favourite Pinot Noir. You were merry, maybe, though quietly so in comparison to these merrier men, who were more inclined to volume and a pantomime of bumping fists and clinking glasses before cheering and downing in one.

That guy to your left, keen to point out he's a good, no great, no *best* friend of your father-in-law, had nudged you with his broad elbow. His mouth was parted and carnivorous. When you followed his gaze, it was the waitress's chest his eyes were fixed upon, not the plates of still-bleeding steak she was carrying in her hands. It was only after she'd given you all your dinner that Bry remembered he'd had something to say.

'You heard Luke Rock is performing later?'

You'd tightened, shrank, even, at the name. 'Luke Rock?' Two syllables. The second, a solid and permanent thing of the past that sits heavy in your present day.

Bry's nod was emphatic. 'Local boy. Shrewsbury born and bred.' There was pride in the way he swiped his napkin across his blood-flecked chin.

That image of your wife again. The outrageously pink bra and outrageously tiny thong. The underwear wasn't new; it was pre-kid, pre-wedding, pre the nights, weeks, months, even, when you no longer struggled to keep your hands off her. Did she buy it when she was with you? Or with him?

Rock.

The extra Pinot was gone already. You'd raised a finger to get the waitress's attention, asked her for a top up – 'plenty, please' – of 'whatever' wine.

When Bry and Paul suggested port during the auction, you were at least two bottles down. And yet, it would have been rude to decline.

'Backinamin.' Your mumble was irrelevant to your fellow diners. Of course, it was; Luke Rock was about to come on stage.

The washroom was quiet, the water cool when you splashed it across your face.

'Man-up,' you'd said to yourself in the mirror, laughing at how pitiful you were because the phrase – like Rock's TV's skits – was stupid. Abhorrent. But you gave it credence anyway. This notion of being dependable, stoic, strong.

You watched him from the back of the room.

His jokes were crass, but you laughed as long as the rest of them because to do otherwise would single you out. And haven't you always made light of your connection to this man who is, to your disgust, as tall and handsome and charming as he is on the telly.

It wasn't your wife or the message you were going to send her that you thought of as you stumbled back to the table, rather your mind was set on the notion of having one last drink. Only Bry was distracting yet another waitress. You'd seen the money he'd been spending, not on a racing-car experience or lunch with a local thriller author, or a golfing day, including a three-course lunch, for four. No, his spend had been more immediate. No wonder this new girl had her back to the rest of you. It allowed her to lean in closer to this man who'd been so lavish with his cash.

Man, girl, each getting what they wanted. Fair play, you thought. Still, though, she *was* your only route to more port.

'Letherdoherjob.' You couldn't be sure if the others agreed because there was too much light in your eyes, then, two yellow beams that came from nowhere, blinding you. 'Wewantheport,' You slurred. 'DoIhavetokeepasking?' Was it the glare of the lights that meant your hand ended up on her arse? Or the fact you could barely sit up straight now the booze had hit home. It was a quick tap, that's all. Two at a push. An attention-grabbing nothing-really pale-in-comparison gesture because you'd wanted a drink. Honestly. No matter what Bry assumed when he pushed your hand from her, it was port you wanted. Nothing more.

She stumbled, turning, her face made visible.

You have never boiled so hot. 'HOW COULD YOU LET HIM TOUCH YOU LIKE THAT?'

Were those words, like your hand, an almost-accident?

She obviously didn't think so because, despite you grabbing her by the shoulders, she's run.

'A little heavy handed there.' Paul's face when you turn to him is *whatever* with just a hint of disgust.

It's true you didn't mean to hurt her.

'Bit full on groping her arse like that.' Bry is thoroughly pissed off. 'Harry, mate, the girls here are up for it, but you have to be subtle.'

'Cass,' you call. But it's true that the word in your mouth is broken.

And it's true, you think as you watch her leaving, that your daughter might now be broken too.

CASS

Girls with smiles at the tables. Girls with drinks at the bar. Girls with men in the corridor. All these gorgeous girls glowing like neon lights above grimy bars, spelling out their offering: *girls girls girls*.

They're in the changing room too. Less shiny here though. Two of them, propping each other up. One of their faces is granite when she clocks me and turns to the other. 'Holly, babe, it'll be ok.'

I can't read Holly's expression. It's mucky with mascara and tears.

Trainers, I need my trainers. Dropping Aunt Sophie's elegant but stupid shoes, I grab my trainers. I need my trainers. I need to be able to run.

Bag.

Coat.

And I am made of collapsing lungs and a heart that beats like techno, running down the hallway and into the lobby. Feet fast then faster faster across the pristine marble floor.

'Wattchit.' A shoulder pounds into mine.

'Sorry,' to the faceless, black-hooded bloke, whose gruff fury drags him in the opposite direction away from me. I run run run towards the door. I inhale only when I'm outside on the broad step beneath a million stars I want to snatch from the sky because their twinkling optimism is a façade, isn't? Money-Clip. Bry. Then Dad. *His* hand on my arse and *his* sour breath on my face made it clear how the real truth, the crux of it, lies in the absolute dark.

'You okay?' A voice behind me. Deep. Male. And, sure, I can hear the smile in it, but there were plenty of smiles in *those* voices in *that* room. In my father's need for more port which was greater than my need for —

What?

What *did* I need in there?

The corner of the folded fifty presses pointed and painful into my skin.

A glance backwards. His mint green shirt and charcoal trousers the uniform of the front desk at the hotel.

It's forward I want now. And away. As quickly as possible.

Again, I'm running. Fast then faster, feet grinding against the stones of the shingled driveway. With every step, the word "Dad" vibrates against my skull and down through my spine and into my toes the way bitter cold gets into your bones and bites you from the inside so you can't imagine ever being anything but numb.

But I'm not the only one escaping. From behind me comes the grating roll of a car across the gravel drive.

'Hey?' That same male voice through an open window at the side of me now. 'There's only country lanes.' He's breathless. 'I can call you a taxi?' His offer is more of a plea. 'There aren't any pavements. These roads can be fatal at night.' We approach the gated entrance. 'Please,' he says. 'You'd be safer to wait inside.'

I stop where the gravel meets tarmac. If I wasn't crying maybe I'd laugh.

'Though you might struggle to get a cab.' The man? Boy? It's hard to tell in this light, leans across the passenger side, the lock on his seatbelt kicking in. The strap goes taut. The only bright thing I can see is the white of his eyes. 'I've finished my shift. Can give you a lift if you like?' His lips curl ever so slightly upwards in a hopeful smile.

'I...'

'Did something happen?' A gentle kindness in his tone.

'He... They...' How to finish this, or any, sentence. No point trying, I rummage in my bag for my phone. The taxi app, unreliable when you're in town let alone in the middle of nowhere, is a fail. Liv doesn't answer when I call.

Mum? What will I say even? About the men and their generosity with their money and their compliments and their hands? Will I narrow it down? To that table? To Bry? To Dad?

I risk the possibility of those words and their fallout. But it rings and rings then clicks into voicemail with Mum's too-happy recorded apology for missing my call.

The man-boy's face strobes in the weak moonlight, refusing to disappear no matter how hard I blink. 'You should at least put that on.' He nods at the green puffer wedged under my arm.

I'd rather be cold.

'Look, no pressure or anything…' The near silence that follows is broken by the clunk of unlocking doors.

The road ahead of me is almost pitch black beneath a thick whispering canopy of trees.

Every direction poses a different kind of risk.

'…I get you don't know me from Adam, but I'm not comfortable leaving you here on your own.'

'I —'

A scourge of hollers from the hotel stops my "no". Men shouting. Running in our direction. Any one of them could be my dad.

'Fine.' I open the back door. Jump in. 'Please,' I say. 'Quickly,' I say. And like some pathetic victim in some pathetic movie, I am made of a hurricane of fear shouting, 'Go! Go! Go!'

EVE

'You're lying!' Charlotte – semi-prone and semi-pissed on the sofa – tosses me one of the chocolate coins I found at the back of the cupboard after she requested something sweet when we got home. 'Do not forget, Eve, I was in your antenatal class when you were presented with a life-size model of a new-born's head alongside a life-size model of a vagina. Saw how quick you were to reassure the rest of us "It'll be fine". Your smile was as rigid then as it is now. Clearly, despite your declarations to the contrary, work isn't fine.'

I dig at the edge of the gold-foil wrapping. A pale-pink chip of gel varnish cracks on my nail. 'Damn you.' I wave my ruined finger at Charlotte, who rounds her eyes, silently urging me to stop procrastinating and spill. My raised finger turns into a waving hand dismissing my friend's concern. 'Seriously, business is cool.' This is true. Harry's lined up more projects than ever. They might not be the most exciting design-wise, but we can't have it both ways. 'Speaking of our antenatal classes though, have you heard from Katharine?'

'Their happy accident?' Charlotte's face suggests in the same situation she'd be anything but happy. 'Can you imagine going back to that stage of parenthood?'

'Hmmm, without it, I wouldn't have met you.' Charlotte and I basically spent the first two years of our children's lives in each other's pockets. I buck my chin to request another coin. 'In some ways, it was the best time of my life. How many kilos of chocolate fudge brownie do you think we ate?'

'We were fucking knackered, Eve. Needed some kind of pick-me-up. I'd have been on the dark web risking my legal career in the hunt for amphetamines if it wasn't for everyone turning up to our mothers' meetings with cake after cake after cake.' Joking aside, those early baby days Cass and I spent with Charlotte and Diya were fuelled on a solidarity that was more precious, even, than sugar. Charlotte takes a pointed swig of her wine and digs in the gold net for another chocolate. 'I love my kids *and* you lot for helping me survive their babyhoods, but there's no way I'd do it again.'

'Thanks!' I say, making the catch. 'Mmm, maybe you're right. Hard as it was though, there was something simple about those early days. I'm not saying it felt like it at the time, but Cass's needs then were pretty basic, easy to fulfil.'

'At what cost though?' Charlotte winces. 'You forgotten the state of your nipples?'

It's my turn to grimace. The memory of that one particular get together.

'Holy shit!' Sophie had said after I'd unbuttoned my shirt and unclipped the cup of my bra. I was struggling to get my new-born daughter to my breast without making a scene in front of the other women gathered in my sister's sitting room for the twice weekly baby group the NCT woman had promised would keep us sane. She hadn't banked on Sophie – who didn't bother with the parenting classes by the way – piggybacking onto my support network because 'you're so much better than me, Evie, at making friends, at making people *like* you.' And 'Just bottle feed already,' she'd said that morning of my baby-wrecked nipple.

I was never sure if our sibling intimacy was too much for the others.

Not to suggest those women – still my friends – and I hadn't been intimate too because, my god, the things we shared. Despite being near strangers, we were ravenous for details of the rips of labour and our leaky postnatal bodies, which we all bared to feed babies, who were as hungry for milk as I was for reassurance that I was doing OK. We were free with our stories about perineal massage and anal fissures, barely blushing as we spoke of wounds to our most private parts.

It was – *is* – wonderful. But this obsession with our bodies went quietly further than the chat. And although Nina – a yoga-teaching could-be model who was back in her Sweaty Betty size eights the first time we saw her after a candle-lit water birth in her living room – did her utmost to reassure us mothering in the 21st century meant we didn't need to worry about the ways pregnancy had made us physically bigger, I'm not sure I fully learnt to focus only on the ways it expanded me emotionally, spiritually, instead.

But I stayed quiet and tried to be beyond such a shallow thing as appearance.

And the running I started as soon as I was physically able post-labour? Well, the fresh air, the movement, the endorphins. It was all so good for my head.

'You want this?' I ask Charlotte now, offering her the dregs of my wine. 'I'm supposed to be going for a run in the morning, which means what I need...' I stand and put my rejected glass on the coffee table. '...is water.'

'Me too, please.' Charlotte's voice follows me to the kitchen. 'God, we're tame.'

I mostly always have been. Aside from those rebel years with Lucien. I shake my head of the carousel of memories. Damn Sophie for bringing him up.

Grabbing our water glasses from the table, I spot my discarded and now flashing mobile.

Three missed calls. One from Cass. Two from Sophie.

Shit. My thumb jabs at Cass's name.

The phone rings.

And rings.

And rings.

It diverts to voicemail.

I'm attempting but failing calm, further rattled because the phone is beeping with another incoming. Sophie again. 'Call me,' I say to my daughter's voicemail before ending that call and jumping to the other. 'What's happened, Soph?'

'I don't know exactly, but there was a man and he—'

'What do you mean there was a man? Weren't there loads of men? What man?'

'Hold on, the police need to speak with me. I think it's probably best if you come.'

I open my blue-ticked but unanswered messages to Cass.

> Me: Call me
>
> Me: Let me know you're OK
>
> Me: I'm on my way

CASS

Does she know? Has Dad told her what he —
Where his hand —

```
Mum:  Call  me
Mum:  Let  me  know  you're
OK
Mum:  I'm  on  my  way
```

No time for kisses just urgent unnamed concern.

'Where should I drop you?' The man-boy twists so he can keep his eyes on the road while pitching his voice behind him. I thought I'd be safer if I sat in the back of the car. 'Patrick, by the way,' he says. Our eyes meet briefly in the rear view. 'I guess I'm taking you home?' And perhaps I startle because, '*Your* home,' he stresses. 'Not mine. I didn't… I wasn't…' His focus is now firmly ahead. 'I'm not trying anything on here.'

```
Me:  I'm  fine
```

I add three x's. Without them the message to Mum is too stark.

```
Me: Not at the hotel, I'm
going to —
```

I start typing but don't finish because where *should* I ask Patrick to take me? The question kicks off a frenzy in my chest. I'm not ready to see Dad or have *those* conversations if I go home. And hasn't Dad, when he's asked me anything, always been adamant we speak the truth.

It's this stupid obsession he has with my name.

The same stupid obsession that led me, two weeks ago on my eighteenth birthday, to a tattoo parlour, where I branded my wrist with a wreath of bluebells because Dad once read somewhere that if you wear one, you'll be compelled to speak the truth. 'Like your namesake,' he said, in reference to the Trojan Cassandra. 'Only unlike her, I hope when *you* speak *your* prophecies, Cass, everyone will believe what you say.'

His hand.

His face.

His hand.

His face.

His hand.

His face.

An already done thing in an undoable past.

I imagine the truth in my mouth. Sticking to my tongue like dry crackers. The opposite of bland though. More like those tiny barrels of Toxic Waste candy Liv filmed us sucking, insisting we go all in on five at once. My lips puckered with disgust.

Not home, then. Not Dad. George? My boyfriend would be the obvious answer…

Shit.

I don't mean this how it sounds because, honestly, not all men, but what I need now is someone who *isn't* male.

'I… Give me a…' I say to Patrick, my fingers sliding across my phone to Recents, to Liv. But I get her voicemail again, and her WhatsApp status too is set to "unavailable". It's *always* set to "unavailable".

Next.

It's hard not to burst when Maya answers on the first ring.

'Offended and Suspended, how can I help you?' My friend's voice, usually merry, is one note.

'Can you talk?'

'NFL.' She ducks into a whisper.

'Not Fucking Likely or Not For Long?' I snap, which is unfair, I know. Maya's insistence on initialisms is usually cute but, right now, I just want to work out where the hell to go.

'Both actually,' she says. 'I'm grounded which, according to my mother, means I shouldn't be on my phone.'

'Oh.' Refuge at Maya's place is unlikely then.

'Can you believe it, Cass?'

The car slows, and we're bathed in the blue lights of three police cars racing in the opposite direction. Patrick lifts one hand from the steering wheel. 'I don't want to pressure you, but...' A subtle but definite lift of his palm, like, *what way?*

I cover my phone's speaker. 'I dunno, towards town?'

'You know Herring's now talking about...' Maya takes an in breath before continuing in our head teacher's accent, plummy with hints of nasally scorn, *'relinquishing me of my responsibilities as head girl.'* I should stop her, tell her what's happened, but the memory is already caked in thick revolting grime. 'Luke Rock's the one telling racist jokes, writing classist books, and I'm the bloody bad guy. Who even finds him funny?'

I shake my head of all those men laughing this evening. I still can't tell her.

'You heard he's supposed to have assaulted women?' Maya is no longer whispering. 'Thing is, when someone like him is making that kind of money, it's not in anyone's interest to care.'

The auctioneer had called on us *girls* to show how delighted we were with the diners when, only a quarter of the way through the auction, their winning bids exceeded a total of £50k.

'I'm sorry, Maya.' I think of how Money-Clip had smiled then patted his knee and can't imagine gouging out the words from the rot to describe what had followed to my friend. 'I'll call you tomorrow.'

'Are you alri—'

I hang up because how the fuck would I answer Maya's question.

Dad's hand. Dad's face. Dad's hand. Dad's face. Dad's hand. Dad's face.

How could I possibly respond to her 'you alright?' with anything but

no

no

no

'Well?' Patrick's working hard to stay patient, but we're approaching another turning. He needs to know what way to go.

George, then.

```
Me: You up
George: ⬤⬤⬤
Me: Can I come over
Me: I can be there in ten
George: Sure 😊💜x
George:    Good    timing.
Parents  are  away... 😊
```

```
George: I'll watch out
4 u
George: meet u at door
```

I go back into my thread with Mum, add one word to give her some peace.

```
Me: Not at the hotel, I'm
going to George's
```

'Left.' I tell Patrick, adding 'Please' and then 'Thank you' because he didn't have to do this. 'Straight on. It's the first one here on the right. I'd give you some money, but...' I look in my purse. Empty. 'The only cash I have is this.' We pull up outside my ex-boyfriend's house, and Patrick tugs on the hand-brake, I dig at my waistband for the fifty.

He catches the flare of the note's red, and I swear he winces. 'The rumour's true then?'

'What rumour?' I lean toward the gap between the headrests, like he's a cabbie, my eyes half on George whose lanky body is a long straight line, a forward slash against the doorframe, one hand in his pocket, and one bare foot bashing its heel repeatedly against the step. I can tell from the angle of his head that his focus is on the front seats of Patrick's car.

'Nothing. Forget it. It's cool, I don't need paying.' The back of Patrick's neck creases as he turns to look at George. 'You sure you're OK here, yeah?'

I glance again at my boyfriend, remind myself he's different from those other men this evening. Safe. Loving. Kind.

'Yes,' I say before thanking Patrick two, three, maybe even four times. 'I'll be fine.'

'Let me give you this.' He scrawls his name and number on the back of an old Cineworld ticket for the Barbie movie. 'I'm not being a sleaze or anything. It's just that dinner you were waitressing at —'

'I'm fine.' I look away from Patrick to George whose chin, when I open the door and half wave, lifts in a greeting that's as chill as his lopsided smile. I slide Patrick's number into the pocket of my bag.

He sits in the car until I'm all the way up the path, like Mum and Dad always do when they want to be sure I've been delivered to my destination one hundred per cent safe and sound.

'Hi.' George reaches out a hand. I take it, grateful for its familiarity and warmth. 'Who was that?' There's an effort to how casual he sounds, his eyes fixed on Patrick's rear lights disappearing around the corner.

'I dunno. Some guy who works at the hotel where I was waitressing.' I don't even want to start on the story of how Patrick's not the one either of us needs to worry about. Or how I ended up in his car. 'Can we...' I raise my eyes in the vague direction of George's bedroom window.

'Sure.'

I hear the assumption he's making, see the excitement in his eyes. It's different though, I tell myself, to the excitement I saw and felt earlier. That was claggy with greedy lust. This, now, isn't like that. *George* isn't like that. This lust, now, I tell myself, step by step on the stairs, is gentle and sobered by love.

EVE

'Harry!'

My husband, six-foot-three and as broad and muscled as the night we met, is a tight and tiny ball on the step of the hotel's grand front entrance.

'What are you doing here? I thought you were out in town? What's happened?' My hand runs across his solid back, searching for a way into his thoughts. 'Harry?'

His eyes when he lifts his head are round with shock. The blue lights of the police car parked on the gravel turn his usually tanned skin a sallowed grey. He mutters "awful", and those widened eyes dart from me to the hotel behind him, resting finally – determinedly – on his shiny brogues. There is a scuff, fresh and flaky, on the left toe.

I look around for Sophie, spot her in the welcoming warm light of the hotel lobby, talking with two young women in white shirts and short black skirts. One of them is crying. My kid sister is as grown-up as I've ever seen her. Attentive, serious and composed.

I turn back to Harry. 'What's happened?'

'Cass?' He closes his eyes, his torso retracting, like there's something dirty or dangerous on the ground around his feet.

'Cass is fine.' Attempting reassuring, I place a firm palm on his thigh. 'She's with George.' A drift of waitresses huddles by the grand pillars of the hotel's porch emanating an andrenalined hum. They are cloaked in dinner jackets, a chivalrous gesture on the part of the men, one of whom appears to be organising their safe passage home. 'Looks like all the other girls are still here?'

Harry's Adam's apple sharpens beneath his taut skin. 'I —'

'Harry!' A man barrels over – 'It is Harry, yes?' – and standing to the other side of my husband, bends and ruffles his hair. 'Great minds!' His large hand comes down repeatedly on Harry's shoulder with several congratulatory smacks. It's only when his boisterous greeting fails to elicit a response and he crouches to gain a better vantage of Harry that I see this guy's face.

'Lucien?'

'Crikey.' His head whips around to look at me. 'Long time since anyone but Mother's called me that.' Lucien – I mean, Luke – assesses my lounge pants and mac but – thank god – doesn't bother moving up to my face. Would he have recognised me even if his eyes had skidded upwards? His focus returns to Harry. 'I remember my agent being as nervous of the potential reaction to my real name as he was about the millennium bug. Personally, I didn't see the problem but, credit where credit's due, he was bang on. The woke brigade would likely take far more umbrage with Lucien Rothschild pushing the boundaries on free speech than they have with Luke Rock. I truly believe —'

And maybe I'll never know what my ex-boyfriend truly believes because he stops to observe two policemen entering the hotel's reception, wielding a handcuffed man in a black hoodie across the reflective marble floor.

'Shut it,' one of the coppers barks at their charge, whose head is tipped back, the thick veins of his neck bulging with the same roiling anger with which he's hurling obscenities while attempting to wriggle free of their grasp.

'Fucking femoids,' he shouts.

Sophie puts herself between him and the two waitresses, her arms gathering them in, her whole body shunting them out of the way when he spits in their direction.

There's so much to fathom but, '*Femoids?*' I ask, standing and flinching at the force with which they have to bend him into the back of the police car.

'Incel attack, they think,' Luke Rock says like this clarifies everything I need to know. 'Your husband here brought him down.'

'*Brought him down*?' I'm looking at Harry, but it's Luke Rock who answers my sort-of question.

'Yes, brought him down.' He enunciates every word as if it will help me understand. I do *not* understand. Who the young man in the hoodie is. What he did. Why Lucien Rothschild AKA Luke Rock is here and apparently thoroughly impressed by Harry and utterly ignorant of me. Or not of me exactly, but of our shared history. How he once called me his original temptress. How he made me want to sin.

Tonight, though, I am inconsequential. The shoulder-slapping and Lucien/Luke's familiar story-telling begins anew, to me, ostensibly, but there's already a patter to it, like all those years ago when, in front of a mirror, he'd run through a new stand-up routine. 'I was mid-set, and the lad in a hoodie ran in out of nowhere, screaming about *femoid sluts* in the room.' He emits a huff of some-thing, dismay probably but, from a scant curl of his lip, could well be amusement. 'Next thing we knew, he'd pulled out a knife and was lunging at one of the young ladies.' He backward glances at the two women still talking to Sophie. 'Before anyone could truly get a handle on the situation, your husband here charged at him and, as I say, brought the intruder down.'

Harry is yet to look up.

'*I* ran at him too, of course. Kicked the knife out of his hand. The two of us restrained him until the police arrived.'

'Sounds like you're both heroes.' That's when I hear it, my sixteen-year-old voice flushed with fan-girl admiration. This, despite making Harry swear never to tell Cass I'd ever been Luke Rock's girlfriend. His politics don't align with hers, or mine even. But, as I've said several times in my own defence, 'Things were different back then.'

I was different back then.

I flatten Harry's hair where Rock tousled it, the strands are stiff with gel. 'Hey,' I repeat, as if we're starting this evening's surreal reunion over, but there's no time for that because a policewoman is approaching, telling my husband they'll need to see him at the station.

'Not now,' she says. 'The breathalyser put you over the limit for interview. But tomorrow if that's OK.'

'Sure.' Harry's nod, like his voice, is small.

'I hear that *you* though —' she's turned to Britain's most outrageous comedian, '— haven't been drinking?'

Luke Rock, who, despite the evident drama, is still as gleaming as he is on the telly – takes a bow. '"Better to sleep with a sober cannibal than a drunk Christian."'

'Great.' The policewoman's patient smile is polite, a sign, perhaps, that she's not watched Rock's YouTube sobriety channel. I've seen enough of his broadcasts to recognise the *Moby Dick* quote with which he opens each show. 'Would you mind coming inside?'

'Absolutely. Two minutes, yes?' There's only the pretence of a question. The woman might be law enforcement, but Luke has no doubt who's in control. He again attempts conversation with Harry, squatting in front of him, determined to catch his eye. 'You did good tonight.' When he still doesn't receive a response, Rock stands and focuses instead on me.

I ready myself for the moment he says my name for the first time in what must be twenty-seven years. And maybe he would have done, but my sister's voice is a shrill and intrusive siren.

'Holly,' she calls to a young woman stood by the police car. The girl's face is smeared with make-up, loathing and fear. 'You, OK? Did that man – the attacker – hurt you?'

Rock watches the waitress shake her head and turn her back on Sophie, who raises her palms as if to say, *I tried*, then joins us, looking from me to Rock to Harry to me again. I'm sure she's twitching to comment on this teen-romance reunion. How long before she realises my first love has absolutely no clue who I am?

'The things these men – these so-called incels – say about women, it's appalling.' Rock's attention is still on Holly, his eyes narrow and his voice thick with concern. 'They could learn a thing or two from Harry here about what it is to be a real man.'

I lay a hand proudly on Harry's shoulder and text Cass a version of what Rock just said about her father. This is the thing about Luke Rock, he always had an inflated style of delivery, but now as then, amid the banter and controversy, there's often something heart-felt and true.

CASS

'I didn't think you'd be over.' George gestures at his bed, but when I sit on the end, feet planted on the floor, hands folded neatly in my lap like Herring had suggested was appropriate for an interview, he pulls the chair from beneath his desk and turns it to face me. 'You alright, babe?'

'Yeah.' It's an answer, but George inclines his head a touch. He's sussed there's something more. When I inhale, the radiator-dry heat of his room catches in my throat, and I cough. I've barely had anything to drink since that early swig of piss-coloured wine. 'I don't think I'm cut out to be a waitress.'

He stands, snatches the water bottle from his bedside-table locker and passes it to me, his pinkie lingering in the exchange, briefly touching mine before he sits again. 'You're OK though?'

I twist the cap of the bottle tighter, its ribbed edge pressing fine lines into my index finger and thumb.

'Cass?' The wheels of George's chair don't roll easily across the carpet. He drags himself closer, though not too close. Maybe I pull back a touch because he's a little awkward, shifting about like that on his bum. 'You OK?'

Do I tell him or not? The choice scalds my gut.

'Your face,' Mum said when she first told me the details of sex. 'I know it sounds a lot. Gross maybe, but it's nothing to be scared of. Honest, it's actually something grown-ups do for fun.' And, 'Your body is for your own pleasure,' she said too, in a mortifyingly frank chat about masturbation. And, 'Your body is something to be proud of,' she's said on multiple occasions as if she legit believes I won't notice the way she pulls her belly in and her shoulders back, though not in the positive way Grandma says will help you fly. Point is, Mum always made a thing of the fact that I shouldn't let others define me. That when it comes to sex, *I* am a strong and modern woman, able to determine the who, where, why and what I want it to be.

So, 'Yes,' I say to George. 'I'm cool, honestly.' To prove I mean it, I straddle him. And we swivel and kiss on his creaky second-hand office chair.

Those men tonight, they weren't sex. They were hands and faces and comments. Their tongues weren't in my mouth like George's is. Their fingers didn't make their way into my pants. They didn't hold me tight and promise this time they really wanted to make me come. What I mean is they didn't get this close to me. This, what George and I are doing, is still precious and mine.

They weren't sex.

They were nothing.

They don't matter.

What matters is *this*.

We are on the bed now. Me and George.

George.

George.

George.

He is on top of me, undoing my shirt, removing my bra, and I want this. I want him and his touch to scrub them away.

'Cass?' He says, but I don't need him talking, I need him licking me clean. 'You don't seem into it. We don't have t—'

'Please.' I grab his hand, put it on my hip and squeeze. 'Harder,' I tell him. There is a satisfying release in the pain. I drag it, then. A scourer across my dirty porcelain skin. 'We should watch something,' I say because even though *they* weren't sex, even though they were nothing, I see them, *feel* them, in everything George and I do.

'I thought you didn't…' His voice, like his hand, drifts. He rolls onto his side. Does he not want to touch me? Can he tell somehow? Do I still smell of them? Of their wine and their meat and their filthy expectation. 'Last time, when I suggested it, a film, you…'

'That was before,' I laugh, imagining myself as a horror-movie clown. His iPad is half hidden by his pillow. I slide it towards him. 'Show me whatever most turns you on.'

'You sure?' George asks so nicely, like he always asks so nicely because he is made of good manners, though those good manners are now spliced with a ten / twenty per cent dash of thrill. His thumb hovers over the home button until I nod, like, *absolutely*, and it's almost instant, then, the image of a six-foot man rutting a tiny but big-breasted woman, while telling her repeatedly how much she loves it up the arse.

It's nothing to be scared of. Honest, it's actually something grown-ups do for fun.

'I can go back to the beginning,' he says.

And, *I wish*, I think but don't say because it's not the movie I'd like to rewind. 'S'fine. Is this what you...?'

'Mmmmmm.' His lips on my neck are gentle, soft, the opposite of what we're watching. 'Only if you want to.'

What I want is to be someone who feels nothing. When I look at the woman, for all her arch-backed wet-eyed groans and grunts and whimpers, her face is kind of blank.

'Yes.'

'I fucking love you,' George says a few minutes later. And, 'You're so fucking sexy.' And, 'You're so fucking hot.' And, 'Tell me you like it,' he says. And I do. Because I almost do like it. The love and the hot and the sexy he sees and feels in me.

'I like it,' I say. 'I love it,' I say, and I'm almost persuaded that despite the pain, or perhaps because of it, this near-oblivion *is* the answer. But then George's hand, which had been on my thigh, glides up and slaps my arse, and I am right back in that manned and monied room. 'Stop,' I say. 'Stop.' Bucking and pulling myself free of him. A clatter as something falls to the floor.

'Shit,' George says and, 'Sorry,' he says. 'I didn't mean — I thought — Shit, Cass, are you OK?'

'Fine.' I'm standing already, desperately searching for something to pull over my disgusting body, but there's nothing. I'm frozen, too utterly naked to run.

Pushing his still-hard penis down like it's something awful he needs to hide from me, George goes to the wardrobe, passes me a T-shirt. 'Cass.' We both hear it, the serrated edge of his voice when he says my name.

I pull the top over my head. Take a breath. It smells so clean.

'Sorry,' I tell him. 'I just need to…' I point towards the landing to the bathroom. 'Sorry,' I repeat when I accidentally kick his phone across the floor.

A bit later, 'It's not you, George, it's me.'

We both laugh at the cliché. It's small though, polite even. Not the belly laugh we'd shared when we were laid on his bed taking online quizzes to prove which one of us was the smartest, and he'd realised I was serious when I'd answered 'Scotland' to his question: 'Where is Dunkirk?'

'It *sounds* Scottish,' I'd said between heaves of laughter that tumbled between our lips and the sheets and the bodies we'd not long touched for the very first time. Maybe we were high.

Now, though, we are low.

'I should go,' I say to George, who looks at me, like, *what the fuck?*

'We don't have to...' He shakes his head like he's annoyed, though I'm not sure if it's with me or himself. 'We'll sleep, yeah?'

'Yeah.' I'm on the right side, and he's on the left, exactly as it's been all our countless times before.

'Cass.' George, like the night, is incredibly still. 'Is everything alright?'

Dad's hand. Dad's face. Dad's hand. Dad's face. Dad's hand. Dad's face.

Not forgetting Bry and all those other men too.

'Tired, that's all.' Knees to my chest, I am a tight tight ball.

''K.' His voice is brittle. I'm not the only one who might snap.

Thirty or so minutes later, George's breathing falls into the steady rhythm of sleep.

Me: You around? I need you.

There's no blue tick. No three dots suggesting Liv's about to reply.

What is it keeping her from me? I've never not felt like her number one.

And then it comes, the glow of an alert on my phone.

Mum: I hope you're safe at George's, my darling. It's been a strange night. I've always known there are dodgy men out there but what happened at Hambledon Manner made me realise they're much closer than I'd thought. Your dad though is one of the good ones. The best even. I love you, poppet. We both do (even if your dad isn't able to say too much right now) xxx

She knows? And *this* is her reaction?

Squeezing my eyes shut, I try to work out where I'll go tomorrow. Liv's. Maya's. Anywhere really. So long as it isn't home.

EVE

My sister and I may have been territorial about our bedrooms when we were teenagers, but there's no such possessiveness about our homes now. We have an open-door policy; any time, either of us can waltz right in.

'Hey,' I say when I find Sophie, phone in palm, face in laptop, at the table. Her breath, when I kiss her cheek, is fetid with Stevia'd coffee. She is a morning person. Not one to be in her pyjamas at 10:30 and never – usually – make-up free. 'You want another one?' I point at her empty cup.

She shakes her head, *no*.

'Anything new?'

'Since you called thirty minutes ago?' She spans her arms the width of the table in a full strained stretch. 'Another two journalists requesting an interview with the heroes of the hour...' She rolls her neck. The loose knot of her bun unravels, and she groans. This – a deep croaky urge of despair – is a peculiar sound in Sophie's mouth, which is more used to solution and composure. 'Will Harry do it?'

'He's still in bed,' I shout above the roar of the boiling water. 'Though if his mood last night is anything to go by…' I place my tea on a coaster, comb my fingers through my sister's hair. 'He didn't say a word in the car home.' I separate the length into three sections and begin winding them into a plait.

'I could really do with him talking, Eve.' She pushes her head back; it rests in my hands. 'Luke Rock's agreed he'll do it, but since that foreign-ade comment went viral, he's not exactly risk-free PR.'

'Luke Rock, eh!' My voice is softer than my thumbs, which I press with firm yet sisterly kindness, the way I know she likes it, into Sophie's shoulders. 'You could have warned me.'

'Nondisclosure.' She lowers her chin. 'Up a bit.' Tilts to the right. 'Oh god, that's it. There.'

'*Nondisclosure?*' My thumbnails pink with the increased pressure. 'It was a charity evening with a bunch of blokes chatting cycling and pension policies and bidding on one-to-one golf lessons, wasn't it? Not some salacious sex scandal!'

'Speaking of salacious sex scandals…' There's a smile in Sophie's tone. 'How did it feel to see *Lucien* after all these years?' She snakes her spine, curling into a cat stretch, and my hands are tossed down to my sides. Good job, trembling fingers do not a decent braid make.

I flick her ear like I used to when we were kids. 'How did *that* feel after all these years?'

She narrows her eyes at me. 'Touché.'

'You were about to explain why you booked Luke Rock. And what's with his penchant for nondisclosures?' It's so ridiculously A-list. Funny how some people just have that mysterious celebrity quality. His was obvious, even back then.

Sophie shrugs. 'What I intuited from his PR is he likes to keep things out of the press so his team can manage the story in their own time.' Her attention isn't on me but her phone. Her shoulders tense again, all my good work undone. 'I didn't realise it was so late. I need to get dressed, Helena will be —' The trill of the doorbell cuts her short. '— here any mo.' Her eye roll is as hefty as her sigh, and she thumps her mobile on the table. 'Eugh. Can you give us a minute?'

'Sure.' I pull her in for a quick hug. 'I'll pop for a wee then head off.'

She's greeting her gorgeous twenty-two-year-old PA, Helena, and I'm almost in the downstairs loo when she shouts, 'And ask Harry about the intervi—'

'Yeh yeh, you've said already.' Mumbling then, 'Good luck with that though.' I close and lock the bathroom door. I *will* talk to him. His silence last night though. He went straight to bed, rising some time later when I was woken by the smudged voices of distant TV.

I found him on the sofa. His scalp when I kissed him smelt of the woody spice of cigars. 'Can I get you anything?' His head moved side to side beneath my lips. I sat down next to him, pulled the blanket from the footstool across our knees, and he'd shrunk away into the armrest, his attention unstrayed from the news. A cluster of life-jacketed men and women, kids balanced on their shoulders, were wading into a sea as drab as the sky.

Cass.

I pictured her on Harry's shoulders at a similar age. Dodging branches, bluebelled and smiling and drenched in her dad's old green puffer. She refused to give it back, wrapping herself in it when he was out. It felt, she said, like he was giving her a hug.

Our daughter is safe, I thought. Those four words in that very order: *Our daughter is safe*. I pulled my phone from my dressing-gown pocket and re-read her message.

`Cass: I'm fine xxx`

She'd somehow avoided all that shit at the dinner. Her life was an even keel.

No war to flee.

No sea to cross.

No journey to make.

She, Liv and Maya are so often ashamed of their middle-class, privately educated privilege. But as much as I get the distaste for their bubble, I'm also grateful for it.

Our daughter is safe.

I reached for and squeezed Harry's hand.

The rolling news descended into its next story.

According to the caption, the young man talking was Noah, Lucy Corrigan's brother.

'She'd just popped to the shop for milk,' Noah said, 'when she went missing.' And we cut to a photograph of the two of them, taken only seven days ago, last Saturday at a gig. It became apparent, then, how it's not only Lucy who's disappeared. The care-free Noah in that picture is gone too, his skin greyed and his features whittled by forty-eight hours of despair.

'If anyone has any information...' He wasn't crying, but the twitchy cadence of his voice suggested he had been. Cheeks puffed, eyes like shattered glass. The camera panned out to reveal his parents who are, of course, Lucy's parents too, the three of them only able to stand because of the hold they had on each other. They were as precarious as dominoes. 'We want to know Lucy's safe,' Noah said.

'She was from Birmingham,' I whispered to Harry. 'Is,' I corrected myself. Repeating Lucy's present tense in my head – She *is is is* – I thumbed from WhatsApp to Twitter. To Trending. To a tweet in response to the BBC update on the #LucyCorrigan story, in which a domestic-abuse expert, who was obviously assuming the worst, stated that sixty per cent of murdered women know the man who kills them.

I showed it to Harry. 'All those stranger-danger warnings we harp on about to our children, and so often the real danger lies closer to home.'

His finger searched for the off-button on the remote.

Maybe he'll be better having slept, I think now, hovering in the hallway, debating whether to interrupt Sophie's meeting to pass on Mum's message that she wants the two of us to discuss last-minute arrangements for Dad's party over late-lunch at theirs this afternoon.

'How could you or security not stop that sicko coming in?' My sister's gnarled tone keeps me this side of the kitchen door.

'There were distractions.' Helena's reply is both defensive and weary. 'Your niece was one of them.'

Cass?

'Cass?'

An extended exhale. 'She and some of the other girls got a little worked up and...'

And? Just finish the sentence already. I take a very quiet step closer.

'One of them was crying in the dressing room, and Cass simply left, scurried out without saying anything to anyone according to Dave. Do we still pay her? The contract specifically stated they needed to stay until the end.'

I'd read her message from last night several times over but check it anyway.

```
Cass: I'm fine xxx
```

She'd left though. Without warning. Why?

I call her on my way home. When neither she nor Harry picks up, I pull over, search for George in the contacts on my phone.

He answers within a few rings.

Before he has a chance to speak, 'Is Cass with you?' I catch myself. 'Sorry, George, I should at least say hello.' When he says nothing. 'Hello?'

'Eve?' His one-word question is swathed in sleep.

'Yes,' I say. 'Hi,' I say, then, 'Cass? Is she there?'

A pause. Fuck's sake. She either is or she isn't.

'No,' he says. Finally. The one word is definite and sad.

'She was with you last night though?'

'Um.' He swallows the noise.

'George?'

A flash of Lucy Corrigan's mother. My heart zigzags in my chest, and I restart the car, suddenly desperate to drive.

'She was,' he says, though barely, sinking then into another long languid pause.

Speak up, I want to tell him. *Just say whatever it is I need you to say.*

'When I woke up earlier she was gone.'

'What time was that?'

'Dunno. Barely woke. There was bit of light so... Half six?'

The clock on the dashboard says 11:22. Almost five hours that she's been...

'Did she say where she was going?' I turn left into our road. *Fuck's sake.* The space I'd left this morning has been taken by a motorbike. I continue further down the street, find a spot seven cars down and, while George gives me not one iota of helpful information, attempt to parallel park.

'Cass?' I'm barely through the front door. 'Cass?' Taking the stairs two at a time. 'Cass?' Bursting into her room.

Empty.

'Harry? Harry?'

He appears, drooped and doughy skinned, on the landing.

'Have you seen Cass?'

His shoulders pull back a tad. And in this hesitant insufficiently urgent voice, he says, 'No. Why? She OK?'

CASS

The barista's debating if she should take my fifty.

'Don't see many of these.' She holds it up to the light then googles precisely what she needs to look for to determine if it's legit.

'Please.' It was meant to be in my head, but desperation trickles out of me, not only in my feeble plea but in the pathetic drag of my body to a table, where I pretty much collapse on a the wonky-legged chair. 'I need something hot.' My eyes sting with the possibility of tears.

'Don't worry about this.' She hands me the note. The first tear falls when she rumples my hair. It could be intrusive, but it's motherly. Her nose wrinkles. 'This one's on me.'

When I try to say thank you, the achy lump in my throat lurches before descending to my belly where it sticks, noxious and firm.

'It's cool,' she says. 'One tea with milk, yeah?'

I manage a nod.

My phone pings with a message.

Thank god it's not another one from George. Sure, I'm a bitch to ignore him, but I can't face his questions. They're so much more patient than I deserve.

I scoff at the paradox. One of the two most important men in my life was too rough with me, and now the second is too kind.

> Maya: You seen the head-
> lines? Luke Rock! A hero!
> And in Shropshire too!

I go to Google, click on a link to a *Mirror* article declaring Rock a hero for "successfully disarming an intruder at a dinner where the British author and comedian was performing." The incident wasn't merely in Shropshire. It was at Hambledon Manor, and from the timeline they include in the paper, it can only have been a few minutes after I left with Patrick. I read about it over and over.

A charity dinner inspiring and funding worldwide change through local action.

Attended by the county's finest and most respected businessmen.

Luke Rock, one of two men to intercept the lone knifeman, is a brave example to us all.

I start typing a message telling Maya there wasn't a single heckle during Rock's gala-dinner spiel but stop half-way through because pot-kettle-black. How could I admit to someone as genuinely brave as Maya that I kept as quiet as the men.

As something to do that isn't read about Luke Rock and everything else that happened at Hambledon Manor, I go to the Mirror's homepage, where the other headlines are mostly a concerned fascination with the missing girl, Lucy Corrigan, or a sneering delight with Lionel Morgan, yet another dodgy MP. And then there's the pull towards the A-list stories focused this morning on some trial in which Nic Pen, the chiselled-jawed guitarist of Mum's favourite 90s rock band Future is suing his ex-wife, Gabrielle Wolf, 25, for damages after she claimed in a live TV interview to be a victim of sexual and physical assault. She didn't name any names, but Pen, like the rest of the world, assumed this apparent assault she was referring to was supposed to have been inflicted by him.

'Awww, he was my teenage crush!' The barista, when she brings me the tea, gawps over my shoulder at the phone. 'There's no way Nic Pen'd do the things that woman's accused him of. You just have to look at her.' She points at the photo, part of a campaign for some high-end lingerie brand. Here.' She puts a plate on the table. 'I've brought you a cookie too.'

'Thanks.'

'You OK, love?' she says.

I nod, cookie crumbs spilling down my chin.

'Just sayin', maybe you should use that,' she points at the phone again, 'to call your mum?' She scans the length of me, from my goose-bumped, blue-veined legs to my smudged mascara and wind-knotted hair. 'Not being funny, I have a daughter about your age, that's all.'

'Will do.' Clearly, I won't be mentioning that I literally just ignored Mum's calls.

Maybe there's karma at play though because Liv's still ignoring mine.

Where is she?

Of course, Life360. After Liv had to move house when her parents split and we could no longer walk home together, there was some dick-flashing perv hanging out by Red Valley Woods, so we both set up the tracking app on our phones. I open it now, expecting to see the little round photo of Liv in reindeer antlers from our girls' Christmas dinner at Pizza Express bobbing its way towards Zara in Telford for her shift at noon, but she's in Ludlow. Ludlow? On a Sunday morning? What on earth is she doing there?

While the night had been cold, it was dry at least, but rain's now spitting against the window.

'You'll need that,' the barista says. My hand brushes across my coat hung on the back of the chair.

I try to smile at her. It's a battle, though, because pushing my arms through the sleeves of the puffer sends wafts of Dad's scent across my face and into my nose. Last winter, when I was finally tall enough to wear the coat without being swamped, I took it from the storage tub in the basement, where, years ago, I'd forced Mum to keep it instead of throwing it away. Despite its frayed cuffs and oozing stuffing, I wore this puffer every day for months. But not before I'd made Dad sit in it for a few hours while we watched TV to get his smell back into the fabric. It became "a thing" we did on Sundays.

I can't think of anything I want less today.

Outside, I start walking to the train station. Sod's law by the time I get to Ludlow, Liv'll be on a train headed the opposite way. Whatever. I'd rather go there with a five per cent chance of seeing her than go home with a hundred per cent chance of seeing them.

I pull up the zip and, just as I do every single time I pull up that bloody zip, I hear Dad's words when he first lent me the coat. I was sitting on his shoulders during that first bluebell-hunting stomp at Wenlock Edge. We'd arrived at a clearing on top of the hill. 'A father has two jobs when it comes to his daughter.' His voice was a mock-wise boom. 'To make her feel safe enough to explore everything that's out there and loved enough that she'll always come home!' He was being intentionally cheesy, but he meant it. I kicked my feet gently against his chest in appreciation. 'How is it up there?'

The world may stretched out huge in front of me, but on Dad's shoulders, I was made of sunnysides with not even a dash of fear.

YOU

You are a good guy, Harry. Honestly. And not only because of the incel-tackling thing. The parents of the kids you coach – for free! – all say so too. That's why they send the end-of-season hampers and crates of beer, yeah?

And hasn't Eve always told you – *and* her mates – that she knows you would never cheat. 'He's not like that,' she said the night you had the NCT lot over for a boozy dinner you all regretted because you'd somehow forgotten how much bigger, keener your babies' cries would sound with a hangover the following day. But even if you regretted it the morning after, the night *of* was fun. The first in a while because... responsibilities. *And* exhaustion. Despite the murky sea of warnings, neither of you had anticipated the bone-dead tiredness of loving a newborn. At least you were in it together. Because *you* did get up and do your share, Harry. You did – and still *do* – do the work.

That NCT night, though. You held court at the barbeque, backing up your over-excited near-ludicrous statements with a wave of your burger-dirty tongs. You'd caught Eve watching you and smiled. And she did too. Because, after the whiplash of her savage labour and the subsequent months of love-filled but energy-sapped parenting, you felt like yourselves again. Like you still do on those evenings with friends when you edge a little closer to each other at the dining table, going harder on the public displays of affection. And the public displays of attention and appreciation too. Not that you're usually entirely devoid of these things, but you and Eve are hyperbolic in a crowd, coming alive when it's more than the mere two of you. As if a party reminds you that you are the other's favourite person in the room. There's an excitable pleasure in that. In this heightened, almost perform-ative sense of you being a team. One of *those* couples who've lasted the distance. Who not only love each other but really like each other too. Loud laughs and eager hands and an energy that suggests a well-sustained heat.

Not that the heat always – or often, even – expands into… That's not the point though, not now. Now, the point is that on those nights, after she's made her public declaration about your undoubted fidelity, or your understanding of not only the domestic but emotional labour of raising a child, or however else you have bucked the gendered stereotype of that evening's friendly but lively debate, Eve will then make a private declaration. That she is so relieved you don't put her down like Craig does with Anna, or how great it is that you've been so present for Cass.

Cass.

You are a good guy. Honestly.

It was the others at last night's dinner who took things too far. While they were – you try to think of the best word for it – inappropriate? You were a little unlike yourself because you were pissed. Because you were thrown by the appearance of Luke Rock. And, sure, you're not exactly proud of where your hand landed, but clearly things would have been different had you known the woman all over Bry was your daughter.

Cass has likely stayed away because she's embarrassed. Because she would rather you hadn't seen her like that: short skirt, high heels, an older man's hand on her knee.

You're embarrassed too, aren't you? It's awkward this kind of thing, between a dad and his daughter.

Give her time; she'll be cool.

You could send her a message? Explain it was a misunderstanding.

And if she asks about the other waitress?

You can't be sure that first girl who served your table *was* crying when she left.

You're a good guy. Honestly.
Have a shower. Get some coffee. Send that message.
You're a good guy. Honestly.
Cass'll be fine.
And so, Harry, will you.

EVE

I'm barely through my parents' front door when Sophie barrels at me, 'What did Harry say abo—'

'My god, Soph, will you give me a chan—'

'This is importa—'

'Stop.' I put a hand in my sister's face. 'He's at the police station giving his statement.'

'And you didn't ask—

'You *did* hear what I said as I got out the car, didn't you?' My forehead's tacky beneath my palm. 'I've still not heard from Cass.'

'Chill.' A ripple of frustration for what Sophie has nicknamed my bogeyman tendency. But then comes the kinder touch of her hand on my arm. 'Most of the bad things exist only in your imagination, yes?' She has, for the most part, been this pragmatic since we were kids. 'You're always assuming the worst. Seeing these terrible things that just aren't there. Cass'll be doing what any sensible eighteen-year-old does on a Sunday, avoiding her parents and hanging out with her mates. That's what Will's doing right now, for sure.'

'But what would have made her leave like that?'

Sophie takes my jacket, hangs it next to the peg that still has her name above it from when we'd argued about whose things should go on which hook. She'd taken a permanent marker over our joint favourite and written in her very best handwriting "Sophie Campbell, age 6".

'Leave where?' She has the same fatigued impatience she has with Will when he refuses to come off his Xbox. 'And like what?'

I dump my bag by the old haberdasher's cabinet where mum has stored all our artwork and exercise books since we started school. 'The charity dinner, Soph. I heard you and Helena this morning.'

She's as petulant as her son sometimes, the way she rolls her eyes. 'Maybe George gave her a better offer?'

'And the other girl? The one Helena said was crying?'

'Oh, I don't know, Eve. Girls cry about shit all the time. *We* certainly did.' Like a Jane Austen heroine, Sophie puts the back of her hand to her forehead. 'Ah, the teen-girl drama!' Maybe she senses the words stuck in my throat because she softens. 'Cass'll be fine.' My sister knows I *hate* it when worries are placated with *it'll be fine*. But she's right, of course. I'm over thinking, over panicking. And, if nothing else, at least she's stopped banging on about Harry doing that bloody interview.

'Sorry, love, didn't hear you arrive.' Mum's bustling down the staircase, one hand coasting the banister, the other clutching her chest. 'Is Harry OK after that dreadful business at last night's dinner?'

I meet her at the bottom step. She kisses my cheek. 'Quiet but, yeah, I think he's —'

'Soph said Cass had already left when that crazy man came in. You must be so relieved.'

And I guess so, but what I really *am* relieved about is that Sophie can't have mentioned Cass's possible – but, yes, unlikely – disappearance to Mum. No use her worrying unnecessarily too.

'Lunch *should* already be on the table, but...' Mum stalls as is her habit when she wants to create possibly unwarranted dramatic tension.

I turn my index finger in circles to imply she get on with it. 'But...?'

'But...' She heads towards the kitchen. 'Your father's gone AWOL.'

'*AWOL?*'

'He went for a newspaper,' my sister says. 'Two hours ago.'

'Two hours ago? Is he OK? He might have hurt himse—'

'I told you she'd panic.' Sophie looks to Mum, lays a calming hand on my shoulder. 'He's fine. Messaged a few minutes ago. Has *some business to attend to*, though I imagine if he gets an inkling *you've* arrived, he'll be home like a shot.'

'Now, now.' Mum whips Sophie's bottom with a rolled-up tea-towel. 'Don't start about favourites. Baffles me why he wanted a paper anyway. As if something printed in the early hours of this morning can give him more info on this missing-girl case than he's been able to glean from bloody rolling news.' Mum's forehead wrinkles. 'He's been taking notes in case there's anything he can do *to assist*.' The tone of the last two words of Mum's sentence is at best sceptical and at worst what Cass would call a legit piss take.

'Is it so bad he wants to help?' I catch the flicker of mild irritation between Mum and Sophie and wait for their calls of *Daddy's girl*.

'The station came first for years,' Mum says. 'So much for retirement.'

'You can take the policeman out of the force...' I pull four lots of cutlery from the drawer and begin setting the table. Sophie does the same with the plates. 'Seriously though, maybe if you invited him on some of your jaunts, he'd be at less risk of spiralling into a true-crime rabbit hole. It's a slippery slope, Mum. If you're not careful, he'll be cosplaying Sherlock Holmes at CrimeCon with his super-sleuth pals from reddit.'

'If it gets him out the house.' She passes Sophie the salad and me the quiche.

I dump it on the table, sneak another quick check of my phone.

Nothing, I mouth to Sophie, whose expression when I looked up at her was, *well?*

There *is* one unread message though. An unknown sender.

Gen…Long time, no see. Why didn't you reveal yourself last night?

Gen. For Genesis 3. For the idea of me as temptress. *Wickedly tempting* was how he'd put it when we'd first met. I'd revelled in it when I was sixteen. When I think about it now, I should probably be angry. Appalled.

I read the message over and over.

Writhing nerves in my stomach. And beneath that, a disconcerting tug of pleasure in my groin.

'Soph, did you give Luke Rock my number?'

Her nod is casual. 'Sure.'

'Oh, yes!' Water spills over the top of the jug in Mum's hands. 'I forgot to ask. Sophie said you'd been reunited.'

'Barely,' I say, wondering if now's the time to remind Mum, whose pupils are rapidly dilating with what I assume is excitement brought on by being within touching distance of a celebrity, that only last week she was appalled by Luke Rock's foreign-ade joke. Funny how fame – and your proximity to it – can allow for such leeway. Not that I should be surprised. Back then, my parents' resistance to the ten-year age gap between me and Lucien Rothschild had mellowed with his increasing success as Luke Rock.

I press the button to lock my screen.

Sophie dishes salad onto my plate before adding oil, vinegar, salt and chipotle chilli flakes, exactly how I like it.

I blow her a kiss.

Mum puts her elbows on the table, rests her chin on top of her clenched hands. 'Despite what you think, Eve, I *have* invited your dad out with me. To the theatre. To book club. A dance class, even. Not interested! Aside from playing bloody detective, there's nothing else that man wants to do.'

A clunk of the door.

'Hello!' A call from the hall.

For all her supposed discontent, when Dad comes into the kitchen, there's a surprising tenderness to Mum's tone. 'You OK?' She goes to him, a soft hand on his back. 'Where have you been?'

'Talking to Eve's friend Charlotte, actually.'

'Charlotte?' I look to Sophie, who's clearly as clueless as I am. 'Why?'

'I wasn't the only one wanting a paper. That kid who stormed your event last night.' Dad cuts himself a large slice of quiche. 'Turns out he's Charlotte's nephew.'

'What?' Soph and I baulk in unison.

The arch of Dad's eyebrows is more self-satisfied than surprised. As if he has personally solved something.

'It was Aaron? With the knife?'

He nods. 'As you can imagine, Charlotte had a few questions, so we went for coffee.' He checks his watch. 'Had no idea of the time.'

Dad is pleased with these developments, or not the developments exactly, rather his access to them. He's back in the game.

I pull out the chair next to me, and he sits. 'Is he alright? Aaron, I mean?'

'*Aaron?*' Sophie's eyes narrow. Her mouth rictus. 'Why would you be concerned about *him*? The boy's clearly a nutjob.'

'*The boy* is clearly troubled. And he's my best mate's nephew, Sophie.'

'*The boy* could have killed someone,' she says. 'If it wasn't for your husband and your ex—'

'Ah yes, I heard Lucien's back in town.' Dad says through a mouthful of quiche. 'And quite the hero.'

'Harry too.' I add, purposefully not looking at Sophie, who'll no doubt have noted my ever-abundant desperation for genuine approval of my husband from Dad.

'Yes, so I hear.' Dad wipes his chin with the back of his sleeve. 'Can't say I wasn't a little shocked when your mum told me about Harry getting stuck in. My son-in-law's hardly known for his brawn.'

Whatever annoyance Sophie felt about my concern for Aaron is dissipated by her amusement about our father's ongoing Harry-bashing. It's all – according to Dad – played with good humour but, honestly, after twenty odd years, it's beginning to wear a little thin.

When I can, I message Charlotte from the bathroom.

> Charlotte: Emma is beside herself. Has no idea what's happened to her little boy. Said Aaron's been quiet lately. But they'd never expected this.

> Charlotte: Can you thank your dad for me.

> Charlotte: It was useful to get that police take on things from someone really in the know

Lunch over, Mum and Soph disappear to drool over photos of the villa to which my sister's headed after Dad's belated retirement lunch next Saturday. The four-week body-transformation retreat in Mallorca is her reward for *surviving wedding season*.

'Dad, can I ask you something?'

'Always, sugar.' His thumb hangs over the power button of the remote for the TV.

'How long would someone need to be…' It's too much to say the word "missing". It's been a few hours, that's all. But isn't every case *only* a few hours at the beginning before it turns into something more.

'Hm?' Dad looks me square in the eye.

'Cass went to George's after the dinner.'

'So I heard.'

As far as I know, George has never done anything wrong, but that didn't stop my dad from taking an instant dislike to him. A muddy and suffocating intolerance that forces Cass to try even harder to show us her boyfriend's good side. Her desperation's familiar. Being at the centre of Dad's universe is warm and empowering, but it's also addictive and sparks an incessant need to please.

'It's just when I called him this morning to try to speak with her, George said she'd already gone. Didn't know what time but guessed it was pretty early. Like six. And she's not replying to any of my messages, which —'

Dad's face hollows. 'He didn't know what time she left?'

'He says not.'

He places the remote on the arm of the sofa. 'Why would Cass not have at least woken George to tell him she was leaving? Or written a note?'

'A note? We're not in the Nineties!'

'A text then. You want me to send someone over?'

'Over *where*?'

That look of his, honed to make a suspect certain of his authority. 'To George's. You said you've not heard from Cass. Don't you think it's important to know if George was telling the truth about when or why she left.'

My sister warned me this would happen. 'You tell Dad, Eve, and he'll be right on it, trying to solve something that in all likelihood isn't even a mystery.'

I check again for messages in the hope of a clear reason to stop this conversation dead in its tracks.

Nothing.

By the time I look back up at Dad, he's already on his own mobile. 'Stump,' he says, his left eye winking. That knack he has of making us conspiratorial, of making me feel instantly safer because I'm part of this tiny team. 'It's James Campbell. Can you do a visit, and I might need you to run a track on a phone too.'

CASS

When we were little, Liv and I one hundred per cent believed we had some supernatural bond and could read each other's mind or, at the very least, sense when the other one walked into a room. Can she feel me now? My eyes drilled on the back of her head, or is the only real magic the accurate tracking abilities of my phone?

Whatever, it says something for our connection that even at, what, thirty, forty feet, I know for sure that's one of my best friends over there, scoffing a late lunch with a man I'm guessing from the bald patch on the back of his head is her father. It's been maybe two years since I last saw him, and Liv's told me repeatedly how his young girlfriend looks even younger since *he* looks increasingly old. They're sitting at a picnic table on the bank of the River Severn as if neither of them gives a shit that the sky's clogged with clouds ready to burst any minute with more angry thunder and rain. Liv's giveaway? Her unrestrained gestures and the near-constant flick of those huge red curls.

This explains it though. How she's literally cringed and been super quick to change the subject if any of us ever mentions the extravagance of her spending, which is weird when you think about it. Because if you were asked to use one word to describe Olivia Blade, it would *never* be coy. Obviously, she's back on the generous allowance from her dad. And, from the way they're laughing, back on good terms with him too, which is what I've been willing for months. God knows the number of times I've banged on about not letting her resentment, no matter how justified, get so huge she loses one of the most important relationships of her life.

So, it's not that I'm not pleased for her. I am. *Really.* But maybe I had an idea when I left Shrewsbury of how the conversation between us after I told her about *my* dad would go.

Fuck them, she'd say. *Who needs them*, she'd grin. And I'd be bolstered by this new shared skill of coping without our fathers.

But she sits down, and they mirror each other, leaning closer. And when it begins to rain, he taps the seat next to him, and she's so compliant, walking around to his side of the table, where she swings her legs over the bench and tips her head against the top of his arm.

I stop maybe twenty feet away. A crap spy semi-hiding behind a tree.

Liv's dad takes an umbrella from beneath the table and opens its huge black-and-yellow canopy to protect them, extending his free arm across her back. His fingers curl around her shoulder, pulling her to. I think about how fury, in the last few years, has kept Liv moving. How Maya, who's studying psychology and so knows about these things, says Liv clearly won't allow herself to stop for just a second because it would mean she has to think.

Caught in her dad's grasp now though, she's still.

And because it feels like a moment, I take a photo.

I know what these father-daughter moments can mean.

'C'mon,' my own dad had said, his voice carrying in the wind, which within minutes of us setting foot on the beach had knotted my almost-waist length hair. 'I'll catch you.'

I was six and taller than my father because he'd hoisted me up onto the groynes. We were on holiday, and Mum was back at the apartment, wanting to make the most of this valuable time for snoozing and reading in bed. At 8.03 AM, Dad made a game of us stuffing "essentials" in our rucksacks then kissed her, saying right into her mouth, which I thought was so funny, that we'd bring back a picnic lunch.

I didn't mind walking if it was special. If there were gulls that sounded like my teacher when she was cross

127

with Josh Garner and pebbles that felt like sea-smoothed secrets in our palms.

'I'll get you a Mr Whippy if you jump!' Dad's head twisted toward the grass bank sloping down from the promenade, where a woman was opening the shutters of a hut. I'd seen on my skip down that its wall was covered with photos and prices of ice cream. 'You can do it, Cass!' His voice, like his hugs, kept me close without being restrictive, like he could hold me steady while also encouraging me to run free. 'Trust me.'

Trust me.

I imagined the sweet soft vanilla on my tongue and nodded my head.

'One… Two….'

My cheek was pressed into his chest by three.

I lean into the tree trunk. Its bark is rough and scratchy against the back of my head. Keeping half an eye on Liv, I scroll through my favourited photos until I find the one.

There.

I zoom in on Dad.

My leap had been met with a whoop and a round of applause.

'Cass!' It was Mum, clapping, almost tumbling, as she made her way across the slippery stones. 'You were incredible. Look!' She'd captured the jump on camera. It wasn't only me in the air though. Cheesy as it sounds, there was actual love in it too. Dad's eyes were fixed on mine, my pupils wide black tiddlywinks with the thrill. And although it wasn't visible, somehow you could see the tether between us. That indestructible rope that meant when Dad was close, I was made of something invincible, and it wasn't possible for me to fall.

Trust me.

Two words said time and again.

I have.

Always.

But Saturday.

'HOW COULD YOU LET HIM TOUCH YOU LIKE THAT?' He said. Like the person *he* couldn't trust to do the right thing wasn't Bry or himself, even, but *me*.

A quiet beep on my phone as Liv's dad settles the bill.

> Liv: SORRY!!!!!!! Pulled an all-nighter. Cursing Ms Morgan for that bloody essay. Fell asleep. Missed my alarm. Late for shift at Zara. In stock room as punishment. Forgot to take do not disturb off my phone.

And I know how stubborn Liv is. How much she hates going back on these vows she makes in her not infrequent flurries of love and lust and despair. And the things she'd said about her father. The names she called him for cheating on her mum. The passion with which she'd sworn 'never to take any more of his fucking money because, I swear, Cass, it's as dirty as he is.' She'd be embarrassed to admit that despite what he's done, she loves him. That no matter the hurt and the heartache, deep down she can't let him go.

EVE

'Is that even allowed?' There's an abrasiveness to Charlotte's voice coming through my car speakers on my drive home. 'Your dad doesn't work for the police anymore, Eve, and Cass has only been gone a few hours. It's not as if she's officially missing.'

'I only asked him about Cass because you asked him about Aaron.'

'That was general stuff. If Aaron would be put in a group cell. If he'd be given access to a psychiatrist. What Emma and Oli can expect to happen next. What you're talking about is, I dunno…'

In all the years we've been friends, I've rarely known Charlotte rise to anger. These, I remind myself, are extenuating circumstances. 'You must be exhausted.'

'Yes,' she says, or sighs, even. 'But that's not the point.'

'What *is* the point then?' My foot is determined to go hard on the accelerator, but I can't risk speeding in town.

'It feels…' Her pause is infuriating. 'Unnecessary. Exploitative maybe. Calling the cops on your daughter's boyfriend on a whim.'

'*A whim*?' My thumb drums against the steering wheel. 'Wouldn't any mother worried sick about her daughter's safety *exploit* any means possible to bring her home.'

'Maybe' Charlotte says. 'I would have thought, though, that the police'd have more pressing concerns than paying a visit to George – a young Black man – because Cass – a young white woman – went out last night and hasn't yet texted her mum.'

'What?'

She says nothing. But even above the noise of the traffic, I hear Charlotte's long exhale.

'What does it matter that George is Black?' More silence. 'Or that Cass is white? I'm scared. Dad wants to help. Why is that so bad?'

Although I'm on the phone with her and she could bloody speak to me if she wanted, my dash displays an alert for an incoming WhatsApp from Charlotte.

'I can't open that while I'm talking with you.' I hear how much I sound like she and I are deep into an argument, even though I have no clue why. 'I'll read it when I get home.'

'Listen,' Charlotte says. 'I can see why you've been fretting, and part of me's glad your dad is able to pull a few strings.'

I'm pulling up outside the house. 'And the other part of you?'

'It doesn't matter. I don't want to fall out.'

I switch off the engine and lose her for a moment while the audio moves from the car speakers to my phone. 'You still there?'

'Yes,' she says. 'Sorry, Eve. It's just with Aaron and everything… The police took his laptop. And Emma heard via one of her school-mum friends that there's been some talk on a group WhatsApp about Aaron telling his mates he feels *unseen*. Emma's beside herself. Thinks with the extra hours she's been working at the hospital over the summer, she's not given him enough attention. Didn't help that one of her so-called friends suggested something similar on the chat. Fuuuck.' The word ricochets in my ear. 'Lunch? Tomorrow?'

'Of course.' The quick slam of my car door. 'Let me know of any developments.'

I walk around to the pavement, glance up to my daughter's bedroom. No obvious sign that she's home. Stepping up to our porch, I go to read the WhatsApp from Charlotte. It's a link to a Facebook post shared by her husband, Shayan. Like I have time for social media right now.

Still, there's so rarely a bad word between us.

```
Me: I'll read it later.
I love you xx
```

The three dancing dots of Charlotte's slow reply.

Charlotte: You too x

In normal times, I would send another message. About Luke Rock and Lucien Rothschild and his thread of WhatsApp questions that punctuated the afternoon. Charlotte would generally be my go-to counsellor. How do I reply to an ex-boyfriend who's asked if I might have time to meet? For coffee, he'd said, though it ended with a question mark, an uncertainty or insinuation that there could be something else. Something more.

There was always something more with Lucien. In the same way people describe his comedy as edgy, or his sobriety channel as ground-breaking, to be with him was to be on a precipice. On the brink of something. He took me places – geographical and physical – I would never otherwise have been. I'm not saying his routines are funny now, but he's right when he says in his own defence that it's important to push things until we're uncomfortable. That in the liminal space between acceptable and repugnant, we might discover a truth about ourselves that may well be the first step towards change.

As it is, I say nothing of these messages to Charlotte and am pivoted from reminiscing anyway when I come through our front door and into the hall.

Harry is in the kitchen.

'I was drunk. Steaming,' he says, a rare knuckle of frustration in his tone. 'There's no way I would have acted like that if I was sober.' He spots me and winds up the call with vague and hurried talk of a drink next Friday. He turns, and my kiss misses his lips, landing instead on his cheek. A light sweat I'm guessing is a copious mix of today's coffee and last night's wine.

'Anything from Cass?'

He shakes his head, though barely. With his back to me then, he fills the kettle, asks if I want tea. Without answering, I'm taking two mugs from the cupboard when my phone lights up with an alert.

'It's her.' I drop the cups to the counter, where they clatter a crude applause.

```
Cass: In Ludlow. Waiting
for train
```

She doesn't pick up when I call.

```
Me: Are you OK? Should I
come to get you? X

Cass: Thanks but here now
and there's one leaving
in ten
```

'She's fine.' I choke, passing Harry my phone so he can read for himself then snatching it back because, well, *is* she? Fine, I mean. The ends of her WhatsApps are usually a cluster of kisses, but these here drift into nothing. And it's not only the kisses. Her excitable emojis and exclamation marks are absent too.

> Me: ETA? Dad or I can pick you up from the station xx
>
> Me: Love you xx
>
> Cass: I'll walk
>
> Cass: Thanks tho
>
> Me: xxxxxx
>
> Cass:

She stops typing. No further messages come.

I close my eyes, expecting the weight of my husband's arms around me. Only he doesn't come, and when I open my eyes, he's no longer in the kitchen.

My mug is steaming. I reach for it, sip.

There's not quite enough milk in my tea.

> Me: Call off the hounds. I've heard from Cass. She's good. On her way back from Ludlow now xx

Dad: Good stuff. The new chap running the department was a jobsworth about tracking so didn't make any headway with that. Just been chatting with Trigger though. He and Stump paid George a visit already. V compliant. They had no reason to doubt what he told them about Cass leaving without notifying him this morning. And he had no issues when Stump asked if he'd mind showing him his phone.

Dad: Sophie's still here and asked me to ask you if you've asked Harry about the interview yet

Before I have the chance to answer —

Sophie: The Sun has called again! They want to do a piece with H and Luke Rock together.

Sophie: Can you tell H
how much he'd be saving
my arse if he said yes?

Sophie: Pleeeeeeeeease 🙏

'I think you *would* have done it, you know?' I pretzel
my legs on the sofa, rub Harry's thigh with my toe.

He looks up, his thumb still absent-mindedly
scrolling through Twitter. 'Huh?

'What you were saying just now? On the phone?'

His shoulders stiffen against the backrest.

'I heard you say you think it was because you were
drunk but —'

'Eve.' He moves his thigh a fraction. My foot stills.
'I don't know what you've heard, but —'

'That my husband's a bloody hero!' Louder. Almost
jubilant. I come onto my knees, reach for him in the
guise of congratulations when, truth is, I still want a
hug. It's too basic though to speak that need aloud.

'A hero?' I remember when Harry's laughs were
from his belly. This one now cracks around his Adam's
apple. 'I wouldn't go that far.'

The cushions shift, and I fall backwards when he
gets to his feet. 'No matter what you say, Harry, I
don't believe it was the drink.'

Lucien always said as much on the mornings after
our own uninhibited nights before. 'Our true selves

emerge when alcohol strips away self-consciousness.' Would he say the same now he's sober? On his channel, he's talked about that younger version of himself as a boy living with unconfronted pain. He'd alluded to something similar when we were together, after sending a taxi to my school to take me to him because he was hurting and I was the only one, he'd said, who could alleviate the anguish. 'That's the hold you have on me, Eve.' I'd not questioned that hold – of a sixteen-year-old girl on a twenty-six-year-old man – because 'You're so mature,' he said, 'And anyway, my first ten years on this earth were so bloody awful, I wiped the slate clean when my father left and life begun anew.' With those tear-wet eyes, he *did* look young. Vulnerable. 'If you think about it, there's no age difference at all.' I'd got it then. Would it sit the same with me, though, if Cass were in the same kind of relationship now?

But this isn't the time for dwelling on Lucien. It's Harry who needs my attention.

I follow him from the sitting room and up the stairs. 'Don't you think there's a liberty in being drunk that exposes our, I dunno what you would call it...' I *do* know, but it feels odd – a little grubby – to be citing my ex verbatim to my husband. 'When we let ourselves go like that, we expose who we really are at our core.'

Harry climbs into bed.

From beneath the duvet, he holds out a hand.

I take it and lay down too.

'You're a good man, Harry Gunn.' I'm staring at the ceiling. 'And what you did last night was unbelievable.'

'You might be right,' he says.

I turn and stroke his hair. 'I'm pretty sure your true self is better than mine. Jesus, the things I've done after too much wine.'

Or pills.

Like I said, there was, *is* – for me at least – a liberty in being drunk. Or high. And sure, it didn't always go in my favour. But with Lucien, I discovered more of myself on those long nights when we were buzzed than I did in any of the time we spent together straight.

Mum always liked to spout that Mark Twain quote about how we should dance like nobody's watching, and it was in Golden and the Hacienda, where everyone's pupils were dark and dilated, that I found I could be exactly that free. In other clubs or pubs, that liberation was leery, beery and loud. MDMA'd hands, though, were rarely roaming, rather the music sailed them, buoyant and celebratory, above a serenely jubilant crowd.

'Yes,' I said whenever Lucien suggested, on our return home, that we drop another half before bed.

Because I knew what was possible, how the pleasure I otherwise found it difficult to ask for came unbidden when ecstasy rippled through every inch of my bones and flesh and skin.

I knew the dangers. I'd seen the photo of the "pretty girl" in hospital, slack-mouthed and dying despite the abundance of tubes. One pill. That's all she'd taken. That's all it took, the BBC and The *Sun* and The *Telegraph* all told us.

Dad said we were never to touch it.

And I meant it when I told him, *of course*.

But I was a good girl for my father *and* for Lucien too.

The release was greater than the fear. My body becoming so entirely my own that when I drifted from the bedroom to the bathroom and looked in the mirror, my reflection was someone *I* loved and desired. And all those other desired things, the ssshhh'd desired things I'd previously dared not even whisper were also made speakable. 'Imagine,' Lucien said, 'if it wasn't just the two of us. If there were someone else to do help me do *this*.' He described a pleasure that might come with more flesh, more fingers, more tongue. 'Another girl.'

I imagined.

My "yes" was an unbound groan.

It was a fantasy we never saw through.

Not together. Not quite.

A thud, fleeting but ferocious when I remember that one particular night.

'Harry,' I whisper, a finger on the buttons of his shirt. 'Should we…'

A hand – his – on my hip pulling me closer, his breath fire on my tongue. I swallow the burn then open my lips wider, wanting more. More. More.

'Eve,' he says. But not the way he says it when he's loose and wanting. Where the air was hot, it's already turning cool. 'I can't. Not now.'

'It's OK. I get it.' I try to imagine the fury that must have driven Harry beyond fear to bring that intruder down. It was silly to expect him to… I push away the needling memory of our combined bodies once being a place of recovery from the extremities of love and terror, pride and guilt, happiness and pain. 'You rest. It will have been exhausting going over it all with the police. I'll check train times, wait for Cass at the station.'

He must be shattered because Harry's eyes close before I've even finished saying our daughter's name.

I leave him to sleep, reach for my phone.

```
Me: Coffee might work.
Tomorrow? 2?
```

Facebook post, originally written by Saira Siddiqui and Shared by Shayan Akhtar

সায়রা সিদ্দিকী'র লেখা ফেসবুক পোস্ট যেটা শায়ান আখতার শেয়ার করেছেন।

'আমার বোন আনাশি সিদ্দিকী আট দিন ধরে নিখোঁজ। আমরা পুলিশকে জানিয়েছি এবং পুলিশ আমাদের আশ্বস্ত করেছে যে তাঁরা তাকে খুঁজে বের করার জন্য যথাসাধ্য চেষ্টা করছে, কিন্তু এখন পর্যন্ত আমাদেরকে তাঁরা আশানুরূপ কোন খবর দিতে পারেনি। এমনকি আমরা কোন প্রেস কভারেজও পাইনি। আমরা সবাই যখন 'লুসি কারিগান' (স্থানীয়) এর নিরাপদে ফিরে আসার জন্য প্রার্থনা করছি, তখন আমার বিশ্বাস করতে কষ্ট হচ্ছে যে, আমার আদরের বোন আনাশি (অভিবাসী) এর নিরাপদে ফিরে আসার জন্য সমান মিডিয়া কাভারেজ ও জনসমর্থন পাচ্ছি না। কেউ তেমন চেষ্টাও করছে না।

আমি ও আমার পরিবার আপনাদের কাছে অত্যন্ত কৃতজ্ঞ থাকবো আপনারা যদি আনাশির নিখোঁজ হওয়ার এই খবরটা শেয়ার করে সবাইকে জানিয়ে দেন এবং তাঁকে খুঁজে পেতে সাহায্য করেন। তদন্তে কাজে লাগতে পারে এমন কোন তথ্য যদি কারো কাছে থাকে, অনুগ্রহ করে আমাকে জানাবেন।

আনাশি, তুমি যদি এই পোস্টটা পড়ে থাক, তাহলে জেনে নিও আমরা তোমাকে অনেক ভালোবাসি এবং তোমাকে খুঁজে পেতে আমরা সর্বোচ্চ চেষ্টা করছি।

আবারও ধন্যবাদ। আমি সত্যিই আপনাদের সাহায্যের প্রশংসা করি!
অ্যামি

My sister Aanshi Siddiqui has been missing for eight days. We have contacted the police who have assured us they are doing their utmost to find her, but so far we have zero leads. Nor do we have any press coverage. This is not for want of trying. While we are, of course, praying for the safe return of Lucy Corrigan, it is hard to witness both the media and public support for her case and not wish we had the same for our dearest Aanshi.

In light of this, my family and I would be hugely grateful if you could please share this post to raise awareness of Aanshi's disappearance. And if anyone does have any information they think might be useful to the investigation, please do contact me.

Aanshi, if you are reading this, know we love you and are doing everything we can to find you.

CASS

'I said I'd walk.' I've no choice now but to get in her car.

'Hello to you too.' Mum's voice is that faux light she channels when she's determined to keep the mood sweet. 'It's been raining on and off all day, and I wasn't sure what you were wearing given what I heard about you leaving the dinner in a rush?' An arched brow like there's questions brewing. Then she eyes Dad's coat. 'I see your father's not let you down.'

I toss it between the headrests into the back.

She glances to check I've fastened my seatbelt.

What am I, five?

She starts the engine. 'He's been so worried,' she says. 'We both have. And I appreciate you're eighteen and living your own life now, Cass, but what with everything that happened last night – with your father –'

And this is it, I think, remembering word for word, because I've read it over and over, that WhatsApp she sent when I was with George.

> Mum: I hope you're safe
> at George's, my darling.
> It's been a strange night.

```
I've always known there
are dodgy men out there
but what happened at
Hambledon Manner has made
me realise they're much
closer than I'd perhaps
thought. Your dad though
is one of the good ones.
The best even. I love
you, poppet. We both do
(even if your dad isn't
able to say too much right
now) xxx
```

'— he could have died,' she says.

I turn to her like, *what?*

'The incel was holding a knife when your dad rugby tackled him to the floor.'

'*Dad?* I thought Luke Rock was the one who —'

'Your dad got to him first.'

Two men. The *Mirror* article had spoken about *two men* intercepting the intruder. But I was so mad, I never even thought about who the other man might be.

So that's what Mum's message was about. The dodgy men she was referring to weren't Money-Clip or Bry or Dad.

146

We wait to turn left out of the carpark, our silence disturbed by the indicator's tick tick tick.

The traffic light remains on red, and Mum huffs with frustration when the pedestrian crossing flashes green. 'So, you *have* heard about it then?' I keep my eyes fixed ahead but can see she's shifted in her seat to look at me. 'The attack, I mean. Only it seemed like you weren't reading my messages, and you didn't pick up when I called.' And, sure, there's accusation in her voice, but there's hurt too. I hear her hard wet swallow. 'You weren't concerned about your dad?'

'I...' How can I tell her I couldn't bear to read any more from her because I thought she'd taken *his* side? Is it even worth mentioning? Because when an evening ends with a knife-wielding incel surely everything that came before that movie-level Bad Guy is, by comparison, tame.

I should move on, right?

Like Liv, who before I turned and left without speaking to her, without shaming her by letting her know I was witness to her reversal, stood on her tiptoes to kiss her father's cheek. It wasn't clear if the peck was an "I love you" or a "thank you" for what I'd I assumed was money. Notes, several of them, pulled from his wallet and placed firmly in her hand.

Move on. I told myself as I walked away from my friend. *Move on.* I thought as I sat, nauseous from the swaying motion of the train. *Move on.* I repeat in this stifling car with Mum.

Move on.

Move on.

Move on.

Dad's hand though.

Dad's face.

'I was busy,' is all I can come up with.

'With George?'

And I wasn't sure how or even *if* I should bring it up, but the way Mum says his name no problem gets the already swollen veins in my clenched fists twitching, and the words are fiercer than my pathetic attempt to keep schtum. 'Did Gramps send someone to his house?'

The question is almost rhetorical. After my call with George on the walk to Ludlow station, I already know the answer. But there's this bit of me that wants Mum to say "no". Thing is, that bit of me that's made of the sweet stuff, the best-of, the silver-linings and the que sera sera of life and of people is shrinking. Like shrinking so fast I can literally feel the contractions in my gut.

'We were worried,' she says. It is and isn't an answer.

Every inch of me tightens.

'I hadn't heard from you, Cass.' Mum rolls her shoulders, keeps her grip steady on the wheel. 'And when I called him to see if you were still at his, George was evasive. Gramps just wanted to be sure.'

'Sure? Of what?' A squeezing of air in my lungs.

'I don't know, that...'

George was crying when he phoned to tell me about "the visit". 'Message your mum, yeh?'

I was so focused on my own jumbled feelings, I didn't immediately catch it wasn't only words he was spewing but tears too. 'I don't feel like speaki—'

'I don't care if you feel like speaking to her.' He snapped. And I heard it then, his snotty horror and fear. 'The police came here asking about you. Mum and Dad were out. These two guys knocking on the door, so I let them in because what other option did I have? I *had* to talk to them. On my own, Cass. You know how scary it is for someone like *me* talking to people like *that* on my own?'

I came to a standstill, pictured George's face, eyes closed and slow breathing like he did when he told me about his cousin, Carter, stopped and searched in London. A stranger's mouth pressed words too sick to repeat in Carter's ear. Knees on his chest. Carter struggling for oxygen, shouting digit after digit to his mate. 'Call her,' he screamed. 'Please,' he begged, kicking his legs up and out, his friend told him later, like a helpless baby. 'I want my mum.'

'You were livid when I told you about George's cousin.' I say to my own mum now.

'That was totally differe—'

'You were talking about going on marches, starting petitions. You called the policemen scum.'

'That was London,' she says. 'Gramps' men aren't like that. The guys at the station are practically family. I was scared, OK?' She presses the button for the window, a cold rush of air whips through the car. 'Emotions were running high. Your dad was in a state. You weren't responding. What was I supposed to think?' She heaves a huge sigh. 'That man last night, he had a knife! I couldn't stop going over what might have happened if it weren't for your dad.'

I draw blood from the knotty inside of my cheek.

'I'll apologise to George,' Mum says.

'Thanks.' I don't exactly sound gracious.

'You know *you* also have apologies to make.'

'What?'

'Your aunt. You can't just up and leave when you're in the middle of a shift, Cass.' When I don't say anything, 'You're not going to offer any kind of explanation? You've seen the news. We were worried, especially when you disappeared this morning too.'

More silence.

'Fine.' She turns on the stereo.

A man on Radio 4 is interviewing a representative from Birmingham City Council. The councillor, 'like everyone', he says, is very concerned for Lucy Corrigan. 'And while the police are confident there is no need for widespread fear, I urge women to be savvy when they're out and about.'

Mum looks at me, like, *see.*

And that's the thing, isn't it, I'd laughed when one of the other girls called the shoes I'd borrowed from Helena "fuck-me heels". I'd willingly undone the top three buttons of my shirt. I served the men more wine even though they were lewd and rowdy. And when Bry beckoned me over, I didn't stop him when he put his hands on my neck, my hip, my knee.

I was not savvy. I was stupid.

'All I'm saying,' the councillor continues, 'is there are precautions a woman can take – routes with street-lights, installing tracking apps, making sure her phone is charged etc – small but manageable tricks to keep herself safe. I say this as a father,' he says, 'a father of daughters.'

I delete the photo of Dad and me on the beach from my phone.

MAIL ONLINE

Did living in the shadow of his star-student sister lead to this near tragedy? Details emerge of the fraught rivalry between 'quiet and gentle' knife-attacker Aaron Jenkins and his high-achieving older sibling Anna.

Eighteen-year-old Aaron Jenkins was arrested on Saturday night after he ambushed a Shropshire gala dinner, brandished a knife and threatened to attack the women working at the event. Jenkins, a student from Oswestry, has been described by his neighbours as 'a quiet gentle loner who keeps himself to himself.'

Alongside an as-yet unnamed diner, Luke Rock, the much-loved British comedian who was delivering an after-dinner speech at the event, restrained Jenkins for thirteen minutes while waiting for police to arrive on the scene. 'He was angry, but as we lay on the floor together, Aaron began sobbing,' Rock said in a statement on Sunday afternoon. Taking to Twitter on Monday morning, the national treasure spoke of how distressed he felt listening to Jenkins weeping about his 'lack of worth' and apparent 'failure at college and with women.'

A friend of Jenkins' sister, Anna, detailed the accolades 'the head-girl and star of the hockey team' received at her £7500 per term private school before moving on to London School of Economics, where she has allegedly found love with the great-grandson of Sir Edward Tominey, the founder of British ice-cream brand Dairy Boys.

Her brother, by contrast, confessed to Rock that he was a 'lonely virgin.'

EVE

'How's your sister?' Sophie has one eye on Charlotte and the other on the young waitress who, having ignored Charlotte's three attempts to get her attention, heads straight over with just a quick tilt of my sister's chin.

'What the...' Charlotte throws her palms in the air. 'How can I hold a jury in the palm of my hand but then —'

'There's only one woman holding the power when it comes to Shropshire's finest wait staff.' Sophie winks before half-standing to kiss the waitress on both cheeks. 'How are you, Meg? All recovered after Saturday's drama?'

'Oh. My. God!' Meg pulls a pen and small notebook from the back pocket of her jeans. 'It was even wilder than usual, right?' Her wide eyes are halfway between terrified and thrilled. 'I was with —' She glances at Charlotte and me, like she's catching herself. 'I wasn't in the room when that dude charged in, but it was mental, yeah?'

'You're OK though?' Sophie – sitting again now – lays a hand on Meg's arm.

'Sure.' Meg flicks her overgrown fringe away from her face. 'I was on my usual table so when Frank and

I came back in, the guys were all super protective. They were awesome, making sure those of us who weren't staying got in our taxis home.'

'That's great,' Sophie says. 'I'm glad. They're good guys.'

'*The best.*' Meg flips the notebook to a fresh page and asks if we're ready to order.

Once we're alone again, Sophie turns to Charlotte. 'You were about to tell us about Emma.'

A sharp slope falls across my friend's shoulders. Her head drops. Charlotte is usually a face-forward person. In social situations, she's all in, not one for examining the floor.

'You know I love Sophie,' she'd said when I phoned from site earlier to let her know my sister would be gate-crashing lunch. 'But I kind of hoped it'd be just the two of us. Emma's jittery enough about me talking to *you*, if she knew Soph—'

'Why's she worried about you talking to me?' I'd mimed to the tiler I'd be taking the call outside.

Charlotte was quiet for a second. 'Your connection to the police. She was already pissed off at me for talking to your dad yesterday. Fretting I will have said something to further implicate Aar—'

'You do know Dad's retired?'

'Retired yet still able to pull significant strings.'

I let her continued gripe dangle.

'Did you read Shayan's Facebook post?'

I did. But speedily and without much after-thought. Charlotte obviously gathered this because, 'Whatever,' she said. 'Emma's convinced you're all in each other's pockets. Said she and Tony were at Hambledon Manor golf club last week and saw Sophie with that Inspector. Saint, is it?'

'Joe Saint? That's Uncle Joe. Sophie's godfather.' It's true the two of them have become close in recent years but, 'As far as I know, their relationship doesn't extend beyond the occasional 18 holes. And between sorting the details for Dad's retirement bash, packing for her *month*-long retreat, and expending an inordinate amount of energy trying to persuade Harry to join Luke Rock in an interview with The *Sun*, Sophie's not going to have time for a round with Joe or anyone else.' I raised a finger at the tiler, who was staring impatiently through the bathroom window, and mouthed *one minute*. 'Honestly, as far as I can gather, any spare second she does have is spent debating the pros and cons of non-surgical rhinoplasty.'

It seems, from the look on her face now though, that my sister's present concerns are more geared towards Charlotte's connection to Aaron than I'd anticipated.

'I only ask about Emma because I was wondering...' The way Sophie pulls her shoulders back suggests whatever's she's about to say is important. 'Do you think she might do me a favour?' She stops, shakes her head. 'It probably doesn't make sense now I think about it.' She looks to the ceiling. 'Only, In the Event Of is being trolled.' Passes me her phone. 'Keyboard warriors wrecking my social media.'

I read through the comments beneath Sophie's photo of Hambledon Manner, which she posted with an outline of what happened on Saturday night.

'Ex-employees ranting about working conditions. It certainly says something, doesn't it, when a man can walk into a hotel waving a knife and shouting obscenities and threatening the waitresses, and it's the woman behind the company running the event who's getting trolled.'

'*Is it*, though? Trolling, I mean. Because what they're saying…' I tiptoe into the possibility that maybe my sister's not fully grasping the situation. 'Is it true?' I give her phone to Charlotte. 'That you told them they should think of their tips when the men got annoying. They put *annoying* in quotation marks, Soph. What does that even mean?'

Her lips are sightly parted, her tongue pressing into the underside of her back teeth. 'That was 2016, which is, what, seven years ago? Pre-Weinstein. Things have changed. *Massively*. But you know what men are like.' She folds her arms. 'They drink, Eve.' Sophie's tone suggests she's stating the obvious. 'And, back then, when they drank, they could get a bit...' Her right shoulder twitches. 'I wasn't suggesting anything other than the girls shouldn't climb straight on to their high horse if someone told them they're beautiful or – god forbid – that they should smile. I also made it very clear if anyone were to get out of hand, I would deal with it.'

Meg appears, puts a bowl of olives on the table. 'On the house.' She smiles at my sister, then places a palm on Charlotte's back. 'The chef knows you don't have too long and has prioritised your order.'

'Thanks,' Charlotte says, though her attention is elsewhere. When Meg walks away, 'One of them here says she was groped.' She holds up the phone so Sophie and I can read the comment. From the knuckle-white force of my friend's grip, I get the sense she's not ready to let go.

Sophie pricks at an olive with a cocktail stick, stabs it first time despite the slick of oil on its skin. 'Look, some of the diners then were...' She pauses, her eyes rounding. 'Old school.' Before I have a chance to ask her exactly what she means by "old school", she puts a hand to her chest in a gesture of mild surrender. 'But you know, maybe I *do* need to take some more responsibility. The event was a new thing for me then, and in those days, I wasn't as selective with the girls as I am now. It can be difficult for those who've not – how can I put it politely? – grown up around money to navigate these kinds of occasions. For them, the abundance of food, wine, bids, it can all be – I don't know – overwhelming.' She waves her hand in a quiet act of dismissal. 'I swear though, there was only one case of what someone might call physical *inappropriateness*.' The way Sophie says this last word suggests even that's too strong a description. 'It was nothing. He pulled her onto his knee, that's all.' The small shake of her head implies if there was any wrongdoing, it was negligible. 'You had worse when you worked in that cafe, remember, and you were only fourteen.'

It was true. I'd bent over to pick up a dropped fork, and my old-man manager put his hand up my skirt. I moved away as quietly, quickly as I could without seeming rude and worked the rest of the shift at a distance, not wanting to cause a scene.

Sophie impales another olive. 'The guy this girl accused was decent. One of your legal lot, Charlotte. It would be putting his job on the line to do something like that against her will. That said, ever the gentleman, he apologised,' she continues. 'Profusely. The waitress said it was fine. I remember calling her the next day to be sure. Asked her outright if there was a problem, and she swore there was no issue. Came back the following year.' A gulp of wine. 'She'd hardly have done that if it was as serious as she's now insinuating, would she. Everyone just wants in on the glamour of the media glare because of that bloody incel.' Sophie reaches across the table to take back her phone. 'And I was thinking that Emma – if and when she makes a public statement about Aaron – could perhaps mention the money the gala has raised for her paediatric unit in the last few years. It's got to be close to £50k all in all.'

Somehow Charlotte rises above Sophie's gall. 'From what I gather, she won't be making a statement.' She pivots to me then. 'We need to hurry this food, don't we? Didn't you say you have to be somewhere by two?'

'Sorry,' Sophie says. 'That was totally insensitive and inappropriate of me.'

Neither Charlotte nor I disagree.

'Really.' Her hand covers Charlotte's. 'I mean it. It's not an excuse but… I just get so panicky about anything damaging the business. After Tommy left…' Her face bloats with the extreme effort she's making not to cry. I can't not put an arm around her. Despite everything she's achieved since they separated, there's something about the hurt her ex-husband caused her that never fails to bring my sister to tears. 'I swore I wouldn't let myself get that close to losing everything again. Thanks.' She smiles, takes the napkin I'm holding out for her and dabs her cheeks. 'Anyway.' Sophie shakes her head and – as if that really is enough to rid herself of any residual upset – offers me a wide-eyed grin. 'This thing you've scheduled at two, wouldn't have anything to do with Luke Rock now, would it?'

'Luke Rock?' That got Charlotte's attention.

Sophie gives her a vigorous nod. 'Eve's first love.' Her elbow nudges my side.

'I did *not* love him, Sophie.'

'That's not what you said at the time.'

She's right, of course. I did say I loved him.

I did, in fact, love him.

Though the love we had was coarser than the love I later experienced with Harry. But Lucien's pills softened things. And his gigs too. In their wake, if they went well – which they did more often than not – he'd be high without narcotics, though that natural buzz would soon be supplemented with the shots he'd get comped – two a pop – in the bar.

'One for me, one for you,' he said, extending his right arm, looping it through mine, the bind insisting our faces come closer if we were to down the vodka. The hot mortification, that first time, when it dribbled down my chin. He licked it – the drink, the shame – off me. The burn in my throat tame, then, with the rest of my body on fire.

'What's so funny?' His eyes darkened. I hadn't yet learned laughter was best saved for when Lucien cracked a joke.

'My receptors,' I said because only that morning I'd been making notes for my GCSE biology exam. 'You're so much stimuli.'

It was crude but true and, for two years, it only got truer. While terrible for my revision timetable, Lucien Rothschild was stimuli to the max.

'Is Harry meeting you too?' Charlotte contributes a fiver to the tip on the table.

'He's not really up for talking with anyone at the moment.' This statement is wholly accurate. 'Still hasn't told me exactly what happened on Saturday night. That's the main reason for meeting Lucien – Luke – if I'm honest.' *This* statement, however, is not.

'Remind me,' Soph says. 'When was the last time you saw each other?'

'I'm not sure.' Another line of fiction.

1996. 17th of August.

That was the month I last saw my best friend Kelly too.

I'm already in the pub when Luke Rock cancels.

```
LR: Gen! Huge apologies.
Last minute PR meeting re
press  opps  around  the
```

```
incel. In town a few days
though. Will check diary
with PA and get back to
you ASAP xxxxx
```

I leave my coat hanging over the back of my chair at the table and order a vodka shot at the bar.

Mr Alan Herring
Uniform
To: All Parents and Pupils
Reply-To: Mr Alan Herring

Dear parents and pupils

Following the completion of our fantastic new Arts & Drama facilities, partially funded by the wonderful Friends of Oakfield, we are experiencing some minor issues with the use of the glass-balustraded staircase. It was recently brought to my attention that from certain angles, it is possible to gain an inappropriate vantage point of those on the risers and that some students have exploited this in a way that is entirely unacceptable.

While we consider our next moves, I am asking all female students who opt for skirts in school to please also wear cycling shorts. This should allow them some modesty while making their way to and from the drama studio.

As you know, we are extremely proud of recent improvements at Oakfied and are delighted with how heartily the students are embracing the new facilities.

With thanks and best wishes

Mr Alan Herring

CASS

'What's the plan then, girls?' Maya moves her coat and bag from the seats she's been saving for Liv and me in the food hall. When we don't immediately respond to her question, 'You have heard what happened to the statue last night?'

Liv shrugs, *what?* And I shake my head. 'Aside from messaging you two, I've stayed off my phone.'

'The sixth form boarder boys had *a clandestine gathering.*' Maya is momentarily posh. 'Snuck in some wine. Probably some of Daddy's 50-year-old merlot.'

'That would explain why it sent them so gaga,' Liv says. 'You really shouldn't keep a Merlot more than three to five years.'

Maya looks at her, like, *who even are you.* 'Aaaaaanway, whatever they were drinking, they clearly had too much of it because some time around three AM, one of the frat-boy-wannabes snuck out of his dorm and painted a bra on the statue of Darwin outside the headmaster's study.'

'A bra?'

'I know, right!' Maya sighs. 'You should have seen Herring's face when he told us at chapel. I honestly reckon if they'd superglued a cigar to the old man's mouth, our eminent headmaster would have been fine with it. But god forbid you emasculate such a hero by adorning him with something so girly!'

'Uh oh!' Liv bug-eyes. 'Girl's got her plotting face on.' Then, through a mouthful of jacket potato, 'It's a few months, babe.' She puts her knife and fork down, counts out October to May on her fingers. 'Eight! Eight months! And a bunch of that is holiday or study leave. So, it's what, four really? Then we're out of here, and you won't have to worry about Herring ever again.' She nudges me like, *tell her I'm right, Cass.* But whenever I look at Liv, I think about how relieved I'd been when she agreed to meet me early at the greasy spoon this morning, and then how my relief had calcified into confusion as quickly as Liv's intrigue about Saturday night had slipped into disregard.

'You know they wouldn't actually hurt you.' She'd said in the café when I told her about Money-Clip and Bry. She'd picked up a sugar cube, not to drop it into her coffee, which would be "rank" but to lick it, corner by corner, until it was no longer a cube but a ball. 'I mean, is it gross that these old dudes wanna chirpse and that?' She arched her brow. 'Sure. But, honestly, ninety-nine per cent of the time, I swear it pays, literally, to go with the flow.' She rubbed her thumb and fingers together to suggest cash, then ordered two more bacon butties to go.

'I can't have another one. You know I'm saving.' Less than 48-hours ago, the fifty-pound note had slipped neatly into the waistband of my skirt. It was sticky at the station yesterday when I'd used it to pay for my fare.

'My shout,' Liv said at my protest 'You do know the thought of a double portion of high-cholesterol sandwiches was basically what got me through my shift at Zara.'

I was tempted to show her the photo I'd taken in Ludlow when she was supposedly slogging her guts at work. It was at that point I decided if she wasn't going to tell me about the latest developments with *her* dad, I wouldn't tell her about those with mine.

'Earth to Cass!' Now, Liv clicks her fingers dead close to my eyes. 'Back me up, yeah. Maya should walk away from this beef with Herring.'

'But there are so many Herrings,' Maya says. 'And it's the principle. He's on the hunt for this "menace", harping on about his CCTV evidence and his "dogged determination" that the culprit is caught and "duly punished".' She wags a finger like Herring must have done in the whole-school assembly I skipped after breakfast in favour of a hushed and lonely corner of the library. 'He was spitting, Cass. Actual flob on the lectern because he was that vexed. But you remember how chill he was about the upskirting?'

I do. There was a *now now, boys* to his tone. A warning, sure, but the angle of Herring's head, of his brow even, when he said taking such photos was unacceptable suggested there was a silliness as opposed to an abhorrence to the perpetrators' behaviour.

'You see the irony?' Maya says. 'That Herring's losing his shit over a statue, a *pretend* man made of metal, having women's underwear painted on him, while he didn't appear to give a genuine shit about a *real* girl's *real* underwear being exposed. It's not even as if Darwin's bra was permanent. It's Oakfield. The *vandals* used oil paints for god's sake. The caretaker had sponged it off with turps by break. Meanwhile, those photos of Yasmin are still doing the rounds.'

'Hide all the matches!' Liv shouts. And despite my Saturday night, and Liv's blasé reaction to it, I laugh, imagining Maya stalking these ancient halls with a flaming torch setting light to anything she deems offensive.

'Anything?' She says when I've relayed my vision 'Well then that green jumper you love so much'd get it too!'

'Oi!' I pout. 'That's a Nineties original!'

'It's inexcusable is what it is. And if you were wearing it now, I'd one hundred per cent scorch it to dust.' Maya pulls a lighter from her rucksack and flicks the wheel to ignite the flame. 'What's the point in constantly rehashing the past. Isn't that the problem we have in this school. Herring regurgitating the same old same old for the simple fact that that's how it's always been. Ouch!' She snatches her thumb away and the lighter goes out. 'Seriously, let's incinerate the lot.' She stands, spreads her arms and feet wide and declares, 'From the ashes will come something new.' A few of the younger kids turn to watch her, and she gives them a determined salute. 'It would get a response at least,' Maya says, sitting back down. And for all her comedy, I'm starting to wonder if she's serious. 'You know what they say, if a woman's being attacked, she's more likely to get help if she shouts fire instead of rape.'

'Is that even true?' I think of Saturday. How no one stopped Bry. How that voice, *Dad's* voice, was concerned not with unwanted hands on my body but with the delay to his fucking port.

Trust me.

And I should. I want to. He's my dad, and he's not like *that*. Like *them*. It was the drink, the auction, the mood.

Maya shrugs now. 'Wouldn't surprise me.'

'Four months, Maya,' Liv repeats. 'Bide your time. You're head girl. By a thread. Keep it that way. Screw Oakfield. What matters is *you*. Bristol awaits, yeh?'

'Yes, Mum.' Maya pulls a face at Liv for spoiling her pyro daydreams but instantly brightens with a fresh and, I'm assuming from her cackle, devilish plan. '*You* should do it, Cass... our gap-year girl here has no uni place hinging on her good behaviour.'

Before I have a chance to dodge it, Maya's lighter smacks me in the face. 'Ow.' I pick it up from where it ricocheted from my cheek to my thigh to the floor.

Maya leans across the table, rubs my lighter-struck cheek with her thumb. 'How about it, Heraclitus?'

Liv's face crumples. 'You what?'

'Heraclitus.' Maya looks at Liv. 'All these times you've bailed on us recently to study, I'd have thought you'd have heard of him. Philosopher?'

Liv is still no clearer.

'He reckons fire unites everything, that everything *is* fire.' Maya clears her throat. '"It ever was, and is, and shall be, ever-living fire, in measures being kindled and in measures going out."'

Liv makes a small circular motion with her index finger by her temple.

'If everything's fire, it means it's in a state of change. A state of progression,' Maya says like this settles it. 'So, you're game, Cass, yeah?' She mimes an explosion with her hands.

'If I'm going to travel, I need a job not a criminal record.'

'And what *I* need,' Maya pokes me in the chest. 'Is some back-up, yeah? I know I'm not the only one who's sick of this place, but somehow I *am* the only one who ever risks taking a stand. Take Callum,' she says. 'You've seen his TikTok?'

Liv scoffs. 'Why would I follow that prick?'

'Erm,' Maya pulls her phone from her pocket. 'Because this school is enough of a bubble, and we don't want to exist in an echo chamber?'

'Don't we?' Liv crumples her face in mock confusion.

Maya shakes her head, plays the video of our beloved head boy 'giving credit where credit's due to Andrew Tate. I mean, he's controversial, sure,' Callum says straight to camera. 'But he's spot on when he talks about the disenfranchisement of young men.' He jabs his index finger at the overlaid text above his head. 'Some facts,' he says, reading the words aloud in a voice that stinks of our twenty-two-grand-a-year education.

Men have legitimate reason to fear being alone with women. Studies have revealed that anything from 1.5 – 90% of rape allegations are false. FACT.

'You can't argue with numbers.' More text.

The results of a survey for sexual activity and contraceptive use among US teens suggested young men are getting far less sex than we want and need. A Pew Research study discovered that over 60 % of men under 30 are single. This is nearly double that of women under 30. FACT.

'Haters are going to cite speculation, but this isn't hearsay.' Callum's face hardens into a frown. 'It's science, lads. It's truth.'

Liv, Maya and I baulk at the cockiness of that pointing finger.

Three quarters of suicide deaths in the UK are men. FACT.

Maya hits pause. 'I hate to say Callum's right about anything because most of what he says is trash, but number three is real, and we should one hundred per cent be doing something about it.' Liv pulls a face, like, *you what*, and Maya gets dead serious. 'I'm not suggesting the rest of what that nobhead said is legit, far from it. But, irony is, the patriarchy he's so desperate to cling to is fucking over men's mental health too.'

Liv lets out a massive sigh.

'JMO, babe, JMO.' Maya hits play. We watch the rest of the TikTok in silence.

'And they wonder why we don't want to go out with them,' Liv says when it's finished. 'Tell me, apart from chlamydia, what is any girl going to get from a relationship with Callum Bell? I'm done with giving this,' she stands tall and waves a hand to indicate her body, 'to twats like him like it's nothing.' A content smile. 'From now on, there's only going to be one beneficiary from any interaction I have with men, and that's me.'

The three of us clink our Diet Cokes. 'Hear hear!'

The bell rings, and we go our separate ways towards class. I'm half way to History when my phone buzzes in my palm.

```
George: Babe, have I done
something? Why you not
answering my calls? X
```

We'd spoken last night when I'd said sorry again for my family's over-zealous efforts to find me. My apology was genuine, as was George's response, which was that his beef was with my mum and Gramps, not me.

'Come over.' he said. I could hear he was still shook. He'd have wanted, needed, comfort. And, no doubt, I owed him, but nausea lumped in my chest, seeping into every inch of me with any thought of being touched.

I close his message without sending a reply.

The rain, when I'm walking across the hockey pitches, is made of dollops so fat, they practically bounce of the astro. I shake my shoes of them and duck into the renovated arts and drama block to keep dry.

A noise, clumpy footsteps, above. When I look up, I can't see anything but my own face reflecting back at me in the glass of the half landing of the fancy new staircase leading to the state-of-the-art rehearsal rooms.

Is this where Dexter stood, I wonder, when he took that photo of Yasmin? Zoomed in to maximise the embarrassment he could capture in one small frame? No one mentions *that* in the glossy marketing material fanned between the arts and drama trophies on the table. How the "exceptional effort that goes into planning your children's all-round development" won't be matched when it comes to uncovering who exactly it was that took an illegal image of your daughter's crotch on his phone.

We all knew it was Dexter. But the picture was shared so many times there was no way, apparently, of tracing it back to the source. Not that the "investigation" continued for long.

The fallout for Yasmin though? That's ongoing.

She used to be one of the bolshy girls in that year group. Now though, she slips through the corridors. Eyes down. Mute. Dexter, meanwhile, like Callum and the rest of them who've laughed at that picture, remains arrogant and shameless and loud.

I take one of the brochures and remove my phone and Maya's lighter from my bag.

One hand works the camera. In the other, the ridges of the sparkwheel are rough against my thumb.

It should be easy to put the flame to the paper.

I tease it closer then closer still, allow the cover to catch and curl in the heat. But by the time I've whispered "fire", my foot is a hard extinguishing stamp.

I am not made of what it takes to set the world alight.

No.

I am made of whispers and weakness and ineffective adrenaline. Not the kind that makes you pumped and powerful, rather the kind that makes you panic and run.

YOU

You're a good man. You know this. Your wife knows this. And from the football WhatsApp group, where they're hurling words like "epic" and "audacious", the parents and the lads in your team know this too.

You'd gone to the bathroom this morning, locked the door and googled "hero" on your phone.

Caped cartoon men and pec-heavy action figures. An utterly male-heavy offering, aside from Mariah Carey's reassuring warble that a hero lies within us all.

To the mirror then, where you looked for signs of this person the dictionary definition insists is admired for their courage or outstanding achievement. Is this what your daughter would see if she were to look at you now?

You wouldn't know because she hasn't looked at you since Saturday night.

It's not that you've been avoiding her. After Eve left to pick Cass up from the station yesterday, Kev messaged to say there was a plumbing situation on site and, sure, he also said he had it in hand, but you're too far along in the build to risk water damage now.

It was at least ten-thirty by the time you got home, at which point your daughter was already in bed. Your wife too. A plus really; she'd only have wanted to go over what happened at the gala dinner and what was it, did you think, that made Cass disappear like that. If only you'd told her when she first arrived at Hambledon Manor on Saturday, immediately explained the "accident" of your hand on your daughter's arse. That word, though, "accident", could you say it aloud, Harry, without the same subtle scepticism with which it's voiced in your head? What you'd said instead several times already was that Cass didn't disappear, not really. She went to George's and then to Ludlow, where her only crime was, for a few hours at most, to not be as responsive as she usually is on her phone. There was no reason for all this concern.

You said it, Harry. But you aren't sure – even though you're a good man who wouldn't intentionally lie to his wife – that you believed it, that your thoughts weren't as grainy and glutinous as the cement in the mixer in those early days on site.

They were churning, *are* churning still when, unable to stay away any longer, you come in through the door to find Eve in the kitchen, telling you dinner is almost ready and asking, even though it's Monday and neither of you tends to drink on weeknights, if you'd like some wine. You shake your head, *no*. She tops up her own glass. It's already half full.

'It's been a day,' she says, turning to the sink to drain the spaghetti. You put your hands on her hips, a gentle tug towards you, but with that comes a strobe of Saturday night. Your hand on another woman's body. Your daughter's body. Cass's body. Her face, when she saw you, shattered in a way that aged her. The opposite of laughter lines. As if, as your mother used to say in moments of anger or upset, she'd seen it all.

In the bathroom this morning, you'd swiped your search for "hero" from the history of your phone.

'Perfect timing,' Eve calls at the sound of the front door opening then closing.

You listen for Cass's footsteps across the floorboards. Their rhythm is one of the many things about her you'd recognise blindfolded. All those tiny details, since her infancy, memorised by heart. You've always sworn you could pick her out of thousands at the sight of a mere freckle, dimple or toe. Yet you saw those bare legs beneath Bry's fingers and had no hint of your daughter. Her sexual availability erased any hint of your little girl.

Now, when she sees you, Cass's mouth, usually utterly expressive, is an unfamiliar, unfaltering straight line.

There is a question you want to ask *and* something you want to make clear.

Why did you let him touch you like that?
And
I *didn't mean to touch you like that.*

But both are gristle in your throat. 'Is that your mum's?' is all you can manage because the black mac Cass is hanging on a peg isn't your green puffer, which she wore every day last winter. You'd been disproportionately touched, reassured, even, when you'd seen her in it on one of the colder days last week too.

It's silly, you realise now, to have believed your coat was a shield that would protect your daughter.

She stares at her bag, picks at her nails.

'Cass,' you start but, head down, she goes to the kitchen before you can say another word.

'How was school?' Eve kisses her cheek, as you would like to.

Would a kiss from you be tainted?

'Fine,' Cass says, flipping to 'Good.' *Fine* will not pass muster; Eve will want details. 'Herring's initiated a man hunt.'

Your heart lurches when your daughter's face softens slightly with an inkling of a smile. You look to Eve, then, afraid perhaps it will harden again if Cass catches your eye.

'What's riled the old fish now?' Eve, who agreed to Cass attending Oakfield despite rather than because of its "antiquated" headteacher, is laying bowls of pesto pasta with greens and pine nuts and extra parmesan on the table. You are topping up the wine in her already empty glass.

Speaking directly to her mother, Cass tells of sixth formers graffitiing Darwin and of the blatant imbalance in Herring's reaction to this versus "the shit show" with Yasmin Grant last term. She only turns to you once she's finished and snatching Eve's drink. She swallows one glug and then another of deep red wine.

'Easy tiger,' Eve says.

Cass laughs. 'God forbid I get drunk and do something stupid.'

A heat scrambles up your neck to the tops of your ears.

'Have a glass of your own if you like, poppet.' Eve, who is standing now, opens the cupboard.

'S'fine. Unlike some people, I know my limits.' It's not quite a slam when Cass puts Eve's glass back on the table.

You want to remind her you were both there. Were both perhaps behaving in a way you'd rather you hadn't.

'Sadly I think you're right, love.' Eve returns to the table with three yoghurts and three spoons. 'I hate to say it, but boys will always be boys.'

But she's wrong, isn't she Harry? Because not all boys.

Not all men.

Not you.

EVE

'You re-think those paint colours and get back to me. In the meantime, the boss man around for chatting rates?'

I'm about to tell Martin, the painter and decorator, he's more than welcome to discuss rates with *me* when my phone rings. And while, yes, it would be good to prove I'm as much in charge as my husband, truth is, I *do* usually leave the numbers to Harry. It was his business before it was ours. Procedures were already in place. I shout for him to come up from the kitchen.

'Hey.' I answer the video call from Dad.

'Hey yourself.' His eyes squint in the sun. 'How's Cass?'

'Alright, I think.' I pass Harry on the stairs. 'I've barely seen her.' It's true. In the four days since the gala on Sunday, Cass has barely been home. 'She graced us with her slightly mardy presence at dinner on Monday.'

Harry clears his throat, pauses on the top step, I look back, mouth *it's Dad* and point to the front door to indicate I'm going outside.

'Not been around much?' The lines in Dad's forehead deepen. 'I'm surprised you haven't asked me to track her again.'

'I didn't ask you to track her the last ti—'

'You know what the lads at the station are saying?' He pauses, but – like Sophie – Dad's favourite questions are rhetorical. 'That retirement's obviously turned me into a curtain twitcher. A bored housewife looking for drama where there isn't any. It's embarrassing.' He blows out his cheeks, holds the air briefly, emits a potent exhale.

'Isn't the main thing,' I say, shutting the front door behind me and sitting on the low uneven wall, 'that Cass is OK.'

'It doesn't matter that my reputation's in tatters then?'

Tatters? 'Until six months ago, you were a highly regarded Chief Inspector with fifty years of service behind you. I think it'd take more than one erroneous request to tarnish your *reputation.*'

'I'm a laughingstock.'

'No offence, Dad.' I remember what Charlotte said when I'd told her Dad was going to ask his old work mates to track Cass down. 'They won't be giving you a second thought. Don't they have more important things to be focusing their attention on. Lucy Corrigan, for example?' And I'd cite Shayan's Facebook post about the missing Bangladeshi girl from Aston, Birmingham, but I can't remember her name.

'Hello, gorgeous!'

There's a muffling and tumbling. Dad, I think, has dropped his phone. 'You're a cute one, aren't you?' My father's voice pendulums between high and low.

'Who're you talking to?'

'Is he a cockapoo?' A flash of Dad's knees. Then fur. A snout, 'Here, boy.' All I see then is sky. 'You like to be tickled, do you!' His tone is as soft as it was on those afternoons after his night shifts when Cass was a tiny baby and he'd join us no matter the weather for my much-needed walk. His spot for his granddaughter is softer, even, than his spot for me, which is saying something given Sophie has always alleged favouritism.

I see four paws splashing in muddy water.

'Where even are you?' I'm almost shouting.

'The river. Mulling over the speech your mother's insisting I make at my dinner on Saturday. Though I think what she was actually insisting on was *some space*.' The emphasis he puts on these last two words suggests they're not originally his own. 'I'm not convinced she's enjoying how much I'm around.'

'Oh?' I attempt surprised.

'He's like the grandfather clock,' Mum whispered when I popped by yesterday evening after she'd ushered me into the laundry and closed the door. 'Always in the same bloody position letting out some noise or other every hour or so to be sure I can't forget he's there.'

'She reckons I need a hobby,' Dad says. 'Managing to piss everyone off, aren't I?'

'Maybe if you had the same upbeat energy around humans as you do around dogs, things'd be easier at home.' I'm only half teasing. 'You do you realise you were verging on jolly just now.'

'What can I say, I'm a different man in the company of hounds!'

'It's a new phase, Dad. You need to find the new you.'

'I miss the old me. The lads at the station wouldn't have taken the piss out of him.' My Dad's shoulders, which have born so much hard responsibility, round in defeat.

'How about I go to the station?' I suggest. 'Tell them the visit to George's was my idea. Apologise for wasting their time.'

He may be shaking his head, *no*, but Dad's forehead unfurrows, his eyes brighten at the thought.

'It's fine,' I say because what's a few words to bolster my father's clearly flagging ego.

'If you're sure.' Before I have time to confirm my intentions, he's telling me it's probably best to go just before five-thirty because Stump'll be leaving for his lodge meeting at quarter to six.

'It'd be easier for me to go this morning, Dad. I've got a meeting this afternoon, and I promised Cass I'd pick her up at five from school.'

'Even better.' His breath is short from the quickened pace. 'Take her along. Facing that lot'll make sure she won't worry you like that again anytime soon.'

'Fuck's sake.'

'Cass!' It's usually her reprimanding me for swearing.

She stares at the dashboard, her index finger tapping repeatedly against her thigh. 'I don't see why we're going that's all.'

I hold off from starting the engine.

She turns to me, her tongue running aggressively across her teeth. 'You said interrogating George was Gramps' idea.'

'It *was*.' It was, wasn't it? *You need me to send someone over*, he'd asked, so, yes, it *was* Dad's idea.

'Then don't you think it should be *him* apologising? To *George*,' Cass clarifies.

'*I* will say sorry to George, okay?' I offer her a mint from the packet in the centre console, but she just huffs a furious puff of air, shakes her head like everything I'm saying and doing is absurd. 'Look, your grandfather…' I start. But that line of conversation is a dead end because what Dad said when I questioned if we'd perhaps acted too hastily was, *You*

can never be too sure, Evie, especially when it comes
to...

'He's...' I was about to say a different generation
but, the mood Cass is in, that clearly won't cut it.
'Gramps isn't himself. He's used to...' I think about
the exaggerated creeping Sophie and I would do as
kids around the house while he was sleeping. And
then there were those rare occasions Mum took us to
the station so we could see 'Daddy at work'. His
uniform was as dark as the pitch-black nights when
he took me – and only me – camping. Daddy and
Evie time. The cold of the night and the warmth of
the campfire we almost couldn't start.

'I'll let you into a secret, shall I?' He rolled the
wheel of our upside-down duff lighter without making
a spark. Tiny grey flecks fell to the kitchen roll he'd
laid on my knee. 'Fairy dust!' He twisted the tissue
into a ball, which he held to the righted lighter. Made
more powerful by the gathered flint, its spark was
now enough to set the tissue on fire. Dad's grin glowed
magic in the flame.

We didn't see that grin at the station. There, he
was more likely to bark. Sophie and I listened on the
chairs outside his office, giggling at his voice rampaging
behind the closed door. 'Austere' she said, her whisper
hot with spit.

I looked it up in the dictionary when we got home.

Sophie was known for her vocabulary. I was known for my smile.

'He's used to being in control,' I say to Cass now. 'Your grandfather is…'

Her eyes round with anticipation of how exactly I can justify the visit to George *and* this trip to the station.

'…in transition.' I throw my hands in the air because, honestly, it's the best I can do. 'It must be weird for him no longer working? It's no wonder he was keen t—'

'Fine.' The click of her seatbelt is confirmation we can go. As frustrating as she might find him, Cass's Gramps is *her* soft spot too.

It's a relief to start moving.

'Thank you.' I reach for my daughter's arm. Her muscles tense with my touch. 'Cass?'

We reach a crossroads.

'I'll do this,' she says, 'But there's something I think I should tell —'

The trill of my phone cuts her short, and we both look to the display on the car's dashboard to see who's calling.

LR.

When he'd sent that first message, I didn't enter Luke Rock's not-so-new name into my contacts. For Harry's sake; he was – *is* – so tetchy about what happened at the gala, it was important to be discreet.

Cass raises her arm, extends a finger; when I'm driving, she often answers for me. My swipe at her hand is rougher than intended. 'Leave it,' I snap.

Without me having to tell her, when a WhatsApp alert appears a minute or so later, she leaves that too.

LR.

My head is full of him. Of me as I was when we were together.

> LR: You really were a
> temptation.

He'd sent that one sentence at two this morning, the first thing I saw when I woke up.

Temptation.

I was.

Then.

Now though?

Now, I drive a Volvo, wear Breton t-shirts from Boden, eat halloumi and quinoa and avocadoes for lunch.

Reversing into the tight space outside the station, the car's sensors rage a manic beep. Like the possible words of his unread message. And the impossibility of that once-tempting me.

'Mum.' Cass's voice is a blunt knife in the now-still car. 'If we're going to do this...'

'Yes?' I turn off the engine, unclick my seatbelt and open the driver door. The second my back is turned from Cass, I check my phone.

```
LR: Seem to recall I
wasn't the only one who
thought so. Are you still
friends with Kathy?
```

Cass and I start walking. *Kelly*, I type, the air in my chest crunchy. *Her name was Kelly.* And *no, we've not spoken since.*

'Mum?'

I look up; too late. She's dropped it now, but Cass had been holding out her hand.

'I was there on Saturday, doing my bit for charity.' DCI Banford, AKA Stump, says when Cass and I pull out our seats from beneath his inordinately tidy desk to sit down. 'Saw what the girls were wearing.'

In my bag, gaping on my knee, my phone glows yellow-green.

This is not the time to think about Luke or Kelly.

'Were you dressed like that when you left your boyfriend's house on Sunday morning?' Banford's attention shifts from Cass to me, eyes casually rolling as if to bring me on side. I am *not* on side. *A different generation*, I remind myself, though Stump is significantly

189

younger than my father. A family friend, then. My nails dig into my palms. We're not here to make more trouble for Dad.

'I don't see what my clothing has to do with any—' Cass starts, but Banford perches on the edge of his desk, putting him slightly above us, and raises his left hand, his wedding ring too tight, it seems, for his finger, which bulges on either side. I reach across and squeeze her thigh, urging my daughter to look at me so she might intuit my plea. *Keep quiet. I hear his misdirected accusation, but these men, while a little old fashioned, are your grandfather's mates.*

'It took time and resources to find you, Cassandra.' He taps his open notebook with his pen. There is nothing written on the page.

Cass's neck – pale and exposed by her loose pony-tail – is elongated when she dips her head. Her eyeline travels to her lap.

'We're sorry,' I say, soundtracked by a whirl of sirens outside.

'Pardon?' Banford strains forward.

'Aren't we, Cass?'

She tugs at a snag in her tights.

'Cass?' I nudge her foot with mine. I know this is painful, but I want us both out of here. Soon.

'I'm sorry,' she says to the stained carpet between DCI Banford's exceptionally shiny shoes.

'No need for apologies.' Banford stands, places the notebook down and sips his coffee 'She's at that age, isn't she?' His conversation, unlike his eyes, is only with me. 'Girls, thirteen to twenty-odd, they're always trouble.'

My laugh is small but definite.

When we're out of his office, I lean into Cass and whisper, 'What's the punishment, do you think, for punching a man of the law.'

She snaps her shoulder away but plays ball when we see Uncle Joe by the help desk, and I nudge her forward to politely return his kiss on her cheek and mirror his pleasant smile.

I do the same. 'Sorry, we have to rush off,' I say and share one last well-mannered handshake with Banford at the door.

Cass and I say nothing as we leave the building.

'What a prick.' I spit once we're in the car.

Cass huffs irritation through her nose. 'I thought you liked him.'

'Are you kidding?'

Silence.

She doesn't answer when I ask if that was Sophie's Range Rover we passed as we exited the car park. In fact, she doesn't speak to or look at me for the duration of our journey home.

CASS

'Fifty-one.' I try not to sound too smug as I lay down the tiles.

'You sure about that, sugar?' My grandfather twizzles the board around, I guess to improve his view.

'Hundred per cent. K on a double letter then triple word too.'

He lifts the K. The cheek. Thinks despite me playing Scrabble with him pretty much once a week since I was, like, four, I can't read the board properly. Or he believes I'm a cheat. Either way, it's a farce.

'Sorry.' I watch him write my score into the little notebook I bought him especially last Christmas. 'It's mostly just luck.'

'Could be.' He looks up at me, smiles. His huffiness when I'm winning never lasts long. 'Or it could be my grandbaby is a genius.' He sits back in the dining chair, assessing his own rack of tiles.

'I dunno about that.' I reach for the bag and pluck out S T P A R L, place them next to my remaining E. A genius wouldn't be so irrational, would she? A genius would be able to process her dad's mistake, accept his apology and move on.

His hand. His face. His hand. His face. His hand. His face. A phrase on repeat in my head since Saturday.

Being here, playing this, is meant to be a distraction. That bag of letters. All these other possible words.

Gramps examines his tiles, chews his cheek in frustration when he obviously fails to form anything decent.

'You should get some extra practice in,' I suggest. 'You know the library hosts a Scrabble club every other Friday?'

He closes his eyes. A bulging pulse in his tightened jaw. 'She hasn't got you at it too?'

'Who hasn't got me at what?' Attempting super casual on the outside, inside I'm utter cringe.

He cocks his head, entering full-on copper mode, like, *we both know exactly who I'm talking about, Cassandra.*

Before I'd left to come play with Gramps this evening, Grandma had arrived at ours, telling me what an absolute godsend I am for giving her a night off from her hermit husband. 'I don't know if it's sad or sweet.' Her tone had switched from piss-take to genuine concern. 'That aside from room-by-room decluttering, Cass, your Scrabble games are the highlight of your granddad's week.' She'd gone into the kitchen then, waving her bottle of Cava and her pot of olives, which are, apparently, essential ingredients for finalising the details of Gramps' party.

'All this fuss,' he mumbled when I'd raised the subject earlier. 'I would really rather it was just the seven of us.'

193

'Me too,' My belly flips whenever I think about returning to Hambledon Manor. And all those people. All that drink. All those men.

I keep telling myself this kind of gathering will be different. There'll be women there for a start. Not that women are always useful. The galloping resurges in my stomach whenever I think of Mum at the station. With that idiot policeman. How it took until we were out of ear shot for her to utter "prick".

My entire life she's come into my room for these bedtime chats. Banged on about the importance of things like self-respect and agency and the necessity and power of speaking my truth. But she saw the way Banford looked at me. Heard what he said about the girls from Saturday night. So much for standing up for our sisters. Mum sat there yesterday and, other than her stupid "sorry", she barely uttered a single word.

And then there's her sister, AKA The Boss.

What exactly did aunt Sophie want or expect me to do when she asked me to work at the gala?

Gramps nudges his rack a little across the table. 'Grandma said I'm boring, didn't she?'

'She did *not* say boring.' I shift my tiles. If Gramps doesn't use that Y, I could place my S P L and A on the board to make SPLAY. 'You do realise it's only because she loves you.'

'What I realise, Pollyanna, is that it's because she wants me out from under her feet.'

'Pollyanna?' The word comes out bitter on my tongue. I catch Gramps' hard stare.

'It's George, isn't it?' Gramps shakes his head slowly like it's obvious. 'You're still with him then?' There's slight accusation in his tone, same as there was a few days after I introduced them at a family BBQ. It was hot, and I was flushed with the beginnings of everything. Summer. Love. Sex.

'George seemed nice.' Gramps was talking to me but looking at Dad, like, *is this young man what you had in my mind for your daughter?* Gramps never said he didn't like George. The opposite actually. He said how smart he seemed. Polite. But there was always this unspoken end to his comments. Thing is, I thought all Gramps needed to accept what he quietly deemed as unbelonging in our family was time, same as he needed when Will came out last year and Gramps was made of small harumphs of not-in-my-day. But, these days, when Will brings his boyfriend, Alfie, to a birthday party or Easter lunch or whatever, Gramps is chill.

Would he have sent his old work mates to Alfie's house too?

Like mother, like daughter, I don't challenge my grandfather's behaviour. I love him too much to even think about calling him a prick.

'Yes, Gramps. We're still together.'

'And you're not upset about anything?'

I shake my head, and Gramps lays down his F and his I above the B of BAKERS. 'Fib,' he says, sucking up the air through his nostrils, like, *I think there's more to this story but, for now, at least, we'll move on.*

I dawdled on the way home, unsure, still, what I should or would say to Dad if or when I see him. We've both done our best to stay out of the other's way.

It's becoming a habit. George's three unread messages and two unanswered calls are pretty solid evidence I've been avoiding him too.

He is a good man and deserves more than my silence, but I don't know how to explain why I let him do what he did to me on Saturday. Or why I stopped him before he was done. Or why I left while he was sleeping.

I should probably try though.

In my bedroom, I open WhatsApp.

```
George: I'm sorry if we
went too far on Saturday x
George: You say you're
not mad at me but you're
behaving differently x
George: No smoke without
fire.
```

Fire.

I watch the video I took when I failed to burn the school brochure on Monday, star it as a favourite because just like getting together with George felt like the beginning of something that small flame does too.

Watching the film, I wish I hadn't deleted the photo of Dad catching me. It was a reminder that he, like George, is good man. Far worse men do far worse things. Proof? Just open Google on my phone.

I search "what did Nic Pen do to his wife", and there is the most recent footage from their trial. Pen's lawyer hurling questions at Gabrielle Wolfe in the witness box.

'How drunk were you at the time of this alleged incident?'

'Why didn't you seek medical attention?'

'Could you tell me about the history of your mental health?'

There's a photo of Pen on stage that evening. He's performing with his band. Funny, right, given those claims that his career's been derailed by his ex. In the picture, he's accepting a beer from a woman in the crowd, who's holding a placard spray painted with 'Who's afraid of the big slag Wolfe?'

There are far worse men than my dad.

I search "Is Luke Rock as bad as people say?", and while there are links to articles about his "distasteful" foreign-ade comment and references to other "misdemeanours", the screen is mostly filled with details of his upcoming book tour and reviews of his previous sell-out show. I do find a screenshot of a now-deleted Twitter thread from @ LetsAllGoToTheLibrary, who suggested Rock's much-praised "diverse cast" in his latest novel, *Bake Off with Bodies*, is actually a bunch of cliches. A Jewish guy who looks after the pennies, an Asian teen who sources ingredients from her dad's corner shop, a fat teacher who hides body parts down his trousers, a glamour model who distracts the crew with her "most valuable assets", and let's not forget the Black guy who dopes the judges with weed. @ LordOfMen75 who's now sharing these observations says @LetsAllGoToTheLibrary 'has a sense of humour as dried up as her unfucked cunt.'

There are far worse men than my dad.

I search "Lucy Corrigan latest". A man, Stephen North, has been arrested. He is a music teacher at Newling Grammar. I scroll my contacts for someone I know who went there. We were good friends in primary and juniors until we went to separate schools.

> Me: OMG Amelia. Is that guy being questioned about Lucy Corrigan your teacher?

Amelia: I know right. Is
it bad to say I'm not
even surprised.

I never actually thought
he was that bad but people
have been staying stuff
since before I joined the
school

There was this one time
though when we were doing
a music through the years
presentation and I was
Kylie - obvs! - and
wearing hotpants and North
was filming it and when
he played it back it kind
of lingered on my legs.

And then another time, on
this trip to Theatre
Severn, he "accidentally"
touched my friend Alyssa's
arse

In the article I read, it says the police have found
significant evidence at North's home in Harbourne
and are searching a cordoned off area near the canal.

There are far worse men than my dad.

All this "research" was supposed to make me feel better, but everything I've read only makes me more sick.

I see one and two and three AM on my alarm clock.

It's worrying how quietly, secretly, I can open and close our front door.

What with all those things I've read, maybe I'm stupid for being outside so late and alone. Maybe I'm *asking for it* by being on the streets in the dark. But I walk anyway. And with each step, I am made of something flamed and furious, my rucksack filled with a stash of the weekend newspapers and Maya's lighter clenched in the palm of my shaking hand.

EVE

As per Dad's instruction, I'm running not on the pavement but on a treadmill. 'Just a thought,' he'd said a few days ago when he phoned ostensibly to tell me about the most gorgeous Rhodesian ridgeback he'd seen on a walk, though it can't have been two minutes before he suggested my running would likely benefit if Harry and I were to get a dog. 'You'd have to go out daily if you did.'

'Dad! I already go out daily. And I run to *escape* responsibility. The last thing I need is a living creature demanding my attention in the one hour that's supposed to allow me to focus on myself.'

'Fine,' he conceded. 'Then it might be wise – what with all this Lucy Corrigan stuff – to think about joining a gym. You can never be too careful, Evie.'

'Maybe,' I'd said, but he sent me a WhatsApp soon after detailing the year's membership he was gifting me at Bannantyne. *And I've booked you an induction on Friday at seven AM.*

The timing is terrible; on top of a scheme I have to finish for Harry's multiple occupancy project, Sophie had already given me a hundred-and-one jobs to do for tomorrow's party, and that was before she scheduled this bloody Sun interview with Luke Rock and Harry at ten.

'Skip the gym then.' Charlotte was pragmatic when I'd cancelled our morning walk with her golden-doodle, Boomer. 'You do realise one workout won't make the difference,' she said after I told her I had to fit into a dress on which I'd spent £125 despite it being slightly too small.' When I remained silent, 'Fine,' she sighed. 'I'll see if I can persuade Emma to join me instead.' Charlotte's sister, she told me, hasn't left the house since Aaron was released on bail.

'Shayan and Tony have been looking at some of the sites on Aaron's search history.'

'And?'

'I'll send you some screenshots.'

I opened the photos while we were still on the call. 'Shit.'

'Bad, right?' Charlotte's voice was viscid with gloom.

'AJLonely is Aaron?'

'Yup. Funny how little you can know about someone.' My friend was talking about her nephew, but I was fairly sure she was also talking about me. About everything I'd not told her of my history with Rock. She's probed, of course, attempting to establish hard facts out of memories, which for twenty-seven years have flickered and trembled, as intangible as light penetrating water through glass.

	Today at 6:30 PM
PowerOfGrey Skull Joined Jan 9 2021 Messages 321	Normies need to chill. I've been to Shropshire. It's a farming county. Totally get how a man living there would want to take a knife to that herd of heifers. Shame AJLonely didn't manage to do any damage.

	Yesterday at 11:00 AM
HardENuff Joined Jan 9 2021 Messages 321	Anyone have CCTV or mobile footage from that dinner? Preferably with sound. I wanna hear those bitches scream

	Yesterday at 09:53 AM
BlackPillage Joined Jan 9 2021 Messages 321	Aaron Jenkins is AJLonely rite? Next time we tell sum1 2 not just kill themselves but 2 take sum femoids with him, can we pls also tell him exactly how 2 do it. Those 2 White Knights fucked it for AJLonely and us

I've begged Sophie to find an alternative venue for the interview. 'I don't understand why it has to be at ours? Your place is so much bigger. Or what about Luke's hotel?'

'*Luke's hotel*, eh?' Through the invisible phone line, I could hear her bloody smirk. 'Seen it have you?'

'For god's sake, Soph. I haven't even seen *him*.'

'Kidding,' she said. 'He's not staying at a hotel apparently. Still has that apartment on Town Walls. Didn't he buy that when he was with you?'

'Maybe.' The effort it took to sound like I didn't remember the flat and everything that happened within its walls.

The decision – not to concede to his renewed request for drinks – had been an effort too.

The hours I've spent googling "Luke Rock early years" "Luke Rock 26" "Luke Rock 1994".

Those hours were *tempting*. Dangerous, even. The what ifs they sparked. The unruly thrum and burn.

I'm sorry, I said in my last WhatsApp. *I can't meet up. Family, work, my dad's retirement party etc Apologies but too much to do.*

It struck me how I couldn't simply write *no*.

Then Sophie announced Luke Rock was scheduled to come to ours on Friday at ten for a joint interview with Harry.

I tried on seven different outfits. The run this morning allowed for the tighter jeans.

'I see you, Eve.' Sophie says when I walk into my kitchen.

I snatch a piece of fresh and thickly buttered toast from her fingers. 'What do you mean, you see me?'

'I see that you're still charmed.'

'Charmed?' My head spins, checking for Harry within earshot. 'By who?'

She doesn't warrant my stupid question with an answer. 'There *is* something about him.' She puts another slice of bread in the toaster. 'The X-factor, I guess. Wrong talent show, I know,' she smirks. 'Despite all those crass jokes, maybe even because of them. I realise arrogance is no longer supposed to be a turn on, but — Oh, Morning!' Her tone, which had been one of genuine analysis, turns honeyed. Cass, already in her uniform, has come through the door. 'You don't fancy making it up to me for scarpering early last Saturday, do you? Join your dad and Luke Rock for this interview with the Sun?'

I run my fingers through Cass's unbrushed hair.

'Can you not.' She crouches in front of the cereal cupboard. My hand falls away.

'She wasn't even there when it all kicked off.' I've reminded Sophie of this a million times already.

'I know. But she could offer another side of the story. Talk about how much she enjoyed working at the dinner?'

'Soph, she enjoyed it so much she left before it ended, risking the wrath of her aunt!' I look to Cass, hoping now might be the moment she reveals why exactly she left in such a hurry, but whatever Cass is searching for in that bloody cupboard must be well hidden because she's still not out of it. I don't press the issue of her disappearance. She's here now. And safe. I was eighteen once. Sometimes we all need secrets.

'Have I really shown any wrath?' Sophie asks.

Cass doesn't answer, merely mumbles something about being late for school. The next thing we hear from her is the sound of the slammed front door.

'Problems with George?' Sophie asks but, before I'm able to say I'm not entirely sure what Cass's problem is, my sister, who's now in Harry's seat at the table, says, 'All that charm aside, I'm surprised you're even interested in Luke Rock after what happened with Kelly.'

I scan the room for a jacket, cardigan, jumper. Goosebumped suddenly. Cold. 'What do you mean what happened with Kelly?'

'Babe.' She licks her fingers clean of crumbs. 'It was obvious. I appreciate you and Luke were relaxed about monogamy, or at least *he* was. Sleeping with your best mate though.'

'What?' Her words are tiny snakes in my hair.

'Luke. He did fuck Kelly, right?'

'It wasn't like that.'

'OK.' Sophie shrugs, leans back in her chair. 'You do remember I was there before the two of you went out – all glammed up – to meet him. And then again when *you* came home – *alone* – the morning after.'

I concentrate on slicing neatly through the butter with a knife.

'Maybe it was inevitable.' She twists the cap from a new jar of Marmite. A waft of salt and yeast. 'You wanted something wholesome, like Dawson and Joey. Rock was never going to be vanilla. And Kelly always did have a dash of Jen.' The *Dawson's Creek* insult that's been marinating for years. This long-held unbudging assumption she holds that I'm too docile. Too dreary. Too prude.

'It was me that slept with Kelly actually.' *Shit*.

'You! With Kelly?' Her screech, her eyes, her flushed cheeks are utter delight. 'You dark horse.'

'Who's a dark horse?' Harry, showered, shaved and handsome in his Lululemon joggers and tee, comes through the door.

'You,' I kiss his cheek, glare at Sophie. 'Hero of the hour.'

My husband doesn't look so sure.

It's not only Rock I've been googling. And in our locked ensuite now, I again type "Kelly Shackleton" into Facebook on my phone. She's not updated her profile since a US road trip in 2015. I've not seen anything else of her since the summer of '96. Early August, I'd returned from three nights with Luke in London and Manchester with two pills in a zip-lock bag.

'Go on, Eve. Let me!' Kelly had come over the evening I got home. She snatched the packet. 'God, your letters! They make it sound sooo good.' For the five weeks since our exams had ended, I'd sent regular updates on my escapades to what Kelly called The Graveyard of Joy but was actually her parents' five-bed villa with a swimming pool in the south of France. When I'd read back what I'd written to my best mate before posting, my descriptions of those nights in Fabric and the Hacienda felt lacking. *Coming up* didn't come close to capturing that sense of physical and spiritual rising as the MDMA kicked in. And how to explain the mellowed edges of everything – people, objects, music, even – you stretched your warm-but-cool fingers to touch.

'No way!'

'Why not?' She was already opening the packet. 'I've been rotting in Montpellier without you. Why don't you want me to have any fun?' She picked one out.

'It's not that I don't want you to have fun, Kel.'

'What then?' She winked, hovering the pill milli-metres above her pushed-out tongue.

She'd have called me a hypocrite if I'd reminded her of the news stories about the eighteen-year-old girl who'd died taking one. If I'd told her it was too risky. If I'd said what was on repeat in my head which was that I didn't want Kelly getting hurt.

'Oops,' she said, and I swear I could see the shape of it impressing the inside of her throat when she swallowed. She handed me the bag. 'Your turn.'

I slid Portishead's *Dummy* into the CD player and took the pill. I don't remember when we laid down, or whose idea it was to stroke each other's hair, or if the pillow was too small for our faces not to be pressed together, though we'd managed OK before. But *before* was irrelevant when we were high. When Kelly's teeth bit gently on my lip, and I heard a soft and sensual sigh I only realised was mine when she put her finger between our mouths and whispered *sssshhhhh*. The gentle combination of s and h that spilled onto my tongue were then what my body was made of, until it was made of her hands and my hands and all our summer-hot skin.

I watched Kelly sleeping after and couldn't wait to see Luke, to show him the Polaroid Kelly took then slipped – 'a secret,' she giggled – into my drawer.

'Here,' I said, two days later in his dressing room in Birmingham.

It was Kelly who'd held the camera for the picture. My hands were busy elsewhere.

Luke's reaction was just what I wanted. 'Fuck me,' he said. And I did, detailing every inch of her body and what I'd done with it. And everything she'd done in turn to me.

'Eve Campbell!' Luke Rock is liquid in my living room. What I mean is he seeps into the gaps between everything, and there's no air whatsoever to breathe.

'Gunn, actually.' Harry is by my side, an arm around my shoulder, the tips of his fingers pressing into my bicep. His nails a sharp pressure through my shirt. 'Eve Gunn.'

'Of course, Harry, of course.' Rock's teeth here in the daylight are primetime TV. I keep my mouth closed when I smile. 'May I?' He spreads his arms and, without waiting for an answer, comes at me with a hug. He smells cleaner and more expensive than I remember, but beneath the sophisticated pink pepper and bergamot, the bodily base scent of him is the same.

My heart contracts. I am no longer rooted to the floor but drifting.

'I should leave you to it,' I tell them, Harry's face falling because he'd said specifically he wanted me to stay. 'The journalist will be here soon,' I add like this is justification for me going, which it is, I suppose, because what if Rock tells her we used to be a couple? I can't face any questions about this man and how he is liquid and how he smells and how I am eighteen again and my best friend is crying and asking *how could you*. And because if the journalist probed into what being with him did to me, would it be obvious, that whatever Rock stirred in me then is stirred in me this morning too.

YOU

You'd never say it aloud, but Luke Rock is charming. Both with the journalist, Shelley Chapman, and with you. People talk about star quality, and what you realise when he tells her about the moment he'd walked back on stage just prior to Aaron Jenkins' arrival is that true star quality extends beyond The Star. To suggest you are bathed in it – dare you say, uplifted in it – is cloying but true. You are brighter, warmer, *better*, Harry, when you join Rock as co-lead, co-author, of his tale.

The word "hero" is no longer absurd.

Shelley glances at her Dictaphone. A lack of trust in it, perhaps, for she takes copious notes too, her pen furious almost in her spiky scrawl across the page. Her eyes remain on Rock, and her writing falters, an occasional drop below the pale blue lines.

Rock's voice is less gaudy than it was in performance on Saturday. His posture adds to the impression that this is something to be taken seriously. There are no flung arms. No hands on campishly jutted hips. Rather his limbs are composed. Contained.

'I obviously can't speak for Harry here,' he says. 'But in my view the night was proving itself very special. We were raising an extraordinary amount of money for important local charities, and the guests, the auctioneer, the wait staff, *everyone*, really, was having fun. There's always something particularly poignant about that kind of event, where we all understand our true reason for being there extends beyond our own pleasure into the greater good.'

Sophie, perched on the windowsill behind Shelley, nods.

Rock, seeking opinion, turns his head in your direction, and you nod too.

Unclasping his hands, he tilts a palm. '*You* should probably continue, H.' To Shelley, then. 'Harry was the first to respond. You were incredibly quick. Thank goodness your attention was on that main door.'

You picture Cass running through it, flinch at the shovelled dig in your chest.

The pain is brief, though. Rock has already moved on.

'I realise this isn't the time or place for overstatement, Shelley. And I promise you, I'm not exaggerating. Harry was like Bolt the way he sprinted across the ballroom. And like The Rock- the *other* Rock,' Luke smiles, 'the way he brought the young boy down. Genuine heroic instinct.' None of the backslapping of which Rock'd been so fond outside Hambledon Manor. A more subdued grasp of your shoulder. Less congratulatory. A genuine check that you're OK.

Eve has obviously, repeatedly, asked the question. But the *Are You OK, Harrys* have dwindled with your unexpansive and, you imagine, infuriating, "yes". To answer her wholly would have been to risk exposing yourself as a fraud.

With Rock, though, in the quiet of your living room, you begin to believe that, while Saturday night was indeed messy, you have, in fact, been brave.

'I did it without thinking,' you say to Shelley. 'Anyone would have done the same.'

'You're underestimating your own courage.' Rock's hand travels to your knee. A conviction of well-deserved admiration in his touch. You're grateful for his ability to bring you out of yourself. To celebrate this valiant man you'd never have thought you could be.

You tell Shelley what it was like to wait for the police. How, listening to Rock ask Aaron Jenkins questions as if they were two blokes catching up over a pint, your heart had slowed closer to its near-normal pace. 'I couldn't have done that,' you say. 'Spoken with that kid as if there was nothing extraordinary about the situation. It was incredible really. As if Luke was able to shut out how distraught the boy was and act completely normal.' You catch Rock's eye then, impressed. 'All the upset, but you weren't at all fazed.'

Rock's shrug is dismissive. 'You'd done the hard bit. All I had to do was lure him into compliance. Don't do yourself a disservice, Harry. You deserve this moment of pride.'

CASS

'Looking fit, Mr Gunn.' Liv removes her leather jacket and wide eyes my dad in a way I hope is not as flirtatious as it seems.

Mr Gunn? I mouth because my parents, ever keen to be perceived as friendly over formal, have always been on first-name terms with my mates.

Liv picks up her bag, pulls a face, mouths, *what?*

'Nice to see you, Olivia.' Dad smiles his big proper smile, the one I've not seen all week and, I know, despite the weird vibe rattling the house since the gala dinner, he's going to do what he always does whenever anyone ever mentions anything to do with strength or brawn. And yep, there it goes, his right arm curling to flex his muscles beneath the top of his shirt. His lips kiss the bulge. 'Not bad for an old dude.'

What used to be funny is now awkward and thoughtless and, honestly, really fucking rude.

Not for Liv though, who's oooing and ahhing, and Dad's saying something about The Gunn show, his same-old lame-old joke. He and I both look away the nanosecond we catch each other's eye.

'Saw today's paper,' Liv says. 'Best hope Maya didn't. She won't be too giddy if she discovers you and Rock are now BFFs.'

'He was actually pretty decent.' Dad's eyes bulge with surprise. 'I'm beginning to understand what your mother saw —'

'Can you not, Harry.' Mum strides from the kitchen into the hall.

'Wow!' I'm momentarily snapped out of the silent treatment, because with her hair beach-waved and in the blue-and-green bold-patterned dress she's wearing, Mum looks beautiful.

'Thanks.' She glances at Dad, maybe seeking a reaction from him too. But he bends to gather the post from the mat and says nothing. Clocking I'm still in my dressing gown, she comes over, slapping me on the bum the way she always did when I was little and wanted me to get a move on. I see Dad catch it, Mum's palm on my bottom. Same body parts. Different intentions. The consequences miles apart.

'Anyhoo,' he says, his Dad'isms on a downward spiral, not quite as jaunty as before. 'The washing won't do itself.' He takes the stairs down to the basement laundry.

Mum disappears back into the kitchen.

'Never mind the fact that he's my dad, how can you even contemplate flirting with someone who says "anyhoo"?!'

'Oh c'mon.' Liv follows close behind when I attempt to flounce up and through my bedroom door without her. 'It's good for them.'

'Good?' I fall onto the bed. 'For who?'

She sits down next to me, knitting her eyebrows, like, *isn't it obvious*. 'A bit of flattery. Old men love that kind of thing.'

'What kind of thing exactly? Over-zealous types with Daddy-issues?'

'I do not have "daddy issues",' she says, and I'm thinking this is the ideal opportunity for her to tell me about making up with her father, but she's focusing instead on why I've got such beef with mine.

'Why you so pissed at Harry then?'

Like her, I don't want to go there.

I traipse after her into my ensuite, pick up the packet of false lashes she's placed next to my toothbrush and pull a face in the mirror.

'Something's got to distract everyone from those bags.' Liv uses a lip pencil to point at each of the haunted grey bulges beneath my eyes. 'Are you sleeping?'

I think of the hours I've spent walking the last two nights in the darkness with Maya's lighter in my hand. Gramps would for sure call me reckless, but maybe Liv would get it? If I explained how I search online for reports of violence against women. If I said how easy it is to find them. How so many *isolated incidents* have occurred within walking distance from here. If I showed her how the printed versions of these news stories catch fire as quickly as the letter on Luke Rock's stage. If I told her in the moment it takes to spark the flame, I've never felt so awake. Exhaustion only tumbles over me once I'm home.

But before I have the chance to answer her question, Liv's double taking at the outfit hung over the shower door. 'Erm, it's a party, not a wake. Seriously, babe.' She runs a hand down the shirtdress I took from Mum's wardrobe last night. 'This is *matronly*.'

That's kind of the point.

She wags a finger at me, and I spot her fresh manicure, her second in as many weeks. The pairs of thin gold lines running in different directions across each pale grey nail are too neat for her to have drawn at home. 'You're eighteen, you're supposed to look hot, yeah?' Moving into the bedroom, she pulls out the pink midi I wore to the summer ball and presses it to my chest. 'This'd work.'

'It's sleeveless though.' That late-September sunshine Aunt Sophie was banking on has failed to appear. And then there's DCI Banford and his *I saw what the girls were wearing* and what that meant to him. How much those girls were, or weren't, worth. 'I'd freeze.'

'So what? This colour's trending.' Liv touches the chiffon, thumbs her phone. 'Look, Gabrielle Wolfe wore a similar shade in court.'

I read the copy beneath the photo Liv's shoved in my face.

Pink to make the boys shrink. Wolfe yesterday ensured all eyes were on her by teaming a grey pin-stripe suit with a rose shirt. Leaving the top three buttons undone to offer a glimpse of her ample assets, the model smiled demurely at the jury before giving evidence in the libel trial brought about by her ex, the Ivor Novello-winning rock star Nic Pen.

'See,' Liv says.

'Who's *Roger?*' I ask when a WhatsApp alert rolls across the top of her screen. 'And why is he saying something about seeing you this afternoon?' I don't have the chance to read the full text because my friend snatches her phone away, and I can't tell if it's intentional, how the wardrobe door creates a brief barrier between us as she struggles to re-hang the dress. By the time it's put away and the door is closed again, Liv's phone has disappeared, and her cheeks have lost their flash of red.

'Well?'

She raises her eyebrows like, *girl, your interrogation's ridiculous, but as I'm so mature and patient, I'll humour you anyway.* 'A friend.' She backs into the bathroom. 'I need a wee.' Closes the door. 'He's a realtor,' she shouts.

'A friend? Since when do you have friends called *Roger?* Or friends who are *realtors?* And unless *Roger* is in *Selling Shropshire*, isn't a realtor in Britain an

219

estate agent? And isn't every *Roger* in Britain at least, like, sixty-five.'

'Knock knock!' Why Mum insists on saying the words rather than performing the action is beyond me. She comes into my room from the landing at the exact same time Liv reappears from the ensuite. And maybe Mum picks up on the tension because, 'You two OK?'

'Not too good actually,' Liv says. 'I don't think I can come.' Her eyes are fixed on the circle her toe is making in the brush of the carpet. 'To the party, I mean.'

'What?' There's a squeak in my voice. 'But you're my plus one.'

Sure, my request had been last minute, but 'I'd love to,' Liv had said when I asked her at college yesterday. 'Though, honestly, I still don't get why you're not taking George.'

'Because he's no longer my boyfriend.'

'That's another thing I'm not clear about.'

To be fair, neither was he.

```
George: You're breaking
up with me?

George: By text?

George: WTF Cass. You know
how this makes me feel?
```

I didn't answer. Couldn't risk the fallout of an actual conversation in which George would inevitably make me feel guilty because no doubt he's as hurt and confused as I am.

So instead of speaking with him, I spoke with Liv.

'I'm gonna need your moxie to distract me from those drunk men.' And from Dad, I thought but didn't say.

'My period,' Liv says now. 'You know how it is, babe.'

I do. I've seen her, heat pad on her abdomen and comma-shaped on the sofa.

This morning though, just now, even, Liv's been fine.

'You want some painkillers?' Mum asks.

'I took some before I came.' Liv doesn't look at me. 'I'll do your hair and make-up, but then I'll...'

'You'll what?'

'I'll probably spend the afternoon in bed.'

Fifteen awkward minutes later, Liv's gone and I'm waiting in the kitchen for my parents. Dad appears, lays The *Sun* article on the kitchen table. Flakes of croissant on his fingers have left greasy marks on the page. 'We still haven't really talked about what happened.'

I look at the words but can't read them.

'I would never knowingly have touched you.' His voice is low yet certain.

'But you would have touched another waitress?' My question, like his statement, is whispered. 'Slapped another girl's bum?

'It was an accident.'

'Was it?' I ask. 'Because if it was an *accident*, Dad, why are we whispering? If it was an *accident*, would we both have kept it a secret from mum?'

'I...'

I count the seconds of silence between us. All the way to seventeen.

'I wanted your attention. Not *yours*,' he corrects himself. 'I didn't know it was you. I wanted a *waitress's* attention.'

This time we get to twenty-two.

'You girls,' he says, and I know immediately I won't like what's coming. 'I'm not saying what I did wasn't a problem but, Cass...' My dad sighs like *he's* the one with a right to be disappointed. 'You girls seemed not to mind what was going on.'

Eleven.

'Am I wrong?' He closes the newspaper. 'If I am then why didn't you say something? When Bry first had his hands on you?'

'Are you serious?' I ask, and his chin doubles with shock at my still-quiet rage. 'How many Saturday mornings did you sit here and read all those Me-Too stories in the news.' I close my eyes, focus on the dragon exhale from my nose. He's still here when I look up. Nothing, not even his understanding, has caught fire. 'I didn't say anything, *Dad*, because those men, *you* men, held all the power.' It's so simple when I put it like that.

'Cass.' His voice is a little louder, firmer. 'Listen, I didn't mean to touch you like that.' It's rushed and pathetic. 'I would never...You're my daughter.' His face, like the air, wobbles.

Unable to look at him, I shift my attention to the window. The kitchen is bright, but the sky and garden are unseasonably dark. 'Is that how it is, Dad?' On my lap, my knuckles turn yellow-white and taut. 'That what your *friend* was doing, what you then did, only became appalling when you realised it was being done to *me*. You know what,' I push the paper as far away from me as possible. 'I think I'll just wait outside.'

He and Mum come out a few minutes later, Mum looking up at the sky and sing-songing about how she really hopes Sophie's plans for fireworks won't be scuppered by rain. Her over-breezy voice announcing she'll fetch our coats is clearly her attempt to steer us into a better mood for a party. She throws them on the back seat next to me. 'In case the worst happens,' she says.

Lightly berating our silence, she turns on BBC Radio Shropshire. A discussion about a spate of small fires set locally and shared on TikTok by an account called @shoutfirenotrape is interrupted with a breaking-news announcement. Lucy Corrigan's body has been found in a disused garage close to Harbourne Canal.

I am made of sulphured expletives. Yet I don't say a word as we drive.

EVE

'I know a guy,' Cass says, 'at reception. I'm just going to go say hi.' It's not only her voice that's diminished, her stature – well, everything really – has been solemn and stiff from the second we pulled up outside the hotel.

'Ah ah ah. Not so quickly,' Uncle Joe blocks her exit. 'Great to see you assuming responsibility for your actions at the station on Wednesday, Cassandra.' His arms open for an embrace. 'You don't always get that these days in the young. So quick to put the blame on others and mark themselves as a victim.'

'Cass,' I mutter. Too late though. From the disappointment on his face, Uncle Joe already caught the turn of Cass's shoulder away from him and the melodramatic roll of her eyes.

'Get perky, Eve!' My sister appears, putting herself between her godfather and niece, which you'd think might cheer my daughter, but Cass continues to stare at the floor. Sophie jolts her chin at the hotel manager who's headed in our direction. 'Your friend's coming.' She loops her arm through Cass's. 'For someone who criticised me for using Botox to appear young and lively to my clients, your hypocrite mother was all for using her *assets* when she heard from Freddie White over there about the refurb of his new office block here at Hambledon Manor.'

'I was not.'

'*Oh, really, Freddie.*' Sophie uses the tops of her arms to squish her boobs together. '*Well, as it happens, Freddie…*' Her stupid imitation sounds nothing like me. '*…design is my area of expertise.*'

Had I been that obvious?

Shit.

Did Cass just shake her head?

'Ladies!' Both Freddie's arms and smile are wide. I don't want to get any closer. His eyes drop to my cleavage as I lean to kiss both of his cheeks. I wish I'd brought that shawl.

'Sorry to intrude.' A tall woman taps Sophie's shoulder. 'Your dad told me I should come to speak with you? Said you'd organised everything and would be the best person to sort me some squash.' Her eyes slant towards a girl I assume is her daughter. 'Felicity's not so keen on Champagne.'

'Well well well,' Freddie says. 'Who do we have here?' His attention is on the child, who is trying to slide behind her mother. 'What's your name, dear?'

'Flick.' *Her* attention is on her glittery shoes.

'Flick?' Freddie pantomimes his confusion with raised palms and rounded eyes. 'Don't mind if I do.' He playfully flicks the girl's arm.

Cass, finally, looks up from the floor.

When Freddie gets down on his knees and attempts peekaboo, Felicity pulls her mother's maxi dress across to form a barrier. Only his hand is next to Flick's on her mum's dress now too. 'Shy, are you?' His wine-blotched cheeks loom close to Felicity's. 'Well, you might be shy, but you're also a very attractive young lady.'

Cass straightens, pulls her shoulders back, and it worries me, what she's planning to do with those wings. I reach for her hand, give it a hard squeeze.

Her shoulders droop. She says nothing just unloops her arm from Sophie's and walks out the ballroom door.

The mic shakes in Dad's hand, his eyes spanning the function room bursting with colleagues, family and friends. I'm surprised, really, by that shake. Our father has faced all sorts: murderers, rapists, gang members. But put him in a suit in a fancy hotel and ask him to deliver a five-minute speech about his time in public service, and the unflappable strong man looks at risk of coming undone.

'The things the men *and women*,' he says, not exactly like the women are an afterthought, but there *is* something in that "and women" that makes them separate. 'The things the *people* in this room have done for me. To support and protect me. In the force, you need to know everyone's got you covered. You

need to be sure – 100 per cent – that you're a team.'
He raises a clenched fist, and a couple of blokes on
the table next to us slap each other appreciatively on
the back. 'For me to have lasted this long though, I
needed a team that stretched beyond the station.
Clare,' he says and there's a shift in my father's voice
that's almost palpable. 'Behind every good man...' A
shift in the atmosphere too as everyone turns to look
at Mum.

Harry reaches for my hand. For someone not
normally prone to outpours of emotion, there's something about a speech that gifts my husband a freedom
of expression. Cass and I will usually place a bet on
the exact second his first tear will fall. Not today
though. Since that encounter with Freddie White, my
daughter has disappeared.

The maître d was seating us for dinner when my
phone beeped with a message to the family
WhatsApp.

> Cass: Apologies to Gramps.
> I'm not feeling well. My
> friend Patrick's going to
> give me a lift home.

I'd looked across at Harry, tracked his eyes reading
the same words on his screen. A not-quite-smile when

he was done, a shrug, *teenagers eh*, before he poured himself a huge glass of wine. He'd glugged half in the short time it took me to tap out a reply.

> Me: I would have preferred you'd come and told me, but OK. We do need to speak tonight though, Cass. You've not been yourself since last Saturday, and I'd really like to know why xxxxx

I hit send, unable to rid myself of those niggling Instagram comments Sophie so easily dismissed on Monday, the claims that my sister had suggested there would be financial benefits for the young women working at the gala dinner who made themselves amenable to men.

Probably because of the stress of what came after, when I asked Harry about the guests' behaviour, he couldn't focus on anything before Aaron Jenkins's attack. 'We were angry,' he says. 'Shocked. Couldn't believe anyone would want to hurt the waitresses like that. The guys there, they were getting the girls blankets and coffees, organising them taxis, making sure they were safe.'

And at the other galas? When I raised it again later, Sophie assured me things were very different post Me Too.

It's true. These days don't we all have a better understanding of consent.

I like to think I do.

Harry fills his glass.

Dad talks about the importance of loyalty.

That word. When Kelly left on that last night, she'd muttered it too. Unlike Dad, though, who's saying the loyalty of his colleagues and his family has been unwavering, Kelly said *my* loyalty was screwed.

A few weeks prior, my comedian boyfriend and I were sweaty in his windowless dressing room. 'Bring her next time.' He was wiping a towel over his cock.

'Who?' The casual way I pretended not to know.

'Your mate.' He pointed at the polaroid still on the arm of the sofa. 'The three of us could have some fun.'

It was a relief to have perked his interest. On the last road trip we'd taken, he'd yawned while I was giving him a blow job.

I'd left that trip dejected, desperate. And, while I'll admit I was aching for attention, it's not like I'd planned to sleep with Kelly when I got home. It was true we'd kissed a few times in Bar Severn, but we certainly weren't the only girls who understood the Pied Piper pull of two young women in full snog on a dance floor. How quickly the men then flocked around us in the hope we'd give them more. Until the pills, though, there was never any suggestion of sex. But when there *were* pills and when there *was* sex, I whispered in Kelly's ear how much I loved being with her like that, and it wasn't as if I lied. Truthfully? Somewhere in the back of my mind, I already knew the story of me fucking her would buy me kudos. That Luke would be intrigued. It would be proof, I hoped, of what Dad is saying now, 'one's partner can be a surprise.'

'Your mother…' Dad's eyes narrow, and he turns to Sophie and me, his voice dropping an octave into authoritative and stern. 'She believed I was a hard-nosed policeman, who took no crap. And that was true, I am, *was*,' he concedes. 'But…' He cocks his head the way I imagine he would have done when questioning a suspect. But rather than holding that obdurate stare, his face softens, his mouth smeared with a smile he wants everyone to think is reluctant but we all know is as willing as the guests accepting the top-ups on their Champagne. 'Well, you girls turned that hard-nosed policeman to mush and ran rings around me until you weaved whatever magic it is daughters weave upon their fathers –' He looks knowingly to Mum '– and women weave upon their husbands – until they get their own way.'

'Hear hear,' someone calls from one of the distant tables. 'Who *are* these people who still believe men are in charge!' The heckle is good natured, piquing a male rumble of jovial discontent.

'Seriously though,' Dad says, 'we are our different selves with different people.'

From different angles, even. I think of the pictures at Charlotte's exhibition. How the model changed with each of the artists' perspective. For no reason but curiosity, I'd captured every image of her on my phone. I've scrolled through them while brushing my teeth at night, pausing longest on the small, pencilled piece drawn from behind. She looks like she knows everything she needs to know about herself and like she's stepping into the room without apology for what anyone in it might make of her.

What self was I with Kelly? With Rock? With Harry? There's no doubt I prefer the self I am with my husband. Not exactly wild, not recently at least. But no collateral damage either. No best friend claiming to be bruised and broken. No lost Polaroid I sometimes wish had stayed in my purse.

'And what I've learned in forty-five years of service,' he pauses. 'Or, if I'm honest, what my very wise granddaughter —' My dad scans the room, for Cass, I imagine, and looks a little dejected when he fails to spot her. '— what my granddaughter likes to tell me is that in a good relationship – be that at the station or elsewhere – if we are to succeed as a team, we must *embrace multiplicity.*' A dubious quirk of his brow. 'Use it to adapt to challenging situations.' Dad's chest rises with his inhale. 'Someone want to ask Clare here how she's adapting to the challenging situation of my retirement! Twenty-four hours a day together!'

Mum exaggerates a grimace, and the crowd laughs.

Not Harry though.

'And while we're on the subject of my adaptive family, I can't let today pass without a brief mention of my son-in-law, who adapted in a way I never anticipated possible last weekend in this very room.'

My heart lurches with pride. Dad's boom of a voice bigging my husband up when, historically, his MO has been to run the script *no man will ever be good enough for my daughter* to knock him down.

Of course, this moment – this toast my father is proposing – is about Harry, but it's about me too. About the satisfaction of a little girl finally getting Daddy's approval of her choice of man.

'To Harry,' Dad says.

'To Harry,' comes the echo.

I lean into him, 'You're a good man.'

'I'm not,' he says. 'I'm really not.' He snatches his face away from me and walks, head down, from the room.

CASS

'Let's just say you're not the first girl I've seen running from that ballroom.' Patrick passes me a mug, and the waft of his slightly spicy aftershave takes me to the night of the gala and the mix of fear and relief I felt to be cocooned in the back of his car. 'Though you may be the first girl I've seen doing it twice.'

'Glutton for punishment.' It'll burn, but I sip the milky tea anyway. Today was a different menu. Different music. Different crowd. But no matter where I looked in that ballroom, I saw them. Bry and Money-Clip. And Dad. Through gritted teeth, I told myself I could do it. For Gramps. Then along came the hotel manager with his actual flick and his *very attractive young lady*, and I was made of raised hackles and arched spine all ready to pounce. But then there was Mum too with her glare and her fear of my bad manners, insisting I join her and the other women in their silence as we all accommodated Freddie fucking White.

'Coming back here was a bad idea.' I say to Patrick now. I should have done a Liv and claimed period pain. Her status is still showing as unavailable on my phone. 'Who are the others?'

'Huh?' Patrick has stepped around the wall that divides the racks and the desk, where he's supposed to be ready and waiting to collect and dispense guests' coats. He smiles when he comes back through. 'The others?'

'Who you've seen running?' I shift about on my bum, the floor's not exactly comfortable, but then it's not meant to be. This room, cubby hole really, is for jackets and bags, not teenage girls hiding from their parents with a guy she barely knows.

'Is now the right time though?' Patrick leans on the rail of the rack above me. 'Like, are you really in the mood to hear?'

'Well, I'm already permanently angry so...' It's funny, how there's this rage coursing through my body and yet, here I am, with my feet tucked and my arms wrapped around my knees, totally and utterly still. A good quiet girl. Wouldn't my family be proud?

Patrick points at the patch of empty carpet next me, arches his brow, like, *do you mind?* And I shrug, all, *sure.*

'I don't want to make your anger worse,' he says.

'I'm not sure there's much that's going to make it better.' My voice strains with the stretch in my neck, my head tipped back against the wall.

'Look, maybe I shouldn't have said anything.' Patrick picks at the black varnish on his pinkie nail.

'They're not really my stories to tell. But I could put you in touch with them? The others? I was friends with a couple of the girls, and one had been working at the hotel. It's always kind of cool to have someone who understands what you're going through. Who you know will believe what you say.'

'There have been people who haven't? Believed them, I mean.'

'Let me message Rhi,' he says. 'She's one of the other women who…' He doesn't need to finish the sentence. We both know where nights like the gala end. 'She'll talk whenever you're ready.'

Fifteen minutes later, with Patrick released from his shift, we're in his car, and I'm trying to imagine what it would be like to tell a stranger. Wondering if she's still soaked in this mucky indignity and shame.

'You OK?' He glances briefly from the road to look at me.

'Sorry,' I say, using the sleeve of my coat to wipe my nose.

'Should be some tissues in the glovebox.'

I release the clip, and the flap drops down along with an entire slice of pizza. 'What the hell?'

'My bad.' Patrick grabs it from my lap.

'You are *not* going to eat that?'

His face crumples. 'I'll wait 'til I've stopped driving.'

'Er, you driving is not the issue!' I snatch it back.

'Oi!'

'How long's it even been there?'

'Since this morning.' A flash of arm, and the slice is in his left hand again. 'I'm not a total sloven,' he says, or at least I think that's what he says. It's hard to be sure with his mouth full.

'This morning!?' I indicate he needs to take the next left. 'I'm not sure what's worse, that you keep pizza in your glovebox or that the pizza you keep in your glovebox is ham and bloody pineapple.'

He pulls up outside my house. 'I was going to put it in my locker at work,' he says. 'But then I thought I should probably store it at *aloha* temperature.'

'As if the joke wasn't lame enough, you're now winking!'

'And you're now laughing so...' He takes another bite. 'Mission accomplished.'

'Oh god.' My sigh steams a patch of the passenger window.

'What?' Patrick leans across to peer into the glovebox. 'You haven't found my half-eaten Curly Wurly too?'

'No.' I slump in the seat. 'It's my ex-boyfriend. He's there, look, on the wall.'

Patrick's chest expands a little. 'You want me to get out with you?'

I shake my head. 'George is cool.'

Only when I've said my goodbyes and thank yous to Patrick, George *isn't* cool. What he is is sad and confused.

'That was that same dude, right? From last weekend?' His eyes track Patrick's car until it disappears around the corner. 'What, you seeing him now?'

'No. He was helping me out. I was upset at Gramps' part—'

'You didn't look upset.' He's glaring at me, and I can't tell if his face is only wet because of the rain. 'You were laughing. Anyway, why did he give you lift back? You told me you going with Liv?'

'Like I say, I was upset. And Liv couldn't come.'

'So, you took your new boyfriend instead?'

'No, George. Come inside, and I'll tell you.' I reach for his hand, but he pulls it away. 'It's not like that. He's a friend who was doing me a favour.'

'Sure.' He's already at the end of the path. 'You always seemed so nice, Cass. You know, decent. Guess I'm finally seeing the real you, eh? I wonder what other people would think if they saw this other side of you.' He turns his back to me. In the middle of the street, his head is down, his fingers already tapping away at his phone.

That's it then, he's made up his mind what kind of girl I am.

I could call him back but, fuck it, I'm done trying to explain.

EVE

'I need to tell you something,' Harry said when I caught up with him in the lobby. Outside now, he gestures I should take the entire canopy of the umbrella he grabbed from the stand in reception. In this sheepish voice, 'I know how much you hate what rain does to your hair.'

'I don't care about my hair. Just tell me.'

'The dinner, last Saturday.' He's trying hard to look at me, but his eyes keep drifting to a puddle on the ground, the toe of his shoe tap-tap-tapping, sending drops of water up into the air only – obviously – to fall straight back down again.

He tells me what the diners were like at the gala, his words making pictures – a movie, even – in my head. Cliched images of old men and young women and hands in places they shouldn't be. Scenes I'd naively believed had no place at an event attended by husband and run by sister.

I don't speak. And, sure, this is mostly because I need to hear this story until its sordid end. But any reaction is stymied by that other voice I hear alongside Harry's too. Dad delivering his speech, those words of wisdom about being our different selves with different people. Is that the kind of person – a silent unmoved observer – my husband becomes when he's with those kinds of men?

I believed Harry – my Head Over Feet – was one of the good ones. Not long after we started going out, when we'd dared have *that* conversation about previous sexual partners, I'd named the eight men, not mentioning Kelly, and was surprised when Harry's list was even shorter. Four long-term monogamous relationships. Just one one-night stand.

'I didn't feel great about it the following morning,' he'd told me, which I took to be a sign of something. A level of respect for women, or a squeamishness, even, about how easily one could be perceived as a user and, in turn, a baseline understanding that women were not there for men to use.

Who knew such simple courtesy could be a turn on? Or that having the sense a man wouldn't cheat on you no matter which company he kept or how many beers he consumed was not only a novelty but a boost to your self-esteem? Or how pleased you would then be with yourself for finding a true ally.

Because here was a man who took you seriously when you told him about that male boss who groped you. Here was a man who listened sympathetically when you cried about the male doctor who, when you went to him to request STD testing because you thought you'd been date-raped, chose to write just two words in your medical notes: "unprotected sex" and in so doing made it clear – and official – he didn't believe you. Here was a man who complained to the school when your daughter, along with the other girls in her class, was issued with a Look Good, Feel Good questionnaire referencing the visibility of her cleavage, the length of her skirt and the unholiness of her knickers. Here was a man you were sure would do the right thing by women. Here was a man you were sure you could trust.

And yet that same man sat in a dining room eating and drinking while his fellow men mauled the female staff.

'There's something else,' Harry says.

I can't even summon the "what".

'I…' he starts. I wait. He starts again. 'I was drunk. It's no excuse, but when someone said Luke Rock was performing, I freaked, Eve. Your ex. And not just any ex but a millionaire national-treasure ex, who, by all accounts, left you heartbroken and pining until you met me.'

'Stop. My relationship with Luke Rock is not the issue right now.' My heart is a wallop in my chest. 'What else do you have to tell me?'

The smell of something burning. Above the hotel, smoke.

Harry's head jerks side to side, up and down seeking the source of the repetitive gun-like popping sound.

The sky is suddenly green.

'Fireworks,' I tell him. They are incandescent despite the rain.

'What I mean is,' Harry is shouting over the booms and bangs. 'I drank more than I would have done usually. And maybe it wasn't only that Rock was there. Maybe the other men were making me uncomfortable. Honestly, I didn't know what to do.'

The darkness gives way to blue to yellow to red.

'You didn't know how to say, "you need to stop that?" Didn't know how to ask to see the manager? Didn't know how to remove *Bry's* hands from a young woman's body?'

A ground-shaking explosion.

A sky full of stars.

'It's not just that,' he says. 'I — she — I didn't mean to touch her.'

'*Her*? *You* touched someone?'

'I didn't know it was her, and I...'

'You *what*, Harry?'

'It was just a slap on the bum. I didn't know it was Cass, I swear.'

'*Cass*? You *slapped* Cass.'

'I wanted a drink. I didn't know it was her. I wanted her to get a move on.' When I don't say anything. 'You did the same to her this morning.'

242

'*Me?*'

'Yes,' he says. 'Chivvied her along. On the stairs.'

I remember. Without question, this is not the same thing.

'Once I realised,' he says, 'it was too late, she ran, I couldn't explain.'

'Explain what exactly? That you're no better than any of *them.*'

'Look.' His hands reach for me, but I take a step backwards. 'I should have done something earlier. Before I realised it was her, but the slap, or tap really,' he says. 'I'm in no way trying to justify it, but it wasn't like I was groping her. I wanted her attention, that's a—'

I hold up both palms to make it clear how much I want my husband – is this really my husband? – to stop. Cass needs me. 'You are going to be quiet now, Harry, and I am going to go.'

Dizzy with shock and Champagne, I stumble back to the porch beneath a shower of falling light.

The guests, laughing and shaking wet umbrellas, are returning to the ballroom via the huge French doors. The music begins anew.

'Eve!' Sophie is winding her hips in a clumsy circle, trying to coax me into her dance.

It was nothing, she'd said on repeat.

Harry may not have *groped* Cass, but he still thought it was OK to demand service by putting his hand on a woman's body. That doesn't sound like nothing. And those other men? The way *they* were touching my daughter? That doesn't sound like nothing either. That sounds like sexual assault.

'I'm not interested in your moves, Sophie.'

'Jeez-Louise!' She rolls her eyes. 'Chill, yeah. It's Dad's party.'

I look across at my father, laughing with his old colleagues, all raising their glasses in a toast initiated by Uncle Joe.

I want answers but, head down, I swallow, summoning all the decorum I can muster not to release my volcanic scream.

The light in her bedroom window when the taxi pulls up outside the house tells me Cass is already home. I can't get to her fast enough, don't bother with the knock-knock and instead run straight into her room. 'I need to talk to you.'

'Later,' she says.

'No.' I sit as close to her as possible on the bed. 'Your dad's told me. *We need to talk.*' I enunciate every letter. 'Now.' Take her face in my palms.

She yanks herself away from me, '*This* is the problem,' swipes at my hand. '*You* are the problem.'

'*Me?*'

'Yeah.' Her eyes darken, and she stands. Broader. Bigger. Louder. 'You tell me *no means no*, but only if no fits with what you want. Only if no doesn't mean making a fuss. Because, when it comes to it, you want me to be biddable. Well, guess what, Mum,' she laughs a sardonic laugh. 'I have been. I was so biddable I said nothing when a sixty-odd-year-old man told a ten-year-old girl she was attractive because, god forbid, bad manners, right? God forbid we teach a ten-year-old girl that when a man puts his hands on you, it's OK to speak up. Let's teach her the opposite, shall we? Like you taught me. I was so fucking biddable I said nothing when those men put their hands on me because you never actually meant it when you said my body my choice.'

'That's not true.'

'Deeds not words, right?' My daughter stops talking, says everything she needs to in the way she glares at me. A glare so fierce I still feel its heat long after I've left and she's slammed the door.

CASS

'So, what, your dad's gone then?' Maya, who I've told about Dad's departure and what triggered it looks around the kitchen, as if expecting to see evidence to the contrary.

'Not *gone* gone. Not as far as I know anyway.' I press the machine for a second coffee, imagining it grinding all my angst as efficiently as it grinds the beans. 'He didn't come back last night though. No sign of him this morning either.'

'And your mum?'

'At Grandma and Gramps's, but...'

'But what?' Maya is opening the doors to various cupboards.

'Looking for anything specific?'

'Cookies,' she says in the voice of *Sesame Street*'s Cookie Monster. 'I get sugar isn't a finite solution to life's major problems but, in the interim, it nearly always helps. Well?'

'Well, what?' I know exactly what. And because my friend knows I know exactly what she bug-eyes me, like, *c'mon, Cass, please*. 'Fine.' I pull a box of M&S Belgian double chunk from behind the tub of Shreddies, toss them to Maya, sit down at the table, head in hands and exhale. 'We're not talking.'

'You and Harry?' Maya tears the wrapping, removes a biscuit, pushes the plastic tray in my direction.

I shake my head, *no*. 'Or me and Mum.'

'Sorry, what now? You're not talking to Eve either? What's *she* done?'

'Nothing.'

'So the problem is…?'

'Exactly that. She does *nothing*. Claims to be some third or fourth wave feminist or whatever, but the wave's irrelevant anyway 'cos it's all just theory. I told you about that guy Freddie, she was happy to stand there and watch Flick burn.'

Maya reaches for another cookie, takes a bite. 'Devil's advocate, babe, sometimes theory's all we've got.'

Scrunched eyes, I look at her.

'OK. No judgement but…' She goes full on debate-face, chewing the inside of her cheek. Then, 'You claim not to give a toss about beauty standards. Railing against women's mags while reading them over Liv's shoulder. Say they're promoting unrealistic body image etcetera etcetera and you're not going to be a slave to that. But then what was that about?' She pokes at the tray; it slides away from her across the table.

'What?'

'Tell me, *honestly*, you didn't want a cookie.'

'I didn't want a cookie.' The pang in my tummy though. The saliva in my mouth.

Her eyes grow even rounder.

'Fine,' I say, devouring one of the biscuits in two greedy bites. 'That make me good feminist, does it?'

Maya licks the end of her thumb, like my mother used, dabs the crumbs from my chin. 'All I'm saying is every one of us is a mish mash of contradictions.'

'*You're* not.' I think of that film Maya made of her setting Luke Rock's books alight outside the library. She doesn't hide behind the night's darkness and a pseudonym handle. She's there with her flagrant fire and her flagrant face and all her flagrant fury.

'Sure,' she says. 'I can do grand gestures. The small stuff though.'

'The small stuff?'

'The personal.' She breaks a cookie in two, holds out half. In the name of good feminism, I take it. 'And parties or whatever are *the worst*, Cass. All that height-ened emotion. Drink. Friends. *Family!* You'd think it'd be easier to speak the truth with them, but that whole blood is thicker than water thing means situations with relatives get gloopy. Last one, yeah?' She eyes the five left in the tray, and I nod, *sure*. 'You know my white Aunt Jenny? Married to my uncle Jade. Two brown kids. We're at a Christening party and Harry Styles comes on the playlist. Her daughter goes nuts. No rhythm but a ton of mad energy. Jenny looks at me, goes, "And there I was assuming she'd be able to dance."'

'She was being funny though, right?'

'Thought she was. And that dude talking to the little girl at the wedding yesterday probably thought he was being funny too. I'm not justifying what he said, or your mum for not calling him out. But I didn't say anything to Jenny either. Just stood there letting it slide because, for me in that moment, letting it slide was the easier thing to do.'

'So, what, I shouldn't sweat the small stuff?' I ask.

'That's not what I me—'

'Maybe you're right,' I say. 'I guess what happened there and at the gala is kind of insignificant when you think about what's happened to Lucy Corrigan.'

'That's not what I meant.' She rests her foot on the seat of the chair, hugging one leg against her chest. 'Some rando at a party being inappropriate with a ten-year-old girl, while obviously not on par with rape and murder, *is* part of the broader *patri-archal* shit.' She picks at the frayed edges of her cuff. 'It's everywhere, and it's exhausting. How would anyone have the energy to go into every single battle?'

'Exactly what battle *is* Mum fighting though?'

'Maybe many. Maybe none. Have you asked her?' As always, my friend's question isn't critical but curious.

An almost non-existent shake of my head.

'Obviously I dunno what Eve is and isn't going through, but I'd guess her telling you *no is no* or *your body is your body* but not being able to live by those rules IRL is less about Eve being a hypocrite and more about her wanting your experience to be different from her own.'

I turn the friendship bracelet Maya gave me with the initials CLM in five slow circles around my wrist then toss her another cookie. 'Take it! Seriously, you've earnt the sugar hit. There's absolutely no one as brilliant or as wise. And if Herring sacks you as head girl, I'm going full on bat shit."

'Prep your belfry then, babe!' Both feet on the floor, both elbows on the table, Maya is one hundred per cent grounded. 'I've requested another meeting.'

'With Herring?'

'Uh huh. I know you and Liv said to sit tight, but how can we let his attitude re the statue versus the upskirting thing slide? Anyway, if Herring chooses to fire me, I'll simply add it to my list. See how the governors respond to that.'

'Your list?'

Like a queen, she rises, flipping her phone on the table so it's screen-side up and opening Notes. 'My list.' She passes it to me. 'Got the idea from that Laura Bates' book I told you about.'

My Sexist Incident List - school

When, on a school trip to France, we played a game of spin the bottle and I refused to kiss Marco Dean so Marco Dean called me frigid. Said he thought *girls like me* were supposed to be more promiscuous.

Same trip. feeling ashamed of being frigid, I agreed to kiss Roman Styles. Marco Dean called me a slag.

Age 14, my photo is one of many posted on an Instagram account where boys from the school rate the girls' like Top Trumps, when I told them I was going to report it, they said it was only because I was pissed off that I scored so low.

When I offered to help Mr Blake move the desks in Geography but was told it would be better for him to wait for "The Muscles" to arrive because he didn't want me hurting myself.

I raised the idea of doing more on intersectional feminism and the white girls told me I should be a little softer in my arguments. I should watch my tone.

When I went to sit down in Maths and Davey Smith put his hand on my chair so as I sat he felt my crotch. Mr Cash told me off for screaming, he said I was being "hysterical".

Head of year always commenting on the length of our skirts. This happened significantly more times to me in the last year than it did to my white peers.

'When you put it in black and white like this...' I stop reading after the seventh entry. It's not that it's too much, it's too familiar. Apart from the race stuff. 'You've got it double whammy, babe.'

'Two-for-one.' Maya takes her phone. 'That's just the school version.' She closes that note, opens another. 'There's one for general life too.'

I shouldn't be shocked, but, 'Jesus, there's loads of them.'

Reading Maya's list, I realise how, for years, my own unconscious equivalent has flowed so consistently through my blood that I am made of its repercussions. And it's easy to assume others will see them, that those repercussions are as plain as the bluebell wreath tattooed on my skin. But while they're obvious to me because I experience and feel them, those who don't walk in my shoes probably won't even know of their existence. Maybe it's no wonder they don't see.

'You too, right?' Maya says. And I recognise that grin. She's not smiling because I've had my own shit to deal. She's smiling because she has a plan. 'I'm thinking if a bunch of us each made one, I could present them en masse to Herring. There's no way he could deny there's a problem then.'

'Hi.' Dad's half in, half out of his seat, arms semi open for a hug he's not sure I'll want. His hesitancy spreads to his hand, which sort of points at the full-works hot chocolate on the table. There are so many predictable things a parent knows about their child. And so many questions they never think to ask.

'Hi.' I'm tempted to avoid eye contact as well as his awkward greeting, but *face him*, I think. *You are not the one who's done anything wrong*. I sit, spoon in hand, but instead of scooping the sticky mass of marshmallows and cream into my mouth, I push the mug away. I'm in no mood for sweet. For sugar and spice and all those other things girls are meant to be made of.

He watches. Wounded. 'Thanks for suggesting we meet.'

The bell above the door dings one, two, three times. Customers arriving with their *mornings* and their orders for take-out and the small change they drop into a jar labelled "tips".

Time passes. Minutes could be seconds. Seconds could be days.

My head swarms with all the hundreds of times we've sat in this coffee shop since I was a kid. My post-swim-lesson treat was this hot chocolate, a cake too when I moved up a level or earned a new badge.

From my bag, I take my notebook, tearing the three pages I scrawled with my own version of Maya's list once she'd gone.

'What's this?' He asks when I thrust them across the table, which wobbles, sending his untouched coffee over the rim of his cup. It pools on the saucer. He goes to mop it up with a serviette, one eye glancing at my notes.

'I'll do that.' I snatch the napkin. I don't want only half of his attention. 'It's a sample,' I say. 'Of shitty things boys and men have done to me.'

Dad pulls his head back, like, *what?*

I'd known when I was writing I wanted to show it to my father. Like Maya suggested, it's a good way for him to conceive he is just one part of a much bigger problem.

I watch his eyes scan the first few lines.

'I don't know if I can read this.'

I snuff something like incredulity from my nose. 'You think it's hard reading it? Try living it.'

'I know,' he says. But I don't think that's true. He *doesn't* know. None of them do. That's the actual problem.

'Which bit's upsetting you?' I pull the paper from him. 'That I've been sent dick pics since pretty much the week I first got my phone? How in Year 9, there was this boy who used to knock stuff off my desk so I'd have to bend over to pick it up and, surprise surprise, when I did, he'd take the opportunity to grope me. Or the guy in McDonalds who, when I spilt my vanilla milkshake, gawped at the white stain on my top and told me how if I enjoyed looking like that he'd be very *very* happy to come on my tits?'

Dad closes his eyes.

'Oh, was it that last one? Maybe some low-level stuff would be more palatable? Look, page two.' I hold it out to him, but he doesn't take it. 'The seventy-odd-year-old man at the party yesterday, who said how amused his wife would be that he was talking to me because she'd noticed how he always seems to end up chatting with the "sexy ones". Tame by comparison to the others really, don't you think? But if that's still too much, we could move away from the sex stuff all together?' I flip to the last page. 'Talk about the PE teacher who pointed me out as an example to his boys who under no circumstances should *run like a girl*. Or when I was ten and asked the TA if I could wear trousers and was reminded of the uniform code. And when I asked why dresses were compulsory for girls, her only reasoning was "well, they look so pretty", and she saw no benefit in such an "inconsequential change".'

He shakes his head.

'Don't worry, I've spared you the worst.'

The movies boys insist we let them show us if we don't want to be considered frigid. Short crude clips they mostly find piss-themselves funny that are as accessible and disposable as any other photo on their phones. I've watched them, intrigued by the guys' apparent lack of embarrassment around pornography and masturbation. Because that's what the videos are for, right? At least that's what's we all thought until some of us started having sex, and the boys the girls were having sex with wanted to copy the kinds of sex they'd seen on screen. Rumours of boys telling girls their orgasms would be better, stronger, if they came with a hand around their throat. About roughing up. Domination. Conquest. Gratification.

Should I tell him? How sometimes you watch something like that and there's an appeal in the woman's absence, how you need so much to be someone different, it's worth risking the humiliation and pain.

'See.' I lay the pages on the table. One. Two. Three. 'It not only you, Dad.'

'It's a lot,' he says. 'An understatement, I know.' He fingers the paper like it's that that's toxic.

'Maya told me if a woman is being assaulted, she's more likely to get help if she shouts fire instead of rape.'

'That can't be true.'

'Says he who sat around and did nothing while another man touched me.' I hold back from reminding my father that he touched me too.

'I didn't know for sure it was against your will.' Who knew whispering could sound so defensive?

'Really? Cos there was a mood in that dining room, Dad.' I move his coffee cup, along with the serviette, to the empty table next to us. 'If I'm generous, I can perhaps believe your perception at the time was skewed by too much booze. But it took you a week to tell Mum what happened. If you were so certain those men, and *you*, had done no wrong, surely you'd have told her sooner.'

'You're right.' He looks knackered. 'I'm really sorry, Cass. For the dinner. And,' he gestures at the paper on the table, 'all this. For everything that's happened to you.'

'*To* me.' I almost smile. 'We talk about these things happening *to* me or *to* other women. Like, Maya has been researching this stuff, and the majority of stats she's found have been about the victims.' I'm usually terrible at remembering figures, but what my friend told me earlier stuck firm. 'At risk of sounding like some feature on Woman's Hour, did you know one in four women have been raped or sexually assaulted?'

Dad shakes his head.

'And nine out of ten girls in schools say they or their friends are receiving dick pics?'

He sighs.

'I might also find those numbers shocking if my friends and I weren't living it. Thing is though, Dad, the boys, the men, they're living it too, right? On the other side? But the numbers about how many of them are raping or assaulting or sending those dick pics aren't so easy to find. How do we fix a problem when we're only looking at one half of it?'

Dad says nothing.

'Take the list.' I lift my chair so its feet don't scrape across the floor when I stand. I'm not after a dramatic exit. 'Read it a few times over. Have a think if you've ever been the guy in any of those or similar situations. Not necessarily the one doing the worst thing, even

if you were mild by comparison or...' I pause. '...
silent on the side lines.'

'I...' He runs a finger down the first page.

'I do love you.' I move around to his side of the
table, kiss the top of his head. 'You're a good man,
Dad. I'm not trying to make you feel bad. I just want
you to see.'

I leave the café, resisting the urge to go back and
tell my father it's fine really, there's no need to bother,
it's a fuss over nothing, why don't we forget all of this
and both go home. I stop to look at him through the
window. His head is dipped over the paper, and for
the first time in a while, I am a different Cassandra,
the one Dad always promised I would be. Powerful
maybe, like people might actually start to listen and
believe what I have to say.

EVE

My sister looks up from Mum and Dad's kitchen table, where – given the empty coffee cup and the plate scattered with croissant flakes – she's clearly been sitting a while. Yesterday's Sun is opened to the double-page spread with a photograph of Harry and Rock. Beside it, with all my unanswered calls and messages, is her phone.

Mum places a hand over mine. 'Your sister was just saying she wishes she'd kept a better eye on Cass this last week.' She pulls the chair by one of its spindles, urges me to sit down.

Typical Sophie, schlepping over here to slip her side of the story to Mum first.

'Oh yeah?' I'm not sure I want to go there in front of our mother. 'What exactly would you have done differently then, Soph?'

'I take it from that grumpy demeanour someone's head's a bit sore this morning.' Like the perfect bloody sibling, she fetches me a glass, pours me some juice.

Despite being parched, I don't touch the drink. 'Why aren't you at home packing for your retreat?'

'Because, dear sister,' – Sophie pulls a croissant from the bread bin. 'Butter? Jam?' Without thinking,

I nod. *Shit.* – 'with whatever it is that made poor Cass and then you and Harry leave early last night, I wanted to check you're all OK.'

'So why didn't you come straight to mine then? Or answer my calls?'

'I thought you could chat more freely here,' Sophie says. That's bollocks. She's well aware I won't to go full throttle in front of Mum. 'I know how teenagers can lurk at that very moment we need some grown-up time.' She hands me the perfectly prepared croissant with her perfectly prepared smile. 'It's not only Will and Cass either. I was telling Mum how even some of the more culturally sophisticated girls we now have working the gala haven't yet mastered reading adult cues.'

And there it is, Sophie's eternal knack of getting to our parents to pre-empt my gripe.

'Eve?' Mum pours me a tea from the pot she somehow always manages to keep full and hot without her ever seeming to leave the table. 'Do you think Cass went missing from George's last week because she'd been drinking?'

'What?'

'It's only Sophie was telling me how some of the younger girls at the dinner get caught up in the excitement of the auction and, despite what Sophie might tell them, they can be a bit too willing to accept offers of drinks from the men?'

'Huh, that's what Sophie told you, is it?'

My sister puts her elbow on the table, her chin in her palm. 'What I said was that if Cass had stayed in place at her assigned table instead of running off, I would obviously have been able to moderate her drink—'

'From the sounds of it, Sophie, it wasn't Cass or the other girls in that room who needed moderating. It was the men.'

She sits up straight. 'Jesus, Eve, not you as well.'

'What do you mean?' It's Mum's turn to lean closer. 'Has Cass said something?'

I glance at Sophie, who's fiddling with her phone. 'Let me show you the guestlist, Mum, then you tell me if you believe the men would need moderating. They're policemen, friends of Dad, for god's sake, property people, architects; it's not like I'm sending the girls into a pack of ex cons.' She thrusts her phone at Mum. 'And his name's not there because he came as a last-minute guest after someone else dropped out, but obviously Harry was also in attendance. Are you suggesting, Eve, your husband needs moderating too? And what about your ex? Be funny, wouldn't it, if the two key men in your life were both dubious or depraved or some other insulting adjective you're so keen to thrust upon my guests.'

'Harry's nothing like Luke.' Mum's voice is a freshly honed knife.

She's right, isn't she? They couldn't be more different. Harry and I first met in a bar, his mates giving it the large one with their inane chat, while he stood out for being quiet. I remember how impressed I was by the way he looked at his friends. The disapproving slow shake of his head. He was a gentleman. Bought me a bottle of Prosecco by way of apology for their behaviour, and so determined was I to prove myself a true Noughties woman, I drank the whole lot before inviting him back to mine. He wouldn't have sex with me until the morning.

Rock on the other hand. He couldn't wait.

'I *was* ready,' I told Kelly when she'd grilled me about that first time – my actual first time – with Lucien. 'It was…' I struggled to finish the sentence. Intoxicating wasn't a word I'd have used at sixteen. What I meant was, he made the undoable doable. Like with his comedy, he would say something provocative but describe it as edgy. And isn't edgy brave and challenging? Isn't edgy shocking, yes, but OK?

'In a club toilet though?' Clearly Kelly didn't approve. 'And isn't he a bit, I dunno, old?'

'Twenty-five isn't old, Kel, it's mature. It's someone who knows what he wants and isn't afraid to go for it. Someone who sees the woman I'm destined to be.' I tried to say it with the same conviction as he had.

I've thought about it since. And, sure, the age gap was significant, but Lucien, as he was when I met him, was persuasive, maybe, but not pushy.

'I was watching you,' he said that first night when he beckoned me behind the velvet rope, the only hint of worldly glamour in an otherwise dingy Shropshire club. 'Saw something I didn't in the other girls.' He recognised I was struggling to hear him above the music. It was only gentle, the tug of his fingers on my hip. 'You're like me.' His lips were hot against my ear. 'You want more than what life's given you. You want everything you know you deserve.' He offered me an already-poured glass of Champagne.

'I…' I started. I'd agreed – begrudgingly – to come with Sophie but had sworn I wouldn't drink.

He must have caught my hesitation. 'Sorry,' he retracted slightly, his fingers dropping from my hip and his gaze drifting to the bar. 'Was I wrong? I wouldn't want to —'

'No.' One smile, and his eyes and hand were back on me. 'You were right.' A small flick of my hair. The bubbles were elegant and sophisticated, were like nothing I'd had before.

'It's dry,' Lucien said. 'I'm glad you like it. I knew you'd understand the advantages of not being too sweet.'

He always encouraged me away from the saccharine. Told me I was capable of being assertive and bold.

I could do with some of that gumption he saw in me when dealing with my sister now.

'You've read the article, haven't you?' Sophie slides the paper across the table. 'It talks about the incredible amount of money the auction raised. Well,' she heaves a dramatic sigh, 'before that boy arrived. You know I've not even heard from Charlotte. What's the latest with Aaron?'

'Can we please stay focused on what happened before Cass left the gala?'

'Um, Eve?' Dad is at the kitchen door. 'Can I borrow you for a minute?' For a man unbothered by the worst kinds of scenarios in his work, whatever he wants to talk to me about has turned his usually weather-ruddy skin pale.

Why would be my cucumber-cool father be sweating?

I hold my breath and stand.

The room is hot suddenly. Small.

Somehow, despite my heart being home to a tornado, I follow Dad into his office. 'Everything alright?'

'I've been sent something.' He coughs before the word "something".

I don't want to ask but, 'What?' I close the door behind me, a sense that whatever's coming should be contained.

'I'm not sure I should show you.' He moves behind his desk. The seat-pad of his chair puffs as he drops onto it, a farty type noise Sophie and I would sneak in here for the sole purpose of making. Juvenile, but even as adults we've found it funny. Today, though, I don't laugh. 'It's a photo.' Dad's voice is even quieter than it was in the kitchen. Another cough. 'Of Cass.'

Shit.

Shit.

Shit.

He doesn't need to say what kind of photo. His face, his volume, says it all.

'Who?' Like Dad, I am not loud. 'Who sent it?'

He shakes his head, turns his palms, shrugs his shoulders, all the signs to suggest he doesn't know.

'You must be able to tell?'

'The email's not one I recognise, Eve.' His finger hard clicks the mouse as if double checking. 'Whoever's sent it says it's a still from a video. They've cropped so it so I wouldn't have to see Cass's face.'

'It might not be her then?' The question is thin, desperate.

'The ring of bluebells on her wrist?'

After failing to talk her out of it, I'd gone with Cass to the tattoo parlour. Her hand squeezing mine, she tried to convince me through wet eyes and gritted teeth that there was no pain.

'You sure about this?' It was my last-ditch effort to stop her. I pointed at the beginnings of one flower. 'Leave now, and no one would even realise those lines were there.'

She'd laughed then. 'Mother knows best, eh!'

'It's just so permanent.'

'And so pretty,' she said.

I wonder if she'll think so now.

CASS

It's funny, right, how a best mate and her shot of hope that I can change things trumps my grudge against Mum from last night. 'I saw him,' I say to her when I come back from Maya's house, where I'd rushed after meeting Dad, this mad buzz and a bone-deep determination to harness that high of feeling heard. I'd called Liv on the way over to see if she wanted in on Maya's presentation to Herring, but she was buried in notes for her Economics assignment, which I'd have thought she'd have finished by now, what with all the cramming in the weeks just gone. 'Dad,' I clarify when Mum looks up from the sofa with eyes like one of those frightened-dog gifs Liv finds so funny. 'And Maya and I, we've spent the last hour or so plotting, and we have this plan t—'

'Cass.' She pats the seat next to her, the way she used to when she was gunning for one of her serious talks. You know, the ones about Father Christmas or periods or the birds and the bees. Only she never called it the birds and the bees. My mother is not a fan of euphemism. *If you're going to say it, say it straight*, she says when it comes to matters with the highest cringe potential. But then I sit down, braced for an extended apology for the Freddie White fiasco and she keeps opening her mouth then shutting it again, like those dumbass fishes Liv's dad used to keep in the giant tank that took up, like, half of their living room.

If things weren't already so screwed around here, I'd be taking the piss, but Mum's open-closed-open-closed non-start to this conversation has my hands kind of clammy, which isn't great for her either because whatever it is she's trying to tell me is so bad she reaches across the sofa and takes hold of my sweaty palms.

'Did you and George...' She begins but stops again, then hearing my sigh or clocking my rolling eyes, 'I'm sorry, I'll come right out with it. Did you and George ever take any photos or films when you were having sex?' Her words are a rush, but that doesn't stop me from noting the fear in them and the way, like those bloody fish again, when she's done she gulps for air.

It's this I want to talk about, not the meaning but the delivery of her question because the meaning is too personal, too ugly, too much. I understand suddenly what people are getting at when they say silence is heavy because the longer I don't answer Mum's question, the more the unspoken words swell inside me and the more Mum's nervousness thickens the air.

Everything is either pressing out or pressing in.

'No,' I say. And then, 'Why?' I ask, not because I want an answer but because I want release. I mean, the answer is obvious, isn't it. There's only ever one reason someone would ask the question *did you make a sex tape?* and that's because something they've already seen has confirmed a resounding *yes*.

'Something – a photo – has been brought to my attention.'

Brought to my attention? She sounds so formal, looks it too now with her straight back and her straight face. The only thing that thaws her stiffness is those hands, still holding, *no*, gripping, on to mine, like when we we've been on a rollercoaster or an airplane take-off and we were each as scared as the other. *I've got you*, she said with that repeated squeeze. *It might not feel like it, but, I promise, we will be fine.*

'These things are designed to keep us safe,' she said when we sat on the runway, and she was right then, technology and engineering were on our side.

Now though?

Technology and engineering make it a shit tonne worse.

My legs, arms, elbows, fingers, knees, shoulders, all of the bones and everything clinging to them are shaking. My voice is all wobble too. 'Who sent it to you?'

It.

A photo, yes, but of what?

Me, yes, but which part?

How exposing?

How identifiable?

How foul?

'It wasn't sent to *me*.' Mum takes a giant in-breath. 'It was sent to Gramps.'

'Gramps?' Everything's spinning. 'What?' Everything's blurred. 'How?'

She tells me it came anonymously. She tells me Gramps doesn't think any less of me. She tells me over and over and over we will get through this. Things will be OK.

We, she says, still able to sit and speak and smile, which means *we* are no longer the same kind of people, or the same kind of creature even, because sitting and speaking and smiling and so many other things are all impossible for me now that the only viable option is to find a hole and crawl inside it until I die of thirst or hunger.

If shame doesn't kill me first.

'Will I even be able to look at them?' We are outside George's house. How can I get out of the car? Because by *them*, I mean George and his family, but there are other people on the street, in this town, on this entire fucking planet. And any one of them could have seen it. Any one of them could have seen *me* like *that*.

'Show me,' I'd said to Mum before we left. How did I agree to leave? To do this? To come off the sofa, where I'd curled into a literal ball, eyes closed and the world still not dark enough to block out the spotlight shining on me because of him. "Shining" too nice a word for it. Too warm. Too positive. The spotlight I'm under is a stark and nasty glare.

'You sure you want to see?' Mum's voice, like everything else, was both distant and close. Maybe I'd have been better off not looking, but isn't it always better to have the full picture? Always better to know? 'OK, then,' she'd said when I nodded, explaining in this too placid way that after Gramps had forwarded it to her, she'd saved the photo to a locked folder on her phone.

She gave me one last out. I refused to take it.

'Just show me,' I said, surprised I could form a sentence that wasn't *Kill me now*.

The photo was very clearly mortifying.

Very clearly anal.

And, because of that stupid fucking tattoo that was meant to symbolise truth, very clearly me.

George wouldn't, though.

So, how? Why? When?

My mind flickered between the photo and the only night it could have been taken. In the hours after the gala. In George's bedroom when I said I liked it. When I said I loved it. When I said "stop" and then I heard something – it must have been his phone – fall to the floor.

It had been years since I actually screamed, but at home on the sofa, my scream was so much a part of me, I didn't think it would stop. In the car now though, as I try to shrink myself to zero, I am the most silent thing on earth.

Mum leans across from the driving seat, a finger under my chin to raise it. I know what she's doing but close my eyes. 'We've all done things, Cass,' she says, and I might be blind to her at the minute, but I can hear the gulp at the end of her sentence, how hard she's trying not to cry. 'Intimate things we did because we felt not only excited by someone but safe with them as well.' The line is too smooth not have been prepared, rehearsed, even, as Mum waited for me to come home. I imagine her trying to quash that inevitable rush of disgust with me while fretting about the right thing to say. 'It's normal to experiment, love. I could give you a whole list of stuff I've tried through the years.'

'Please don't,' I attempt but fail to laugh.

'You are not the one in the wrong here.'

Does Gramps think that?

Will Dad?

'I can go in without you if you prefer.' Her finger on my chin turns to a flat palm on my knee. 'Whatever you want,' she says, but we both know what I want is impossible. This will not just go away.

'I'll come.' The alternative is worse. George telling them his side without me there to put his assertions right.

Like that time when I was twelve and Mum took me to get my ears pierced, I go into autopilot, opening my eyes, letting her lead me by my elbow, telling myself it's going to be uncomfortable, but it's my choice, and the hurt can't last forever. Things heal. The pain will go away.

Unlike then, I don't believe it, but somehow I make it out of the car and to the door.

'Cass?' It's George's mum who answers. Her left slipper is almost worn away at its toe. 'You OK, angel?' I can't do it. Look at her, I mean. 'I'm Pam,' she says. To Mum, I assume, because Mum's giving her name in return then asking if it's possible for us to come inside.

Pam's feet take three steps backwards. 'Of course. Tea or coffee, Eve?' Whenever I was here with George, Pam was always warm. This offer of a drink now though is no more than polite.

'I'm good, thank you.' To anyone else Mum might sound normal, but there's an undercurrent in her 'thank you', which is usually only "thanks."

'George?' Pam shouts. 'Can you come down, please.' Quieter then but no less purposeful, 'He's not been himself since he received that visit from the police.'

Mine is not the only mother who's angry.

I watch Mum's left thumb pick at her pinkie nail and wait for an apology that doesn't come.

Footsteps above us.

'What about you, Cass?' Pam's voice is softer with me. 'I've made some of those cheese scones you like.' She was constantly feeding me when I was here.

Afraid of what will happen if I speak, I shake my head.

'I think perhaps they've come to apologise, George,' Pam says when the footsteps move to the stairs.

'Hardly.' Mum snaps. I raise my eyes to glare at her. What we're here to talk about isn't Pam's fault. I don't want Mum to draw any more negative attention. I don't want her to be rude.

'Cass?' George is clutching onto the banister, standstill on the bottom step.

My face is hot. Not just my face though. *Everything* about me is appalling and red, including my mouth, which spits the word *why* at my ex-boyfriend again and again and again.

'What?' Confused lines so deep in George's brow, his skin is almost folding.

'The photo, George. Or film, maybe?' Unlike me, Mum is stone cold.

'What photo? What film?' Pam's eyes flit from Mum to George to me, and at this point I'm back staring at the carpet because it's impossible, isn't it, for me to explain. 'George?' Rolling slowly from his mum's tongue, each letter of his name is audible, as if Pam already knows what kind of photos, what kind of film.

'What was it? Revenge because you thought I was with Patrick? Thought you'd get your own back by showing other people what we'd done?'

'I haven't shown anyone.'

'But you did take a picture?'

He's in front of me now.

'Don't touch her,' Mum says when he attempts to take my hands.

'Sorry.' George's apology is not defensive or dismissive, it's real. Or at least it sounds it. Though I can't trust myself to believe anything he might say. 'I swear to you, Cass, I would never. I promise. I'll get my phone if you like.' He disappears briefly before returning, holding it out to me. 'I'll admit I did film you. It's in a folder there, see. But look.' He scrolls through the apps, 'Whatsapps, emails, whatever. I've not sent anything.'

In his messages I search for my name. All I find are his mates taking the piss out of how lovesick he's been since our split. I jump back to those between him and Ellis last Sunday morning when I'd left without saying goodbye.

> George: Gutted. Think Cass is going to end it.
>
> Ellis: A girl shouldn't just leave like that bro. She's not playing fair
>
> George: Maybe
>
> George: Worried about her though. She didn't seem herself.
>
> Ellis: Hope you at least got some 🐾 out of it
>
> George: Not funny yeh

'You know I'm not the sort of guy who...' He stops when I jump to the "Cass" folder in photos and play the video – not just a photo but a video – of him doing *that*. The volume's up high and George's *I love you* is paired with my scandalous groan. I hit pause.

I could die.

'Not the sort of guy who what?' I suck in air between jagged breaths, oxygen somehow finding its way to the right parts of my body so I can say what I came here to say. 'I didn't think you were the sort to film me without my permission.' I angle the screen, like, *right here, see, is evidence to the contrary*. 'Just tell me who you sent it to.'

'No one,' he says.

Pam stands by my side in front of her son. 'Now is the time to be honest, G.' Despite how dirty she must think I am, she places a sisterly hand on my shoulder.

I'm still flicking through the photos, mostly goofy selfies we took during a picnic in the park.

'I *am* being honest.'

'So how would it have got out then?' It's such a simple question, but he has no answer, just shakes his head. If before shame made me quiet, right now it's making me shout. 'Someone sent it to my granddad. It was your video. Your phone. And what was it you said last night? About other people seeing this *other side* of me. Well, good job, you've showed them, right?'

'Cass,' Mum comes between the two of us. 'I think we leave now and give George a chance to think about this.' It's Pam she's looking at, eyes all, *I'm begging you – please get the truth from your son.*

Tonight Will Be Fine @MSTWBF
In light of all the advice to women in the wake of
Lucy Corrigan's death, thought I'd share these words
of wisdom from @SVCCork

EVE

'She's been up there since we got home.' I pass Dad a coffee, think about leaving Harry to get his own but press the button on the machine despite my petty instincts. No matter how much the gala dinner and the photo feel like part of the same problem, I can't lay this all on my husband. There's George. The diners. Sophie.

Me.

'He didn't force me,' Cass said in the car on the way back from George's. 'Into trying…' She was swallowing sobs. 'I already felt so grubby.' Her hands scrubbed invisible dirt from her thighs. 'I didn't say yes to the filming though. But then he didn't ask, so it's not like I actually said no.' Her hands balled, and she began to punch her chest. 'Who does something like that? Shares that kind of photo of someone they're supposed to love?'

I reached across to the passenger seat to take hold of her beating fist.

It's Cass I need to focus on. But Kelly keeps creeping in.

It was different, I tell myself now. *It was Kelly's Polaroid camera. It was Kelly who said we should take the shots. And it wasn't digital. You had control of who saw it. You weren't putting Kelly in any danger. It couldn't be re-shared.*

Where is it now though?

Random food items I've taken from the fridge in the hope of hashing together dinner, sit untouched on the kitchen counter. Cass said there's no way she could eat. Like her, I don't think I'd keep anything down.

No matter where I look, I see George's photo and hear the soundtrack of the longer more explicit film.

'It's hardly surprising she's hiding,' Dad says. 'You wouldn't catch me venturing out.'

'You think she'd let *me* in?' Harry takes the mug, his fingers briefly but intentionally touch mine. It's as much of an olive branch as he can muster in front of my dad, who – as yet – knows nothing of my husband and his mates at Hambledon Manor. Does all that pale into insignificance now?

'What would you say if she did? Because they count,' I tell Harry. 'Those first words she hears from you.' Like imprinting – the crucial moments for a new-born animal when it forms attachments and a concept of its identity – how we respond to our daughter's sexuality made public could impact the rest of her life.

Did George not think of the consequences?

Did you?

It was different.

Maybe, but there were still consequences.

A week or so after I showed him the polaroid, Luke – and he *was* insistent everyone call him Luke by then – had invited Kelly and me – VIP passes – to watch him perform. Tickets to a club after. Two pills wrapped tight in cling film. It wasn't me he gave them to, though. Rather, in his dressing room in the immediate aftermath of the show, he greeted Kelly on her right cheek and then her left – so grown-up and cosmopolitan – and slipped the tiny gift into her hand.

'Cheers,' she said, on the edge of the dancefloor maybe thirty minutes later, lisping, laughing, not yet drinking but dropping her jaw to reveal half a pill on her tongue. Another was pincered between her thumb and forefinger.

I snatched it, swallowed it, less for the high and more because I didn't want Kelly getting caught. 'Are you mad?'

'Maybe. Dance?'

I knew she was coming up when she took hold of both of my hands.

I knew *I* was coming up when I heard her voice – the way we'd always sworn, if we tried hard enough, we could hear each other's voices – without her saying a word. *You,* she said, and *You,* I mouthed back to her, relishing the light and freedom of her moves.

She kissed me in the cubicle of the ladies, the door vibrating with the music that was weekend-loud even though it was a Tuesday. 'You're still together then?' Her mouth so much smaller, softer than Luke's.

'Sure,' I said, which wasn't a lie exactly. Despite his obvious boredom, Luke hadn't officially ended things. Not that he'd ever officially started them either. We still, I thought, had a chance.

And then, 'Did you tell him about us?'

Again, I didn't lie, not really. I said nothing, intuiting the distraction of my fingers on her spine, along her neck and in her hair.

After the club, his apartment. Kelly and me on the sofa. Luke on a chair in the corner. For a change, he was relatively sober. 'Don't you still have one more pill?' When Kelly didn't answer. 'I'm going out for a bit anyway.' He grabbed his coat. 'You girls chill.'

The silence when the front door closed was swollen with anticipation. 'What do you think?' I asked. We were on the start of a gentle comedown.

'May as well,' she said. 'If he'll be a while?'

We took the pill.

Kelly told me I could do better than Lucien or Luke or Lucifer and grabbed Rock's landline, requesting *You Oughta Know* on The Box and moving to the floor, where we waited. Both to come up and for our video to appear on his state-of-the-art TV.

We were on Luke's bed, peeled of clothes and inhibition, by the time Alanis was singing, her visceral anger turned visceral desire surging through the darkness towards us via the open bedroom door, where the only lyric in my mouth was Kelly's name. The hard K and the soft Y on my tongue pressing against her bones, seeking more and more and more of her. All breath and strength and skin.

Her palm cupped the curve of my skull and urged me down.

A loud groan, and she was gone. No longer laid before and beneath me but upright against the headboard, grasping for sheets and asking did I hear that. 'It wasn't me', she said. 'That groan.' It was too deep, too distant. Her fingers were on switches. There was light.

Too much light.

'Don't stop.' A voice from by the wardrobe. Luke Rock sitting, erect penis in hand, on the floor.

'Eve?' My name no longer hunger for Kelly but a question.

'C'mon girls. I'm nearly there.'

'Eve?'

'She said she'd like me to watch.' Luke's eyes were glazed. 'Isn't that right, Gen?'

Was it? With Luke I said a lot of things I knew he'd like to hear.

Kelly's face then. The one that screams betrayal.

The best I could do was to help my friend find her dress, to ask Luke for money for her taxi, to say sorry in the hall and on the communal staircase and again on the dirty path outside.

It's Cass I need to focus on not Kelly.

It's now I can try to fix. I can't do anything about what happened then.

In the kitchen, I dither, not knowing who – my husband or my father – to sit next to at the table. 'Look,' I say, attempting a voice somewhere close to normal. 'Kids experiment. And as far as we know, what George and Cass did – until the filming that is – was something they both wanted.' I pull out the chair beside Harry. 'And, yes, it's not something we would choose to think about, let alone witness, but what I'm very sure of is that it's *not* something for which I want my daughter to feel disgraced.'

My father makes a noise like a little pig.

Before I have time to curb my irritation, 'What does that mean?'

'Eve.' Harry puts what I think is supposed to be a calming hand on my arm.

Deeds not words.

'No.' I snatch it away. 'I'm serious, Dad. What did that little snort mean?' I've never been very good at knowing what to do with anger, especially when Dad is at its core. The fact he'd threatened to confiscate the Morissette album because of her "angry swearing" made it clear that kind of intense female fury wasn't acceptable in his domain. The thing is, anger manifests differently when it's not you but your child your father is judging. I make myself bigger. 'You told me you were coming over to *help* Cass, not cast judgement upon her for whatever sex she wants to try.'

'And I *am* going to hel—'

'You've seen the worst of people – murderers and paedophiles for fuck's sake – and had less of a reaction. Is your granddaughter doing anal really more shocking than the grooming gangs you investigated in Telford, or that bloke in Shrewsbury you put away for multiple rape? Have you really never done anything that – if you were caught – you might regret?'

Surely Cass was only doing what I wanted her to: being open about sex and bodies and understanding we shouldn't be afraid to find pleasure in them, that experimentation – when it's safe and consensual – isn't something to be feared.

Kelly had sent me a letter after.

You made me feel special, Eve. I'd never slept with a girl before. You made me believe it would be OK.

It's pathetic, how relieved I am for the distraction of a beep from my phone.

> Sophie: You with Dad? I've
> been trying to call him
> but he's obviously preoc-
> cupied with whatever sent
> you off without saying
> goodbye this morning. Can
> you tell him I've been
> ringing Uncle Joe but n/a.
> I need to speak with him
> before I leave for the
> retreat tonight.

And there are far *far* more important things for me to think about right now but, 'Dad,' I say, about to relay my sister's message, but he holds a hand in the air. It could be a shut-down, there's something soft and sympathetic, though, in his palm.

'I love Cass,' he says, 'more than anything. Any disappointment you're picking up on is in the mere fact she trusted that boy.' His hands clasped as if in prayer. 'I knew from the beginning something was off with him.'

Harry raises his head. 'George was nothing but lovely with Cass *and* with us. How could she have known he'd do something like this?'

Both palms in the air now, any hint of Dad's clemency is gone. 'Because that's what boys these days do, Harry, even the nice ones.'

Whatever audacity my husband had corralled to challenge my father dissipates with a point that obviously hits too close to home.

You were my best friend, Eve, Kelly had written.

Massaging a spot at the base of his own neck, Dad grimaces. 'I'm not judging when I say this, Eve, but girls need to protect themselves from that.'

I look at Harry. How much faith I had in his goodness.

How much Kelly had in mine.

That was different.

'I dunno.' Harry's shoulders broaden as he inhales. 'Should it really be on the girls to protect themselves?' He pulls a piece of paper from his pocket. 'When I met Cass this morning, she gave me this.' He flattens it out on the table, slides it towards Dad. 'Hardly light reading. She asked me to think about times I may have been complicit in any of this crap, and it's...' His lower jaw pulses. His foot tap tap taps on the quarry-tiled floor.

'I'm not saying it's all on them, Harry.' Dad runs a finger down each item. 'Of course, we have to do our bit too. Why do you think I became a policeman. This man she says flashed her when she was sixteen, I bet that's the one we caught. The boys at the station are constantly on the lookout for dodgy behaviour. I'm not pretending we can fix all of this, but we *are* doing our utmost to keep women safe.'

'You honestly believe that?' Cass. Her tone is one I've never heard her take with anyone, let alone her grandfather. She's at the kitchen door, and even with how red and puffed they are, the outrage in her eyes is clear, pure. 'George just called.' Her whole body's shaking. I rush to hold her, but she shoves me away, cranes her neck to keep her view of my dad unblocked. 'There was someone else who had access to that video.'

'Who?' Harry and I ask in unison.

A flash of her furious eyes at me, 'When *you* thought I was missing and *he* —' she jabs a finger at Dad, '— sent his men to George's house, remember?' She takes a step closer to her grandfather. 'It was made very clear to George then, Gramps, that, on *your* instruction, he had no choice but to give *your* policeman mate his phone.'

CASS

Maya rolls onto her side to look at me instead of my ceiling, which is what she, Liv and I have been staring at for well over half an hour since they finally stopped me crying by promising not to leave my side for, like, the rest of my life, which is a big promise, but if anyone would see it through, it's these two.

Even Liv with her extreme study habits has sacked off everything in the last two days to be with me, all three of us risking sanctions for absence from school. Unlike Maya and Liv, though, I've had no stroppy emails from matron, which makes me wonder if Mum's told Herring what's happened. Joke is, on Sunday, I thought it couldn't get any worse. But you picture your headteacher learning about your sex tape and then it does. And then it does. And then it does.

It was Maya who, after four back-to-back episodes of *Glow Up*, suggested the meditation app. And the lie-down. And the holding hands, which, honestly, all sounded a bit claustrophobic but was, as it turned out, alright. As much as anything's been alright since *then*. There was a sort of peace in laying with my friends either side of me, no words, just the music and the blank white space of the ceiling with its spotlights bleaching my vision so I could pretend, briefly at least, that I'd never see anything again. That'd be good, right? Like when I was a toddler and the simplicity of 'if I can't see you, you can't see me' made it so much easier to hide.

Everything was easier when I was tiny. When the worst thing I could do was snatch a toy or pinch a friend or take a crayon and scrawl on the wall.

Mistakes could be painted over, were momentary, punishable by naughty step or no ice cream for pudding, and any falls were quickly kissed better by Mum.

Or Dad. He also made things better then, is trying to make things better now too, dropping hints about his version of The List. Ten out of ten for effort, but whatever lifted between us in the café is bearing down again, the shadows of all the ifs and mays from that night.

If he had stepped in

If he hadn't been so drunk

If he hadn't slapped me

If he hadn't asked HOW COULD YOU LET HIM TOUCH YOU LIKE THAT

If he had said 'I'm sorry' and 'I'm here for you.' instead

I may not have run to George seeking a state of nothingness.

I may not have said yes to watching and emulating that video. I may not have left early in the morning.

Mum may not have worried.

Gramps may not have instructed his policeman friends.

There are too many ifs and mays to see my father and not see cause and effect.

I do my best, then, *not* to see him.

'I reckon we should go to the press.' Maya bursts the thin tranquillity the mediation duped me into feeling.

I am immediately made of dread. 'Why?' What I mean is *no* because, even with my avoidance tactics, I've heard Dad fielding calls on his mobile. Since the The Sun article, local papers and radio stations have wanted more details of his heroic escapades with Rock. And there's the problem. It's him and Rock they want to talk about. *Their* bravery, *their* camaraderie, *their* instinct to save the young women in the room. Aaron Jenkins? With his knife and his apparent desire to at best hurt, at worst kill, those young women? He's what my English teacher would call a subplot. Interesting but let's not get too caught up in his tale. Put this, my sordid story, in the limelight, and whoever sent the video would be boring legal crap. It's me who'd be the protagonist. Me and my naked body are where the juicy bits lie.

'The police are dealing with it, Maya.' I toe the party line even though the party is fractured. Aside from official communication re any required action, neither Dad nor I are talking to Gramps. Mum is another story.

'That's impossible,' she said on Sunday when I barely held myself upright to tell Gramps it was one of his mates who'd sent the video to himself from George's phone. There's no evidence. Not yet. But there must be hundreds of these kinds of images shared every single day. How many of them end up on the desk of a retired Chief Inspector, who happens to be the victim's granddad? You don't need to be a detective to spot the coincidence, or the simple chain of events.

'You really think the police are going to do anything when it's them who are guilty in the first place?' Maya is as measured as she is when she's repping the debate team at nationals. 'Babe, it's not in their interest to uncover the truth. Not that journalists are always much better. I read that story about Luke Rock and your dad.' She's pulled the article up on her phone. 'Don't get how *I*, a schoolgirl in Shropshire, can have heard all these rumours about Rock while the national papers remain somehow oblivious to all his,' she makes bunny ears with her fingers, '*alleged* crap. Who writes this shit?'

For me, now, it's irrelevant. But Maya is zooming in on the byline. 'Shelley Chapman?' She chatters her teeth the way she does when she's thinking. 'How do I know that name?'

I lie down, nuzzling my head into Liv's shoulder, wishing we could wind back time, if not ten days then fifteen minutes when there were no questions, just that blank and blinding light.

'Twitter!' Maya slams a hand down on my thigh in victory. 'She liked a retweet of the video I posted of me burning Rock's books.' Her fingers go mad busy on her phone. 'I can't find it. I'm sure it's her though. Do you remember, I was buzzing thinking a journalist was going to scoop the story and I'd go viral?'

I do not want to go viral.

The TikTok trolls have been spitting sick suggestions of what exactly they'd do to any girl who shouts fire not rape. To any girl who shouts anything really. Truth is, they don't want us to speak at all. It was fuel at first, their vitriol. Petrol to my midnight flames. George's film though made me realise the flimsiness of anonymity. TikTok pseudonym or not, nothing offers one hundred per cent protection from the words or stunts of every nasty hateful man.

'No press.' With my held breath and clenched fists, I'm sure I'm keeping the panic in, but something's obviously leaking because both Maya and Liv take hold of my hands, telling me again and again there's no pressure to do anything I don't want to, everything will be OK.

Mum says the same later during her habitual hourly check-up. 'It'll be OK,' she says. I know she wants to bolster me, but I am made of punctured hope and suspicion of her optimism. For days, her voice has been too quiet for me to trust that even she believes what she's saying is true.

She keeps telling me to not to apologise, says I've done nothing wrong. But she also insists I'm unnecessarily punishing my granddad. 'The men at the station. They wouldn't. I grew up with them, Cass. They're Gramps' friends, decent guys.' I heard it though, her wobbling note of doubt.

Minutes turn into hours. Hours turn into days. Days turn into almost an entire week off school. And even though no one says it, not at first anyway, the obviousness of the bad timing, of it being my second year of A Levels, means I can't avoid the place forever. Means five days after I first learn my granddad's colleagues have shared an illicit video of me, I'm sitting in my headmaster's office wishing, for the millionth time in those five days that I was dead.

Mum is onto this. To the lure for me of a place that isn't this one. She's barely left the house and hovers, silent but persistent, on the other side of my bedroom door. From time to time, she'll knock, ask if there's something I'd like to eat, a programme I'd like to watch. She'll suggest she paints my nails or plaits my hair. For the most part, I go along with it because she looks knackered.

We *all* look knackered.

'This is clearly a difficult time for you, Cassandra.' Since we started the meeting, Mr Herring's done this little cough at the end of every sentence. And in the silence that follows there's been an uncomfortable swallow too. 'And for you, Mrs Gunn.'

Cables from Herring's phone and computer run down the back of his desk into sockets embedded in the floor.

'I understand the police are doing their utmost to…' Herring pauses. Perhaps, like the rest of us, he's unsure exactly what the police do when it's their own men at fault. 'To resolve the situation,' he says. And I wonder if I should tell him what I've learnt from the hundreds of accounts of other similarly exposed women and girls I've read online. How they say because you can't track who's shared the video and because you can't really be sure it's been deleted from various sites and phones, mine is a situation that will likely never be "resolved". I *don't* tell him this. To do so would require talking, which would prolong the meeting when what I want most is to go home.

Herring continues. 'I want to reassure you everyone here at Oakfield is on your side. We've spoken about best steps—'

I imagine them in a meeting held specifically to discuss me. How much detail did they go into?

If I tied those cables around my neck, would they be strong enough to take my weight?

Mum squeezes my hand, and shame upon shame pulses through me.

'— Miss Standing and I think it would be best if we issue a warning about sharing this kind of content generally. We wouldn't mention any names, Cassandra. And Miss Standing will host a PSHE class with the older girls, in which she'll talk about the potential consequences of allowing oneself to be...' That cough again. '...filmed,'

The girls? Of course, it's the girls getting the lesson. Of course, it's the girls who need to learn. I'm too tired, too unsurprised to kick off.

'That's good.' Mum's tone implies otherwise. My eyes move from her feet to her hands, clasped now on her lap. The tendons repeatedly flatten and bulge.

'I also want you to know you can come to see me any time you want to, Cass.' Ms Standing, who took a seat on Herring's side of the desk when we first came into his office, must lean forward because something, a pen pot maybe, is knocked and there are a few seconds of gathering things up, of putting things in order. 'I appreciate how difficult it is for you returning to school after something like this.' Even though my eyes are down, I see Ms Standing's head dip as if trying to put herself in my line of vision. I look to the left, to Herring's shelves, neat with ancient books, red, green and blue hardbacks with gold titles embossed on their spines. 'If there's any hint of students sharing the video or making reference to it in a way that makes you uncomfortable, I'll come down on them like a tonne of bricks.' Standing's voice is pointed and slow.

'Well, yes, absolutely.' Herring stands, and I see his hand held out for Mum's, like, *meeting's over*.

'And those PSHE classes.' Standing says. 'I believe, *strongly*, we can learn lessons from the way we handled the upskirting iss—'

'I think you mean the issue with the theatre-block stairs.' If Herring's tone carries a warning, Ms Standing won't heed it.

'Oh no, I mean the issue with upskirting.'

I look up for the first time and see the way she stares at him.

My heart races. My eyes are filled with tears.

'It's important to call it what it is, don't you think?' Standing turns to Mum.

'Absolutely,' Mum says. 'Cass? Do you agree?'

I think of the message I received from Yasmin Grant last Tuesday when the rumours about me had slunk, hot and juicy, into every nook and cranny of the school.

> Yasmin: I know you don't know me, and what's happened to you is
>
> worse than what happened to me but I have at least a sense of what you're going through. So if you ever want to talk
>
> Yasmin: I hope the police act better than the school did. Herring was more worried about his repu-tation than my dignity. Easier to think it was the architects not under-standing the negative impact of a glass stair-case than him not understanding the nega-tive impact of (some) boys

If this were a movie, I'd be moved by Yasmin's vulnerability, bolstered by Standing's conviction. I'd pull my
shoulders back and immediately feel bigger, stronger,
winged.

Yes, I'd say, refusing to let the word wobble. *We
must call it what it is.*

But there's only one movie I'll ever be in, and that's
the one doing the rounds with the revolting policemen
and scuzzy schoolboys who, never mind that Mum
was with me, made their amusement clear with their
smirks and their murmurs the second I walked
through the gates this morning.

There's no epiphany. No inner strength. Just a 'sure'
and a glance through the window to the clock tower,
and a calculation of what the damage to my body
might be from a "fall".

EVE

There are niceties. Cups of tea. Coffee. Neat discussions about what we will have for dinner. A behind-closed-door conversation about how I think the meeting went with the school.

Painful.

Standing gets it.

Herring – typical man – has no clue.

The way Harry moves about the house reminds me of the robot lawn mower Mum gave Dad for his birthday, all straight lines and quiet efficiency while sticking to stringent yet barely visible boundaries.

'Cass is in her room,' I tell Harry, unnecessarily perhaps because, until tomorrow when she'll return to her job at Subway – else you're fired – you can bet her room is the only place she'll be. 'You're not going anywhere, are you?' He knows what I mean by this.

It's unsafe to leave her alone.

'No.' He looks up from his book, one of the huge and heavy ones – photographs mostly – we buy each other for Christmas. The remoteness of the cabins was romantic when I chose it. Now, the woods in the picture it's open to look ominous, filled with camouflaged risk.

Harry's been sat with it at least half an hour. He's not once turned the page. 'Are you?'

'Meeting Charlotte.' 'Oh.' One syllable, but his voice is off, like he can't quite stick to this script we've conjured of tolerance and shattering but deeply concealed hurt.

'Will you check on her? In twenty minutes? See if there's anything she needs?'

When she was a baby, I'd lament Cass's scalpel-sharp cries at night, and then, when they came – eventually – lament the silent nights more. The quiet when I woke in the solid black should have been honeyed but was instead so implausible it tasted sour. Like the breath of the sick, or the dying. I'd leap, then, from our bed, tripping on discarded slippers and sick-stiff muslins until I was stood over Cass's cot with a hand on her chest for the most rudimentary evidence she was breathing.

'I ordered a baby monitor.' My throat contracts with the stupidity. Of searching. Of purchasing. Of admitting the split-screen and its two tilting, zooming cameras will be delivered tomorrow. 'We can keep an eye on her. Check she's not...'

Harry's nods, like he understands. But, 'I'm not sure that's the solution,' which is something I, of course, already know.

'What else is there though?'

The sound of the radiator on the far wall.

'We should...' Harry says. 'We need to...' he says but looks up at the ceiling we'd sworn we'd replaster when we moved in.

'What, Harry? We should... what? We need to... what?' Impatience whirls in my stomach like the jagged and imperfect Artex circles above.

'Talk.' He shrugs like he's aware this suggestion is unremarkable but has nothing else to offer. 'I know you probably have been talking.' I follow his eyes to a speck of dandruff on his shoulder. 'To Charlotte. Or the other girls. Or your mum. Only I've not,' he says. 'Spoken to anyone, I mean.'

'I didn't realise we were supposed to be keeping things secret.'

His sigh is silent. 'We're not. It's just...'

I allow his ellipsis to hang.

'When shit happens, Eve, I usually talk to you. I don't...' Harry lets out a small noise. '...have anyone else,' he says. 'I don't have anyone but you.' Humiliation floods his cheeks with blood. 'You can say it.'

'What?' Though I know what. The I told you so. Because we've had conversations in which I implied – no, stated – that this, my husband's lack of real mates, was a problem.

'It takes effort,' I said once. 'To make friends. And vulnerability.' Harry's laugh made it clear my plea was a lost cause. The nerves underpinning his jovial tone stretched back too far. Roots, if you like. And as much as they are the inheritance that hamper him, so too are they the inheritance that allow him to stand stoic and tall. As much as he might, after three glasses of Pinot Noir, concede to bouts of loneliness, he wasn't going to take this – my effort to make him expose himself in less obvious ways – seriously.

Now, I don't say I told you so. Don't say anything really because as much as I am sorry for my husband, I am angry with him too.

Outside, the early evening sun is the colour of a lemon. The temperature is bitter, has lost its warmth.

'Inside, I assume?' Charlotte opens the pub door, but I shake my head, no.

'I need air,' I tell her. 'And wine.'

'Fine.' She buttons up her coat for dramatic purposes. 'I'll grab a table; you grab a bottle of red.' When I return with a full-bodied Syrah, 'How are things?'

'Cass is barely talking. I don't know what to do. No one does.' I pour. 'Meanwhile, Harry's praying for time travel.' Like a dog, he'd followed me this evening to the door.

'I wish I could go back,' he said, his whole body stiff and stooped, like his blood had petrified.

'Says he'd return to the gala. Not drink.' I make a show of swigging my wine. 'He would make different choices.'

'You sound sceptical.'

'Aren't we just an exaggerated version of ourselves when we're out of it?' I give voice to that incessant question in my head.

You making moves on me, Eve? Kelly asked that ecstasied summer. Was it me who'd suggested we move from the living room to Rock's bed?

Charlotte's shrug is non-committal. 'Sure, it can loosen our inhibitions, but—'

'I think I've done something bad.' I move my hands from the glass to my pockets. The evening's growing colder, darker too.

'Fuck's sake, Eve. Not Rock?'

'What?' A stupid but firm fear that my friend is somehow reading the memory playing in my head.

'You were going to meet him last week but then – thank fuck – he cancelled. Please tell me you did not make other plans?'

Plans with Luke Rock were never definite. They were loose. Open to last-minute change on his whim.

Back at his flat, the same night I showed him the Polaroid in his dressing room, he'd asked to see it again. 'Go on. If you let me, I have a surprise.'

He placed the photo on the glass coffee table next to two neat lines of coke. After showing me how to snort it, he told me it was my turn.

The tiniest shake of my head. 'I—' I started, but with the press of his hand on my back, I bent over and copied his long hard sniff.

He said he loved how my body looked with Kelly's and slipped his fingers inside my knickers from behind.

'How would you feel if I watched you?'

'Fucking hot.' I was rushing.

'No,' I say to Charlotte now. 'I've deleted his messages.' What I should do is delete his number. It's a mystery to me why I don't.

'Thank god for that.' Her eyes crease. 'Why were you ever with him?'

'Gratitude.' The answer comes without thought.

More wine is my only answer. And a switch. 'What's happening with Aaron?'

She shakes her head.

'Lonely apparently. Emma mentioned a while back Aaron'd been citing some Andrew Tate type ideology.' Maybe it's the increasing dark, but Charlotte looks smaller than her five-foot-eight. 'Mostly motivational stuff. A strong mind equals success; not giving into weakness; seeking out heroes

living the kind of life you're after. Not bad, right?'
Her voice is calm, but her posture is crumpling,
defeated. 'So, while she didn't like the association
with Tate, Em wasn't overly worried by Aaron's
interest. And Shayan and I were all, it's fine, you're
a feminist, our family bangs on about equality all
the time, there's no way Aaron'd ever be sucked in
by any of that misogynist shit.' Charlotte tips her
head back, her chin angled towards the stars, and
is still for just a moment, before looking back at
me. 'And we meant it, Eve. I'd heard the more
extreme stuff Tate was saying. It was ridiculous.
Women belong in the home. Demo videos about
how to attack a woman if she accuses you of
cheating. Women should "bear some responsibility"
for being raped. Attention-grabbing bollocks; no
way any one of sane mind and liberal, feminist
upbringing would fall for it.' A sip. A swallow. A
sigh. 'None of us took it seriously because it seemed
so… out there.' Incredulous raised hands and sad
narrowed eyes.

'I'm dreading the "but" that's coming…'

'But.' Charlotte's smile is wry. 'It wasn't out there
at all because they – these online communities – they
make it so plausible. Stats supporting this idea that
Me Too is part of a bigger feminist conspiracy threatening men and making them the oppressed minority.'

A nearby couple turn at the rise in Charlotte's voice.

My elbows grind into the table. 'You said about him being lonely?'

'Lonely. Depressed maybe? No girlfriend. No job. No money. None of the success feminists reckon comes so easily to young middle class white men. The same success the papers are pointing out has come easily to Aaron's sister. And the groups he's been in make similar comparisons. Play on him feeling inferior. Aaron's still not telling us too much about it, but Shayan and Oli have done a fair bit of digging, and it's scary, Eve. Like, hugely scary.' She leans back in her seat, downs half a glass in one.

'I saw the screenshot you sent. Do they seriously encourage men to take their own lives? And murder women?'

'Oh, they don't see them as women,' Charlotte says. 'They're roasties.'

'Roasties?'

'Women they deem promiscuous. Someone obviously heard rumours about what happens at Hambledon Manor.' A too-long and almost too-taut quiet falls between us. I pour the remains from the bottle of wine. 'You know if it was one of our nephews on Shayan's side, the news would be completely different, right? If a brown-skinned boy had stormed the gala, the press would not be suggesting his anger is because of insecurities about his sister.'

A waitress, apologising for the intrusion, lights the candle next to our empty and moves quietly away.

Charlotte stares at the flame. 'They found Aanshi Siddiqui.'

'The missing Bangladeshi girl?'

'Yeh. Her sister and aunt discovered her body in the boot of her husband's car. The police were still reticent to set up an official search.'

'Shit. That's awful.' I rub the corners of my mouth for sticky tannins. My fingertip's colour of a bruise.

'Isn't it? Police, eh.' Charlotte looks up from the candle, drags her chair closer to the table, holding my gaze. 'Your dad still claiming his men wouldn't share a sex tape?'

I watch my thumbs drumming my lap.

'Well?'

'Those men went to George's to help Cass.' I repeat Dad's defence pretty much word for word. 'Another bone of contention with me and Harry.'

'He doesn't share James' faith in the force?'

'No. Says he understands Dad's faith in them but expected better from me..'

'Wow.'

'I know, right. The irony of Harry wanting me to see the best of him but assume the worst of my dad.'

'Eve.' Charlotte's tone verges on reproachful. 'Harry's very different from your dad.'

'The gala sure proved that, didn't it?'

'You know that's not what I meant. I have a lot of respect for your father, but —'

'Maybe just end that sentence there.'

Charlotte leans back, slides down a little in her chair.

'Sorry,' I say. 'The last couple of weeks have thrown up a lot of questions.'

My friend nods, like she gets it. To a point, she does. Dad. Harry. Aaron. She doesn't know about Kelly though and the questions those memories have thrown up about me.

YOU

You watch your wife leaving, make yourself coffee, which you take to the unlit sitting room, where you self-flagellate by replaying her departure.

There was no kiss goodbye.

'It's just a drink,' she'd said. 'With Charlotte.'

What will they talk about, you wonder.

You, probably.

Cass, definitely.

Rock?

You're not generally a jealous person. It's not in your nature, you'd explained to Eve years ago on a surprisingly hot afternoon as you left site. You could smell the sun on the tarmac. Your entwined fingers were rapidly gathering heat.

You were new but already living together – you'd invited her to move into your house – working together too – you'd invited her to join your business. Everything had so easily fallen into place.

The month prior there'd been celebratory drinks for the end of the first project you'd run as a couple. Snagging was done, and an invitation was extended to the lingering tradesmen who'd brought your shared vision to life.

'The house is sold,' you announced in the pub, getting a second round in because you're a good guy, a good boss, who recognised this success wasn't yours alone. You'd carried one vodka-and-orange and five beers on a tray back to the table, froth as thick as the laughter rising from the banquette seating, where your girlfriend, Eve, was wedged between the plumber, Darren, and his son, DJ, the apprentice. A decent kid, who never grumbled about making the tea.

In bed that night, after sex that left you narcotised, sweaty and splayed, Eve propped an elbow on one of the pink and yellow scalloped-edge scatter cushions she'd brought with her when she'd left her rental for the house you'd purchased and renovated two years previously. Like a lot of her *finishing touches*, you hated those cushions in isolation. But with the striped box-pleat lampshades and the bright glass candlesticks she'd put – no, arranged – on the bedside tables, somehow, they worked. Your bedroom, like the rest of your life, had so much more colour with Eve in it.

'Earlier… When you were at the bar…' She kept shifting, unable, it seemed, to get comfortable. You rolled onto your side to face her. 'Darren put his hand on my thigh.' She didn't blink and, in the dim bedroom light, you were distracted by the kingfisher-blue of her eyes. 'Asked if I have *a thing* for older men.'

'And have you?' Your voice was teasing. You doubt now if that was the response she was after.

'Not generally, no.' She hadn't moved, but the whole of her was momentarily distant. It fell quiet between you, then, until she turned off the lamp and whispered, 'I *do* have a thing for *you* though.' You were both in your twenties. You hadn't thought the seven year-age gap made you significantly older.

You reached for her. Touching multiple parts as you fell asleep. Fingers. Toes. The crook of her elbow. The hard round cap of her knee.

'Darren? *Really?*' She said, three, four weeks later as the pair of you left the two-bed semi where she'd just walked in on a meeting to discuss the viability of moving the bathroom upstairs. 'You're having *him* quote?'

'Sure.' You threw an arm around her shoulder. 'I'm many things, Eve, but jealous is not one of them.' A statement that was mostly true until now, and still not in the way others might think.

Charlotte.

That lucent satisfaction she and Eve have in each other's company, the fluency of their conversation, the ease with which they create in-jokes, never purposefully excluding but sometimes, *often*, not quite widening the gap between them so that someone else can press themselves in.

It feels childish to wish you had a friend like that.

You're not friendless. But on Saturday, after you'd told Eve about the gala dinner and she'd said she didn't want you at home, you couldn't think of a *best* person to call. You scrolled the hundreds of contacts in your phone. There were men you'd ask for a round of golf or Saturday-night beer, but no one in whom you'd confide, like, *really* confide, about that.

You *are* friends with Shayan and the other NCT lads. You've been on camping trips, taken muddied walks with their kids and cockapoos and chocolate labs on New Year's Day. The women, in hooded macs and near-matching Hunter wellies, would link arms and jump straight in to the nitty gritty of three, four, five days mostly cooped up with family. The deep shame of a lost temper during Malbec-drenched Monopoly with the in-laws. The unbearable sadness, hidden from the kids, of a first Christmas without a now-dead parent. Irrational after a failed attempt at a bird within a bird within a bird. They couldn't *not* share. Couldn't *not* step away from the path for a consolatory hug. Couldn't *not* do their utmost to temper the inevitable shit-show of life with their sympathy and raucous, sometimes dirty, laughter.

You – the men – were, *are*, part of that group but, handshakes aside, there's no touching. It's not only your bodies that aren't so intimate. The conversations are stoically distant too.

Florian Grove Proposal - The Lost Boys
To: Luke Rock
Reply-To: Florian Grove

Hey Luke

Hope you're not feeling too worse for wear today!

Saw you on the Daily Mail's Sidebar of Shame this morning. Birmingham's Sobar is a great night, eh? Good for you to let off steam after what, for many reasons, has been a difficult few weeks but, as your agent, I'm dutybound to mention we don't want your recent swing back into public favour hampered by what some might consider compromising photos. Let's just say I hope the young woman pap'd getting into your car had some proof-of-age ID. 😉

In other potentially exciting news, Gabe Danser from Buddy Productions has been in touch. He and Seb are keen to progress with a new project. Will forward more details shortly.

Regards

F

CASS

'Cass.' George, running out of Subway, is all limbs, or arms mostly. They hang, long and bent at the elbow like he wants to hug me but can't. We've managed an entire shift without speaking.

'Yes,' I say, eyes darting down St Mary's and Castle Street, checking for whispers and stares. I pull at the sleeves of Dad's puffer. Not my first choice. I'd baulked when Dad insisted on it. He wasn't wrong about the weather though. and Maya is predicting the vigil for Lucy Corrigan will go on late into the night..

'Can we chat?'

I shrug. Nod. 'I don't have long though.'

'It's kind of difficult to talk.' George is breathless. 'If you keep storming ahead, I mean.'

'I'm not storming.' You need strength or spirit or whatever to storm. I don't have any of that. 'It's just… people, you know?' I walk a few steps ahead down Pride Hill, turning right and then right again until we're at the river.

'Where we going?' He asks.

'Somewhere quiet.'

George might also be in the video, but he's unidentifiable. That's been obvious all morning, in his ability to ask customers about the fillings for their sandwiches, in how happy he was to be front of shop, grinning and taking money at the till.

My boss had made it clear any compassionate leave was over. His compromise was I could stay out back.

George and I cross the bridge and walk the perimeter of the cricket fields until we reach the trees at Poplar Island.

Not too far in, there's a felled trunk. Sawn at each end, it's a near-perfect cylinder, its core pale, though still brighter than the boneish colour of my skin.

'What do you want, George?' I'm so tired. When I sit down, I imagine the reddish-purple lines the hard ridges of the bark will depress into my thighs, think how perfect the scar-like marks are for my life right now.

'I feel awful,' he says, hovering until I gesture to the make-do seat. 'Thanks.' He sounds surprised I'm allowing this close proximity and is a little wary, edging away from me when he does finally sit. 'Honestly,' he says, and though I'm staring at the ground, at the fallen leaves that aren't yet the colour of real autumn, I know there are tears. 'I feel so guilty.'

So you should, I think but don't bother to say.

He removes his arms and shoulders from the straps of his rucksack, digs into the front pocket. 'You want some?' A Yorkie bar duo. A peace-offering. The kind we'd always share. When I shake my head, *no*, 'You look like you need it,' he says.

George is not the first person recently to imply I'm too thin.

It's like when I had Covid. There's no taste to anything. I'll eat with Mum and Dad at dinner to curb their fussing anxiety, but the food's just texture. What's the point.

'I'm sorry.' George says, and I can hear the chunk of chocolate, how it's wedged between his jaw and cheek. 'I know it's not enough. I should never have taken it. Should have got rid of it. The video,' he adds, as if everything doesn't now always come back to that.

'Why didn't you?'

'I enjoyed looking at you,' he says, like it's that simple. 'At us.' His trainers, the ones he goes to such great lengths to keep spotless, are covered in dirt. 'I don't know how to say this without it sounding weird but...'

'Just say it, George.'

'Fine.' His left foot taps. 'I meant it when I said I love you. And maybe it's wrong that I got off on watching the video, but I did. I love you. Love that you were up for trying new things with me. Because that made me feel like you loved me too.'

'I did,' I say. 'I *did* love you.'

317

'So what went wrong? Because you ended it before all this shit happened. And it was a mad shock. Like, totally out of the blue.' We both look up from the small pit he's ground into the mud. 'Was it the...' Our eyes drop at the blank spot, the point at which he would have said "anal". 'Because I remember asking. I *did* ask. I *always* ask about anything like that.' He tucks his thumbs inside his clenched fists. 'And I remember you saying you wanted to. I remember you saying yes.'

'I did. But you don't George.' When he looks confused, '*Always ask about anything like that*. You didn't ask me if you could take the video.'

On the walk here, I promised myself I wouldn't cry. From his rucksack, he pulls a pack of tissues.

Our fingers touch as I take one. That connection would, not very long ago, have been a jolt.

'Ever the scout,' I say. We both laugh, not fully but it's something. A nicer memory from when we were a couple. From our first time, when he told me he'd take care of everything. A promise he didn't renege on. He booked a hotel room, ran me a bath, gave me a massage and, when the moment came, his weight pressed on top of me, took a condom from that very same rucksack he has with him now.

This is it, I thought then. And maybe he sensed my nervousness because he paused and, trying to be funny, lifted himself onto his elbows to release the pressure. 'You can take the boy out of the scouts...' he'd said. Then, 'Be prepared.' His attempt at a salute had thrown him off balance, and he fell backwards onto the mattress beside me. 'You know we don't have to?'

'I know.' I pulled him back closer. 'But I *really* think we should.'

'There's something else,' I say now. 'That night, the Saturday we...' Like him, I can't use the word either. Pulling my hood up to protect from me from the rain, I tell him, this boy I loved and trusted, about the gala and those men and my dad.

'You should have told me.' He's hurt, but it's not an accusation. 'At the time. We could have talked instead of...'

'Maybe.' I turn my knees so they're pointed towards him. 'That's separate though.' I take the second half of the Yorkie, snap off a square and give it back. 'From you filming me without asking.'

When George reaches for my hand, I don't flinch or pull away.

'I really am sorry,' he says.

'I know. But, fact is, you being sorry doesn't change anything, does it? The video's still out there. Probably always will be.' When I stand up, his hands drop to his lap. 'End of.'

The rain's stopped by the time Maya and I arrive in Harbourne. But the air in the park when I WhatsApp Liv to tell her to call me if she thinks she can join us is damp with the weight of grief.

When Maya suggested we come, I told her I couldn't face being in a crowd. What if people have seen the video? But she was right; no one is looking at me here.

A man and woman everyone recognises as Lucy Corrigan's parents are walking to the mass of floral tributes laid in memory of their daughter. Her dad puts an arm across her mum's rounded shoulders, tries to remain tall.

I squeeze Maya's fingers, doing my best to hold in the wail because even though I don't know these people, even with all the shit that's happened recently, I've never felt this sad.

We watch them crouch in front of the row of luminous-jacketed policemen to read the notes and the posters and the cards. Can they feel our eyes on them? Or have the last few days and this awful ending turned them numb? When he stands, I see patches from the soaked ground have formed on the knees of Lucy's Dad's trousers. It's this, something trivial in the grand scheme of things, that forces me to look away.

There are so many of us. Girls and women, mostly, huddled and weirdly quiet. It's not the same, because there it was noisy and joyful, but there's something about this evening that reminds me of the Harry Styles concert last May. What I mean, maybe, is we are bound together by one person none of us really knows but are connected to. A shared feeling, strangers united in an emotion, but on opposite ends of the spectrum because that spring night what we felt was ramped-up euphoria, tonight it's hushed despair.

'Cass?' Maya passes me a candle. And she's got the lighter ready to go when there's commotion twenty/ thirty feet away over by the path. A man, held steady by others, is standing on a bench.

'My sister,' he says, sucking his bottom lip to curb, I think, the surge of emotion visible in his wet wide eyes and his hands, which clench into and out of fists around the pockets of his jeans. 'My sister,' he starts again, looking to his mum and dad, who are beneath him now, each with a hand on his leg like they're afraid that this child too will be taken. He nods at his parents and inhales a deep breath as if he under-stands just how much depends on what he's trying to say. 'Lucy was kind,' he says. 'Lucy was funny. Lucy was loud. Lucy was adventurous. Lucy was hard working. Lucy was a brilliant daughter and sister. Lucy was a wonderful loyal friend. Lucy was annoy-ingly good at maths *and* the sciences *and* languages but would have admitted I was better than her at art.

And you'd think if that's what I'm good at, I could paint you a picture of my little sister, but to capture the whole of her in paint or words is impossible. Because Lucy was so many things. And now the over-riding thing Lucy is in the press and on social media is dead.'

He stares across the tops of our heads. The world around him is momentarily still.

'We're so grateful to you all for coming. But we don't want what that man did to be our overriding memory of Lucy, who deserved better. So we ask you to remember more than what you have seen on the news. To remember Lucy was our daughter, our sister, our friend, who was lovely and made us laugh every single day she was alive. Thank you.'

The applause is gentle, no one sure if it's appropriate but searching for a way to show Lucy Corrigan's family we agree. We will try.

I turn to Maya, 'Should we—' I was going to ask if we should light our candles, but Maya's face is frozen and her eyes a sort of grey. 'You OK, Maya?'

She doesn't answer, only her eyes move. I follow her startled sliding gaze to her right side. An elbow at the back of her waist and a hand slipping out from between the tops of her thighs.

The thigh and the hand are different. The thigh is hers. The hand is his. A man behind her is touching her. Assaulting her. Here of all places where girls and women have come to mourn.

We came for Lucy Corrigan.

Maya came for Lucy Corrigan.

But he, this man who is so normal looking with his blonde hair and his freckles and his Sainsbury's bag for life, he throws us off track.

His need or his greed or his lascivious exploitation causes a standstill that throws me back in time. To *my* thigh. To *Bry's* hand. Slowed down and stretched out like a movie recorded at 0.01X speed. Bry's swollen face and Bry's amplified voice suffocating any hope of me telling him *stop*.

And then that other hand too.

My father's.

The good guy's.

Fuck's sake.

We can't even trust the good guys.

Snapped back to the park, here is Maya. My bold and beautiful friend, who fights for so many causes but, like me, is silenced when it comes to her own.

'Oi,' I shout. All eyes on me now for disturbing the peace.

'Ssshh,' someone says.

'Where's your respect.'

I stretch for the hand, *his* hand. 'Oi, I repeat, hard. Loud.

I hate him.

People are shaking their heads. Someone tells me to calm down.

Then, thank god, a policeman.

'He touched her.' I point at the man, who ten seconds ago had his fingers on Maya's crotch and is now walking away from us through the crowd. It parts for him. His exit is swift and uncomplicated. 'He's right there.' I point until the policeman puts a hand on the top of my arm to lower it.

'You need to be quiet,' he says. 'This is a peaceful event.'

'I *know* that.' I hear my tone and know too it's not sugar or spice or whatever stupid word he or someone else might use to describe what a girl or her words should be made of. 'This is disgraceful.' The word is ridiculous, pompous even, but the fact that a man touched my friend right here right now and this policeman is *watching* him leave *is* disgraceful.

'He assaulted her,' I say, but he doesn't listen. 'HE ASSAULTED HER.'

The policeman doesn't like my volume, tells me he has other, more important, things to do.

The women around us take a few steps backwards, their necks twisting and stretching to look for a disappeared man.

Maya shakes her head. She gets how useless my pleas are.

'No need for hysterics, young lady.' The policeman slides his jacket aside to reveal a baton strapped to his belt.

I stare at his hard empty face.

I'll say it one more time.

But he's barely paying me attention.

I remove my coat and grab the lighter from my friend's hand.

'HE ASSAULTED HER.' It's not just *my* voice now but a chorus of women around me. 'HE ASSAULTED HER.' Together, we are rhythm and heat. 'HE ASSAULTED HER.'

'Ladies, you need stop shouting.'

I raise my dad's puffer above my head and roll my thumb over the spark wheel of the lighter. The policeman has turned his back to me when the flames spread across the sleeves of the coat.

I scream, then.

Louder.

Wilder.

The only words I know might save us. The words I am now made of:

'FIRE! FIRE! FIRE!'

From: Gabe Danser <gdanser@buddyproductions
.com>
Subject: Luke Rock / Buddy collab
To: Florian Grove
Reply-To: Gabe Danser

Hi Florian,

I hear congrats are in order! A girl! God help
you, eh!

Following the huge success of SOBERING – still
crossing our fingers for an NTA nom for Luke btw
– Seb and I have been chatting about possible new
ventures. The reaction to SOBERING on socials
made it clear how much viewers loved Luke's unique
mix of comedy and vulnerability while confronting
what it is to be an addict on the world stage.

Post Hambledon Manor, there's been significant
chat in the nationals and online about what would
drive a decent middle-class boy like Aaron Jenkins
to take such drastic steps for attention. Luke's
tweet acknowledging the pain Jenkins was feeling
prior to and during the attempted attack garnered
a lot of sympathy for the kid.

We think Luke, with his recent first-hand experience of the real-life consequences of under-served

young men in today's potentially women-centric society, would be the perfect person to front THE LOST BOYS, in which we hope to get to the bottom of why males – white males, especially – are currently feeling so disenfranchised.

Given public opinion has very much swayed even further to Luke's advantage since his heroic action in Shropshire, we'd like to move quickly and are hoping he'll be as excited by the prospect of THE LOST BOYS as we are.

Could we fix a lunch in next few days to discuss?

Gabe

EVE

'I'm here for Cass Gunn.'

'Cass Gunn.' The man on the front desk repeats her name – loudly – a statement as opposed to a question. Two guys behind him, necks craned and laughing, swiftly put away their phones. Were they watching the video?

God knows how, but I bite my indignant tongue.

'She and her mate are in the Sarg's office,' one of them tells me. 'She's lucky the officer was able to grab the coat from her so quickly. Not a single burn. We won't be pressing charges.' Is that a hint of disappointment? 'I'll take you through.'

Cass stands when she sees me, allows me to hold her, leaning into my chest, clinging and shivering. Unlike the Cass we saw on the news, here, she is quiet. Cold.

My phone had been open to the live feed of Lucy Corrigan's vigil. The connection to Cass tenuous but, without physically following her to Harboune, the BBC's cameras would have to do. I showed it to Harry and – personal quarrels momentarily quelled by our shared terror – we listened to Lucy Corrigan's brother describe his sister then watched him climb down from the bench to his ruined parents. Needing to do something other than sit, I got to my feet, agitated with the inclination to wash away my discomfort with drink.

'Shit!' Harry jumped from the sofa. 'Eve.' He thrust the phone in my face.

The camera at the vigil had swung away from the journalist to a tribe of fury-faced women, mouths wide in a long, banded scream. It took me a second to recognise the foremost figure as our daughter. I'd never seen Cass that kind of fuck-you fierce. I'm not saying I wasn't immediately frightened, but with the rage that fuelled her entire body, for a livid second it fit that she was on fire.

Until reality or sanity kicked in, and I was shouting, then, as loud as the hysterics on my screen.

Now, though, at the station, we are calmed. Hushed voices and lowered eyes, scouring my baby girl for damage but seeing none.

None?

As if there's none.

In the car, Maya tells me what happened. 'Another incident,' she says, 'to add to my list.' And I hear the same resigned almost-laughter my school friends and I would fall into thirty-odd years ago, when one of us relayed *yet another* story about *yet another* dodgy man. And here we have it, no different, Maya's innate shrug-your-shoulders understanding that this is – *still* – just the way it is. Were Charlotte and I wrong, then, when, only a few weeks back, we lauded our daughters' generation as the one that'll get things done.

This doubt of mine is muddled, though, wrong. For my disbelief isn't in Cass and Maya's conviction rather in the possibility of any true shift in the situation they want to change.

The situation?

Call it what it is, Eve: The fucking immutable men.

A change in gear, the skin pale and taut across my knuckles with my furious grip on the stick, and it's not Maya's voice I hear now but my father's. *Anger is a dangerous emotion behind the wheel. If you're going to survive learning to drive, Evie, you need to rein your feelings in.*

A long inhale.

Maya's still talking, raging. I was stupid to have questioned her resolve.

I shoot a glance at Cass in the rear-view. Her friend may well be a lioness, but this evening my daughter is a tortoise withdrawn into its shell.

I check on her at eleven PM, go to her bedroom window, where the curtains are shivering with the outside hum of gentle but persistent rain. The sash is clunky, sticking to the wet frame so I have to shunt it, aware if I push too hard, the glass may shatter or crack.

I perch on the edge of the bed, and my itch – no, *burn* – to hold her, to bind her even, is tempered only by the cool of the raindrops spattered across my skin. The simmering inside-monster-mother in me wants to swaddle and coddle and keep Cass away from everything. But away mostly from men.

And, of course, I'd hashtag *not all men*. And, of course, I'd hashtag *some women too*. I've learnt, it isn't as simple as us versus them. There is no clear line.

I tread carefully, wanting to stop at 'I love you.' But Dad's caution about curbing emotions extended beyond the confines of a car. 'You need to be so careful,' I whisper to Cass now. And then, 'And I know you're angry, but what you did today was dangerous. I don't want you getting more hurt.'

She closes her eyes.

'Will you sleep?' I ask.

Her bony pyjama'd knees urge me off the mattress, and she contracts, shins to chest, making herself tiny then tinier still.

A tentative kiss on her forehead, still dirty with sweat and smoke. A whiff of her teddy, Grumples, squished and working overdrive to keep her safe and loved and calm. She holds him like I want to hold her. Fierce and ready to defend. Quiet and incredibly still. You

331

can see her love in his flattened fur and cuddle-bent nose. A mark-making love that assures him and warns others she has his back. She will never let him go.

In the sitting room, the TV is on low. When I put the mint tea I've made for Harry on the table, he hears the chink of china on wood and looks up.

'You were right,' I say. 'About the monitor.' I can't protect my baby. She and the world are too big for the camera's lens to capture everything.

I sit next to my husband without looking at him, eyes instead on the TV, where the newsreader is ending on an upbeat story about the MP Lionel Morgan.

'More token gestures,' I say, not specifically to Harry, though he is the only other person in the room.

'Huh?' He's been sitting right here – no book or phone – but hasn't been listening to the news.

'Our MP. He's the one who made that shitty comment about the Ofsted inspector a few weeks back. And now he announces his involvement in a charity fun run. In aid of women and children. Throwing dirty money and fake concern at his repu-tation because, god forbid, a man like him make a genuine apology.'

'I know *my* apology wasn't good enough.' Harry shifts, removes his feet from the footstool to the floor.

I hadn't been making a dig, but, 'It's not only you,' I say. 'Can we go to bed? To talk,' I clarify because his face... What *is* that expression exactly?

'OK.' He looks at me, as in *really* looks at me, for the first time in days upon days upon days. 'That would be good.'

Harry and I are on our backs with the lights off, two true lines, each on their side of a super king, the bedsheet beneath us still cool.

'Was it me?' He asks. Even though we are supposed to intuit so much from body language, Harry and I hear each other more clearly when we remove the distractions. We have better, more honest conversations in the dark. 'I made her take that bloody coat.'

'It wasn't the coat, Harry. Or it *was* the coat, but it was everything else too. You. Me. Bryan. George. A stranger at the vigil. Aaron Jenkins. Stephen North. Lionel fucking Morgan.'

'What?' Only my husband's mouth is moving, every other inch of him is still.

I want to run downstairs – two steps at a time – to get my phone. To break the dark with the scroll of news that's rarely really news. Rather it's the same old same old shit against women and girls. And our daughter is one of them. Has – despite all my best intentions – been one of them since the moment she was born. A privileged one, sure. With her white skin and private education. But even with those advantages, my baby is still one of them.

'She could have been so badly hurt,' he says.

My heart cleaves. 'She already *is*.'

'I'm sorry.'

'I know you are, but you failed her,' I say. "We both have. God!' I tense every muscle, the way you're supposed to tense every muscle during the meditation practice Sophie likes so much. The one she's probably revelling in right now in the cocoon of her Mallorcan retreat. This is not like that. 'I didn't think I'd be a perfect mother, but the thing I was sure I'd be decent at was giving our daughter the tools.'

'Tools?'

I turn my head towards Harry, whose face, now my eyes are adjusting, is visible. 'To defend herself. Not rape alarms or pepper spray or whatever else we're supposed to carry. I wanted us to raise a daughter who would shout at men like *Bryan*.' His name is petrol in my mouth. 'Cass was right to be mad at me for not stepping in when Freddie White was inappropriate with that girl at Dad's party. I've set her these my-body-my-choice rules, but I've never managed to live by them.'

Harry puts his hands together, as if praying, slides them between the pillow and his cheek.

'But tonight, *she* did say something, Harry. And not because of anything we've taught her, but out of sheer frustration and fury, tonight she *did* say something. And you know what the policeman called her? Trouble.'

'Well, we know what the police think of young women, don't we.'

'Not that,' I say. 'Not now.'

We join the force because we want to protect people, Dad said when Harry asked him why he was so certain it wasn't Stump who shared that video. *You seem to have forgotten who the good guys are here.*

From downstairs, the whirs and clunks of the coffee machine dispensing its final dregs.

Harry is so still. 'Isn't this your point though? The gala. The sex tape. The vigil. The *police*. Aren't they all part of the same thing?'

'Yes,' I say. Then, 'No,' I say. 'I know you're convinced otherwise, but Dad's colleagues wouldn't do that. And no matter what Cass thinks, she needs to be careful.'

I'd called my father on the way to pick up Cass in Birmingham.

'I understand she's frustrated,' Dad said, 'but there are channels. Procedures. What Cass did tonight was vigilante.'

He was right. And I don't dare quote Dad to Harry but, 'Setting her coat on fire at the vigil was crazy,' I say. 'Desperate, probably, because I didn't give her the voice she needs. And that silence has bullied her into a corner, pushed her into doing something so extreme she's now practically mute again. And how sick is it that her reticence feels like the better, safer option?' I bite the inside of my cheek so hard I'm tasting blood. 'I so wanted Cass to be different from me.'

'In what way?'

'I don't know how to describe it.'

He pulls one hand from beneath his face and puts it near to – without touching – mine. 'Can you try?'

The edge of the pillowcase crumples in my fist. 'I don't have the words.'

An hour or so later, Harry is sleeping, as is Cass when I go to her room.

I watch her and pray for an awake version of this slumberous peace, though even this is disturbed by the glow of a TikTok notification piercing the darkness with its yellowish-green.

You have 37 direct messages.

Before she turned eighteen, I had full-access rights to Cass's phone. Her birthday was only three-and-a-half weeks ago. Isn't the date and her age redundant really? Wouldn't it be neglectful not to check her messages. Especially now.

Trusting me and my promise, she hasn't changed her passcode.

The phone and the app open. User273212344547854384 has sent 7 direct messages in the last hour.

U shout fire. I shout whore

Whore. Someone has called my daughter a whore. Somehow *whore* is tame though. The uninvited and unanswered comments that follow are increasingly violent, increasingly sexual, increasingly impossible to read. I delete delete delete, but my fingers can't work fast enough; when I go to her inbox there are more more more. Every message something about fire fire fire. As if I didn't already know how rapidly heat on women spreads. I go to her profile intending to delete her videos, all those images of her dancing with Liv and Maya that allow sick strangers to see her body, her face, her tattoo.

Only the grid isn't her usual book reviews and dances, and the name at the top isn't CassGunnBooksAndFun. The grid compromises six films of contained but persistent burning, and the name of the account is Shout Fire Not Rape.

Shit.

I go to her bag. Inside are strips of paper and a lighter.

What kind of mother am I not to have known the vigil wasn't the first time my daughter's protest made the news.

The last Shout Fire Not Rape TikTok was posted seven days ago. The night before we found out about the sex tape.

She must have retreated then. Must have understood the dangers of being female, vocal and exposed.

But then that idiot man at the vigil drove her to even greater extremes, and whether or not anyone connects last night with these smaller acts of objection, the DMs are proof of the anger she's inciting.

'I know I've always told to use your voice,' I whisper. 'But you need to keep quiet. Please, my darling. It's too dangerous. You can't rile them like this. You have to stop.'

CASS

I count the seconds then minutes until Mum's gone. She must have been here an hour at least, her whispers repeating the importance of silence, and her hand stroking my hair. The pretence of sleeping gave me time to think. The same thoughts I've had on loop since the policeman cuffed me and told me, 'Time to shut the fuck up now. You're a disgrace.'

Clearly Mum's got it into her head that my quiet's a good thing. I get where she's coming from. It'd be easier, wouldn't it, to keep my head down. But what Mum can't have looked at when she thought she was so covertly messing with my phone just now was my camera roll, where only a few seconds before I heard her padding across the landing, I'd saved a photo that's doing the rounds online. Like *that* video that left me thinking I'd never want to see another picture of me again, this photo was taken without me knowing. But this time it's not an invasion. It's a release.

In almost every other photograph I've ever seen of myself, I'm playing ball. Posing as directed. Obediently smiling and saying "cheese". There's no cheese in this picture. No saccharine grin. I am not well-behaved or polite.

I am utterly myself, and I am seething. Made of the fire born of men's arrogance and expectation.

I don't want to be good or quiet. Like in the newsworthy image of me from the vigil, I want to burn this fucking world down.

'I'm gonna get them,' Four words. Only together they're more than a sentence. They're a declaration that cuts the stale air in my parents' bedroom with sharpened grit.

Mum and Dad raise themselves up on their elbows on the bed, look from me to each other, their faces all, *what the hell?*

I climb onto the mattress, show them the photo. 'Better than the other picture doing the rounds, eh?' I'm laughing. Not because anything's funny but because, well, I'm nervous, already on my feet again and buzzing with saying out loud what's been in my head for the last four house since Mum left my room at two AM. 'At the vigil, it hit me how little they listen. I know you think I should keep schtum, Mum. And maybe you're right. Maybe it's more important to be clever than loud.'

Mum is fully awake now. 'What do you mean?'

'Dad, you keep saying how you wish you could go back and do things differently.'

My father sits, stiff and upright against the headboard, nods.

'Well, me too,' I stand taller. 'So, I'm going to re-do the gala dinner,' I say, like it's that easy. 'I'm going to get those diners back, be the Cass in that photo and make those men live and *feel* our fear.'

'No way,' Mum says for, like, the gazillionth time. I'm guessing from his silence over his juvenile bowl of Cheerios that Dad agrees. 'Even if you had the money and the contacts and the space, it's not safe, poppet.' Fucking *poppet*. 'Do you really think we'd allow you to take that kind of risk.'

'*Allow* me?' The veins in the backs of my hands turn purplish blue. I flatten my palms against the top of the kitchen table.

'What did you mean?' Dad's voice strains with the effort of sounding calm. 'When you said earlier about them feeling your fear?'

What I think but don't say because it sounds crazy is that I want those odious creatures to be cowed. The plan had been clear as glass by 4AM. Lure the men to a dining room and give them exactly what they thought they wanted. Willing girls in shorts skirts and huge supply. More and more and more of us clambering onto their laps and clasping at their disgusting bodies until they don't know what to do with all of our hands on them, our nails clawing at their skin,.

I sit on my fingers. 'I haven't quite figured out the details.' This feels like a better answer if I'm to get my parents on side.

'I understand you want resolution,' Mum says. *Actually, what I'm after is revenge.* 'But, it's like your

341

granddad says, Cass, we need to find the proper means.'

I quash my full disdain. 'Like the police, you mean? Or shall we call Sophie, as she was in charge of the dinner?' I flip my phone screen side up, make a show of opening contacts and finding my aunt. 'Oh, I forgot, poor thing, it's so exhausting running events for perverts she's on a month-long retreat to recover and would rather not be disturbed.'

My parents look at each other, united in confusion and concern.

'Cass...' Dad's shaking. 'Honestly? I think you're right to do something,' he says, and Mum's face is one hundred per cent if-looks-could-kill. 'And I respect your guts, but you do not need to go near those men to fix this.'

I laugh. A witch's cackle. 'But it's not just *those* men, Dad. It's so many men. So many. It was even you.'

'It was,' he says. 'And I can't tell you how sorry I am. But, Cass, what you said to me in that café. About the list. It made me think—'

I lean across the table, tower over him. 'I don't want you to *think*.' The room shrinks, its air sucked out, and he chokes on my whisper. 'What I want is for you to change.'

YOU

She looked down on you. Physically, yes, but meta-phorically too. The girl who once looked up to you. Who in a Year Six essay about 21st century heroes made you – ahead of Malala Yousafzai, Jonnie Peacock and Jacqueline Wilson – her number one.

Shropshire Local Is Hard as Rock

What do headlines matter when your daughter believes you're a degenerate?

It's not only the dinner, the hands on Cass's body, the silence as other men put their hands on other women's bodies too. Those may sit at the top of this list you're compiling, but there's a lifetime of smaller, less obvious behaviours you would never have considered questionable. The list is mental, as in you can't quite bring yourself to put it to paper. You tried, but seeing them on the page like that, the words making each act at the same time both ordinary and extraordinary, your ability to think objectively was hindered by the discomfort of shame.

The hours you've spent on your phone. Trawling through old messages, scouring for times you could have held your friends accountable. You were relieved to discover they weren't rife. Only one flurry of texts in response to the news that a pensioner had killed his wife in the early stages of lockdown.

> Pete: To be fair, mate, I've come pretty close
>
> Chris: Now now, gents, let's not forget women deserve equal rights (and lefts) 👊
>
> Pete: At least lockdown's given me a chance to fix that whining noise in my car… opened the passenger door and kicked her out.

There's no crying with laughter emoji to indicate you found this funny. But there's no other response either. You chose silence.

When you think about the men who shared the video of Cass, you're able to dissociate. There are things you're certain you wouldn't do. There's comfort in this. Hope too. If you'd have been sent that kind of movie, you would surely have said something. At the very least, you would have protested by leaving the group.

George, though. You cannot separate yourself from him. The opposite, really, is true. He's a good kid. You saw how considerately he treated your daughter. Not opening doors or paying for dinners – neither she nor you are bothered by details like that – rather, you liked how relaxed she was in his company. How when she talked, he listened. How he took his time to really think about what she'd said. How he appeared willing to be swayed by her opinion. How unencumbered he was by stereotype. How he'd cried while watching *A Man Called Otto*, unembarrassed when you clocked his tears. How kind he was with Cass's grandparents, neither squeamishly deferential nor patronising the way some people are with those they consider old. How while it triggered mixed and muddied emotions, you were proud of Cass for talking to Eve about contraception and the fact that she was ready because George was a man with whom she felt safe to have sex.

When Eve told you about the video, the channels between your teeth and cheeks flooded with saliva. You swallowed because you didn't want Cass to know she'd made you sick.

You told yourself she wasn't the reason. She is an adult, and the problem she is facing right now should not be that the kind of sex she'd chosen. The problem she is facing right now is that the filming and sharing were done without her consent.

But you keep returning to the vulgarity. To the baseness of your daughter's desire.

You wonder if you would make the same judgement of a son.

You do not want to see George.

Your father-in-law said he'd kill him. You agreed. Took solace in the obviousness that your roiling anger was shared and therefore justified.

Your focus now, though, must be on Cass. Her fire and her quest for retribution. You've given your reasons why the re-do is not an option, but she's adamant you're wrong. Something *needs* doing.

Her friend Maya is corralling their fellow students to write their lists. There is power in the collective, Cass said, and you're inclined to think that's true. Though there's power in the personal too.

'Eve,' you say to your wife after Cass has scorned your offer of a lift to her first full day back at school. 'We should support her. In this re-do. I think we can make it work.'

She will not have any of it.

'It's guilt talking,' she says. 'You want to placate her. But the reality of her being anywhere near those men is absurd.'

'*I* was one of those men,' you remind her. 'If the girls are able to explain the impact of their behaviour. Like Cass did with me. Encourage them to think about their own list. There's a good chance, no, that they might see?'

'No.' Eve says this like it's end of story.

For you, though, Harry, *your* list is just the start.

EVE

'She's going to do it with or without our approval.' Harry presses the X in the corner of the file to close the Gantt chart on his computer.

It's funny how work carries on as usual. How despite my regret for not speaking out against him, I've managed to spend hours designing an office-refurb scheme for Freddie White. It's not pride or excitement I've felt, though, in the seconds since I hit send.

'It's not like she's working in isolation.' Harry takes a sip of his coffee. 'She might not have us on side, but she's got the full support of her friends.'

He's right; Maya has been at ours every day this week. I was, at first, reassured by her presence. A constant comfort for Cass since her no doubt torturous return to school. But, last night, with Liv also tow, they'd disappeared upstairs again, hyped like they were when I took the three of them camping. They were thirteen. I barely slept. The canvas of their tent was no barrier to their late-night screeching or to the gentler buzz of their incessant chat. Boys! Star signs! Taylor! Their midnight plan to sneak into the woods, where everything – despite the dark and the shadows and the monsters – would be OK because, no matter what happened, they had each other's backs.

When I unzipped their tent in the morning, they were sleeping, three tightly packed spoons.

I'm so grateful to those girls. To the saving grace of their friendship, but there's worry too. The rock-solid belief they have in each other has proven itself good and powerful these last few weeks. But they're eighteen. At eighteen, when you have that strength of faith in your collective, you brave the danger, you take the pill, because – fuck it, right – invincibility is real.

'She needs to keep her head down, Harry. Until the spotlight moves onto something or someone else.'

'And then what?' My husband rolls back on his chair. 'You heard what the woman on the helpline said. You can't know the numbers of people who've shared the video; it never truly goes away.'

'What happened at the gala was something different though.'

'It was.' Harry toys with the clip of his green Lamy pen 'But, like you said, it's all connected. Maybe the main difference is that with the gala, Cass can claw back some control.' His tongue runs across his teeth.

'You're wrong,' I say. *There are channels. Procedures.* 'Dad's concerned about the legality.' That's putting it lightly. 'You can't honestly think she should do this.'

'Practically speaking, I don't see how she could. The logistics'd be mental.' His shrug is as blasé as if we were debating takeout or restaurant dinner. He gathers his papers, closes his notebook, knocking the Newton's Cradle Cass bought him for Fathers' Day the year she turned eight. Harry watches my index finger settle the slightly swaying balls. 'But if she wants any sort of *closure*…' He winces at the word. 'Perhaps what Cass needs *isn't* to keep her head down. Think about what you said the other night. I hate to throw your own words back at you, Eve, but you said you wanted us to raise a daughter who would shout at men like Bryan.'

I *did* say that, but any idea involving *them* and Cass in a room together will never make sense to me. What would she even say to them? 'I understand her list is a way for her to spell out what's been done to her,' I concede. 'Seriously though, do you honestly believe there are words sufficiently potent those men will understand the consequences of what they've done?'

The question's rhetorical. Both Harry and I know the answer is "no".

Is it though?

What about Kelly's letter?

'I'm going for a bath,' I tell Harry.

I hear the rhythmic clicking of the balls in new motion and close his office door.

In our locked bathroom, I open the envelope for what must be the tenth time today. Until Sunday, it had been untouched in the same box for years.

I made a choice to be with you, Eve. I was given no choice about Luke. How can I trust anyone with anything now? Did you show Luke the photo too? You made me feel special, Eve. I'd never slept with a girl before. You made me believe it would be okay.

Maybe there *is* some sense in Cass's plan. On first reading them, these fifty-two words had drenched me in guilt because I understood how I'd hurt her. When he next invited me to his flat, I'd taken the letter to show Luke. I didn't know then it would be the last time I saw him. After a quick scan of the page, he'd let the paper fall to the floor. 'Gen,' he said, 'your friend Kelly is just a girl. It takes a woman to do what *we* were planning. Not everyone is as sexually evolved as you.' I loved how he saw me, how his hands possessed every inch of my body, how his mouth was done with words, already deep into a long appreciative groan.

I didn't speak to – or of – Kelly again. Not with Harry. Not with anyone until Rock reappeared a few weeks back and asked if I was still friends with Kathy. It had been twenty-seven years. Could I really expect him to remember her name?

It was me who was best friends with her.

Me who slept with her.

Me who first sowed the seed of a pill.

Was Luke right?

Was I evolved?

Or blinded by desire?

He's sober these days. Would he remember differently?

Double checking the lock is bolted, I type LR in the search bar of Contacts in my phone.

CASS

'Were you told to wear red nail varnish or black?'
Rhi's question blooms in my brain. Since I called
Patrick to organise this Gathering of the Gala Girls,
I've run through that night so many times I thought
I had the minutiae locked in, but, honestly, I can't
remember.

When I don't answer, 'They were black,' Liv says.
I glance across at her, like, *how would* you *know*.
'When I saw you on the Monday, I made a point of
looking, OK?'

Rhi's eyes wrinkle at Liv like some detective on a
TV drama. 'You're the one who's worked the event
before, aren't you?'

Something about Liv's 'Yeah' is off. Not unfriendly
exactly, but any true camaraderie is missing for sure.

Patrick appears with another round of hot drinks.

'The varnish was a tell.' Rhi glances at my fingers
then her own. We're both unpolished. She smiles then.
Not broad and bright but purposeful.

'A tell?'

'It's a poker thing.' Liv, being Liv, rolls her eyes. 'I
think what Rhi means is the varnish was a clue to
those in the know as to whether or not you were

353

invited to the after party. Red, you were in.' Is there smuggery in Liv's tone?

'There was an after party?' It's fucked up, right, that a part of me wants to know why I didn't make their stupid cut.

Maybe Rhi sees that sick something in me because, 'I'm not sure how they decided. It might have been different this year. But, honestly, I wasn't the only one surprised *I* was there.'

Maya who, as per, is poised with a notebook and pen, snuffs a whole load of *I hear you*, and shakes her head. 'Hmm, you're not exactly traditional Shropshire.'

'Tell me about it,' Rhi says. 'What was it one of the *gentle*men said? I was the *spice* apparently. Not to everyone's taste, but someone would give me a go.'

The sound of a nib scratching on paper.

'It was there, anyway, that it happened. If you thought the main event felt off, the vibe in that suite was another level.'

'And it was…' I'm unsure how to put it. 'Like, still an official part of the night?'

'Look.' Rhi takes a sip of her tea. 'I don't know for sure what those women who run the night knew, but what I *do* know is that when I rocked up that evening, I was told, repeatedly, there was no *official* end to my shift. There were *opportunities* to stay longer if I wanted to earn more cash.'

'And did you?' Liv's voice is shot with shards of glass.

I want to grab the napkin Patrick's tucking into the neck of his actual sweater because, well, muffin crumbs, and shove it in Liv's mouth to stop her talking. What is her problem?

Rhi eyes Patrick, clearly wondering if his judgement re whether she should have come this afternoon was skewed. Then hard-staring Liv, 'Did I *what*?'

'Want to earn more cash?' Liv doesn't quite reach the end of the question before her own stare falters.

'I didn't understand what that entailed.' Rhi holds her voice, but barely.

'Didn't you say you had to be somewhere?' I tilt my head as if this softens the unsubtle hint I'm throwing at Liv.

Another 'Yeah,' and she checks her watch, kisses my cheek, then Maya's. 'Nice to meet you,' she says to Patrick and Rhi.

'You too.' Neither of them sounds convinced.

The bell of the café door dings when Liv opens it.

'I'm sorry,' I tell them. 'She's not normally like that.'

'It's fine.' Rhi steals a fallen chocolate chip from Patrick's plate and pops it in her mouth. 'We all draw different lines, I guess.'

Through the window, I watch Liv disappearing down the high street. Despite the low-level music, old-school P!nk, I think, my heart is a boom in my ears. I turn back to the three of them. 'You were saying… about the after party.'

'I think maybe some of the girls weren't overly surprised by the men's expectations. Maybe they'd been there, or similar occasions, before.' Rhi looks away from the window and pours herself water from the jug. 'I'm not judging. If they were on board with that, then, I dunno, that counts for a lot, yeah? You know, choice.'

'Yeah,' I say without really understanding what I'm agreeing with.

'But I *wasn't* there for that. I mean, I *was* there for money, but not for *that*. But when I said as much to Bryan, the man I was talking to, he said he'd been promised a night to remember and…' She pauses, and I think she's gathering her thoughts. When I look up at her though, 'You OK, Cass?'

There I was, thinking I was concealing my shock well. 'This guy, Bryan?'

'Yeah?'

'What was he like?'

'Pfff.' Rhi huffs out a breath. 'Not that different to the rest of them. Old. White, if you don't count the blotted cheeks from all that booze. Stank of it too. Hands that were giant for his body, but that last bit might be untrue. Maybe it just felt that way.'

'And he…?' I don't know how to phrase it.

'Got me into one of the bedrooms, pinned me down on the bed. Said he was surprised he could manage it. He'd heard women like me were dominant. If only, eh?' She attempts a laugh. 'He didn't actually, you know…' Rhi's fingertip squishes the round muffin crumbs flat into the plate. 'But what he did do…' She rolls her bottom lip beneath her top one, and there's a beat while it unfurls. 'It was lot,' she says. 'But the police, when I went the next day, they were dismissive. You know, it was a party, and I'd been drinking along with everyone else so….' Her eyebrows arch, like, *classic*. 'Said it would be difficult to prove without evidence.' She holds up her wrists. 'They didn't acknowledge the bruises. White guys, obviously. Like my sister said, probably don't understand how bruising is different on Black skin. Not that I'm making excuses.'

'I'm sorry.'

'It's not you who needs to apologise.'

'I get that. But I am. *Really*.'

She slides her palms beneath her thighs, pressing hard against the unyielding seat of her chair.

'That apology?' I say. 'I think you deserve one.'

'From what Patrick tells me, you do too.'

'About that,' Maya says, pulling a ring binder from her bag. You've got to love my girl's commitment to planning. 'It's ambitious, but Cass had this idea to re-do the dinner. To get all the men back. Then stage some sort of coup!'

'Coup?'

I jump in. 'Look, I get there are risks, concerns or whatever. Believe me, my mum's detailed every single possible bad outcome, like, a thousand times, but my Aunt Sophie —'

'The one you said runs the gala?' Patrick looks concerned.

'The gala's not her only gig. And some of her ideas are much better than others.' I open YouTube. 'She used these guys at a wedding she planned a few weeks back.'

In the video, a maitre'd goes mad at a waiter who drops an entire tray of Champagne intended for the top table. Voices are raised, glasses are shattered, and guests' jaws are literally dropped at the unexpected drama. The maitre'd sends his minion packing, literally throws him out of the room, and then just as someone's about to intervene, he turns to the crowd and starts singing *Another One Bites the Dust*. Thirty or so seconds later, in comes the waiter, now dressed as Freddie Mercury and, within seconds, the entire room is on their feet clapping along.

Patrick turns to me. 'I don't get it.'

Rhi, though, is smiling. 'They're undercover.'

'Exactly,' I say, so sure of my plan. 'We find other women like us, who've had similar experiences at the event and invite them back too. We all pose as regular wait staff, like those guys in the video. Let the men think it's business as usual, then halfway through the night, we start the show.'

'What kind of show?' Rhi, while several years older than me, is still significantly younger than Mum. But her tone suggests the same jaded scepticism.

'That's the bit we're still workshopping.' The solid in-my-bones certainty that we can do this turns mushy with the disbelief spreading across Rhi's face. Before the silence that's fallen at our table can get too thick, I keep going. 'The singing waiters aren't the only thing I've been watching. There are all these protest videos.' I scroll my history. 'Have you seen the thousands of Chilean women who gathered on streets across the world to sing a song about rape culture and victim shaming? And then there was a feminist group in Paris who posed topless with the Ukrainian flag painted across their chests.'

'Topless?' Rhi's trying and failing not to laugh. 'Sorry, hun. But the last thing any woman who's had a bad experience at the gala is gonna want to do is get her tits out in front of that lot. I think maybe you two read too much fiction.' She shakes her head, like, *sorry*. 'I'm not saying it's entirely impossible, but before we even get to how we'd protest, there were, like, 100 odd men there. For canapes, four courses and drinks. How would you even fund it for a start?'

I look to Maya, crossing my fingers there's some kind magic money pouch in that folder.

'We were hoping, given what happened at the actual gala, with Aaron Jenkins, suppliers might offer their services at cost?' What had been a reasonable assumption earlier now comes out of Maya's mouth as a question. Clearly, Rhi's doubt is infectious. For someone who's usually so sure of herself, my friend is tentative as she reveals a spreadsheet with all the contacts we pulled from my aunt's computer. It hadn't taken much to convince my cousin, Will, that the re-do was an effort to restore Sophie's tarnished reputation.

Even Helen, my aunt's assistant, seemed open to it. Told us to come back when we had more of a plan.

Rhi takes the paper, but her glance across it is cursory. 'I don't want to piss on your parade because, honestly, I love the idea of that lot getting their come-uppance.'

'But?'

'*But...* even if you were only paying cost, you're still talking thousands and thousands of pounds.'

I slump back into my chair, teeth sinking into the fleshy inside of my cheek.

'Hey.' Rhi leans forward, rests her elbows on the table. 'I love that you've come to me, Cass.' With a word like "love" in a sentence, you'd think there'd be softness in Rhi's face, but what I see when we really look at each other is rage. 'There's something in that,' she says. 'In you seeking out other women. In you wanting solidarity. I shouldn't have laughed because your ideas aren't silly, they're brilliant. If we had all the time and money, I'd be in.'

'But.' I shrug because, she's right. We don't.

She sits upright. 'What about the after party?'

'What about it? My varnish was black, remember. I don't know.' I pick at the skin around my thumb.

Rhi turns to Patrick. 'Was there one planned?'

'I think so. My mate in housekeeping said she was dreading the mess she'd face the next morning up on the top floor.'

'But it never happened?'

'Can't have done. From what I heard, everything stopped the second that mad kid arrived.'

'OK.' Rhi drums her thumb on her thigh. 'I can't believe I'm even suggesting this, but how about instead of re-doing the dinner, we do the after party that never happened instead? Still get all the girls on board, but when it comes to the men, we pick out the key players and invite them to an *intimate soiree*. See how they take to being outnumbered?'

'Cass?' Maya looks at me, like, *what do you think?*

What I think is it feels powerful. Dangerous. And, right now, powerful and dangerous are good.

EVE

'Looks like we made a good call.' Luke Rock stands in the communal entrance of the Edwardian conversion he bought in the year we first met, moving to the side and sweeping his arm to invite me in from the storm. In my WhatsApp, I'd suggested we meet this morning for a walk. But his calendar was chock with Zoom calls, and if it was OK with me, he said, he'd rather not talk outside because, well, *fans*. His actions at Hambledon Manor have resulted in an increase in the request for selfies whenever he "braves town".

Photos are the bane of my life, he'd said in our flurry of texts.

He was talking about photos in plural. I think of my daughter. Of Kelly. Of the power – the consequences – of one.

Maybe I'm naïve for assuming he's kept it but, if nothing else comes of me being here, I'd like the Polaroid back.

'You're drenched.' His thumb hovers near my temple. Something decides him against wiping away the rain. Maybe it's the dark sky, or the badly lit hallway, but his smile is more sincere than it seems on the telly and brighter than on his sobriety channel, where they carry a certain a solemnity. This is in keeping, I suppose, with the distance he puts between his life now and the sometimes-temerarious habits of his past. *Temerarious* was his word choice, by the way. He always did have a broader, better vocabulary than me. I looked it up: reckless, rash. Was I one of them, his undesirable obsessions? Sure, we dabbled in drink and drugs, even, but our wildness, he said to me, was bohemian. It wasn't highs we were chasing but truths. I was his route to understanding himself and the world more fully, his temptress *not* his mistake.

'C'mon in.' That hovering hand again. A burn in the small of my back where he *doesn't* touch me. 'You know the way.'

The instinct of muscle memory. I climb the one flight of stairs and turn left.

'Drink?' There's a glass on the kitchen side. 'One shouldn't presume, but…' The fridge light yellows the tiny room. '*I'm* a changed man and don't drink, of course, but I seem to remember *you* like Champagne.'

What I'd like to say is that it's not only him who's changed since I was a teenager but, 'You remembered right.'

'Tanners.' He makes a display of uncorking the bottle. 'Better than the cheap stuff we'd knock back as kids.'

'Kids?' I hold the glass as he pours. 'You were twenty-six.'

'Was I?' He laughs. 'A mere child. God, to be young. Though you still look it, Gen.' His eyes grow wide, the heat of a magnifying glass held over a leaf in the sun. 'Let me take your coat.' He moves behind me, his hands just above my shoulders. I manoeuvre myself from the sleeves. 'Muggy, isn't it,' he says from the bedroom, where I can see he's laid my wet mac on his unmade bed. He's removing his jumper. A glimpse of his torso, the coarse hair above the belt of his jeans. It had looked and felt so adult when I was sixteen.

He steps into the kitchen. It immediately shrinks.

I remind myself I'm here for a reason. Rummaging among the matches and lighters I've gathered from around the house to in a token attempt stop my daughter's burning, I remove Kelly's letter from my bag. But when I look up, 'Oh my god, is that…?' I point at his top.

'Is it?' With his head cocked like that, Luke is almost boyish. 'As always, you made the decision for me.'

'There was only ever one option.' We clink glasses. Flute and tumbler. 'It was never the Gallaghers.' I'd bought him the Daman Albarn T-shirt to settle any debate re Oasis v Blur. Funny though, after he left,

I wasn't bothered about listening to either. Instead, I tore my room apart searching for Alanis Morissette. 'I can't believe you still have it.'

'Why wouldn't I?' He leans against the counter. 'Those were important times. Fun too, of course.' He sips his water, tops up my Champagne. 'I don't get back here often, so, as you can see from the décor, it's pretty much as it was in the Nineties. Wardrobe and all. Anyway, they call it vintage now.' He straightens, holds out his arms as if his clothes are a case in point. 'The good old days.'

'About that,' I say. 'I wanted to speak with you about Kelly.'

But his back is to me. 'Shall we?' He's already in the front room.

'Er, wow!' Luke wasn't kidding about the décor. It's a time warp. 'Literally nothing has changed.'

'I know, right. How does it feel, Gen, to be eighteen?'

I'm right there again. Obsessive. Insomniac. Mad.

I wanted him so badly. At my most insane, when he was on tour and I had no way of reaching him, I cut out a photo from a TV Times article about up-and-coming comedians. Maybe it was because the picture was the size of a stamp that I licked it. In truth, I wanted whatever I could get of him. Any bit of him near my lips and pressed to my tongue.

'I can't remember.'

He looks up at me from the armchair, his eyebrows arched like he detects the lie.

I sit on the sofa. On its arm, a stain where Kelly had spilt her tea. 'I hoped we could talk.'

'Of course.' He leans back. His legs come further apart. 'I'd hoped so too. Like I said, this place.' He gestures to the room. 'I heard through your sister you're an interior designer now.'

I almost spit out my Champagne. 'If my husband heard you call me that...'

'What?' Luke shrugs. 'It's true, isn't it? You *do* design the interiors of your renovations.' He's chill. I'm upright. 'Success is all about how you define yourself. Like when we first got together, you were so in the shadow of your sister.'

'Huh?'

'You remember. The velvet rope.'

It wasn't enough for Sophie that she'd persuaded me to a nightclub. She was gunning for the VIP.

'I spotted the two of you from the bar.' He raises a foot onto his opposite knee. 'She was so trussed up. So obvious. You, however...'

'What about me?'

'*You* were more interesting,' he says. Behind me, the rain is heavy on the windows. 'Your confidence was there but undiscovered. Once we were alone though, without Sophie telling you what to do all the time…' That contemplative shrug again. 'You grew up, Gen. Started to do things for your own benefit. Found your own pleasures. Or maybe those pleasures found you.' He coughs, then, as if embarrassed by the intimacy of his memory. 'Anyway, my point is, I was thinking you could perhaps restyle this place for me. The city's great but, you know how it is.' The way he looks at me like he's so sure I get him. 'It can be lonely. It'd be good to have somewhere more welcoming to retreat to. Dare I say it, somewhere like home.' On his chat show, Luke has a reputation for boisterous conversation and incessant fidgeting. Now though, he's quiet and still. 'And, if the flat goes well – and I don't see any reason why it wouldn't – maybe you could work your magic on my London house too. Sophie said you'd dreamt of something bigger than Shropshire but were restricted by where Harry's been able to buy.'

'*We.*' My nail scrapes at the stain. 'Where *we* have been able to buy. The business is both of ours.'

'Of course. Sorry, I didn't mean.'

'S'fine.' Even the smell here is the same.

'Let me get you more Champagne.' When he returns, I see I've already drunk half a bottle.

'Easy.' I sip the brim to catch the overflow of foam.

'You still love it here then? Shropshire, I mean, not my flat. Saying that though, you are beginning to look more at ease.' This time, when he sits, it's next to me. 'You did the viewing with me, didn't you? Fuck me, that estate agent! Am I wrong or did he talk for approximately fifteen hours about plumbing.'

'You're not wrong.' I'd never felt taller than when I held Luke's hand while surveying the kitchen. Look at me, I thought. With this man in this flat he can afford to buy with money he's made from his work on stage and TV. I was sixteen and a woman. My imagination swung between homely roast dinners on Sundays and what he said when he'd shown me the particulars. How if he bought the flat, he'd need to fuck me in every corner of every room.

I'm laughing now, like he and I did after sharing a just-kill-me look behind the agent's back. He was giving us a history of the cast iron bath. Luke and I rolled our eyes in unison. He had this way of bringing me into his circle. It wasn't only him who deserved better than the middle-aged man's lecture. I did too. *I want you*, he mouthed, and I swear I loved him so much I would have said yes if he'd suggested he strip me naked and piss on me right there on the tatty carpeted floor. 'I was kind of deranged when I was with you.'

'Nah.' He twists to better look at me. 'Not deranged, Genesis. You were playful. Tempting. And let's not forget hot as fuck.'

'Shit.' My shirt – the white one I chose after forty minutes of deliberation – is soaked in Champagne. Like *true love* and *together forever*, *hot as fuck* was something Luke would often say. And I'd been so happy to believe all those phrases of his were true. After though, when he no longer returned my calls and I read in *OK!* magazine he was dating the actress Jessica Alderford, I wondered if the things he told me were *hot as fuck* were actually just perverted, and if he was now doing the things he'd said were special to us with someone new? The article put Jessica at 21, three whole years older than me. For the first time since I'd met Lucien Rothschild, I felt like a stupid kid. I examined Jessica's womanly curves, sophisticated dress, and professionally styled hair. No wonder he didn't want me.

'Sorry,' Luke says. 'I shouldn't have said you're hot as fuck. Not that you're not, you *really* are but...' He drops his head as if embarrassed. 'You're *wet*. Borrow something of mine.'

A mortifying wobble when I stand. Forty-five and still can't handle my drink.

'It's those heels.' Luke points at the wedges. Another agonising decision. 'Take them off if you like. Here.' He kneels before me, his fingertips brushing my feet as he unbuckles my shoes. I step down from their three-inch platforms. His mouth is level with my cunt.

Shit. That word. I *never* use it. It's too much, too vulgar. But with Luke Rock, wasn't that always the way?

A question, then, other bad words, raw and unformed and forbidden: If he unzipped my jeans?

He doesn't. A good thing. I can't risk becoming that mess I was when he went away the last time. He never knew. Should he? Should I tell him of the cross I carried that stank of our lost love and all our hard and *temerarious* sex?

I'm dizzy, and he's steady and holding my elbow and leading me into his room.

'This one?' He pulls out a green Stüssy T-shirt from the wardrobe.

'My nightie.' Everything is a flashback. This time, him behind me, slow and tender against the wall. I haven't been touched in so long. I undo my top button.

His eyes drop. 'I'll give you some privacy.' He turns to the door.

He should, I think. He should know. He really ought to know.

'Luke?'

'Yes?' And although he's not left the room, he keeps his back to me.

And I want to scream how much his broken promises hurt me, but I want his eyes on me, his *hot-as-fuck* need for me, too.

The second button. The third. 'You stopped calling.'

'You told me to.'

Is that true?

The fourth. And the last. I am removing my shirt. My index finger runs across the lace strap of my bra.

'I was so sad.' On his dresser, my Champagne glass. I tip my head back, desperate for dregs.

'And now?' He's in front of me, and I'm crying because —

Because what?

Because I'm here again?

Because he said we'd be together forever?

Because I haven't been here for twenty-seven years?

Because I never liked Oasis *or* Blur, and yet I want this man to hunger me like he did when I was sixteen?

'You really are beautiful.' His warm hand is on my jaw, his little finger on my neck.

I'm tilted towards him. I could and I would, but —

'I licked your photo,' I say, and this is so unbelievably funny I can't stand up for laughing.

He catches me, lowers me to his bed. 'We were crazy for each other.'

'Were you though?' I can't tell what the noise is between my words. If I'm crying or giggling or both. 'Crazy for me, I mean?'

'Eve,' he says, 'You were – *are* – my Genesis 3.'

And the noise in my mouth is neither crying nor giggling but groaning because Luke Rock is kissing me.

Me.

Older.

Fatter.

Hairier.

Me.

'I —'

'Sssshhhh,' across my breast and stomach and hip. 'Sssshhhh,' he says. 'You're better than I remember.'

He *does* want me.

Still.

Even.

Now.

'Eve,' he repeats. And, like me, the fly on my jeans is undone.

Somewhere, a warning. But in his hands, I am invincible.

'Eve.' His familiar voice in this familiar room and his way of moving me beneath him on his familiar bed that surrenders to the weight of this familiar pleasure and pain. He pushes my legs apart and my mac falls to the floor and his fingers are inside me and he's telling me, 'Wait.'

If there's a gap for too much thought, I will end this, so, 'No,' I tell him, 'don't stop.'

But his right hand pins me to his bed, and his left hand is in the bedside cupboard and, 'Look,' he says, 'I kept it.' He's emptied a box onto the mattress. 'Shit.' Is rummaging. 'I know it's here.'

I twist my neck and see a scourge of magazines and photos spilt across the sheet. Pink, black, brown arses, tits and flesh. One by one, he scans them. 'Nah,' he says, 'nope,' he says and tosses them to the floor.

'What...' I try to lift myself onto my elbows.

He pushes my shoulder back down with his knee. 'That girl you fucked? Kiko? Was she Japanese?'

'Kelly. No, British.'

He drops a photo, not a Polaroid, onto my chest and takes a swig of his water before continuing his search. If I raise my head, I can just about see them. The two girls in the picture. One white, one Asian. Neither of them is Kelly nor me. 'Luke?'

'Call me Lucien,' he slurs, his mouth a smeared hunger across his determined face.

I twist from beneath him onto all fours, aware of the folds in my belly and my sagging hanging breasts. 'What is this?'

374

Among the porn magazines, another fifteen, maybe twenty photos he hasn't yet checked.

I see it before he does. A little faded, but it's definitely me and my friend. In the pictures around us, all these other girls. When I look at us, we *were* – all of us – girls. In a photo tucked beneath ours is someone I recognise from the year below me in school. She would have been fifteen.

My hand on my mouth is unable to contain everything coming up and out between my tongue and teeth. There is yellow stinking vomit on the pillows and on the sheets.

'Fuck's sake, Eve.' He's disgusted but not enough to give up on his search.

I snatch our photo and manage to roll away, to get to my feet and stand above him and his vile collection. 'I thought —' But I stop talking, understanding the naivety of the words before I speak them. *I thought I was special. You made me feel special. You said I was different from all the others. So sexually evolved, you said, One of a fucking kind.*

I stumble, looking for my jeans and find them in the corner. The same dark corner where he sat and watched us. In the aftermath, he'd told Kelly I was in on it. But, like her, didn't I think he was out?

When I read him her letter, 'It takes a woman to do what we were planning,' he said. I didn't remember planning anything, but he was insistent, reminded me of what I'd said when I'd first shown him the Polaroid. When he gave me the coke. 'I asked how you would you feel if I watched you and you said – your words, Gen – that you'd feel fucking hot.'

What I realise now is that was it. I never said yes to anything involving Kelly because Luke didn't ask me about it again.

'You're leaving?' He barely looks up, is still rooting through the last few photos.

I don't speak as I button up my shirt.

'Spoil sport.' He throws his arms in the air and collapses in a defeated heap by the sick-drenched bed. 'See you then.' His face contorts into a leer. His hand a mocking wave goodbye.

'Are you drunk?'

'Me?' He sits up, tries to reach for his glass. 'Fifteen years sober.'

I get to it before he does and sip.

'S'water,' he says.

Twenty-seven years ago, despite all evidence to the contrary, I would have believed his every word.

Thu 21 Sep

Heads up. Journalist for
the sun interview is
shelley chapman

FFS
Sort it

Let me see what I can do

Advised the editor SC has
history of liking provoc-
ative tweets about you
but he assures me she's
keen to portray you in a
positive light

Her non fic is publishing
with Lawson & Cook next
year. Given how much £
your books make for them,
I'd like to see L&C's
marketing budget for SC
if she slates you in the
press

👍

Today

Missed voice call at 17:41
Missed voice call at 17:58
Missed voice call at 18:23
Missed voice call at 19:00
Missed voice call at 19:13

> Luke, you need to pick up. Trying to avoid putting this in writing. Our legal department has received a letter from the mother of that girl Holly who you spoke with at the Shropshire business mens dinner. I don't want to have to explain over email. Call me asap

CASS

I walk into the living room, where I find Dad on the sofa in his dressing gown with a plate of toast.

'I finished the list,' he says, scrambling to press the off button on the TV remote and reaching for his laptop as if wanting to prove his Sunday morning lounging hasn't been purely chill. 'Shall I show you?'

'I don't need to see it.' I didn't mean to sound critical, just matter of fact. I'm pleased he's listened, acted, but if he's expecting love and light for his efforts, he's missed the point. 'It was for your benefit, Dad, not mine.'

'Oh.' He's like a child who's worked for hours perfecting a painting only for a parent to dump it in a drawer.

'I'm sorry,' I say and, to his credit, he tells me I've nothing to apologise for.

'I'm the one who needs to make amends.' He points at his computer, 'There's something else though,' then opens the laptop. 'I've been thinking about the re-do.'

Here we go. He and Mum have been made of naysaying and caution all week. *It's too dangerous, Cass. It's not for you to teach them a lesson. Your granddad says there are other things we can do.* But my granddad, who's still claiming his men 'were not in any way involved with *that* video' can do one. He's either as bad as they are or a blind idiot who has no clue. Given he was top dog at the station, I'm not sure which one's worse

Dad's face now though is kind of pink with excitement, rather than the recent standard pale with fear. He beckons me over, nods at the screen. It's some kind of horizontal bar chart.

Clocking my confusion, 'It's a task-management system,' he says. 'Thought it could help keep you on track with everything you need to sort.'

'For the re-do?' I ask, but my question's answered by the title of the file: Cassandra Speaks.

'That list,' Dad says, 'it's really made me think. I know your mum has her worries —'

No shit. Sure, Mum likes a drink or two at the weekend, but how drunk she was when she got in last night was another level. I was brainstorming with Maya on Facetime, trying and failing to figure ways to fund our plan. I hung up when I heard Mum stumbling around the kitchen for water, found her a few minutes later attempting, badly, to silent-sneak up the stairs.

'You ok?' I asked. Unconvinced by her nod and her "fine". I fetched her some paracetamol and a Diet Coke for the morning, left them outside the spare room door. I couldn't sleep after because it was me, wasn't it, who'd done this to her. Put her in such a state she'd drunk herself stupid because of what Gramps calls my hairbrained plan.

Dad, who must think otherwise, is still talking, '— but I honestly believe if we could get other men to think like this, maybe we really could see some change.'

'Thanks,' I say. But it's not only Mum and Gramps' objections that have me stymied. Looking at the to-list on Dad's fancy chart, Rhi's concerns about paying for any kind of re-do, no matter how small, are multiplied. 'But it's a no go. We don't have the cash.'

'*You* don't,' Dad says, closing Cassandra Speaks to reveal a website for our local MP. 'But *he* does.' He clicks on a link to a news story about Lionel Morgan signing up for a fun run. 'It's not the race he wants to win, Cass, it's public favour. The man has bridges to build, and if he believes your event will make him look like someone doing his bit for feminism, I reckon he might be all in.'

'Oh my god.' I grab my phone from the arm of the sofa. 'I need to call Maya. This is genius. If he stumps up the money, it'll get us publicity. And with someone like him on board, we'll have more chance of persuading Luke Rock to come back too.'

'No.' It's Mum, still in last night's shirt and jeans, glaring fire at us from the living room door. Her eyes are as wide as her voice was fierce. 'No.' The opposite this time. A whisper. 'Not him,' she says 'No.'

'But he's perfe—'

'I forbid it.' The declaration is Victorian.

'Forbid it?' I'm laughing because she sounds ridiculous.

'Yes,' she says. 'I forbid it.' Loud again. A wedge of crazy in her tone.

'Eve.' Dad is cool and calm in her fury. 'I think if you listen to Cas—'

'No.'

Dad turns to me, 'You go upstairs, love.' He lays a hand on my back. It's the first time I've not flinched when he's touched me. A small smile like he also recognises this progress. 'Go on,' he says. 'Let your mum and me talk.'

YOU

This is not what you were expecting. Your wife in the kitchen, pulling at the sleeves of her shirt. She's less painful to watch than she was a few minutes ago when she was pulling at the lengths of her hair. You peeled her hands from the strands and asked if she was able to explain.

The explanation she offered had the cold oozing creep of anaesthetic eased into a vein.

She hates him, she said. But what she also said is that last night she was *this close* to fucking him. She was specific with that word. Not *sleeping with* or *having sex with* but *fucking*. The hard K with its kick and its cruelty.

It's in his name too, of course. Luke Rock. Those single-syllable monikers a punch in your deadened gut.

You want and don't want the details. The *does want* pushes on regardless, no time for contemplation. 'Where?' You ask. 'When?' You say. 'Why?'

She was drunk, she tells you. What she tells you too is she hasn't forgotten what she said. She repeats it verbatim. 'When we let ourselves go like that, we expose who we really are at our core.' That steely eye contact. 'Looks like, deep down, I've always been a naïve little whore.'

It's *whore* that makes you cry, Harry. Your wife and this word she's always refuted because it's a dated and loaded weapon used mostly by men to degrade women they hate. It's *whore* that makes you reach again for her hands.

'Tell me everything,' you say, 'that happened.' You aren't angry or begging when you add, 'Please.'

'I —' Her eyes close. 'He —' And open. 'We —' They drop to the table, fixed on a gouge in the wood. She does as you have asked and tells you, every image returning your numbed body to life. Whole and hurting, you want to flip the table. Take an axe to it. You want to chop and destroy.

What you do, though, is listen.

It's not that you're not sore or furious. You are both of those things, but you are also sorry for Eve, who is sore and furious too. Time is a funny thing, Harry. You have known this woman twenty-four years, but it's really only in the last few weeks, in the dark-room conversations and in the kitchen now that you are even beginning to truly understand her.

She pulls a photograph, a polaroid, from her jeans but won't let you look at it. 'It's of me and Kelly,' she says. You don't recognise the name. 'We're...' She stops. You follow her gaze to the ceiling. The cornicing is grey with dust. 'I was so stupid to love him. To trust him. He made me feel like a grown-up, but when I saw this last night, Harry, Jesus. I was a baby. I was eighteen. *Sixteen* when we first got together. He was a man, who sent taxis to pick me up from school so we could have sex in my lunch hour.' A breath catches in her chest. 'And I wanted it. I wanted it so bad. I wanted it then, and, I'm sorry,' she says, 'but I wanted it yesterday too. I can't tell you what it felt like to have him need me. Sometimes...' The grand-father clock in the hallway strikes its eleven gentle bongs. '...there's been, or I've felt... I don't know, like, this polite obligation to just bear it when a man puts his hands on me. Not wanting to make a fuss because it's probably all in my own head anyway. All these good manners of keeping still and hushed because to do otherwise would be to make *him* uncom-fortable.'

You don't take your eyes off her.

She too refuses to look away. 'And that's the thing, right? I've never been able trust my own discomfort. Couldn't name it as anything more than a dread in my gut. How do you act on *that*? How do you call it out before it's too late? Before the man has either left already, or his hands – or worse – have pushed even further. It's that, Harry, that I wanted Cass to avoid.' Her eyes scrunch tight. 'With Rock though, and not only him but with him especially, it was more complicated than even that.' In whispers she tells you how as much as she hated that leering attention, sometimes she wanted it too. 'I fucking hate myself for saying it but, a lot of the time, it was – *is* – only when men notice me that I feel of any worth.'

'I'm sorry,' you say because what other word is there.

'Me too.' She rolls her eyes at the phrase.

'He's not a good man, Eve.' It's so obvious it's stupid to say it, but your wife agrees.

'I can't have him in the same as room as our daughter. She thinks she's ready to take him and the others on, but there's no way they'll listen. Before I left last night, I asked Luke about the girls in all his photographs, and he just shrugged like they – *we* – were inconsequential. In his mind, he's done nothing wrong.'

'OK,' you say. 'Maybe not him then. The others though. The lists – Cass's *and* mine – are a powerful tool, Eve.'

'I can't give her my blessing. I know it's a lot to ask after what happened, but can you back me, please?'

You are trying so hard to do the right thing, Harry, but when the two most important women in your life are in opposition, how do you pick a side?

CASS

I stand on my bed to read this latest news aloud. *'Lionel Morgan has, with great pleasure, agreed to sponsor your fundraising dinner at Hambledon Manor, 21 October 2023.'* Maya claps. 'I know, right!' My heart squeezes with the optimism oozing from her like the bright-green glittered slime Liv and I were obsessed with as kids. *'As a life-time resident of Shropshire, he is always keen to support local businesses, especially those with a keen interest in women.'* God, he's eager. I only sent the email a few hours ago. *'Shrewsbury Refuge Services is a charity of utmost importance to Lionel, and he is therefore offering to cover the full cost of a three-course meal for up to ten guests. Please note, the funds will be transferred via Lionel's consultancy firm, Morgan Strategy, and are donated on the understanding that he will be named as principal supporter of the event in any associated PR.'*

'Oh, I'll gladly name him,' Maya says.

'Me too!' I smile. 'I mean, thanks to *Lionel's* timely indiscretions and Dad's suggestion that we exploit them, we might actually pull this thing off.'

I call Helen, who's delighted with the news. 'This is awesome, Cass. Sophie will be super pleased In the

Event Of has another opportunity to raise money for such a good cause.' Together we'd decided Shrewsbury Refuge Services will benefit from any money raised on the night. 'Only hitch,' Helen says, 'is we have a wedding on the night of the 22nd.'

'Oh no.' It's my best impression of disappointment. Truth is, when Will gave us full access to Aunt Sophie's computer for the contacts, we made a note of key events in her calendar too. 'You know what though?' I'm rather enjoying pretending I'm conjuring solutions on the fly. 'Our friend, Patrick, who works at Hambledon Manor, said their internal events manager is happy to lend a hand. Obviously it would have been great if you could have joined us, but with their help, I think we'll be fine.'

After a few minutes of promising to keep Helen in the loop, I offer the others a massive grin. 'I'm pretty sure Sophie's tendency to hold Helen responsible for any managerial misdoings at the gala has worked in our favour. Poor thing's so determined to restore her boss's reputation, she's pretty much given us a massive green flag. I reckon so long as we make her feel included, she won't ask for much in return at all.' A round of high-fives. 'Now to check Patrick can get us that room.'

'Patrick?' While keen to help, Liv's not been to all of our many meetings, which is to her detriment, because Rhi's arrived at each one with the very best home-made biscuits or cake. Today, brownies. I offer one to Maya, who declines.

'He's got a mate in the events team at Hambledon Manor,' she says. 'Reckons he can swing us the private-dining space FOC.'

'Free of charge,' I clarify. 'Speaking of FOC... Liv?'

My mate barely looks up from her phone.

'You think your dad's company could do us some official invites? And we have this idea for table centres. But they'll need printing on decent card. Several copies, and maybe some bound versions too?'

Without even asking for details, 'No can do,' she says. 'Still not talking.'

'What?' I don't get it, this odd lie Liv insists on tending.

Her head's already dipped again, her thumbs tapping out a message on the screen. What's with her? Why's she so apathetic when the rest of us are practically flying with the battle-ready energy of this room?

Not wanting to make a public thing of it but also not wanting to let it slide, I go to photos and WhatsApp Liv the picture I took of her and her dad in Ludlow that Sunday after the dinner.

```
Me: I know you're back in
touch with him. Can we
```

```
chat about this later. Just
want to know everything's
ok ♥♥♥♥♥
```

I watch her open it. Glance at the same photo on my phone. There's no denying it's her. The tumble of red curls pressed into his shoulder beneath that huge yellow and black umbrella he's holding to give them both cover from the rain.

'What the —' She starts but doesn't finish. Her eyes shrink. Her face is a new kind of harsh.

Maya senses the switch. 'You alright, Liv?'

'Yeh.' A sudden gloss to her tone, Liv tosses her phone into her bag and stands. 'I need to get off, that's all.'

'We've ordered Dominoes!' I grab the menu from my pillow as evidence. But Liv's on the landing then down the stairs already, turning only when her hand's on the catch for the front door. 'Pepperoni passion. We got thin crust because of you.'

'Sorry,' she says without sounding it. Kinder, then, 'Thing is, Cass.' One foot crossing the threshold. 'What you're doing's amazing, yeh, but I don't think I can... you know... be involved.'

'What? Why?'

That infuriating shrug of her shoulders. 'Too much on.' She pulls up the hood of her mac even though the air, like the barely-there hug and the kiss she half gives me, is bone dry.

'About your dad though?' The front path is cold beneath my feet. 'Liv?'

The metal gate creaks with the shove. She hurries through. 'Message you later.'

'Cool,' I say. But she's pulled out her AirPods from her pocket.

Conversation over then, I watch her walk down the path until she's gone.

'So...' Rhi says through a mouthful of pizza, near-neon orange juices running down her fingers and onto the paper where she's started another list. 'Who are we inviting?'

'I have a few contenders, first names only though, from the night I was there. But I'd one hundred per cent recognise their faces if I saw them again.' My skin burns at the thought of their spittle-flecked mouths and flesh-seeking eyes. I wonder, not for the first time, if this whole idea is as insane as Mum insists. Or worse. The plan we have for the men now, though, is far more tempered. Far more legal. I look at Dad's Gant chart I imported onto my iPad, try to think logically. 'How about we cross reference Sophie's guestlist with google-image searches on the names. Pinpoint the worst offenders?'

'Sounds good.' Maya opens the lever arch. 'You two want to do that while I contact Mr Rock?' I didn't tell the girls about Mum's reaction to my suggestion we invite him. 'If there's anyone who

could do with a lesson in how not to treat women…
I'm sure, like Lionel Morgan, there'll be something
Rock's done recently that'll need some reputation-
restoring PR.'

Rhi takes my iPad and reads the names, organised
by company, from Aunt Sophie's spreadsheet. I simul-
taneously google on my phone.

There's Bryan, obviously, and another guy David
Hargreaves from the same table. Rhi confirms
Sebastian Cornish, Bobby Sparrow and John Welch,
who attended in 2019.

'Ha! Repeat offenders,' she says when I recognise
their faces from the table adjacent to the one I served
for most of the evening. 'Roger Mannering next,
Weston & Mayfair.'

I type. Hit search. 'Eugh.' I zoom in on the first
photo, a LinkedIn professional headshot of Roger,
suited and well shaven against an expanse of grey. His
thick-rimmed glasses have the whiff of an old-man
attempting cool. 'Money-Clip.'

'Who?'

'This dude who had some fancy engraved clip for
holding his massive stash of notes.'

'Let's have a look.'

I tilt the screen so Rhi can see him. 'Generous tips.
Seemed OK at first, but I could feel it, you know.
He wanted something in return.'

'So, he's a tick, yeah?' She puts a mark next to his name. Zooms out. 'Pff. I always knew I was right about golfers.'

'Huh?'

'Your guy Money-Clip, there.' She points at a photo two rows down. 'My dad was this mega Tiger Woods fan, could cope with all Woods' marital cheating but lost it when he spat on the green! You know there's this website that ranks Tiger's *round* of 18 mistresses…'

Rhi's voice fades as I try to zoom in. My stupid shaking fingers. Got it. 'Shit.' I double-tap the home button. Switching between my camera roll and Safari, the same yellow and black umbrella in both.

'What?' Rhi asks.

Back and forth. Back and forth. I click on the Google image and zoom again, focusing on the branding splashed across the brolly's canopy. Back and forth. Back and forth. Zoom in on my photo, the one *I* took in Ludlow. The same umbrella. The same logo.

I Google Weston & Mayfair. 'They're an estate agents.' I mumble. 'But Liv's dad runs a stationery business.'

Back and forth. Back and forth. The same build. The same bald head. One from the front. One from behind. It's the same man in both.

'It can't be.' I look to Rhi, double, triple, quadruple check the name

'Yeah, Roger Mannering.' Rhi points at the screen, like, *you literally just typed it.*

My heart roars as I remember.

'Who's *Roger?*' I'd asked Liv as she helped me get ready for Gramps' retirement party.

'A friend,' she said. And then Mum had come in with her *knock knock* and her convenient timing.

I go to WhatsApp. To Liv.

```
Me: Where are you?
Me: We need to talk.
```

EVE

'I can't be long.' Charlotte passes me Boomer's lead while she closes and locks her front door. 'Emma and Oli are coming over later. I'm prepping dinner. They're bringing Aaron. They don't trust him enough yet to leave him home alone. And Anna, who still doesn't feel safe returning to uni, by the way, refuses – understandably – to babysit her scarily misogynist brother.'

'I get that. I'm not sure I'd be happy being on my own with someone who so clearly hates women.'

Charlotte takes Boomer and starts down the path. 'Like you were alone with Luke Rock yesterday, you mean?'

I think how he couldn't take his eyes off those photos. 'He doesn't *hate* women.'

'You sure about that? Just because he wanted a shag, doesn't mean he actually likes you.'

We turn out of her private road onto The Mount. 'I don't think I like him either.' And yet my phone, since last night, has been a body part, a small but repugnant tumour still aching for him to message or call. 'Fucked up, isn't it.'

Charlotte shrugs. 'Isn't everything? Sex. Power. The law. You know with a good lawyer, Aaron could get as little as two years.' She moves us both to the side of the pavement to let a girl whizz by on her scooter. 'If his crimes were racially or religiously motivated, that sentence would be notably longer but, because it's only women he hates, those enhanced sentencing powers don't stand.'

I watch the girl – so speedy, so vulnerable – disappear down the road. 'Is that true?'

'Yep. We're not a minority therefore how can it be an issue. It's more complex than that, of course, but what the government fails to recognise is the forums Aaron was in, they're not insignificant in number. It's like Shayan said, if it was brown people chatting about hurting white folk on religious grounds, you'd bet the perpetrators would face the harder side of the courts. White boys like my nephew, however, they're not prejudiced, merely troubled pitiable souls.' Charlotte stops so Boomer can pee. 'It's not that I don't feel sorry for Aaron. I do. He was a good kid, who somehow got caught up in all that Men's Rights shit. He says the only place he felt able to vent was online. But it's not like he didn't have friends.'

I'm certainly not defending Aaron, but 'Even with friends,' I say, 'sometimes it's not so easy. Especially for a boy.'

Harry had implied as much earlier when, despite everything I'd told him about Rock, he was still arguing in favour of the re-do. 'You're underestimating the power of talking,' he said.

'These men are dangerous, Harry. I think you're oversimplifying.'

'And I think *you're* over complicating. *And* forgetting.'

'Forgetting what?' I was already tired and irritated – we'd been going round in circles about the gala and its fallout for hours – but there he was, during one of our most important conversations, playing with his bloody phone.

'The power of vulnerability,' he said. 'I've been reading about it.' A small smile that seemed to acknowledge what I've been getting at all these years. 'Watching YouTube even.' A contrite quirk of his brow. 'There's a lot of talk about the importance connection.'

'Harry, are you about to mansplain vulnerability to me?'

'No. What I'm about to do is say how right you were. I *don't* have connection. Not much of it anyway, and without wanting to *oversimplify*, my guess is most of those dangerous men don't have it either.'

'What, and it's our daughter's responsibility to help them find it?' I shook my head, let out a kind of snort. 'As if the pressure on young women isn't already great enough.'

'No, not *Cass's* responsibility, Eve. *Mine*. And not only mine but men's generally. I'm not saying this whole fucking mess can be solved by talking but, honestly, if we could create a space in which men can be genuinely open about their full spectrum of feelings, maybe so many of us wouldn't end up being such utter dicks. You know what?' My husband, who in the last hour had exposed a pretty broad spectrum of his own feelings, was suddenly in a state of emotion I can only describe as giddy. 'I'm not just going to *support* the re-do, I'm going to *attend*. Be vulnerable. Explain to those men what I've done.'

'What could I say?' I ask Charlotte now. 'Harry's proving himself Cass's true ally, which is clearly more than I'm prepared to be.'

'Eve,' she says, 'How abo—'

'But don't you think he'd be better letting the police deal with the grown-ups, and he could focus on helping kids instead. Like Aaron, or the boys in the football team he coaches, young men in waiting who will still be open and able to change?'

Charlotte stops, pulls me into the alley that would take us down to the river, only she's not walking, rather she's telling Boomer to sit. 'And how is this newly vulnerable Harry?' Despite my intense irritation, my friend remains as calm as her dog. 'After what you told him about you and Rock?'

Confused.

Generous.

Kind.

'Forgiving,' I say and see Charlotte prickle at my irked tone.

She begins to make her way down the steps to the fields below. 'And that annoys you, why?"

From my bag, the Uplift ring tone assigned to Harry's calls. 'Speak of the devil, do you mind?'

'No.' She smiles, 'Of course not.'

Harry doesn't bother with hello but is straight in with, 'Your dad called,' His voice is a desert dry. 'It's official,' he says, 'one of the officers is now being questioned about the video of Cass.'

'Stump,' Dad says. The nickname of the accused policeman – the same policeman who lapped up the apology *I* forced Cass to make – dangles between us like a carcass on a butcher's hook. It's meaty, and it stinks.

'And you worked with this guy for, what, thirty years?'

'Twenty-nine actually.'

'Sorry – my bad – a mere twenty-nine. No wonder you didn't spot *Stump* was a wrong'un.'

Dad looks from left to right, probably checking for eavesdropping neighbours. Not for the first time, he attempts to usher me inside.

I don't budge from the porch. 'Twenty-nine years and no indication?'

'I was aware his humour could be a little…' He coughs. '…Blue.'

'When you say *blue*…' My lips remain pursed, and I wait.

'You know, bant—'

'Don't you dare say banter.' Something barbed and rooted swells.

'He may have made comments from time to time.'

'What kind of comments?' There's only ever one reason why someone would be this vague.

'What you have to understand, Eve.' Dad sighs, rolls his eyes like he did when I was a child and unable to comprehend what he deemed simple maths. 'The job's stressful. We see things. Have to handle things. The jokes and that, they're a way to let off steam.'

'For fuuuuuuuuck's sake, Dad,' I watch his eyes grow wide at my tone. 'Oh, that's what bothers you, is it, hearing your daughter swear?'

'I think you've misunderstood me, sugar. I never saw anything like that video or those photos. What I was witnessed was harmle—'

'Harmless?'

He has the decency at least to hold his tongue.

'That fucking word.' I speak in slow searing whispers. It's either that or scream. 'It's never fucking harmless. Was that not obvious to you in all your fifty years of work? How many women, Dad? How many assaulted, raped and murdered women did you deal with in your time? And you never thought to connect any dots? Never thought to ask how the perpetrators had been allowed to get that far?'

'Evie.'

'Don't touch me.' I push him away. 'You didn't believe her. Cass told you it was one of yours, and you refused to believe her. And that meant *I* didn't believe her either. Your gaslighting is so fucking good sometimes we can't even believe it ourselves.'

'Eve?' It's Mum. Like last night, I'm in a time warp, only I'm not even sixteen now, I'm eight. And I've told my father there's a boy at school who keeps chasing me and stealing my sandwiches. *He's mean*, I said. But Dad shook his head and told me, *No, sugar, he's not mean. He likes you. Just doesn't know how to show it.*. My mum looped her arm through his, nodded at her husband's world-wise lecture. *If he does it again, don't let your emotions get the better of you. The best thing you can do is smile.*

'Men like you persuade us it's nothing. And then wonder why we're so angry. Why we don't go to the police.'

Mum comes to the doorway but doesn't stop by Dad, rather walks past him and stands by *me*. 'Up,' she says.

I am taller and stronger with my wings. 'I didn't think I'd ever encourage my daughter to take the law into her own hands, but what else is there, Dad? When the law, like everything else in this fucked-up world, has let her – and the rest of us – down?'

CASS

I'm walking home from Maya's when I see her. Running full pelt in her lounge pants and winter coat, black handbag swinging, its top gaped like everything's about to spill. Mum's mouth is open as if she's calling me, but she's made of so much panic there's no room for noise.

In a movie this kind of scene would be accompanied by rain.

But as Rhi keeps reminding me, this is *not* a movie, we can't rely on a happy ending. No matter how meticulous our plans, everything may go to shit.

So, there's no rain, only autumnal sun, bathing Mum's distraught face in its low yellow light.

She bends double, hands on her knees, gasping for air, raises an arm, waves her phone.

I read the breaking news. 'I *knew* it was them.' And it's true, I *did* know. I feel no better, though, for being proved right.

'I'm sorry.' Mum is all arms, holding me tight then tighter like I'm so broken, if she lets go, my body will literally fall apart. 'I'm sorry.'

I lean into the galloping thud of her heart.

Back home, she reaches for her hot chocolate. I can't drink mine. It's too frothy. Too sweet. Side by side on the sofa, we read the article and its scant details, leaked by a whistle-blower, about the policeman who went to George's house and most likely used his own phone to film the video of me he played on George's. We click on the embedded links to other similar cases. An investigation into policemen who went "talent spotting" while on patrol, grading women for their "fuckability" A senior officer telling a colleague he'd happily rape her. A top surgeon grabbing a junior doctor's hand and placing it on his genitals, reminding her he had the power to make or break her career. Link. Link. Link. It's not only the emergency services. It's everywhere. The law. The media. Politics. Schools. And it's not only misogyny, the pervading hate is racist, classist, and homophobic too.

'You were right,' I sink into the cushions. 'It's stupid. To think one night could change anything.'

Mum shakes her head. 'It might, it might not. But, honestly, I don't see what else we can do.'

'You want to do it? The re-do?'

She lifts my chin with her finger, nods.

'But what if we fail?'

'At least we won't have failed to try.'

I am all eyeroll and groan. 'You sound like a fridge magnet.'

'Oh?' She laughs. 'I thought I sounded wise.'

'That too.' I let my head fall onto her shoulder. 'What about Gramps?'

'What about him?' Mum's question is mutinous, but there's a faint wobble in its delivery.

'He's going to be mad, right?'

'Yep.'

I pull at a length of frayed cotton on her sleeve. 'And you're OK with that?'

'Not really.' She runs a finger around the rim of her empty mug. 'You know what he said to me just now when I told him I saw no option but the re-do? He said it was madness. That if I went along with it, the only thing I'd prove is that I'm not the kind of woman he raised me to be.' She pulls away, puts her cup on the coffee table, looks me square in the eye. 'My whole life, I've feared his disapproval. The only truly rebellious things I've done were the things I did with Luke Rock.'

'*Luke Rock? What?*'

The eye contact is gone. 'I was with him,' she says to the floor. 'Two years on and off.'

'*When?*'

'I was younger than you. Sixteen. It was…' She stops. 'I wasn't going to tell you the details but, Jesus Christ, Cass, you've been through worse.'

It could be icky, hearing about your Mum's experience of sex. With a man. With a woman. With consent. Without. And maybe it *is* a little cringe, but she's careful with details, though they are sometimes scary. Or sad.

'I basically went from seeking one man's approval to another,' she says. 'Gramps. Rock. Trying so hard to be a version of me they wanted, even though those versions were almost complete opposites . I don't think I really thought about what I wanted myself.'

'What about Kelly?' I ask. 'Did you want her?'

'Yes.' Mum sounds surprised, looks it too. Her eyes flitting, like she's seeking certainty, about the room. 'I loved her,' she says. 'But what first happened between us became so embroiled with Rock, I couldn't see it for what it was, or what it could have been: exactly the kind fun moment of self-discovery and realisation we should all have in our teens. Whatever it was with Rock was —' Her hands clasp, and her thumbs steeple and rub at her brow. 'I don't know how to describe it. I was possessed, and I treated my friend so badly.'

She shows me a message she's been drafting to Kelly on her phone.

'Take out the bit about Rock,' I tell her. 'How you didn't know he was planning to watch.'

Her thumb hovers over the cursor. 'But I want her to know.'

'I get that. But you've not spoken with her for twenty-seven years, Mum. If I was her, I'd want the sorry to be for showing him the photo. Apologise for what you *did* do. Don't water it down with what you didn't. That can come later. If she wants to talk.'

She deletes, rewrites, passes it to me, asks if I can do it for her. Hit send. 'Thanks,' she says. 'You know you deserve an apology from the people who've hurt you too.'

'We all do. And maybe with your help, we'll get it.'

She stands. And when she reaches for my hand and pulls from me up from the sofa like she's ready for action, I am made of greenlights and courage, and only a dash of fear.

Florian Grove

Shropshire Business Men's Dinner – The After Party

To: Luke Rock

Reply-To: Florian Grove

Hey Luke

Further to our conversation yesterday, I would strongly recommend we accept the below request that you attend the belated After Party for the Shropshire Business Men's Dinner. If we are to secure the THE LOST BOYS offer, we need to retain public approval and your presence at this fundraiser will do just that.

It would, I think, be helpful to organise a meeting with Holly for while you're in Shropshire. While the mother appeared satisfied with the arrangement*, a photo depicting you and Holly together, with her clearly comfortable in your company, might prove beneficial in the future. I'll get someone from legal to speak with the mother about that today. I assume you're happy for us to increase our offer if needs be?

If we proceed with The After Party, it would be on the condition that In The Event Of makes your unpaid involvement clear in all press material and that we have permission to use any footage of your performance in the doc. Whether Buddy Productions would want this footage is, of course, at their discretion, but as far as I'm concerned you returning to Hambledon Manor, AKA the "scene of the crime", could provide a key moment of vulnerability on your part and would remind viewers of your personal drive – not to mention eligibility – to front a documentary on the diminishing confidence of young men.

Best

Florian

* The legal department is sending the documentation today and payment will be made on return of signature

EVE

My feet are a rhythmic thud on the treadmill, my gaze fixed on the in-built TV. Susannah Reid and Richard Madeley deliver the news that a Romanian court has eased geographical restrictions placed upon Andrew Tate after he was charged with rape, human trafficking and founding a criminal gang to sexually exploit women. He can now move freely around Romania. I, meanwhile, am running inside on a conveyer belt in a dark sweaty gym.

'What the fuck?' I hit the red button, come to a jerky standstill and pull out my earpods. The woman on the bike next to me asks if I'm OK. 'No,' I say. 'I hate running machines. They're so boring. Screw this.' I grab my water. 'I'm going outside.'

The fresh air *is* better but, even now, by the river, I'm not exactly loving the repetitive plodding or the faint but persistent stab in my right knee. It's been there for years, almost every single time I run, a twinge that's mostly bearable but occasionally excruciating. I've always allowed myself to rest when the pain turns overwhelming but then I'm back on the road ASAP because... I drop to a walk, move to the edge of the path, where I force myself to be still. *Because what,*

Eve? It's that voice, the mean one who speaks mostly when I look in the mirror. *Because you're scared of what will happen if you stop?*

Am I really that basic? Despite all the body-positivity chat I've thrust upon my daughter, am I – a forty-five-year-old woman – really so terrified of fat?

Yes.

My answer is quick and simple and true.

By the time I return to the health club to shower and change, the pre-work rush-hour is over. Through the glass, I see a woman lifting a barbell loaded with giant weights. Her grimacing face is scarlet with the effort. Her muscles flex and bulge.

In a changing-room cubicle, I take out the Polaroid. It's silly, probably, but I'm too afraid to leave it anywhere, even at home. The Eve in the photo is like the Eve in every photo and every reflection I've ever known, posed to make herself smaller, stomach sucked right in. She has never not tried to look like something she isn't, no matter how young or how thin.

I slide the Polaroid into the zipped pocket of my bag and look instead at my phone, at Charlotte's nude model. She is striking for her confidence, beautiful for her take-me-as-you-find me, distinct from but as equally extraordinary as the woman lifting what must have been the equivalent of her own body weight in the gym.

411

'Good run?' Harry asks, his head jerks at the painter waiting in the kitchen. Our meeting was scheduled to start five minutes ago.

'Fine,' I say. 'But it was my last one.' His face crumples in confusion. 'I've booked in a PT session for weightlifting.' Fuck it, I told myself in the shower, I'm done with wanting to be skinny when what I *need* is to be strong.

Without any further discussion, I go to Martin, run through the paint schedule for the downstairs reception rooms and hall.

'Nah, you want it neutral, love, if you're doing it to sell. Have a look at this job I did a few weeks back.' Whatever photos he shows me are redundant, and not only because of the light from the large drawing-room window, which causes an obscuring glare on his screen. 'There,' he says, 'see'. He looks up, expectant, wanting gratitude for his uninvited "wisdom".

'This is what I want,' I say, surprised by how alien the words sound. 'Green Smoke for the walls, please.'

Martin shakes his head. 'And for the woodwork?'

'Like I said, Clunch.'

I'm anticipating a rebuttal but, 'Sure,' he makes a note of the colours on his pad. 'Cool.'

I'm finalising my order on the website when Harry appears. 'Eve?' He's tentative. 'Do you have time for a walk?'

Given the length of my to-do list, the answer should be *not really* but, beyond telling my husband I'd changed my mind about the re-do, last night we didn't really talk.

We're in the park before he says anything. 'You told Cass about Rock then?'

'Yeah.'

'About last Saturday or the stuff when you were a teen?'

I glance up briefly before looking again at the pavement. His shoulders are stiff, despite his best efforts to sound cool.

'Everything,' I say, then, 'I'm sorry. I should have spoken with you first. Are you OK with her knowing?'

'Knowing what? That I'm a cuckold?' For a moment, I think he's serious, but in Harry's voice, there's the hint of a smile. 'There are worse things I could be.'

I gesture at the coffee hut near the river. He nods, and we get in the queue. 'I don't think either of us has been at our best lately.'

Despite the fact we're no longer moving, Harry continues to look ahead, his eyes fixed on the bright yellow cap of the man in front of us. 'What do you think all this means,' he says, 'for us?' I have to lean closer to catch his whispers. 'I don't doubt Rock is a manipulator, Eve, but I can't help but wonder if part

413

of the reason you wanted *him* is because you no longer want *me*?'

A boat passes by on the water.

'I feel like I've lived my life like that.' I point at the rowers, their backs to the direction of travel. 'I don't know if I've ever really been in control of where I'm going.' The cox is shouting, steering, keeping the crew on route. 'I went from pleasing Dad to pleasing Luke. And then you, Harry.' I reach for his hand. 'And you didn't make demands of me like they did. You were so different but, trouble was, I was the same.'

The couple ahead of us moves up to place their order. She can't decide between ice cream or cake.

'I was so used to shaping myself into what others – men, society – wanted and expected of me, I didn't give what *I* truly wanted a second thought. You asked me to join your business, and I did. You asked me to move into your house, and I did. And I'm not saying either of those were bad or wrong decisions but, with hindsight, I don't know if those decisions were ever really mine. Or if I went along with them because I thought that's what would make you happy. And if you were happy, you would want me, so chances are, I would be happy too.'

'But you're not?' He rubs his finger across my thumb.

'Ice-cream,' the woman says. 'With a flake.' She turns, excited, to her partner. 'I don't think I've had a flake since I was fifteen!' She takes a bite, chocolate crumbles on her lips. 'How on earth did I forget how good they were?'

I look at my husband. 'When I was fifteen, I wanted to be a set designer, source all the props and furniture for TV and film.'

'I didn't know,' he says.

'Because I didn't tell you. I don't think I'm generally very good at saying what I want out loud.'

'Time to practice.'

I order one Americano, one milky tea.

We wait in silence for our drinks, thank the man for making them and begin our walk back to site.

'I *did* want to marry you,' I tell him.

'Good,' he says.

I think the problem is, though, what was more important – what drove everything – is that Harry wanted to marry me.

CASS

'What you've failed to realise, Olivia, is the upside of me having a sex tape released into the wild is I've sussed out all the best hiding places in school.' I prod the thigh of one her crossed legs with my trainer. 'And the cricket pavilion is a kind of obvious choice in this rain.'

'Busted.' Liv puts her hands in the air like some criminal on a cop show.

'Can I?' I point at her bag, and when she nods, shunt it along the slippery wood of the veranda with the back of my heel and sit down next to her. I tuck my knees to my chest. What had been drizzle is now a driving wet sheet. It's hard not to take the angle of its drive personally. 'I assume you checked the door isn't locked?'

Liv looks at me for the first time since I found her, like, *I'm not stupid*.

'Who is he then?'

She doesn't bother to ask *who*, but then nor does she bother to answer, just stares at the open pages of her textbook. The thin-paper corners are curling in the damp.

'In your message you called him "a companion", but I'm not even sure what that means?'

'Someone I spend time with.' Liv's utterly neutral. Utterly unruffled. She takes the pencil from where it was resting in the crack of the open spine and underlines a word.

'What kind of time?' What I'd seen in Ludlow was tame enough. A lunch, that's all. Though the way Liv leant her head against his shoulder suggested an intimacy that's lost its innocence now I know the shoulder didn't belong to her dad. And when I track back to the time I first saw Roger Mannering, when he was Money-Clip, there's that one specific line, sticky now like meat going bad.

Let's just say I have something especially sweet waiting at my hotel.

'I keep him company,' Liv says.

The wind whips through the veranda. I'd usually huddle into her, but Roger's twelve words expand into any gaps between us.

'How?' I'm quiet. Even so, my impatience howls louder than that wind.

'How do I keep him company?' Liv is a grown up weary of a child's incessant dim-witted questions. 'What are you asking me, Cass?'

'Did you meet him at the dinner last year?'

'Yes.' It's concise, but at least it's a solid answer.

'And then?'

'And then he offered to meet up after.'

'So, a 60-odd-year-old man asked you to meet up with him and you —'

'He's 54.' Like those six years make all the difference in the world.

'OK.' I refuse to let her pedantry rile me. 'So, a 54-year-old man asked you to meet up with him and you said yes because…'

She closes her book, slides the pencil into her coat pocket and shifts on her bum to face me. 'Because, Cass, I know exactly where I am with Roger. We have an understanding. An arrangement.' She points her toes, her legs at full stretch so they poke out beneath the canopy of the roof as if to prove a point that this *understanding*, this *arrangement*, makes her invulnerable to everything I'm exposed to. Including this fucking rain.

'And this *arrangement*, it involves money?'

'Yes,' she says. 'And experiences. Gifts.'

'Look at where you go to school.' I throw my arms up. The pavilion alone is the size of a four-bed house. 'It's not like you need the cash.'

'No, I don't *need* it.' She extends her fingers, twirls a jewel-studded ring. 'I *like* it.'

I drop my head, try to hide the disgust brewing on my face behind my hair.

'What?' Liv dips her own head, her eyes determined to catch hold of mine. 'That bothers you? It would

418

be more palatable, would it, if I was doing it because I had no choice?'

We sit in a silence that isn't really silence because of all the heavy weather and the kids in the distance with their lunchbreak screams for the ball.

'This is a positive choice for me, Cass.'

I'd like to believe her, but there's what Mum told me about when *she* was eighteen. With Luke. 'I'm worried about you.'

'Why?' Her laugh is quiet but telling. My reaction, she thinks, is predictable. Prudish. Naïve. 'I'm more in control with Roger than I have been on any other date I've been on. We both know exactly what we're getting out of it. That's more than you did with George.'

Ouch. 'But the money.'

'What about the money? Maya went for a drink with a guy who asked her to refund the £4.50 he'd spent on a coffee when she said she didn't want to see him again. If a man doesn't pay for my aunt's dinner on a first date, then he's...' Liv makes a slicing motion with her hand across her neck to suggest he gets the chop. 'There's always money, Cass. Think about your mum and dad and that proposal story they've told us, like, a hundred times. You don't seriously believe his house and his business and his job offer didn't play at least some part in him sealing their *romantic* deal?'

'That's different.' I swallow. There's a roaring separate from the wind in my ears.

'Why? Because they love each other?'

'Yes.'

'And how's that going for them?'

She might not know the very latest, but she knows enough. In normal circumstances I'd tell Liv, *well, actually, now you ask, it's going to absolute shit. Everything that stems from that gala dinner is a thermonuclear bomb.* Mum may now be all for the After Party but, with the silence at dinner last night and breakfast this morning, I don't know if she's all for Dad.

'And I hate to, you know, rub salt in the wound, but weren't you and George in love too?' Liv shrugs, like, *you see what I'm getting at*, and my stomach cramps like thunder. 'If Roger wanted to film me, we would have a conversation about that like we do about everything else.'

'What, to discuss your terms?'

'You spit it like an insult, babe, but yeah. We discuss my terms.'

Again, that story of my teenage Mum. 'You sound like you're OK with it now, but how will you feel about it in the future?'

She glances upwards, and her eyes reflect the dark of the sky. 'Maybe I'll be glad I tried it but wish I hadn't got caught.' There's a hint of a smile. Long strands of her hair catch in the wooden slats on the pavilion wall when she rolls her head to the side to look at me. 'You know, a bit like you might feel about anal.'

I am made of a thrumming heart pumping shame-drenched blood, but I don't bite. 'What would your mum say?'

'If you're trying to humiliate me into giving it up, it won't work.' She lifts her water bottle to her lips, sips like everything about this is one hundred per cent normal. 'Mum's not stupid. She noticed the manicures, the jewellery, the nights away.'

'And?'

'*And* at first she was a little…' Liv eyes my hands, which are turning aubergine purple with the cold. 'Upset,' she says. 'But she'd been with Dad for years without loving him. Understood how it works. The convenience, you know, of a relationship with a man with money. *And*,' she repeats, 'She knows I'm a bright young woman who will have thought about what I'm doing. *And* she trusts me to do what I think is right and comfortable for me. For *me*, Cass.' She reaches out and rubs my fingers the way she does sometimes when it's proper frosty in winter. 'I get this wouldn't be for everyone, and other women aren't doing it out of choice, but *I* am. *I* feel empowered. Like *I* am the one in control.'

With the shit show of my life right now, I get the appeal of control, but...

The bell for lessons rings in the distance. Liv gathers her things.

'Does he have other girls like you?'

'*Like you*,' she mimics, perfectly catching the judgement I thought I'd quashed.

'I'm sorry,' I say, and I *am* sorry, which means I should leave it there, but, 'Is this why you've not really wanted to get involved? With the After Party. Because you don't think those men did anything wrong?'

'When have I ever said that?' She's standing before I am, bigger now than she looked in that photo I took of her and Roger. 'Those men think they're entitled to get it for free or to take without asking. Of course, I think they're wrong. They're shitbags, and you should go ahead and do whatever you need or want to do, babe. I just can't be there when it kicks off.'

'Why?'

'Because Roger is friends with some of them, and I don't want to compromise my arrangement. I'll help with the planning though.'

I too am on my feet now. I just wish I felt steadier. Wish I felt with Liv like I've always felt with her in the past. Like I know her, *get* her. And ditto. Like she really has my back.

EVE

There are ten men. The majority thrilled with both "the girls" and themselves for being chosen. I've heard them. Their slightly hushed tones when they pause one of the three waitresses in her tracks to take a canapé, yes, but to say too what an honour it is to be here. A delight. Their eyes are only briefly on the platter of smoked-salmon-and-dill blinis. And once they've popped the treat onto their thick pink tongues, their hand is free again. To touch a shoulder. To rest, briefly, in the small of a back.

I think of Boomer on my walk with Charlotte this morning. Cocking his leg. Scent marking lampposts and gates.

'Gentlemen,' I say, inviting them to take their seats at the large round table. Rhi, Maya and Lily circle, graciously pulling out the chairs.

We ummed and ahhed about whether Rhi should start the evening. If we were risking Bryan recognising her and questioning why she would be here after her official complaint in 2019. Rhi – rightly it seems – was sure Cass and I were over estimating Bryan's ability – or inclination – to differentiate one Black woman from another.

'Anyway,' she'd said, 'I was wearing a wig that night. I'd bet you all the money he threw at our shitty situation he won't have a clue who I am with my natural hair.'

My own role tonight also felt precarious. Speaking in front an audience is one thing, but when *he* is in it. And with Harry there too.

'Just pretend you're Aunt Sophie,' Cass suggested at breakfast, guessing – correctly – the reason I was pushing the yoghurt-soggy clumps of granola around my bowl was nerves.

Harry nodded. 'If you could harness just a smidge of that woman's gall!'

Mum, who's been staying with us since news broke of Stump's involvement with the video, cast a disapproving stare. While willing to believe her husband culpable of collusion, she's not ready to think her eldest daughter is in any way to blame.

'Welcome,' I say now to the diners. Two of them look up at me. The other eight – Rock included – continue to talk among themselves. I allow my gaze to drift over their heads towards the gold-framed mirror on the wall opposite, where I see myself as they would see me, if they only bothered to look. A few weeks ago, this would have irked. Now though, I wonder if this invisibility may well be a superpower. If older women might wreak unseen havoc as men's attention is inevitably drawn elsewhere.

When Maya, Rhi and Lily come to stand next to me, I begin.

'I would like to reiterate our gratitude for your support this evening. Your willingness to attend at short notice is greatly appreciated, as is your generosity in agreeing to pay a not insignificant sum for your place at this very unique table.'

Their teeth are bared as they grin, less at me, more at each other. At their shared sense of being men who do the right thing.

I press the button on the remote clenched in my palm to begin the slide show on the large screen behind me. A carousel of images from galas of years gone by. Close-ups of smiling mouths, raised arms and clapping hands as the diners drink and bid and cheer their own good will.

'We are particularly indebted to Freddie White – manager here at Hambledon Manor – for the complementary use of this beautiful room.' He laps up the compliments about the grand hotel that scatter gun from around the table.

'Enormous thanks too to Luke Rock and Lionel Morgan.' His name rolled more easily from my tongue than I'd expected. Adrenaline, for once, on my side. 'It's down to Mr Rock's offer to waive his appearance fee and Mr Morgan paying for tonight's food and drink that we're able to donate all your other contributions, in their entirety, to our nominated charity, Shrewsbury Refuge Services.' I tip my head in a sign of reverence the politician especially appears to enjoy.

Bryan slaps our MP on the back. The other men offer a hefty round of applause.

Rock takes a seated bow.

'Good man,' someone says. 'Splendid.'

'Should you be interested in learning about this organisation's invaluable work in supporting women who experience violence, there's plenty of information about that and other associated stories in the pamphlet on your tabl—'

'Well, hello!' It's Bryan, whose head has been turned by the arrival of another two waitresses, dressed – like Maya, Rhi and Lily – in the same low-buttoned white shirts and short black skirts the all-female staff have worn at every preceding gala. Clocking their trays are laden with twenty glasses of pastis, Bryan beckons the girls over. 'It would rude not to tuck in.' He takes a pair of drinks. 'Two to one,' he says. 'Same ratio as us to the waitresses now, chaps.'

'Spit roast, is it, for the main?' Rock's voice is pure showman. He swigs from the bottle of Evian he's kept tucked out of the way on the floor.

As she hands an aperitif to his immediate neighbour, I watch the youngest man at the table take a sly photograph of Maya's arse.

'Hey.' My interjection is instinctive and loud and premature because Maya hasn't reacted.

'We need a sign,' Cass said a couple of days ago in the sitting room at ours. It was hot and strained by the twenty-three bodies willing to go only so far to prove a point. 'I realise we want the night to feel authentic until we reveal our actual purpose for being there, but what if one of them...' It didn't matter that my daughter failed to finish her sentence, we all knew how that and the night might end. My skin burnt as I watched Harry's resolve melt into the truth that our plan was at best mad at worst dangerous. Perhaps Cass saw it too for she stood quickly before conviction could seep from the room. 'We'll all be together,' she reiterated. 'They can't really do anything. A sign would be a precaution that's all.' She double tapped a clenched fist twice against her head.

If the mood hadn't been so tense, I would have laughed. Mum had shown that very sign to Cass and me that morning when she'd baulked at an Amazon link Maya had sent Cass. It was for a scrunchie. But this was no ordinary hair accessory, rather it doubled as a cover to place over a glass to prevent anyone from spiking your drink in a bar.

'You'll need a bloody rucksack for all your protective gear just to go out dancing.' Mum was scrolling through RightMove, 'I'm not saying it was better in my day, but at least we could see what the men were up to. My friend Babs and I, we had none of this fancy modern stuff. Just good old British Sign Language learnt from her deaf sister. A so-called gentleman got silly and we'd —' Just like Cass had demonstrated, Mum banged a fist twice against her temple. 'Means "idiot,"' she said. 'No matter how much fun the other of us was having, how nice the other companion might have been, we'd leave.'

Decades – centuries, even – of women's plans to escape men lie behind us.

Bryan, oblivious to the younger man's camera, looks up at me, at my admonishing, 'Hey.'

His palm slides from the curve of Maya's buttock. 'Oh, cry me a river,' he mutters, making a show of pulling a hanky from his top pocket and tossing it at me. 'It was only a hand.'

I draw on years of good manners and smile.

CASS

'He's taken photos,' Mum says. 'I'm not sure how many, but it's worth checking.' The back of her hand dabs at her brow. The warmth in this prep room has been ramping up with the girls coming in and going out again, humming with whispered confirmations that the men are mostly as expected. "Normal" conversations about frustrating golf, plunging stocks and flashy vehicles are punctured with occasional comments and wandering eyes.

Maya nods at my phone. 'You've got a message, Cass.'

'Well?' Mum asks.

I open WhatsApp. 'The angles aren't ideal, but they're good.' I hold it up so she and Maya can see. Two pictures. At a glance, the first is innocuous, the shot largely obscured by a doorframe, but beyond that is Bryan's colleague, David Hargreaves. Smart. Handsome. Focused. Follow his gaze, and it's clear where it lands. Right on Rhi's chest. It's not incriminating. But it does say something. Enough, I think, in context, to prove my point. The second is mostly tablecloth, but to the side of that is Bryan's hand, cupped and pressed against black fabric, which is clearly on a woman's arse.

'You alright, Maya?'

My friend's eyes gleam with loathing. 'Honestly.' Her tone is sober. Cold. 'I'm really glad I'm here.'

'Should we tell him to stop there?' I ask. 'Not Bryan,' I clarify. 'George.'

Persuading my ex-boyfriend to come had been easier than expected.

'I think you need men on the ground,' Dad had said. 'Allies. And not because you can't handle yourselves. There'll be enough of you for that. But when it comes to it, crap as it sounds, they're more likely to listen if other men back you up, confirm what you're telling them is true.'

When I asked him to meet for a coffee, I'd warned George Dad would be coming too. I didn't want him turning up, clocking a wronged father and thinking it was some kind of ambush.

After I explained what we were doing, it was George who suggested he take photos. 'I get it's kind of funny,' he said. 'Me and my camera.' His face was as overcast as the morning. 'But we've seen the power of pictures, right? How quickly they spread.'

'We could do with a few more,' Maya says now, watching me forward the images to my laptop and adding them, then, to the rolling Powerpoint of photos on display in the dining room. 'There'll be more of us to distract them now.' The clock on the computer reads 20:14. 'It's time for the main.'

430

'You two twins?' Freddie White calls when Maya and Rhi, with their plates of meat and two veg, enter side by side.

The men are outnumbered. We are up to fifteen now.

'You girls multiplying out there?' One of the men quips, and the diners' necks twist to take in all the waitresses.

'I'd like to watch Attenborough's special on *that*.' Morgan's lips are dappled purple after a greedy swig of wine.

Dinner is served. Men are eating. Another five girls come into the room, and the twenty of us form a circle around the table. Mum taps a glass.

'Cassandra here would like to have a word.'

The diners are bemused.

Each of us places a hand on a man's shoulder.

'What is this?' Bryan smirks. '*The Traitors?*'

Aside from Harry and George, only two of the diners appear nervous. The others are all raised eyebrows and winks. You can almost hear the swallowed 'oi oi's'.

Bryan shifts forward away from Rhi's and another girl Stella's grasp.

'It's only a hand.' Mum's voice is the bruised and quieter side of angry. She reaches out, a reassuring touch on my elbow before she leaves the room.

The men who've heard her sit up a little in their chairs.

'I wanted to thank you again for coming.' When I start talking, there's a flash of something like recognition on Bryan's face. He looks to my dad, who, already leading by example, has his eyes fixed firmly on me. As promised, he's listening. 'The reasons we are gathered here this evening are important to me personally. I wonder if any of you has taken the opportunity to read the literature mentioned earlier?' I gesture at the pamphlet, still resting, untouched, against the simple hessian-wrapped thyme centrepiece.

'We've given rooms, money, time. Job done.' Freddie White says. 'You don't honestly expect us to read too.'

A jovial chorus of hear-hears.

I inhale, grateful for Maya's arm around my waist, for the defiant lift of her chin.

Dad reaches across the table for the booklet we've been compiling over the last week or so and passes it to me.

'Of course,' I smile at Freddie. 'I can read it for you. Anything to make your lives easier.'

'Don't I know you?' he says, and before he has time to place me as the young woman at Dad's retirement party, I begin.

YOU

You're a confident man, Harry. Not loud, necessarily, but in your day-to-day, you're well versed in telling people – men mostly – what you need them to do. On site, you insist everyone abides by the rules. Identifying risks. Protective helmets. Unobstructed paths to safety in case of emergency. You have a voice and, to keep things running smoothly, you use it.

Here, though.

Something about *them*, the attention-grabbing funny boys, compresses your easy sense of authority. Your gumption as mangled as the fatty bits of steak Freddie White yanked from his mouth in the main course.

"Admire" isn't a big or strong enough word to define how you feel about your daughter, who is standing before them, summoning the moxie you too will need to muster to tell them what's what.

'All the women here have put a lot of thought into this,' Cass says. 'We were prepared to get personal for the sake of something bigger.'

You've never been so aware of your heart. Of its raw function. Its hollow centre filling with viscid fear.

'I hope you'll think carefully about we're asking of you.'

Your eyes remain on Cass, but it's impossible not to see Lionel Morgan lean on the two back legs of his chair, arms folded in sweet satisfaction. 'Prepared to get personal, eh? I heard there might be an auction,' he says. 'But I didn't think the lots would be quite so attractive.' His voice has an excited wobble that was absent when he spoke last night on BBC Radio Shropshire, reassuring the audience he will 'support the highest penalty for those found guilty of writing or sharing abhorrent views about minority groups. *And*,' he added, 'I will do my utmost to eke out the lone miscreants from the force.'

Cass refuses to let Morgan's comment shake her. If anything, she appears bolstered by its timing. 'In this book – and we have a copy for each of you – are twenty lists, one from each of the waitresses working this evening. These lists are a compilation of our experiences at the Shropshire Business Men's Dinner and beyond. We're not here to deny the enormous sums of money raised for important char- ities, but we *are* here to make you aware of the toll these nights have taken on the women who've served at them.'

You listened as she rehearsed, a formality to her words she hoped will give her gravitas.

Like the other men, you follow her finger as it points to the big screen, controlled by Eve, who's backstage now. There's a montage of the pictures taken tonight on George's phone.

'Jesus. Anyone else see where this is going?' Luke Rock closes his eyes as if willing Cass and her friends to disappear.

You wonder if it's time, Harry, for you to step in, but before Rock has a chance to elaborate, Cass invites Rhi to speak.

'I was assaulted.' She looks straight ahead, eyes unveering from the women standing opposite. You'd heard them talk about the importance of strength in their number. 'In 2019,' she says. 'At the after party, though it began before that really. At the main event when men seemed to think it was OK to touch me without my consent. To—'

'Seriously?' Rock is on his feet. 'You saw my show the last time we were here, gents. I made it very clear then what I believe needs doing to *woman*splaining drivel like this.' He snatches the A5 booklet from Cass and mimes an explosion.

You open your mouth, but, 'Leave, then.' Cass says. 'This is an invitation, Mr Rock. Unlike what some of us here have been subjected to, no one is forcing you to stay.' She breaks the circle only to show him the door. The comedian is gone, but she continues to hold it open. 'You're free to leave any time,' she tells the others. Morgan shifts in his seat. 'You're all good men though, aren't you? And good men listen to women. Rest assured, if anyone asks us about this event later, that's what we'll say.'

No one else moves.

Returning to position, Cass makes a show of unbuttoning the cuffs of her shirt, rolling up both of her sleeves.

In your throat, your glottis swells.

Your daughter is ready to fight. 'Anyone else have anything they'd like to add?'

The men, including you, are quiet.

'Can you continue then, please, Rhi. I think these gentlemen are ready to hear your story.'

'Hold on a minute.' It's Freddie White. 'I *do* know you.' His lips are a thin smug smile.

Cass nods. 'From my grandfather's retirement party. We could chat about that too if you—'

'Maybe,' White sneers. 'But it's not the party I was thinking of. Your tattoo's the giveaway.' He pulls out his phone. 'This little presentation is all very interesting, but I'm not sure you're the best person to be stood here preaching to us about what is and *isn't* decent behaviour when we know you're perfectly happy doing this.' He doesn't need to hold up the screen for you to know what's coming, Harry. 'This *is* you, isn't it?'

Your hands are a hard sharp slap on the table.

There is movement by the door. Eve. Has she heard what's happening? Come to persuade you from committing murder?

But if not to protect, what is the job of an ally? Of a father? Of a man?

'Don't, Dad.' Cass says, calmer than you can ever imagine being because, despite always having declared yourself a pacifist, you are wondering how it would feel to squeeze this man's neck so tight there is no hope for him of air.

EVE

I'm supposed to stay in the prep room. There are headlines, reddit threads, Instagram posts in a second slide show I'm due to load when I get the sign.

But something, mother's intuition maybe, draws me to the dining room, where *that* man, Freddie White, is playing *that* video on his phone.

I go to speak. Only this time it's not good manners stopping me calling out Freddie White but thick lava'd fury that scrambles my blood and brain. Harry was so confident in the power of speech, but I can't summon it, and even if I could...

Deeds not words, Cass spat that night I let her down.

Charlotte was right, our girls really are the generation that'll get things done.

But that doesn't mean I shouldn't do my bit too.

I grab Rock's Evian bottle and trust the women *and* men I respect to do what's needed in this room.

'I think it's *White* – not his hotel – that needs a renovation,' Cass said earlier after he'd insisted on taking us to his office so we might quickly run through my proposed scheme.

'I wasn't sure at first,' he'd said as he commandeered us through a door across a small courtyard from the main hall into the decrepit old coach house currently serving as his workspace and general storeroom. 'But you're actually rather impressive, Eve. If you're still interested in the office refurbishment job, tonight's a good opportunity to show me what you're made of.'

'You have no idea what we're made of,' Cass whispered so only I could hear.

On his desk now are the A3 printed versions of everything I thought White's office needed to make this room comfortable, but I'm done with prioritising the comfort of men like him.

In the days and nights of planning this evening's gathering, we'd talked about what we wanted. And though it was, of course, ironic, part of me was sorry Sophie wasn't there. Because in those messy chambers of your brain where memories linger, I could see and hear my sister and me in my bedroom when we were seventeen. Before Rock convinced me Alanis wasn't my type. *All I Really Want* we screamed at the tops of our voices was common ground.

In the lead up to the After Party, a common ground between us and the diners had felt possible.

But Luke Rock's premature departure and Freddie White's pompous nerve have proven they're incapable of listening.

Now, like Alanis at the end of her tether, what I want above everything else is justice.

From Rock's bottle, I pour liquid across the desk and on the scraps of ancient carpet covering parts of the otherwise bare floor. I could be wrong; my ex may well be the reformed character he peddles on his channel. Licking my finger though, it's obvious, this man makes a lie of everything, even water.

In my bag is one of the lighters I confiscated when I feared Cass hadn't fully given up on the idea of an inferno. I run my thumb across the spark wheel and growl, 'Enough.'

But the tiny action bears no flame.

Like a trick, I pull Bryan's handkerchief from inside my sleeve. Just like my father taught me all those years ago, I turn the lighter's thumbwheel and watch the flecks of flint fall to the hanky below, twisting it then, into a highly flammable ball.

Life doesn't drop to slow motion when I put the flame to the Polaroid I'm still carrying with me. Rather it escalates. I drop the blazing picture to the desk, where my best laid plans immediately burn too.

'Shout fire not rape,' I whisper.

Shoulders back, wings spread and with the heat increasing in the now fervent fire behind me, I don't walk from Freddie White's office, I soar.

CASS

'This is *you*, isn't it?' White's self-satisfaction oozes from between his lips. He fake smiles and holds up his phone.

A meaty smack of palms against the table.

'Don't Dad.' I try so hard to be cool, but the words are hot in my mouth because I get it, his thunderclap reaction to me on that screen.

White is too far from me for clarity, but I know the minutiae of that film by now so when I hear that first long groan, I feel its rhythm and see the flesh and the hair and that tattoo.

That stupid tattoo.

'Wear one,' Dad said when he made me a wreath of bluebells all those years ago, 'And you'll only speak the truth.'

A red visceral part of me wants to scrub my skin clean of it, so I can lie. So I can tell White *no, that's not me* with such conviction that he and everyone else stops watching, and the thistles of worry that live in my guts now will soften to mush.

'*Dad*? You're her *dad*?' White, dripping in faux sympathy, looks across the room at my father, presses the phone into the space between them at the same point as video-George asks me if I like it.

'Yes,' video-me moans into the present silence.

White's laugh is a snigger with teeth. 'You must be so proud.' This statement is a rough shove into a wall.

I close my eyes. Wish I could close my ears too, but...

'Honestly,' Dad says. 'I couldn't be prouder.'

His voice carries a different volume, a different intention to that reactive smack of his hands. It's slow and deliberate and removes the oxygen from White's incendiary attempt to shame.

What was teetering steadies. And if that old man comes at me again, I know *my* voice is just as strong. Stronger even, because all these women around me and my dad and my ex, who is standing now, his own mobile held at arm's reach in White's direction, every one of them has my back.

'Yes,' I say to White. 'That *is* me. And I'd like you to stop playing it, please; I never consented to being filmed.'

I follow White's lazy gaze around the table. Like him, I'm expecting sly grins and dirty jeers, but the other men's heads are mostly hung. Disgusted, I think. By White. Or by themselves. Maybe I'm deluded by camaraderie and adrenaline, but despite White's best efforts, I don't think they're disgusted by me.

In the circle, without speaking, we women make clenched fists of our paired hands.

'Go on,' I say to Rhi, who continues from where she was cut off a few minutes ago. Louder, this time, to diminish the sound still emanating from White's phone.

'Some of you know the details,' she says. 'Some of you were there when it happened. Right here, in this hotel.'

Bry makes to stand, but George puts a hand on his shoulder. The diner to Bry's right does the same. Under only a little pressure, he sits back down. 'This is an exaggeration,' he says. 'We had some fun that night. You're talking like it was rape.'

Freddie White is made of spread legs and folded arms at his side of the table. His head tilts back, exaggerates the width of his jaw. 'Bry's right,' he says, but whatever attention he had is ruptured by the rush of feet and a scream of 'FIRE!' and the start of a long weaving alarm.

'What?' White is the loudest. The fastest to the door, where Mum is urging him and everyone else to get outside.

Confident the room is empty, she comes behind me, the tail end of what should be, if we followed instruction, an ordered evacuation. But there are too many jostling elbows and shunting shoulders to form a line. Too much charging forward for anyone but Mum to even think about looking back.

She scans the crowd gathering on the lawn. Our party is mostly divided in two. 'Any idea where Rock went?'

Her question can't compete with fire.

The coach house is small in stature but huge in light and frenzy. One of its two windows glows scarlet and amber, smoke pouring like gravity-defying liquid from the cracks around its door.

'Everyone back!' It's Patrick. Fluorescent yellow bib and megaphone. 'The fire service is on its way.'

Guests are talking in panicked breaths into their phones, or else attempting to hold them steady, zoomed in on all that red-hot danger. Screams then, as the full moon, whole and silver, is splintered by flames punching through the tiles, determined to ravage the sky.

Sirens in the distance. Blue lights at the end of the drive.

'Did *we* do this?' I ask. I don't know how or why it would be possible, but there was momentus power in that room.

I'm expecting 'don't be silly' or 'of course not' or a short and simple 'no', but Mum is open-mouthed, words sucked out of her by the roar we've felt inside us that's now raging and real and loud.

'Get back!' Patrick calls through the megaphone.

Ignoring him, Mum takes one, two, three, four steps forward. 'The store-room window,' she shouts.

'Shit.' Her head is a spinning top the way it desperately looks around. 'There's someone there.' She runs towards the searing heat.

I am stuck still. Only my eyes move. In the backroom window, there's the harsh white flashlight of a phone, which suddenly swings up and away. Glass flies. Wood snaps. The frame splits and protrudes like broken bones.

Through the hole comes a foot, a calf, a thigh.

A body bent double, and a hand clutching a high-heeled shoe.

I *know* that shoe. And it's almost funny, this fairy-tale thought that stabs at me, but I *know* that shoe. Like Cinderella, I ditched it so I could run away.

'Sophie?' It's not only me but Mum too calling her sister's name.

My aunt, upright now, is in a rainbow: moon white, fire orange and fire-engine blue. She is barefoot and limping, madly pointing at the coach house from which she's come.

'What?' Mum asks her.

But Sophie's voice is gone. Stolen, maybe, by smoke. She continues to a jab a finger toward the burning building.

'Is there someone still in there?'

Sophie nods. Her silk blouse is gaping. Crimson spatters on her neck, chest and cream lace bra.

Two fire-fighters run to the coach house, where a figure is waving blindly at the gap in the window, unable to force themselves through.

Mum wraps her arms around her sister. 'I'm sorry, I'm sorry, I'm sorry.'

But Sophie refuses to sink into them, 'He can't…' she croaks. 'I…'

The firemen lift a man through the window to safety.

It's only when they're far from the building and lay him flat on the grass before us that we can see his face. Or part of it.

'Rock?' Mum asks because it's not immediately clear. A stiletto protrudes from his eye. Its soul is the same red as the blood seeping from his socket. 'Sophie,' Mum whispers. Gags. 'Is that your other shoe?'

SOPHIE CLAIRE CAMPBELL

PART 2 OF RECORDED INTERVIEW

Date:- 23/10/2023
Duration:- 23 minutes
Location:- Shrewsbury Police Station, Clive Road, Monkmoor Road, Shrewsbury SY2 5RW
No. of Pages:-

Conducted by Officers from West Mercia

POLICE   You say weren't supposed to be in the country on 22nd October?

SC   No, I was on retreat. In Mallorca. But a friend of mine had become increasingly concerned about an event being organised by my niece.

POLICE   Can you confirm your niece's name, please, Sophie?

SC   Cass Gunn. Cassandra Gunn.

POLICE   Go on.

SC   Cass was organising a small party for my company In the Event Of and I felt compelled to return.

POLICE   Could you tell me which friend was talking to you about this party?

447

SC   Roger Mannering. He's a director at the estate agents Weston & Mayfair. He'd been invited but an associate of his had advised him against going. She'd said the organisers were planning some kind of protest.

POLICE   What kind of protest?

SC   Roger didn't have the details, but this associate thought—

POLICE   And who was his associate?

SC   He didn't tell me. She just thought it would best if he wasn't there. That it might not be good for his reputation.

POLICE   In what way would it not be good for his reputation?

SC   There have been some questions around the safety of the waitresses at the Shropshire Business Men's Dinner. It's an annual event. I've been hosting it for eight, no, nine years. There was an incident at this year's gala, I'm sure you're aware, a young man entered the building with a knife, which, as you can imagine, was terrifying. It got people talking about the dinner online and some of the women who'd previously waitressed for me alluded to inappropriate behaviour.

POLICE   Who was behaving inappropriately? You?

SC   No. Well. The comments – on social media – were mostly about the guests. The men. That they could get...

POLICE   They could get?

SC   I thought we were talking about last night.

POLICE   And we are. We're just trying to build a bigger picture. We'll come back to that. Let's return to your decision to end your retreat early and attend the after party yourself. What were you hoping to achieve?

SC   I was worried.

POLICE   About the attendees?

SC   Yes and, if I'm honest, about my company. My reputation.

POLICE   OK. And what did you intend to do when you arrived?

SC   I wanted to be there at the beginning, but my flight was delayed so by the time I arrived home and changed, I wasn't able to get to Hambledon Manor until gone nine.

POLICE   And the shoes – Louboutin, size 39 – very high heels. They formed part of this outfit change?

SC   Yes. It seemed important to look professional.

POLICE   Go on. What happened when you got to the hotel?

SC   I knew from the invite Roger had forwarded that it was in the Boudica room so I was heading there but as I walked past the hotel manager's office and into the main building, I ran into Luke Rock. He was coming out of the Elizabeth room.

POLICE   And what kind of event would you usually host in the Elizabeth room?

SC   I don't. Use that room, I mean. Not normally anyway. It's such a small space, it only sits four, five.

POLICE   And was it in use for last night's event?

SC   I'm not sure.

POLICE   I see. Tell me then, what is your relationship with Luke Rock?

SC   It's a business relationship. We know each other from the September dinner, where he did an after-dinner speech.

POLICE   And you liked him, didn't you? There's an article in the *Sun* in which you're quoted as saying *We need more men like Luke Rock. Men who are prepared to put themselves on the line to protect women.*

SC   I did say that, yes, but I was talking specifically about his actions on the night of the knife-attack. He and my brother-in-law, Harry, had restrained the intruder. I was so grateful to them both. To think what could have happened.

POLICE   So prior to the after party, you had no concerns about Rock's conduct?

POLICE   Can you answer the question, please?

SC   There was something.

POLICE   Go on.

SC   I've had some communication from Rock's legal team about one of my waitresses. Holly Garner. They asked if I'd witnessed any inappropriate interactions between the two of them at the September dinner.

POLICE   And had you?

SC   I was on a call during some of his performance.

POLICE   And, in your absence, who was in charge?

SC   Helena Brown. My assistant.

POLICE   And did you speak with her about Rock and Garner?

POLICE   Sophie? Did you speak with Helena Brown about Rock and Garner?

SC   Yes.

POLICE   And?

SC   Helena confirmed Rock had made reference to Holly during his performance. A joke about her bush. He had her number on a serviette apparently. I know nothing else other than Holly was seen crying in the girls' dressing room.

POLICE   And did you, as director of In the Event Of, make any effort to speak with Holly yourself?

SC   I was dealing with the fallout from the knife attack and then preparing, among other things for my father's party, and then I was on retreat.

POLICE   Is that a no then, Sophie?

SC   I intended to call her when I got back from Mallorca, but I had a second email from Rock's legal team telling me the matter had been sorted.

POLICE   And what do you think they meant by sorted?

SC   I assumed she'd withdrawn the claims.

POLICE   So what happened when you ran into Mr Rock outside the after party?

SC   He was ranting. Drinking. He had a bottle of Evian. I always ask the hotel staff to leave four of them in the green room. I assumed he'd got it from there, that it was water, but the way he was slurring his words made me wonder if it was alcohol. He was saying he'd been duped and the world was dominated by 'snowflake femi-nazis'. He was swearing and loud and there were people arriving at the hotel and I didn't want him attracting attention so I suggested we go into Freddie White's office.

POLICE   To clarify, it was you who instigated going somewhere more private.

SC   Yes.

POLICE   And what happened when you went inside?

SC   He had a booklet. Something the girls had printed apparently.

POLICE   The girls?

SC   The waitresses at the after party. They'd each written a list of incidents at previous events.

POLICE   And what kind of incidents?

SC   I didn't have chance to read the whole thing.

POLICE   But what you did read?

SC   Comments from the men.

POLICE   What kind of comments.

SC   Lewd. Sexual.

POLICE   And anything else?

SC   There was some physical stuff too.

POLICE   Can you explain what you mean by physical stuff, please, Sophie?

SC   As I say, I only had chance to read a couple of items on one of the lists.

POLICE   And what were those couple of items?

SC   One of the girls said she'd been pinned to a sofa. One of the men had forced himself upon her.

POLICE   And were you aware of this incident? Prior to reading about it in this booklet?

POLICE   Sophie?

SC   Yes.

POLICE   Can you tell me about that, please?

SC   One of my waitresses, Rhi Makawa, after the 2019 dinner, she contacted me the following day to tell me she'd been assaulted.

POLICE   And what did you do?

SC   I said I'd speak with the man in question, which I did, and he'd said the interaction was consensual. That Rhi had smiled and thanked him for his healthy tip.

POLICE   Did you speak with the police, or encourage Rhi to do so?

SC   Rhi said she was going to so, yes, I also spoke with the police but it was more of a chat really. Informal.

POLICE   Informal?

SC   Inspector Joe Saint is a family friend. My godfather. I spoke with him and

POLICE   And?

SC   He said he'd sort it.

POLICE   Sort it how?

SC   Fuck it. Sorry. I wasn't sure how much to tell you but fuck it. I'm going to end up in all kinds of shit, aren't I?

POLICE   Are you?

SC   Joe and I had an arrangement. He would handle these kinds of situations and I would give him cash.

POLICE   He would handle them? Handle them how?

SC   If girls came into the station to report anything from the galas, Joe would, well, I don't know what exactly he would do, but let's just say nothing ever progressed.

POLICE   OK. As you can imagine, we'll need to come back to this. But the night of the after party. Rock's shown you the list. What happened then?

SC   I was pissed off.

POLICE   With Mr Rock?

SC   No, with my niece. My sister. My staff. Cass and Eve had been messaging me about their plans. And because I'd sworn to the retreat's spiritual leader that I wouldn't work while I was there, I'd not been involved. I was grateful, even, to them for doing me what I thought was a favour. They'd pitched the after party as a way to raise more money for the charities and to help In the Event Of's reputation.

POLICE   But the booklet. That wasn't in your favour?

SC   By its very existence, the booklet suggested I was negligent.

POLICE   Did you express this irritation to Mr Rock?

SC   What I think I said was that the girls were jumping on a bandwagon. That it was all blown grossly out of proportion and I would ensure the booklet wasn't disseminated any further.

POLICE   I see. And was Rock satisfied with this response?

SC   Sorry, I shouldn't laugh. None of this is funny. But of course he was bloody satisfied. Said he'd finally found a woman who understands men "unlike those bitches in the other room".

POLICE   Thank you. And then?

SC   And then...And then he came closer, put his drink on the desk and took the booklet from me, slid it back into his pocket and put a hand on my shoulder. Said it was a shame to let his trip go entirely to waste. I tried to move away but he was pinching the sleeve of my blouse and was clearly looking at my cleavage and smiling and he asked if anyone had ever snorted coke off my breasts. I laughed and told him no and he said he was surprised because, and again I'm quoting, "they look ripe for it". And would I be up trying it tonight.

POLICE   I understand what's happened is upsetting, Sophie. Would you like to take a short break?

SC   No. I just want this done before I change my mind. When I said no, he said he was disappointed, said he thought he'd found a kindred spirit and his hand moved from the sleeve of my blouse, along its trim to the top button.

POLICE   Did you ask him to stop?

SC   No.

POLICE   So you were happy for him to do this?

SC   No but ...It's not like I don't see the irony.

POLICE   The irony?

SC   I froze, OK? He's...He's...Important is the wrong word. And he's a big man. Tall I mean. Broad. And...sorry, I'm not explaining this very well. It's not as simple as it seems. His hands were on me and I couldn't think straight but then I thought I saw someone outside. I told him this, thinking it would make him stop but he looked at the door, the internal one, and said he thought maybe we should go somewhere we were less likely to be disturbed. I said I thought it would be better if I went to the after party to sort the situation but he said we should have an after party of our own and again I said something about leaving but his hands were on me and he was leading me to that other door.

POLICE   And you went with him?

SC   Yes, but

POLICE   Did you want to go with him?

SC   No. I've told you, I said I should go the party.

POLICE   And the external door, the one to the courtyard, that wasn't locked?

SC   No, but his hands were on me.

POLICE   Was he holding you with force?

SC   No, but...

POLICE   But?

SC   He had this look and although he was whispering, he seemed I don't know, determined?

POLICE   Determined to what?

SC   You really want me to spell it out for you?

POLICE   We need to be clear what you feel Mr Rock was determined to do?

SC   Touch me. Kiss me. Who knows exactly what he was determined to do.

POLICE   And even though you knew there was someone outside, you didn't call for help?

SC   No.

POLICE   And do you know why that was?

SC   I He I've told you, his hands were on me. I froze.

POLICE   So, you say he was leading you to that other door? For the purposes of the tape, the other door Ms Campbell is referring to is the internal door of Mr White's office that leads to a small hall, where there is a second internal door to the adjacent storeroom. Is this right, Sophie?

SC   Yes.

POLICE   So Mr Rock was able to take you through two doors, which must have required him taking at least one hand off you to open them, and you didn't attempt to leave or call out for help?

POLICE   Sophie?

POLICE   I'm simply trying to clarify the details.

POLICE   Is this what happened?

SC   Yes. Though he actually took both hands from me. Before we went into the storeroom, he said he knew exactly what we should do to stop the dissemination of those booklets.

POLICE   Go on.

THE SUN

LUKE ROCK IN A HARD PLACE Injured TV and literary star Luke Rock probed re assault and arson charges

Family favourite Luke Rock was this afternoon questioned by police in connection to a series of assaults against women and Saturday night's fire at Hambledon Manor in Shropshire, where he was attending an intimate dinner with other "VIP" men, including the MP Lionel Morgan.

Only last month declared a hero for intercepting an attack by Aaron Jenkins at the same five-star hotel, Rock has fallen sensationally from grace after women working at the Shropshire Business Men's Dinner claimed he and other male attendees were sexually inappropriate and aggressive.

One of the waitresses, who has asked to remain anonymous, told The Sun that when faced with a pamphlet she and her colleagues had written detailing the diners' alleged transgressions, the comedian "stormed from the private dining room".

Details have emerged of a meeting that immediately followed between Rock and

Sophie Campbell, the director of In the Event Of, the company hosting last night's dinner. Ms Campbell, who has herself been accused of lack of duty of care towards her staff, claims in a recent hastily deleted Instagram post that the tee-total multi-million-pound funny man and author not only assaulted her too but was so incensed by the accusations made by the waitresses he dramatically SET FIRE to the pamphlet.

While the exact cause of the fire in the hotel manager's office has yet to be confirmed by official investigations, mother-of-one Ms Campbell said, "He took a swig of his drink, which spilt on the desk. He then pulled a lighter and the booklet from his pocket and set it on fire." According to Campbell, whose post also included an apology to all the women she has personally failed, the sobriety guru dropped the flaming paper on the desk before pushing her into the adjacent storeroom.

The striking brunette, who claimed she had by now been shoved to the floor, was forced to think outside of the box. In scenes more familiar to Hollywood than the sleepy

Shrewsbury, she desperately scrambled for anything she could use as a weapon and was able to grab her favourite Louboutin shoe, which she says was intended only to shock Mr Rock. But as she explained in her lengthy post, "I was desperate. I smacked him once on the head with the side of the shoe, the surprise of which enabled me to roll from beneath him. But I only got so far before he grabbed me again, which was when I smashed the shoe into his face, not knowing the heel would penetrate his eye."

Campbell maintains she didn't intend to cause such drastic injuries and, despite everything he's done, hopes Mr Rock's rumoured partial blindness is only temporary.

The drama, however, did not end there. Witnesses say, with no other means of escape, she used her other shoe to smash the glass of the storeroom window, which she was then able to kick through and climb outside to safety.

The fire service was in attendance and thankfully able to extinguish the flames before they spread to the main hotel building.

While the investigation into the cause of the fire is as yet unfinished, video evidence obtained by The Sun suggests such pyromaniac antics are indeed Luke Rock's schtick. Dramatic mobile phone footage from September's Shropshire Business Men's Dinner shows Rock mocking correspondence from his ex-girlfriend, the model Daisy De Souza, before belittling her well-intentioned sentiments by setting fire to the handwritten letter and dropping it into a portable fire pit on the stage.

While Rock's agent has been keen to point out the comedian's proclivity for setting things alight bears no relevance to recent events, is there ever really smoke without fire?

EVE

I lay the iPad between us on bed. Shelley Chapman's article, which she first published on her personal website, is now live on the *Guardian* online. She'd called in the wake of the After Party in search of an exclusive with Cass but then got speaking with Harry about his own list. A week later, she'd interviewed the pair of them, taken her time with both her questions and how she interpreted their answers, which were, in tabloid speak, warts and all. Only this isn't tabloid, it's considered and nuanced and brave.

'I'm proud of you, Harry.' I look down at his head on the pillow below me.

Because it's easier for us to talk like this, we are, as per, in the dark.

'Listen.' He rolls from his back onto his side. 'I know we said we'd support Cass through the court case before we focus on what happens with us, but...'

I sink back into the headboard.

'Only with your mum...' He says, and the room – the house, even – is heavy, like the boxes Harry and I spent a few hours yesterday carrying from my parents' house – or what *was* my parents' house – to the van we'd hired to help Mum move.

She'd looked around their bedroom, drawers emptied of books and jewellery, clothes in piles on the floor. 'God, I've made a mess of things.' She'd patted the mattress to suggest I sit next to her on the bed. 'I keep going back over it,' she said. 'When you first started seeing Rock.'

'I don't want this to sound like an accusation.' I put an arm around her to soften the question. 'But why didn't you stop me?'

'Eve.' Her eyes filled with tears. 'I tried, but you wouldn't listen.'

'You didn't seem so bothered about us being together once he was famous.'

She shook her head. 'I went to the police.'

'What?'

She nodded. 'Your dad told me not to. He was embarrassed, I think. Thought the officers wouldn't take him seriously as a boss if they knew he had such little control of his daughter.' My placid mother kicked a rubbish bag across the floor. 'Not that it made any difference. You were sixteen. If Luke Rock was sleeping with you, he wasn't technically breaking the law. I had no choice. I risked losing you if I continued to fight. I decided, instead, to bide my time.'

'I'm sorry.'

'You don't need to be sorry. Your father though…'

Unlike Mum, Dad is still refusing to use the word divorce. While she was moving, he was supposed to have gone out for the afternoon, waiting for a text from Harry confirming we were done. But there he was, on the pavement, watching us load the kitchen table, the one piece of furniture Mum wanted to take with her. He'd returned, he said, because it was getting dark. 'I'd suggest taking that suitcase out before y—'

'It's fine.' My back was to him. It's easier, I've noticed, if I can't see his face.

We did, eventually, remove the suitcase. As usual, Dad wasn't wrong. Not this time. That other time though. That time when it really counted. It wasn't that he didn't think his colleagues would do that to a woman, he conceded, rather he didn't think his colleagues would do it to *him*.

Him.

On the opposite side of the road, the exhausted sigh of a stopped bus.

'Forty-nine years.' Mum said in the passenger seat of my Volvo. Harry was behind in the van. 'We were almost but not quite golden.' A fraction of pride in her voice that was also resigned and sad. 'You think you know someone.' I nodded, like it wasn't the hundredth time she'd said this exact phrase.

'If this is going to work, I want to know you,' I say to Harry now. 'Like, really know you.'

We've lowered the blinds, pulled the curtains, but now the iPad has gone into sleep mode, I see a thin line beneath the window, a crack of yellow light.

His hands are warm from the cocoon of the duvet, but that's not why I yield to them when they pull me closer. His fingers, in the gap between my t-shirt and jeans, press into the small of my back. It's new to us, this delicate skin on skin. I expect him to tell me he does know me. That twenty years of marriage will do that. Instead, he says, 'So where do we start?'

I shrug because it feels impossible. 'By under-standing, we'll try but there are no guarantees for us.'

'OK.' He doesn't whisper it, this acknowledgement of our perhaps most important – most vulnerable – truth.

'Sophie?' A roll of waves in my stomach on seeing her and saying her name.

'Hi.' My sister steps back beneath the canopy of the door.

'What are you doing here?' The gallery space isn't yet open. It's quarter to; I'd arranged to meet Charlotte's art tutor, Nicky, at six. Charlotte had mentioned to her about the photos George took at the After Party, the idea he had of manipulating the images to form the basis of a small exhibition. He and Cass have had very tentative conversations about using blurred stills from the video too, contrasting them with new and consensual nudes. I've tried to lean into what Cass pitched as "empowerment" and "reclamation" but instinctively – viscerally – I resist. Maybe her distance from the objects of the pictures is what allows Nicky the enthusiasm she's shown for the project. I don't know if I could ever see any naked image of my daughter – consensual or otherwise – as art.

Sophie removes her sunglasses. 'Mum mentioned you had this appointment, and I thought maybe I could help. You know, with the planning?' The tenacity of her eye contact is too much. 'I may have closed In the Event Of, but I still have contacts, could likely get some good press? This kind of female-empowerment is hot right now.'

'Hence your new business?' The sharpness of my tone is blunted by the shallow inhale that quickly follows. When it comes, this bare authentic bitterness is still so remarkable, I find it difficult to breathe.

'I want to help, Eve.'

She said the same in the press release for HERA. *Holistic Empowering Retreats with Authenticity.* 'Having been on her own recent journey of self-discovery, HERA's director, Sophie Campbell, wants to help other women do the same. HERA will serve women, who are ready to examine their own failings so that they might then empower *all* women to thrive.'

'There speaks a white-feminist saviour.' Cass mimed sticking her fingers down her throat when she read it. '*All* women, my arse.'

'I've said I'm sorry, Eve,' Sophie says now. 'Privately *and* publicly. And I took a course on Monday too.'

'I saw,' I say. 'You posted about it on Insta. *Combatting Sexism in the Workplace*. Amazing, really, how much you can cover in a day.'

'Yes, well.' Sophie pulls at the zip of her green leather shoulder bag. 'I found it very helpful.'

'So you said.' *On social media*, I want to add, but is it fair to keep questioning my sister's motives when she totally saved me with her quick-thinking gumption by blaming the fire at Hambledon Manor on Rock. 'I do appreciate everything you've done, Soph. Your head must have been all over the place after what that man did.' It's a shame, though – I think but don't say – that it took for her to be a victim to view Rock's behaviour as problematic. 'I'm genuinely sorry he put you through that.'

'Not as sorry as he is,' she says with a short but definite laugh.

'I'd better go.' I tip my head toward the glass. Inside the gallery, Nicky is smiling, waving her key. 'And thank you for the offer of help but, grateful as I am, I'm not ready to let everything else go. Not yet.' My back's to Sophie before I've finished talking.

'Eve.' A hand on my shoulder.

'*What?*' I turn, angry now, because wasn't my sister one of the first people to tell me I should be more assertive about what I want and need. Yet here she is, about to steamroll me with a barrage of reasons why she should be involved in organising and promoting the exhibition.

But, 'This is yours,' she says. In her hand is a cassette tape, she flips it so its red, blue and green cover is on show.

'*Jagged Little Pill?*'

She nods. 'I *did* borrow it.' There's something childish in the way she passes it to me, an apologetic admission of guilt in the tilt of her head.

I run my fingers across Alanis's face. '*Steal* it, you mean.'

She shrugs. 'I've given it back now.' I'm saying hi to Nicky when she adds. 'Track nine, Eve; I didn't get it then. Now, though, I think it's you.'

'I realise,' Nicky says, taking my right hand in both of hers in a handshake that's more sympathetic than business-like, 'how hard this must be for you, as a mother, to get behind. Cass is very lucky to have you.'

I wonder if – and hope – that's true.

'Sorry to interrupt.' A knock, and a woman's head appears around the door. 'I'm a little early,' she says. 'Just wanted to check I'm OK to go upstairs?'

'Of course.' Nicky releases my hand and opens her arms to welcome her. 'I think we're done, aren't we?' I nod. 'Come in. Eve, this is Simone, and Simone,' she says, 'this is Eve.'

'Have we met?' I ask. Simone's face is familiar. It's more than that though, there's something very specific about the way she stepped into and immediately owned the room.

'Possibly,' she says, 'My memory's always been appalling, but since perimenopause...' She frowns, makes a noise like *ay ay ay*. 'If you're a regular here, though, it could be...' She points at a picture beside the reception desk, a hotchpotch collection of works, each one a single piece taken from a different exhibition from the last year. I recognise the charcoal immediately.

'That's you?' I'm blushing, perverted suddenly. Turns out, I've been looking at a nude Simone nightly on my phone.

'It is,' she says, angling her head to get a better view of her charcoaled torso. I think how I analyse every single photo of myself, rarely happy with the result. Yet here is a woman confronted with her own full frontal, and there's no sigh, no frown, not a hint of disappointment or disgust. Instead, she's smiling. 'Did you go to the show?'

'I did.' I don't know whether to look at Simone in her belted woollen trench coat or at Simone in absolutely nothing on the wall. I flit, obviously awkward, between the two. 'My friend Charlotte took the class,' I say, as if this rushed ridiculous justification for having been here precludes me from voyeurism or kink.

'You don't fancy trying it too?'

'Me?' I cross my arms across my chest. 'God, no one would want to paint *me*.'

'I meant the drawing, not the modelling.' Simone's laugh is warm, loud. 'But why not?' She takes a step back, palms raised, not trying to hide that she's looking me up and down. 'You're beautiful,' she says, her hand dismissing my scoff. 'I swear.' She's dead still now. 'It'd be the best thing you've ever done. I never don't come away on a high. Seriously.' Her eyes are wide with her determination that I trust her. 'No one ever believes me until they do it, but it's spiritual.' And like all this is absolutely normal, 'There's a class now. Why don't you come up and see.'

'She does this all the time.' Nicky's shaking her head. 'You *would* be very welcome to watch though, Eve. No pressure.' A little quieter then, 'I wonder if it might help you find a different way into thinking about Cass and George's show?'

Thirty minutes later, Simone walks into the centre of a circle made of nine women and five men. Without ceremony, she removes her robe and strikes her first short pose. She's standing, her left foot slightly in front of her right, her left arm draped over the top of her head. As pencils scratch on paper, it's impossible to look at only the "polite" parts of Simone's body. My eyes drift from her hips to her vulva. From her neck to her breasts.

I am looking at a naked woman. The same line on repeat in my head.

Without any prompt from Nicky, in two minutes, Simone moves, lays on the yoga mat, her face tilted toward the opposite side of the circle, her back arched slightly away from the floor.

Her nakedness is almost normal now. And I understand why the artist with the oils in Charlotte's group decided to go abstract because Simone's body really is just an assemblage of shapes.

Three minutes in, her internal clock prompts another shift in position. She nods to Nicky, who brings her a chair. Feet firmly on the floor in front of her, Simone leans forward, elbows on knees, head in hands. Her hair is in her fingers and there is fat in her folds, and she is fine with that because, 'You saw the pictures at the exhibition, didn't you?' She'd asked as we climbed the stairs to the studio. 'How different each of them was? I looked ancient in one. Tiny in another. And that's the point. No matter what you do, you can't control the perception anyone will have of you.' She stopped on the top step, her brow raised like she was on the brink of a life-modelling life-lesson ta-dah! 'Everyone will *always* bring their own bias to what they see.'

She'd shrugged when I'd asked her what she thinks about when she's posing. 'Occasionally, I'll be so relaxed, it's an out-of-body experience.' She pulled a Yorkie bar from a rucksack. 'Most times, I'll be planning what to have for my tea.'

When was the last time I was in a room with someone – who wasn't Harry – without their clothes on? Someone so utterly at home in their skin. Years ago. With Cass probably. Before she hit puberty or read magazines or scrolled Instagram and became mired in self-consciousness and shame. The freedom with which she used to run naked – giggling – through the spray of a garden hose.

'You shouldn't have to pose naked to feel empowered,' I said when my daughter, whose body has already been sprawled across the internet, first broached the idea of creating an image, or images, with her consent. 'Surely there are other ways to regain your self-worth.'

She'd looked at me like I was mad. '*Regain* would suggest I had self-worth in the first place.' A wry laugh that made me – and her, I think – sad. 'And there may be other ways, Mum, but mustn't the body, this thing we are born with and live in, be the thing that comes first.'

'I get that,' I said.

That laugh again, 'Do you though? *Really?*'

When I get home, the house is empty. I go to check messages, looking in my bag for my phone but pull out Sophie's – *my* – cassette tape instead.

What was it she'd said about track nine? I check the listing on the back.

'Alexa,' I say. 'Play "Mary Jane" by Alanis Morissette?'

A year into my "relationship" with Rock, my head of year, Mrs Taylor, asked me if anything was up. 'Eve,' she said, 'you've lost your sparkle.' I laughed about it with Kelly and Sophie after because, with my celebrity boyfriend, wasn't I at my coolest, at my sexiest, at my peak?

I worked so hard to believe in that theory, to believe everything I was doing – the drink, the drugs, the sex – were *my* positive choices, which meant when it failed – when Rock stopped calling – it was never about him or his issues. It was only ever about me.

The first bar of "Mary Jane" plays, and I am seventeen. But as the song progresses, and Alanis sings of losing your place, of no longer dancing or dreaming, of losing weight and censoring truth and sitting in a rollercoaster careening off track, I am twenty-two, thirty-eight, forty-five. Because Alanis's question hasn't changed. Who exactly am I doing these things for?

I shouldn't have taken it, Sophie says when I message her a screenshot of the lyrics. *I just couldn't stand your crying whenever you listened to that song. But now, honestly, I think it was telling you something about what being with Rock was doing to your confidence. If I'd not taken that album, maybe you would have figured it out. I'm sorry.*

It's not your fault, I tell her. She might be responsible for many things but me staying with Rock isn't one of them. I don't think a song has ever existed that would have persuaded me to leave him because *he* was so dangerously persuasive in making me stay.

I play it again. On my phone this time, so I can listen on the stairs, in the bathroom, in my room, searching for my earpods so nothing gets between me and the end of the song, so I can properly pause, like Alanis does – music and vocals at a brief standstill – before the penultimate verse. This negative space is the breather, the time to choose – *really* choose – change.

What's important, the voice sings, is freedom.

'I want to know you,' I'd said to Harry, which is true. I *do* want to know my husband, but for freedom, for moving forward, what I need to know most – to *love* most – is me.

Alanis sings as I stand in front of the mirror. She sings as I take off my clothes. She sings as I look at my reflection with no tucking or posing or blaming. She sings as I let everything hang as it's meant to. She sings as I let myself go.

Police officers found guilty of sharing grossly offensive WhatsApp messages

9 November 2023 | News

Two West Mercia police officers have been found guilty of sending grossly offensive messages on a WhatsApp group.

DCI Jonathan Banford, 52, and DC Luke Trigg, 45, were both found guilty by Birmingham Magistrates Court today and will be sentenced on 24th November 2023.

Anika Johns, head of the CPS Special Crime Division, said: "It is inconceivable that police officers would share such grossly offensive messages among their colleagues.

"By these verdicts, the court has agreed that they were not, as claimed 'excessive banter', but that they were indeed criminal offences.

"Where there is sufficient evidence and it is in the public interest to do so, the CPS will always prosecute these offences robustly."

The prosecution followed an investigation by the Independent Office for Police Conduct (IOPC).

Investigations into other officers are ongoing.

CASS

The After Party is still national news. And, sure, the fire and the stiletto and the celebrity are what first got us the attention, but it was the pamphlet and its delivery and the juiciness of our secret scheming that made it stick. Or so I hope. One month on, and people are still talking.

I am still talking. Or am about to be. I am waiting at our kitchen table on the video call for Anita, the *Woman's Hour* presenter, to appear.

'Be yourself,' Mum whispers. The advice would be simple if the last four, five weeks had made me clearer about who I am. Thing is, some days I am made of absolute conviction that I've got this. That what I am is a fourth-wave feminist, who knows her shit. Others, I'm a girl whose body is still naked and writhing on the internet.

'On those days...' I start to tell Anita but stop. Mum takes my hand. I don't think she'll ever get used to hearing me talk like this. As hard it is though, she nods, like, *go on*. 'On those days,' I repeat, 'when the intrusive thoughts come like that, I have to remind myself I don't actually want to die.'

'What do you want?'

My voice, when I tell her all I really want is to be heard and believed, is a march forward. It trembles, but Anita smiles over the screen, posing questions and actively listening to their answers. She could teach Herring a thing or two.

I was summoned to his office yesterday.

'I hear you've been invited to talk on the radio, Ms Gunn.' Since his failed attempt to block the article I wrote about the sex tape for the Oakfield paper, our headmaster has insisted on calling me by this name. 'While I understand these are very important issues you're raising, I would appreciate you bearing in mind our reputation.'

On his desk was the pamphlet. Not the one from the After Party, though Maya and I have given him one of those too. The one resting on the stack of unread magazines in his inbox was our second version, collated by members of the newly expanded FemSoc in school.

'We wanted to talk about sexism at Oakfield,' I tell Anita. 'But it's slightly different to the After Party document. We invited contributions from everyone.' Am I rambling? The producer was so encouraging, but is this something people genuinely want to hear?

Sitting to my left, away from the laptop camera, Mum reaches and squeezes my thigh.

'Go on,' Anita says and even via Zoom, I can see she is made of reassurance and belief.

'We'd been chatting about what happened at Hambledon Manor, and while we know what we told them *did* positively impact some of the men there, we wondered if it would be better, if the boys, or people generally, would respond better if we broadened our focus. My friend, Maya, she was going to come on the show, but she's at a uni open day this morning. She's a proper activist.'

Anita laughs, then, 'If there's one thing we can all agree on, Cass, it's that you're a proper activist too.'

Am I? Is this who I am now? An activist. Three syllables.

Three words: Vigilant, loud, bold.

'Maya said, and she was right, I think, that if we want change, it can't only be us who are striving for it. And that if we want *them*, the boys I mean, to be on our side, we need to expand the conversation beyond why the patriarchy is so awful for women and include why it's not great for other genders too. And that's not to belittle the experiences many of us girls have had in school because, of course, we want the catcalling and the groping, the everyday sexism to stop. But that's more likely to happen if we move away from this either / or.'

Anita isn't challenging but curious when she asks, 'What do you mean by the either / or?'

'Some of the boys, they're aggressively anti-feminist. They're watching people like Andrew Tate and buying what he says about wanting to save young men from a society that's too women-centric, too woke. Aaron Jenkins, the man you mentioned in your intro who tried to attack some of the female staff at the dinner in September, he'd been watching Tate-type material too. And, sure, his reaction was extreme, but the day-to-day impact of this general sentiment is huge. And we have to wonder where that trend for young men to buy into this kind of thinking comes from. Sorry,' I say, clearing my throat and taking a sip of water. 'You asked me about the either / or. And I think my point is that while it's imperative we make things safer and more equal for girls, we don't want to make boys feels demonised or somehow less in the process. As Pollyanna as it might sound, we want to be looking out for everyone. That's true equality, right? So, while we did call for girls to contribute lists like the ones we put in the After Party pamphlet, when it came to school, we invited the Pride and BAME clubs to work with us and asked all their members to get involved too. And we appealed to the boys to think about the ways in which the patriarchy might also be detrimental to them.'

'And did they respond? With their thoughts, I mean?'

'We've had some really insightful pieces. One from a guy who, amazingly, has now joined FemSoc.'

'Could you tells us about him perhaps?'

'He said his friends think Tate is king, that he's bang on with his theories about women and where we belong. And this guy, he finds it difficult to speak out against that. His mates say he's pussy-whipped if he ever tries to defend even the most basic of women's rights. And this one time, when he then got upset, he was called gay, which obviously, shouldn't be an insult, but that's part of the issue, right? The way society is teaching boys to be, or *not* be, emotional is helping no one, least of all the boys themselves. And if we're wanting to create a safer world for girls, we can't ignore the fact that it's men who are more likely to be victims of male violence. We have to think about where and why those violent tendencies begin.'

'And on that note, I want to turn now, Cass, to your dad, because I know you're not the only one in your family to be broaching this subject of how men can benefit from, and be involved in, feminism.'

'That's right. This is a team effort. Not just my dad but my mum and even my ex-boyfriend too. He and Dad are hoping to create something, a workshop maybe, to take into schools and colleges. To generate these kinds of conversations in which they can make clear the real-life consequences of the kinds of behaviours my friends and I were subjected to at the dinner. But what's just as important to them is making a safe space in which boys can talk freely about their own beliefs and worries because, a lot of the time, that anger young men are feeling might be fear that they just don't know how to communicate.'

'Thank you,' Anita says, smiling at me via the camera. 'That was Cass Gunn there, a young woman unafraid to make herself heard.'

I'm still buzzing from the interview when I arrive for my Scrabble game with Gramps. Maybe, like the rest of the family, I should still be giving him the silent treatment. But if he doesn't see me as only the girl in the video, I don't see him as only the policeman who made a mistake. A big mistake, sure. But his wife and daughter have disowned him. As punishment goes, isn't that enough.

I don't want to have to ask but, 'Did you hear me? On the radio?' What I want is for Gramps to come straight to the front door and tell me how proud he is, to tell me I am made of all the things he's ever wanted in a granddaughter and more.

He does none of that, just smiles and says 'sure,' and I don't press him, but he does later say, 'You were good.'

After a victorious win with 72 points on a triple word-score with PHOENIX, I swerve by Liv's on the way home. Despite the late hour, my friend's insisted she absolutely has to see me.

I'm not expecting to see Maya too.

'You weren't the only one who was busy today,' Maya says. She and Liv both hold out their right arms. 'We were thinking about what you said in that PSHE lesson on Monday. When you were talking about the tape and how you feel like you're stuck with it. After what Freddie White was saying about recognising you because of your tattoo.' She pulls up the sleeve of her jumper. 'What if you're not the only one with a ring of bluebells on your wrist? You never know, if someone else sees it, they might think that girl in the movie was me.'

'Or me.' Liv, like Maya, is newly inked.

'Thank you.' A tear drops to the clingfilm wrapped around Liv's wrist. 'The Black skin or red hair might be a bit of a giveaway.'

'We know that,' Maya says. 'They're more symbolic than they are convincing, but—'

'They're perfect. As are you.' I pull them both in for a hug.

Later, when Maya has left and it's just me and Liv on the bed, 'I know you don't agree with what I have with Roger, babe.'

'I don't.' I think about all the things I don't under-stand when it comes to relationships and wonder if maybe not understanding everything is OK. 'I might never get why you do it.' I rest my head on her shoulder. 'But we can still love each other, can't we, even if we don't agree?'

'Fair.' The mattress shifts when she gets to her knees. She looks down at me, shakes her head. 'I'll tell you what I definitely *don't* agree with.' She points at my puffy eyes. 'Are you sleeping?'

'Not much. Pre-*Woman's Hour* nerves.'

Truth is though, it's not only last night and the interview. It's the incessant thinking, talking, defending, consoling and then there's the news too. The constant roll of it. Lucy Corrigan. Aanshi Siddiqui. The police with their WhatsApp photos of women's bodies. The male MP suggesting women make up stories of sexual assault for money. A TikTok'er ignoring sexual advances to then be subjected to monkey noises and called a Black whore. That was just yesterday.

Some days, some hours, I have what it takes to fight this.

And others, I am full of despair.

It's the never knowing what you're walking into that makes it so difficult.

The morning after the interview I enter the common room at school.

'Here she is,' Callum Bell is all rolling eyes and burly sneers when he looks at me. 'Oakfield's wannabe activist. No TV appearances yet then?' When I shake my head, 'Not surprised,' he laughs, 'Face and tits for radio, that one.' He scans the room as if expecting applause.

But, 'Don't be a dick, Callum.' It's one of his cronies. 'Did you even listen to the interview?'

'Yeh, Callum,' his other mate says. 'It was decent.'

It's only a few comments from some kids at school, but it *is* something, isn't it? That I spoke. That they heard. That their response suggests a small significant change.

'You're right,' I say to them.

It – *I* – *was* decent.

Because *I* am Cassandra. And I am made of voice and power and truth.

Lawson & Cook bags 'addictive' tell-all memoir from Luke Rock

RIGHTS   MAR 20, 2026 BY KATH-LEEN HANSON

Lawson & Cook has acquired *Time Will Tell*, a "searing memoir" from comedian Luke Rock.

In a significant high six-figure deal, publishing director Max Freemantle bought UK and Commonwealth rights from Florian Grove at the Grove Agency. *Time Will Tell*, Rock's non-fiction debut, will be published summer 2026 to coincide with his expected release from his 42-month jail sentence.

Freemantle said, "I've not read many memoirs that have me roaring with laughter and crying with despair. Rock's writing, with its blend of social commentary and acerbic wit, is a timely take on what it means to be a man in the twenty-first century."

Before being jailed for arson, Rock was a hugely successful comedian and author, who also fought and won a legal battle with several woman claiming to have been sexually assaulted. *Time Will Tell* promises to take no prisoners when it comes to exposing the dangers men now face in the wake of #MeToo.

Rock said, "I am delighted to be working with Max and the team at Lawson & Cook. These last few years, I've literally had to learn to see things differently. I hugely admire Max's bravery in taking this on; in these times of significant social change, it's imperative men's voices can and will be heard."

For more unmissable reads,
sign up to the HarperNorth newsletter at
www.harpernorth.co.uk

or find us on Twitter at
@HarperNorthUK

**Harper
North**